NEW DAWN RISING

SCOTT GAMBOE

Medallion Press, Inc.
Printed in USA

Previous accolades from *The Killing Frost*:

4 HEARTS

"At last, a space opera sci fi novel like the good old days. It is so hard to find good sci fi adventure, but *The Killing Frost*, fits the bill. We follow a special ops military unit of the future as they battle an alien race and political traitors within the ranks of their government, including amongst their own people. This is a fast paced story that keeps the tension up until the very end. All the elements are there: imperfect protagonists, heroines, villains we expect and love to hate, treasonous friends and loyal friend, an evil alien race that may not be completely evil, and constant changing technology. It includes warrior ethos and idealistic values."

—Bob Spear, Publisher and Chief Reviewer
Heartland Reviews

"From hand-to-hand combat to spectacular battles in space, *The Killing Frost* packs a punch and knows how to keep those pages turning . . . this was a very satisfying read. Message to Mr. Gamboe, 'please keep Arano Lakeland in your thoughts for future work. That's one great character.'"

—Shawn P. Madison, The Eternal Night

NEW DAWN RISING

SCOTT GAMBOE

DEDICATION:

I would like to thank my wife, Jill, my daughter, Erica, and my entire extended family. Their continued support has made my new career as an author much more enjoyable, and I couldn't do this without them.

Published 2009 by Medallion Press, Inc.

The MEDALLION PRESS LOGO
is a registered trademark of Medallion Press, Inc.

Typeset in Adobe Garamond Pro
Printed in the United States of America

ISBN 978-193383695-9

10 9 8 7 6 5 4 3 2 1
First Edition

ACKNOWLEDGMENTS:

I would like to thank prolific author Robert E. Vardeman for his expert advice, for his friendly correspondence, and for taking the time to read and critique my work. He is definitely a gentleman and a scholar. Further kudos go out to Medallion Press author Rick Taubold, who has provided invaluable feedback on my writing. Last, but of course not least, I would like to thank the staff at Medallion Press. They are a very supportive group, and they make the writing process as painless as it could possibly be.

CHAPTER ONE

THE AGING FREIGHTER CREAKED IN PROTEST, the decrepit inertial dampers unable to fully compensate for the braking maneuvers the helmsman was executing. He bit his lip and held onto the flight controls until the ship finally settled into a more stable approach. The docking computer beeped for attention, and the helmsman turned back to his controls.

"Captain Feng, there's a message coming in from Darin Station," the communications officer announced. The helmsman took advantage of the distraction to steal another admiring glance at her while she worked the subspace Comm, her brown hair pulled tightly behind her head, framing her stunning features.

"Patch it through," Captain Feng ordered with an imperious gesture.

The screen crackled to life, and an emaciated Kamling smiled back at them. "Welcome to Darin Station! We can put you in docking port four. If you would please cut your engines, we'll use our tractor beam to bring you in the rest of the way. Our crews are standing by to unload your cargo."

"Acknowledged," Captain Feng replied. He nodded curtly to the helmsman, who cut the engines and allowed the ship to be guided forward by the station's tractor beam. There was a sudden, sharp jolt, and the freighter's nose slipped home in the station's number four docking port.

The helmsman pressed a final button on his control panel, then rose from his station and left the bridge, the communications officer close behind. They were met in the fore of the ship by an oddly assorted crew. There was a Kamling, his green, amphibian features appearing somewhat darker in the low lighting. Next to him was a leathery-skinned Tompiste, her diminutive size contrasting sharply with her oversized head and almond-shaped eyes. On the opposite side of the hatchway was a Gatoan, his pointed white teeth gleaming from his fur-covered visage. He stood with a hawk-beaked Tsimian, whose fur was distinguishable from the Gatoan, being so fine it was almost featherlike. The Tsimian, with the superstitious air common to his race, weaved his fingers in the air before him, making the Tsimian sign for good luck. There was even a Bromidian, the insectoid race which, until recently, had been the enemy of the Coalition.

The helmsman smiled grimly at his shipmates, even as the Gatoan handed him a laser rifle. He waited until they had taken up positions on either side of the entry hatch before he released the locking mechanisms, allowing personnel from Darin Station access to the ship.

The door slid open with an angry *hiss*, and three Humans charged through the entryway, laser pistols in hand. They were met by a storm of laser fire, and all three fell in their tracks. The Bromidian stepped forward briskly, knelt, and checked the bodies.

"They are dead," he announced. "Let us proceed, Viper!"

Captain Arano Lakeland discarded his helmsman's smock, shedding his crewman persona and exposing his Coalition uniform. His teammates followed suit. Lentin was dressed in his Bromidian Intelligence Chapter uniform, the Coalition emblem on his sleeve a silent testimony to his status as an assigned observer. Lieutenant Videre Genoa was the first Avenger to step through the docking vestibule and onto the station, and the rest of the team soon followed. Arano looked both left and right, checking for any other enemies who might be lurking in the area. The hallways were a uniform gray color, with access panels interspersed at regular intervals. The thin plastic sheet covering the walls had chipped off in places, evidence of the lackadaisical attitude commanders on frontier stations typically had. Even the carpeting had worn thin from the passage of booted feet, and the metal subfloor showed through in places. Without turning, he jammed his thumb in the direction of a nearby control panel, and Videre immediately set to work.

Arano kept a sharp eye out for more of the pirates who had overrun Darin Station. His rifle became an extension of his arms, following his every movement, always ready to aim and fire. Down the gray, empty corridor, just around the bend, he would find docking bay number five on the right, and beyond that, a secondary hallway to the left leading to the central core. In all likelihood, that was where they would find the rest of the raiders, but Arano was never one to leave anything to chance, if he could help it.

"Finished, Viper," Videre whispered, sidling up to the team leader. Without having to verify Videre's work, Arano knew his Gatoan teammate had tapped into the station's security system and disabled it. Arano took another look around the dimly lit halls before motioning to his wife, Captain Alyna Lakeland. While Arano led Lentin, Videre, and Lieutenant Lain Baxter to the central core, Alyna and her squad made their way to the shuttle pads to prevent an escape.

Arano glided smoothly, soundlessly, across the carpeted floor, cheek pressed firmly against the stock of his rifle, elbows pressed securely into his sides. The corridor continually bent noticeably to the left, following the curve of the station's perfect circle.

Just ahead, the sub-corridor leading to Operations came into view. Arano took a deep, calming breath, then lurched around the corridor, Lentin at his side. To his relief, the passage stood empty. He gave an inquiring look to Videre and Lain, eyebrows raised with the unvoiced question. Both nodded curtly and turned to opposite sides of the corridor. They removed the covers for the station's ventilation system and immediately crawled inside, one circling the station's core to the right, the other to the left. Arano and Lentin replaced the covers behind them before they crept closer to Operations.

Arano stood stoically, watching the door to the operations center in case it should open. Behind him, Lentin kept watch in the direction they had just come. The closed portal before him was different from the others they had seen to that point, with a spiral pattern of narrow metal slats converging in the center. The red and blue striped logo of the Coalition had been painted on the door, but even that patriotic mural had been allowed to fade into disrepair. The control panel unlocking the door hung askew by a single screw, and Arano's brow creased in concern. He hoped the door would easily open when the time came.

The awaited signals arrived almost simultaneously, and Arano licked his lips in nervous anticipation. With a low hiss to Lentin, he stood to the side of the doorway. Lentin took up a flanking position, weapon held ready. Arano released his left hand from his rifle, reaching out with a device strapped to his arm and touching it to the door's control panel. After a moment's pause, the lights on the panel flickered to life, danced about in succession, then turned green. With a metallic grinding noise, the door irised open, the metal slats recessing into the wall and allowing access to Operations.

Arano and Lentin leaped through the open doorway, weapons ready. "USC Avengers!" Arano shouted. "Hands in the air!" There were six pirates on what passed for the station's bridge, and all froze in shock at the sudden intrusion. One, a Kamling wearing a filthy shirt that had likely once been some hue of white, reached hastily for the weapon dangling from his waist. But Lentin's rifle barked twice, and the man fell to the deck, a plume of smoke rising from the gaping hole in his chest. Apparently, that was enough for the others, who raised their hands in submission. Arano stepped forward to take them into custody, but froze, his danger sense warning him something was amiss.

A crashing sound from behind him brought Arano around swiftly, and he dropped to one knee as he spun. A Tsimian rose from his place of concealment, his pistol tracking toward the veteran Avenger. A shot rang out from above, and the pirate's body lurched backward across the bank of computers behind him, his pistol spilling unnoticed to the ground. Arano spun back to the others, knowing Videre's rifle had found its mark.

But the distraction had done its job, and pandemonium erupted in the operations center. The five remaining pirates dove for the cover of nearby banks of equipment, firing madly into the air in an effort to confuse the Avengers. Hellish beams of colored light streaked through the room, sending showers of sparks from computer systems unlucky enough to be hit. Arano fired off a rapid burst of laser energy, punching a hole in a narrow wall of metal and exposing the leathery torso of a Tompiste pirate using the thin bulkhead for cover. Another blast from Arano's rifle silenced his foe.

Lain opened fire from his vantage point on the opposite side of Operations, catching the pirates from behind and sending a Human spinning madly to the ground. The deadly crossfire was too much for a pair of Human pirates, who threw their weapons down and shouted their surrender. The last pirate, a dark-haired Human, dove through an open doorway, his rolling form narrowly escaping shots from Lain and Videre. The door sealed behind him with a hiss, and Arano climbed cautiously to his feet, Comm in hand.

"Alyna, this is Viper."

"Go ahead."

"What's your status?"

"We've secured the shuttle bay. We encountered a pair of Bromidians, and we had to neutralize them. The hard way."

"You may have another Human heading your way. We have four KIA's here in Ops, and two prisoners. The last one escaped during the firefight."

"I copy that. We're watching for him."

A warning klaxon sounded over the intercom, accompanied by a sudden flashing of red lights. Videre literally flew to a control panel, hastily scanning through a situation report on the station's computer. His eyes flew wide, and his fur-covered fingers froze in place.

"Viper! Our fugitive just activated the station's self-destruct sequence! Other than escape pods, access points to the station have been locked down, including our entry point!"

Arano rushed to Videre's side, motioning to Lentin and Lain to keep watch over the prisoners. "Can you deactivate it?"

"Maybe, if I had a station security card."

"I have one," a prisoner said in a trembling voice. "It's in my left cargo pocket."

With Lentin scrutinizing the prisoners' movements, Lain dipped down, his dry, green, reptilian hands smoothly checking the man's pockets. He produced a small, white card, which he tossed to Videre. The Gatoan Avenger inserted the card into a slot in the computer. The computer beeped and hummed in response.

The station's main computer spoke over the intercom. *"Five minutes to self-destruct. All personnel to evacuation zones."*

Arano jammed a button on his Comm. "Alyna! Leave someone watching the shuttle bay and get to the escape pod area! Our fugitive is probably heading there now!"

"Copy that," she replied. "We'll meet you there, if you can't get the self-destruct sequence stopped."

Arano returned his attention to Videre, who was scouring the computer panel for something that was eluding him. "What do you need, Vid?"

"They have too many security protocols in place. I could work around them if I could connect my datapad, but I can't find a connection port. I may have to hard wire them together, if I can find a way into the computer's casing."

Arano slung his rifle and, drawing his smaller, less powerful pistol, aimed and fired. With a shower of sparks, a hole opened in the black metallic cabinet supporting the computer. Videre looked at the opening, then at his team leader, then back at the opening. He shook his head, managing somehow to laugh before he went to work again.

"Three minutes to self-destruct. All personnel to evacuation zones."

"Viper," Lentin said calmly. "If you are planning to use the escape pods as a last means of escape, we had better do so soon. It will take us at least a minute to reach the pods, and we would still need to have enough time to move away from the station before it explodes."

Arano shook his head. "If these pirates didn't kill the station's occupants, there are at least twenty people being held on the station somewhere. We won't leave them to die."

Lentin considered that; his hard, insectoid features narrowed in thought. "I agree. To do so would bring dishonor on us all."

"Alyna to Viper!"

Arano activated his Comm. "Go ahead."

"I hope you can do something with that auto-destruct sequence soon. The fugitive has already escaped, and he ejected all the other pods. We're stuck here!"

"Acknowledged." He took a deep breath and let it out slowly. "Videre, status?"

Videre grunted in reply, not bothering to speak. He punched keys on his datapad more swiftly, stopping occasionally to wire his pad to a different component of the station's control system. The computer announced the one-minute warning, and Videre sat back on his haunches, lips pursed, considering his next move. He made small gestures to himself, apparently running several courses of action through his mind. Impatience finally got the best of Arano, and he knelt next to his lieutenant.

"What is it, Vid?"

"There is one more protocol to bypass, but I can't figure out where to connect in order to do it. I have it down to three wires, but if I hook up to the wrong one, it will blow out the circuits in this computer."

Arano smiled and slapped a hand on Videre's shoulder. "Best guess, Lieutenant!" He looked up, glanced around the battle-scarred operations center, and took a deep breath of the acrid, smoke-filled air. "Wow. I didn't realize how much I missed this job."

Videre gave him a withering look before returning to his scrutinizing of the computer circuitry. His eyes flew open and, with a sudden flash of insight, he dove back into his work.

"Thirty seconds to self-destruct. All personnel to evacuation zones."

"Well, you didn't destroy the terminal, so I guess you did

something right."

Videre didn't even bother to look back. "Ah-hah. You are a funny, funny man."

"*Ten seconds to self-destruct. All personnel to evacuation zones.*"

Arano squeezed the grip on his pistol until his fingers hurt before he realized he hadn't put it away. He slid the weapon back into its holster and snapped it in place.

"*Five seconds. Four. Three. Two. One.*"

Arano squeezed his eyes tightly shut, his face lifted, waiting for the end, but it never came. He opened one eye to look around, and he saw Videre facing him, arms crossed, his face split in a wide, toothy grin. Arano slowly brought his hands to his hips, cocking his head to one side and fixing Videre with a knowing stare.

"Oh, did I forget to tell you, Viper? Because I bypassed the normal protocols, the audio countdown continued after I shut off the sequence."

Arano folded his arms across his chest, letting out a disgusted breath. "How long ago did you shut it off?"

"Oh, I don't know, ten or fifteen seconds before the end of the count."

Alyna's voice crackled over the Comm, and Arano remembered he hadn't closed down the link. "Not funny, Videre. I almost needed to change my uniform down here." Her announcement sent Videre into hysterics, and even the normally silent Lentin chuckled. Arano joined in, shaking his head and motioning for Lentin and Lain to secure their prisoners.

The troop transport *USCS Casey* revved its Rift Drive engines to life, and the swirling vastness of the artificial wormhole formed in front of them. The intermingled red and blue hues raced around the surface of the tunnel as it reached out toward them, almost seeming to swallow the ship. Arano's team gathered in the dining hall, discussing the mission with Commander Laron Alstor. The commander was alone with them in the room, so the atmosphere was quite relaxed.

Videre had to pause in his narration, laughing heartily once more. "I couldn't resist, Laron. After his helpful suggestions, what else could I do?"

"My suggestions?" Arano protested. "Such as?"

"Oh, I don't know. How about, 'Best guess, Lieutenant'?"

Laron was laughing openly, and Alyna buried her face in her hands in mock disgust. Arano rolled his eyes, looking to Lentin for support.

"Lentin, do you see what I'm up against?"

The Bromidian managed a smile. "Videre is a formidable opponent, for a teammate."

"Not you, too?" Arano said, raising his hands helplessly to Laron. "Hey, Alstor, is it too late for me to take that promotion?"

Laron gave him a wide smile. "Sorry, Viper, you're stuck with them. So, how was your first mission after such a long time off duty?"

Arano reflected briefly on Laron's question. Four months prior, Alyna had given birth to their daughter, Nicole, and both she and Arano had taken leave. Arano's Aunt Nebra moved to Immok City, finding a vacancy in the house next door to her nephew. She took great delight in being her great-niece's nanny; in fact, upon the announcement of the pregnancy, she had told Arano and Alyna, in no uncertain terms, that any time they were sent away she would keep Nicole with her. Nevertheless, it had taken three months before either Arano or Alyna could bear parting with their family's new addition.

At Laron's command, the one surviving pirate who had been cooperative was brought into the room. A security detachment used shackles to confine him to a chain at the far end of the table. The man stared continually at the table in front him, eyes unfocused. He had dark hair, shot through in places with streaks of gray, and his face was partially hidden by a scruffy-looking beard. The guards saluted Laron and left the room.

"What is your name?" Laron demanded harshly.

"Nesis Penter."

"What were you doing here?"

"We were boarding freighters for weeks—now that we have a new buyer. He buys up everything we can put our hands on, and he always wants more."

Laron leaned forward, placing his arms on his thighs. "And you say that the man in charge of your operation is the one who escaped?"

"Yes. We never knew his real name. We just called him Ament."

"Ament?" Lentin asked, running a finger along the dark exoskeleton of his right arm. "That's a Bromidian word."

Kish Waukee, the Tompiste lieutenant, looked at him curiously, her double eyelids opening wide in curiosity. "What does it mean?"

"Roughly translated, it means 'Boss.'" He gave a Bromidian frown. "Actually, it doesn't translate well. It falls a bit closer to 'Dictator,' but it's not quite that either."

Laron gestured to Nesis, who picked up his narrative once more. "Ament came up with an idea that seemed like it would work. If we took over Darin Station, we could have ships dock, strip them of their cargo, and have no one any wiser. We would lock the freighter crews up in the station's main cargo hold, where we had hidden the station's regular crew. After about a week, we could leave here with one or two of the larger freighters carrying all of our new cargo."

Laron looked up from his hastily scribbled notes. "Was this Ament's entire operation, or did he have more than one crew working for him?"

"Several, actually. We were his favorite."

Laron placed a notepad and pen in front of Nesis. "You will provide us with the location of all of Ament's bases of operation, as well as any of his contacts you can remember." Seeing Nesis hesitate, Laron bore down on him. "As it stands right now, you are facing charges of piracy and theft. If you fail to cooperate, you will be charged with other crimes by means of vicarious liability."

Nesis looked up at his interrogator, jaw dropping open in confusion. "Other crimes?"

"While you did drop your weapon immediately, your co-conspirators fired upon members of Avengers Team 5. In addition to this offense, you can also be charged with the deaths of the men who Team 5 had to kill in the course of defending themselves. I can assure you, with some degree of certainty, you would be facing the death penalty within a year or two."

The shabbily dressed pirate was trembling noticeably when he reached for the writing utensils in front of him. Arano turned and pretended to examine a datapad in order to hide the smile tugging at the corners of his mouth. Apparently, Laron hadn't lost his interviewing skills.

While Nesis scribbled away on the notepad in front of him, Arano motioned Lentin off to one side of the room. The two warriors helped themselves to a pitcher of water and seated themselves at a table.

"Lentin, what do you think is the significance of these pirates' having Bromidians in their group?"

"I'm not entirely sure, Viper. I conducted DNA scans on them, and I sent a request for identification to the authorities on Rystoria 2. Hopefully, by the time we leave the wormhole, they will have some answers for us. Most likely, they were looking for an easy way to make money, but I've never heard of Bromidians belonging to these types of groups. I suppose the war could have changed their situation, making them more desperate."

The *USCS Casey* dropped out of the wormhole, emerging in the Immok System in a vibrant swirl of colors. Almost immediately, Lentin's Comm indicated a waiting message. Arano watched the bulky Bromidian manipulate the controls, waiting anxiously for the information from *Rystoria*. The data crawled across the screen, but Arano was unable to read the oddly shaped letters and symbols of the Bromidian script.

"Well, this explains why they joined this band of pirates. They were both members of Rising Sun. With the destruction of their base in the Solarian System, the operatives who either escaped the Coalition sweep, or were off-world at the time, vanished into the galaxy's underworld elements. People like them would've naturally gravitated to thievery." He tapped a few more buttons, and the information continued to scroll down the screen. He frowned, scratching the hard shell of his face. "This makes no sense. According to our intelligence reports, shortly after the war, these two became senior operatives in an organized crime family."

Lieutenant Pelos Marnian sat back in his chair, his beak slightly agape. "If they were in the upper echelon of an organized criminal organization, why would they be working as simple deck hands for a group of pirates? Shouldn't they have been in charge?"

"Maybe their group was dissolved by arrests, or even eliminated by competitors," Kish suggested.

"It's possible," Lain conceded. "But I suppose it's also possible that they were here on behalf of their organization. Ament might not have even been aware of who they really were."

"Lentin," Arano said, rubbing his eyes in exhaustion, "can you make a translation of the information? We'll put it together with the other data we have and figure out our next step. I don't like people escaping from me. I want Ament, and I want him now."

CHAPTER TWO

ARANO EASED HIMSELF ONTO A BENCH NEXT TO his wife, who immediately held out her arms. With a regretful sigh, he passed Nicole to Alyna, who covered her baby in hugs. Arano picked up his glass of tea and surveyed the assemblage. His entire team was there, along with Laron. They were joined by a great gathering of Coalition military officers, especially Avengers. Lentin had stopped by with a few Bromidians, comrades of his who were also attached to Avengers teams as observers. Arano chuckled.

"What's so funny, Captain Lakeland?" Alyna gave her husband a friendly nudge.

"Nothing, Captain Lakeland," Arano answered, grinning broadly when Alyna's brow furrowed in irritation, as he knew it would. "I was just thinking that, two years ago, if you had told me I would have a bunch of Bromidians stop by my house for a party, I would've laughed."

"Not to mention saying that you would be a married father of a baby girl," Alyna added.

"Ah, the good old days," Arano said, accepting her playful punch with a devilish grin.

He rose and wandered through the mob behind his house. A popular form of Gatoan music was playing softly, barely audible over the gabble of the crowd. The sides of his yard were lined with tall xental trees, providing a comfortable amount of shade for the revelers. He found Kish fairly quickly and, as he had expected, she was debating religion with a pair of Humans who were members of the Coalition's Security Police. Arano almost dropped his glass when he heard Kish's next statement: With the security officers expressing secular views, she was refuting their every expostulation, explaining the impossibility of their ever proving their atheistic viewpoints.

Arano chuckled and moved on; Kish never ceased to amaze him. He wondered suddenly where her religious views really fell. Just as in a religious society, there would be those who didn't believe the teachings of their religion; in a secular society, such as the Tompiste, there would still be those who believed.

Arano found Pelos Marnian next, and as he had expected, the big Tsimian was discussing finances, this time with a group of Gatoans. Judging by the group-wide nods and raised eyebrows, Arano surmised that the Gatoans were fairly impressed by Pelos's economic abilities. Pelos acknowledged Arano's approach with a nod.

"Pelos," Arano said loudly enough for the entire group to hear, "I wanted to be the first to congratulate you on your recent purchase."

Pelos gave a crooked smile, his long, sharp beak making the expression seem somehow distorted. "Which one?"

"Transcorp Shipping. I hope everyone realizes the value of your hostile takeover."

Pelos shrugged, his grin somehow spreading wider. "Their assets were seized following the war, due to their connections to Event Horizon. I don't like to brag, but I paid less for a fleet of freighters than you paid for the *Intrepid*."

Arano held up one finger, turning his head slightly to the

side. "Less than Balor Tient paid for the *Intrepid*."

Pelos laughed. "Transcorp Shipping is now Marnian Freight. If you need anything shipped in bulk, let me know. I might be able to work you a discounted rate."

Arano raised his glass and saluted, then moved on. He neared the stone patio at the rear of his house and was somewhat shocked to see a pair of Kamlings holding Lain Baxter upside down, his head dangling drunkenly near the beer dispenser. Arano's eyes darted about wildly, but he just couldn't resist the temptation.

"Hey, Lain. I almost hate to ask, but what are you doing?"

"It's ancient Human tradition. They called it a 'leg-stand.'"

"Never heard of it," Arano said carefully, taking a sip from his cup to hide the laughter.

One of the Kamlings glanced over at Arano. "Actually, it's called a 'keg-stand.'"

Arano's laughter got the best of him, and when he walked away he was giggling openly. Arano glanced at the newly dug hole in his backyard, and he found himself reconsidering the wisdom of adding a swimming pool at any gathering involving Kamlings and alcohol. He continued to meander through the crowd, stopping occasionally to speak with friends and coworkers. Finally, with the sun setting, he sat down to dinner with Alyna and their daughter. Videre and Laron joined them, and the four chatted about work while they ate.

"So the anniversary is next week?" Laron asked.

"Yeah," Arano replied. "Rather than celebrate the first anniversary of their liberation, the Bromidian people decided to mark the anniversary of the establishment of their constitution. Hawan told me Alyna should definitely come, and they said to bring one other person. I couldn't really see pulling another person off my team, so I chose you."

Laron looked to the sky in mock disgust. "Thanks a lot."

"What will you do with Nicole?" Videre asked.

"Aunt Nebra, once again," Alyna told him, looking fondly at the child in her lap. "I hate to take off again, but duty calls, I guess."

Lentin strolled over, arms laden with food. "Are you discussing the commemoration next week?"

Arano nodded. "Laron just volunteered to go along with us."

Lentin smiled, chuckling softly. "I see you Coalition soldiers have as much use for ceremony as I do. If we have to mark a date, we should be observing the day of our liberation, not the day some politicians signed a piece of paper."

"Humans tend to agree with you," Alyna said, playfully tickling her daughter. "Our civilizations on Earth tended to celebrate their days of independence, not the anniversary of the establishment of their government."

"We should have held a remembrance ceremony for the day Hawan plunged his knife into Vagorst VIII's cold heart. That was the day the true Bromidian government was born. The rest was just details."

"How have things been going for you with the new government?"

Lentin rolled his eyes, dabbing at his mouth with a napkin. "Oh, the usual troubles. Probably the biggest barrier has been theft. For the last several months, we have had a rash of thievery, mainly targeting surplus military items, but with some food and medical supplies being taken also. Some people are suggesting we resort to the methodology used by Vagorst. Brutal, but effective."

Arano set down his fork, leaning forward on his elbows. "Lentin, I've been meaning to ask you something. It didn't hit me right away, but those of you in the Rystorian Liberation Front always called the emperor by the name 'Vagorst.' Wasn't his name really 'Gorst?'"

Lentin smiled, laughing slightly. "The truth is, referring to him the way we did was a sign of our contempt. Since 'Vagorst' technically means 'Gorst's World,' we were showing our disdain for his belief that he was the ruler of the world; in his mind, he had *become* the world."

"I'm glad you cleared that up. I had been wondering about it and . . . Now what?"

Arano pressed a hand to his forehead and stared at the sight of Lain, who, to the roaring encouragement of his supporters, was engaging in his next "ancient Human ritual." Bent over at the waist, Lain and another Kamling were spinning in tight circles with their foreheads pressed firmly against short poles. The staggering effects of the alcohol, combined with a self-inflicted dose of dizziness, produced rather predictable results. The two Kamlings tried to race across the yard, but the best they could manage was a sharply zigzagging course. Lain crashed into a picnic table and rolled across the top, dumping several plates of food onto the ground. The other Kamling fared no better, running headlong into a tree. Neither was able to regain his feet, and instead both lay where they were, laughing uncontrollably. Arano gave a heavy sigh, hoping Lain's antics for the evening were over.

Early the next morning, President Siator Bistre emerged from his shower, preparing for another long, meeting-filled day. He studied his aging features in the mirror, noticing the gray hairs that seemed to be invading his fur in a dozen places at once.

He had made up his mind, prior to the war with the Bromidians, to retire from politics after his term was finished. However, his time in captivity with Rising Sun changed his mind. When he was freed by a valiant team of Avengers, he had learned how poorly the government had fared without him. He came to realize just how few politicians in the Coalition government were above the petty bickerings of party politics and the machinations of the devious elected officials. The government had sputtered and faltered without him, nearly allowing the Bromidian Empire the edge it needed to defeat the Coalition entirely. Once the war was over, he had resolved to remain in office for at least one more term while he worked with the Ethics committee to try and straighten out the web of treachery.

Wrapping a robe about his aging frame, he entered the living room, frowning into the darkness. He could have sworn he had left the light on. He padded over to the wall controller, casually flipping the light back on. He never felt the awesome explosion that tore through his house, ending his life.

Videre's computer terminal beeped, the data he had requested dutifully scrolling across the screen. He skimmed through the information, making a few notes on a nearby datapad.

"I've got it, Viper. It looks like Ament must've had more help than we realized. One of the captured freighters was already removed from Darin Station before our arrival, and it was carrying selected items from the cargoes of the other ships they had boarded."

Lines of concern creased Arano's forehead. "What did they get?"

Videre read the list once more, frowning. "Several barrels of assorted chemicals, a cache of weapons, mainly laser pistols and small laser rifles, and some communications equipment." He scrolled down the list farther. "They also stole a load of equipment the Coalition had seized from Biomek. I imagine some of it would fetch a nice price tag on the black market."

"We need to figure out where the freighter went, but Ament is *mine*."

Without looking up, Videre told him, "Remind me not to get on your bad side."

"I've downloaded the sensor data from the station's computers," Lain said. "It should be a simple matter to figure out where the freighter went. Of course, they could've jumped in a false direction, dropped out of their wormhole, and redirected to their true destination, but I doubt they would bother. When the freighter left Darin Station, they had no idea we were onto them."

"Nice work, Lain. Keep me posted."

"Well," Lentin said, squinting at his computer screen, "here's something. A single occupied escape pod left the station while we were there. It went directly to the second moon of Drania 2, which would be the closest planet to Darin Station."

Alyna looked up from her workstation. "Isn't Drania 2 a mining colony?"

"Yes," Kish told her, leaning back in her chair to stretch her legs. "With all the volcanic activity, it's a hazardous duty post, but apparently the pay is enough to draw some people in. If I remember correctly—" Kish had to pause to allow Videre to sigh heavily in mock disgust, as he always did when she made light of her photographic memory. She continued, "The people there are a bit lax about security. They are more concerned with seismic shockwaves than they are with smugglers."

"Well," Lain said, "within a few minutes of the escape pod touching down, a personal skiff launched and went into a wormhole. According to their last trajectory, the most likely destination would be"—he touched a few controls, and then his eyes flew open wide—"here!"

Lanta Nupez, the Tsimian who was selected as the successor to Grand High Councilor Balor Tient, pulled a light jacket about her shoulders. The weather wasn't especially brisk, but she was never a fan of cooler weather. She activated the Comm in her study, speaking briefly with her aide before casually strolling out to her waiting transportation.

She stepped into the back seat and was about to close the door when she heard a distant rumble like thunder. She looked up at the sky, puzzled; it was a beautiful, clear day, with not a cloud to be seen, though a noticeably cool wind was blowing. With a shrug, she closed the door and signaled to her driver. Her limousine backed out of the driveway to begin the long ride to the council chambers.

Several minutes later, her Comm gave an urgent beep, and she activated the video link in her vehicle. Her top aide appeared on the screen, his face pale; quite a trick for a Tompiste. "What is it, Rolan?"

"Madame Grand High Councilor! I . . . we just received word that the president's house has exploded! There is no word yet about President Bistre, but the house was totally destroyed!"

Lanta sat open-mouthed, unable to express what she was feeling. She was still trying to form a coherent answer when the bomb exploded under her seat.

"Ament was coming here?" Arano asked incredulously.

"While it's likely," Kish said, "it's not certain. The timing of the skiff launching from that moon could have been coincidence."

"I don't think so," Videre replied, peeking over Lain's shoulder. "The skiff was the only ship to leave that moon in the last three days, and the freighter had the same destination."

Arano spun on his heel, slapping a control panel to open a Comm channel. In a voice sounding just a bit harsher than he had intended, he described the situation to the harbormaster and sent him the identifiers of the two ships. Within minutes, they had received the confirmation Arano was expecting: both the freighter and the skiff had landed, within a few hours of each other, and the skiff's pilot had specifically requested a berth near the freighter. Arano's eyes went flat at the news, and he immediately reached for his pistol belt.

The main Comm panel for Team 5 flickered to life, and the speaker sounded a critical alarm. Alyna activated the screen with the touch of a button. The screen flickered, and a battle-scarred Tsimian face materialized. His beak was pressed firmly shut, and the featherlike, dark fur on his neck was bristling. "Avengers teams, I have some terrible news. There has been a series of bomb attacks against ranking members of our government. The president, the Grand High Councilor, and the entire Military Committee have been killed."

A sudden silence fell over the room. Arano reached a numb hand out for a nearby table, leaning on it for support, and Pelos covered his heart with a fur-covered hand, a Tsimian gesture meant to ward off bad luck. Arano slowly lowered himself into a chair and buried his face in his hands. Alyna sidled over to him and placed a supporting hand on his shoulder.

It was some time before Lain broke the silence permeating the room. "Arano," he said in a quiet voice, "I was just looking at the list of chemicals stolen by Ament. Three in particular stand out: rudamine, tolium nitrate, and gallium oxide."

Kish gave a low whistle in surprise, but the rest of the team sat waiting for the explanation. "These three chemicals," Lain explained, "are fairly unstable. But if you combine the three, they produce a violent explosion."

Arano's eyes narrowed, his hands clenching into fists. "How long after they are combined would they explode?"

"Immediately."

"Then how could you make a bomb with them? Any thoughts?"

Surprisingly, it was Lentin who provided the answer. "The RLF used to produce such a bomb. It could be as simple as attaching the bomb to a light controller. The victim flips the switch, the chemicals combine, and the bomb explodes. As for the vehicle bombs, any of the switches could have been rigged to trigger the explosion."

"We need to speak to Ament," Alyna said in a menacing tone.

"I think I know how," Arano said, his eyes thoughtful. He spun in his chair, tapped a few keys, and activated the Comm. The screen hummed to life, and moments later a grim but familiar Human face appeared.

"This is Special Agent Imatt Deeps, Galactic Bureau of Intelligence." He blinked his eyes and leaned closer to the screen. "Arano?"

"Imatt, how have you been?"

"I've seen better days. As you can imagine, things are a bit hectic here right now."

"I think we can help each other on that point, my friend. I'm sending you some internal sensor data from Darin Station."

Briefly, Arano told Imatt Deeps about the events occurring at Darin Station. "I would love to put my hands on Ament. If he's our man, we'd be solving a number of problems at once by catching up to him. I was hoping you could use some of your resources to get a better identification on him. I'm sure Ament isn't using his real name."

Imatt studied a nearby datapad while Arano's data streamed across the screen. He connected it to his main computer interface, and uploaded the information. "This may take a while," he warned them. "I'll contact you when I have something. In the meantime, I'll send his picture to the spaceports and main intraplanetary transportation centers. If he shows up, an alert guard might catch him."

Arano terminated the link, but his Comm immediately beeped once more. With a sigh and a shake of his head, he flicked the switch to complete the connection. He relaxed when he saw Commander Laron Alstor looking back at him.

"Viper," Laron said. "I just spoke with General Timor. He wants to put the best possible face on this situation. Although the fleet is making a show of force around Immok 2, the rest of us are supposed to continue with any planned military exercises. This includes our trip to Rystoria in a few days."

"Are you kidding me?" Arano protested, throwing his arms into the air. "I think we're making some progress on these bombings."

Laron strummed his fingers on his desk. "Okay, here's what we'll do. We're under orders to go to Rystoria, so we're going to have to keep that engagement. I will go, and you, Alyna, and Lentin will go with me. The rest of your team can work on this with Captain Pana's team. They're shorthanded because Captain Lanson is pregnant. Again." He glared past Arano to where Alyna sat looking innocently at the ceiling.

"Don't blame me," she said innocently. "I had nothing to do with it."

"It must be something in the water. Anyway, we'll still go to Rystoria, but we'll come back as soon as we can. I'll tell Pana to have the remnants of his team help yours in our absence. Keep me posted." The screen went blank.

Arano sat silently for a few minutes. "Okay, let's make the best of this. We'll talk to Pana and coordinate things with him." He grinned slyly, casting a superior gaze in Videre's direction. "Sorry, Vid. I was going to destroy you in our chess match, but now I guess you've been given a reprieve."

Videre raised his hand in reply, but Lain spoke first. "Not necessarily, Viper. I've modified a pair of our old FM radios, giving them a direct FM link to orbital subspace converters. You can make your move, send it through the radio, and in about two hours Videre will have it. He sends his move back to you, and you keep going until he wins. Or whatever."

"Will that work on Rystoria?" Arano asked. "After all, they are still rebuilding from the war. I don't know if their new subspace converters are even in orbit yet."

"They are, Viper," Lentin told him. "In fact, they were put up about four months ago."

Arano sighed. "I think I smell a conspiracy."

After a tearful good bye with their daughter and Aunt Nebra, the two Avengers endured the long ride to the spaceport. They were taking a standard military transport to Rystoria 2; the *Intrepid* would be staying with his teammates in case of an emergency. In fact, the only weapons they were bringing were their sidearms, and they wouldn't even bring those to the ceremony. Lentin and Laron met them at the bay housing the *USCS Augustus*, and together they walked up the boarding ramp.

They entered the spacious crew quarters assigned to them, and they selected their bunks. It would take two jumps and over twenty-four hours to go from Immok to Rystoria, so they would make up for a night that had been short on sleep. The modified FM radio Arano had brought along beeped once, and he rolled his eyes as he pulled it out.

The control screen indicated a message was waiting, so Arano called it up. As he had expected, it was from Videre, taunting Arano about their chess match. *You're going down, punk.*

Arano laughed out loud and typed a message back to Videre. *Bring it on.*

CHAPTER
THREE

THE *USCS AUGUSTUS* ARRIVED ON TIME IN THE Rystoria System, and an hour later it had landed in the Bromidian capital. They were escorted to the residence reserved for visiting heads of state. Lentin was also housed in the sprawling mansion, and was given a room adjoining Laron's. Arano and Alyna shared a room across the hall, and the intimate surroundings appealed greatly to Arano. Alyna noticed her husband's wicked grin and rolled her eyes.

They gathered in a small but functional office, which they designated as their meeting room. The plain white walls were decorated with drab paintings, and Arano assumed they were the Bromidian equivalent of watercolors. While his friends settled in, Arano spent several minutes poring over a computerized chess board. Finally satisfied with his strategy, he typed his next move into the computer. The modified FM radio hummed, sending out a signal to the subspace converter.

Videre paced impatiently in front of his team's main computer, anxiously awaiting the DNA test results. Despite Imatt's best efforts, he had been unable to identify Ament based upon his picture alone. However, on an inspired plan concocted by Kish and Pelos, a number of GBI agents had conducted an intensive search for unexploded bombs. The two Avengers had suggested that devices such as those they believed the culprit to have used didn't always work. Sometimes they failed to properly combine the chemicals, and therefore the mixture wouldn't explode. Two more bombs had been located; both had been triggered by their intended victims but had failed to detonate. They sent the bombs to the crime lab, where they were being tested for traces of DNA.

The computer chirped happily, and several pages of data rolled across the screen. To simplify the analysis, Videre printed several hard copies, allowing the nine Avengers and Imatt Deeps to each have a copy. According to the report, the only DNA on the bombs belonged to a Human named Treng Gomid. The picture provided in his file, while similar to the pictures of Ament taken on Darin Station, were not entirely the same.

"Most likely," Videre said, "if Ament and Treng Gomid are the same person, then he wore some type of disguise while with the pirates. But that begs another question: why would he hide his identity from his cohorts?"

Imatt bobbed his head, staring blankly at the floor. "My guess would be that he was working, primarily, for someone else, and the disguise was a contingency plan. This way, the pirates we captured would be unable to identify him other than by the alias he gave them."

"Let's go over what we know about Treng," Pelos suggested.

Videre nodded, rapidly skimming through the compiled data. "He was born on Subac 3 Prime, held a few odd jobs, and went into the military. He went through the Avengers training program, but was washed out in the final phase. He specialized in counterterrorism and explosives. He left the military after failing the Avengers program, and there are no more official records of his location, aside from a few scattered arrests."

"Now what?" Kish asked. "We can put out a system-wide alert for him, obviously. But I would be very interested in putting my hands on his employer. Obviously, the whole pirate scheme was secondary. According to later interviews with the two men we captured at Darin Station, Treng had only been with them for a few months. They knew very little about him."

"I have an idea," Imatt volunteered. "Let's put out our bulletin for him, but on a notification basis only. We can monitor him from a distance and see if he'll lead us to his contacts, or even his employer."

Lon Pana nodded approvingly. "I think we have a plan. Let's get on it."

Arano sat impatiently in the elevated, padded bleachers provided for the special guests of the ceremony. His arm was still sore from the vaccination he had received, a preventive measure against the detrimental effects of the sun's rays scorching through an atmosphere short on ozone. All around him, Bromidian generals sat in their crisp dress uniforms. Colorful banners hung from the bleachers and the building behind them, announcing the festive atmosphere of the day.

Although the air was cool, the intense Bromidian sun beat down on him like a hammer. Leaning over to Hawan, Arano whispered his request for something to drink. Hawan looked at the time, shrugged, and motioned for Arano to follow him. They left the stands and moved inside a nearby hangar, where refreshments were being provided.

"What is this stuff?" Arano asked. "It looks and smells like tea, but tastes a lot better."

Hawan smiled. "I'm glad you like it, Viper. This is a drink called *kati*. It is made by boiling certain herbal leaves in water for a period of time. The taste and beneficial properties of the leaves are leeched out into the water."

Arano nodded appreciably. "Very similar to Human herbal tea, then." Despite the dark glasses he wore, he shaded his eyes from the bright Rystorian sun, trying to get a better look at a squadron of Bromidian fighters roaring overhead in a test run for their performance later. "You Bromidians put on quite a show."

Hawan sighed. "It would be a shame if we weren't able to get back to our seats and had to wait out the show in here . . ."

"With the *kati*," Arano said, smiling.

Several minutes and another glass of *kati* later, Hawan regretfully told him it was time to move back to their seats. Arano drained his glass, squared his shoulders, and motioned in the direction of the bleachers. Before they had moved two steps, a rhythmic stomping brought them up short. A column of Bromidian soldiers marched in, stopping behind the bleachers and effectively preventing Arano and Hawan from returning to their seats. The two exchanged a look, grinned broadly, and returned to the drink table.

Alyna looked out from the empty hangar where she, Lentin, and Laron were to watch the ceremony. The walls of the building were hung with various spare parts and repair tools. The lack of doors inside the hangar struck Alyna as odd, and gave the foul-smelling building the appearance of a prison.

She wasn't certain about the source of the feeling creeping over her. Perhaps she had spent so much time with Arano that she was beginning to imagine she, too, had a danger sense. But whatever the cause, she had an uneasy feeling growing stronger by the minute.

The sound of rhythmically tramping feet brought her out of her reverie, and she was startled by the appearance of a company of Bromidian soldiers carrying laser rifles. She reached for her own pistol, only to remember they had come to the event unarmed. Her eyes went flat, and she cast about for a weapon, but the soldiers executed a flanking maneuver and turned away from the hangar. Alyna sheepishly relaxed, hoping her friends hadn't seen her reaction. The laughter coming from behind her spoke volumes about the chances of that happening.

Arano stepped up on a footstool for a better view over the ranks of soldiers in front of him. Only he and Hawan remained in the hangar, the other revelers having returned to their seats when the show began. Although the air outside had a slight chill to it, the temperature inside the hangar was noticeably warmer. Five Bromidian fighters streaked low over the parade grounds, flying in perfect formation through a series of intricate maneuvers.

A lone Bromidian soldier stepped in front of the stands, saluted the crowd, and retrieved his projectile rifle from a cache of weapons. He took up a prone firing position and aimed across the barren, kilometers-wide field before the stands. He fired at a number of targets, some static and some moving, all at different ranges, while a voice on the public address system droned on about the various capabilities of the rifle itself.

The bodiless voice continued its oration, describing the different pieces of artillery in the Bromidian arsenal. As if in tune with his words, distant artillery pieces fired with a low *bump*. The shells hissed overhead to land with deafening explosions a short but safe distance into the field. Heavily armored Bromidian tanks rumbled into view, racing onto the parade grounds and firing their shells unerringly at their targets. Simultaneously, several attack hovercraft raced into view, firing rockets into the target zone. Heavy laser cannons mounted on their sides belched a blizzard of laser fire into the havoc. The artillery came alive again, and the Bromidian soldier in front of the stands fired his rifle once more. He had been surreptitiously joined by several other soldiers, and together they fired the stunning array of weapons at their targets.

"That's the house," Lain whispered. "The green one with the black shutters."

Videre nodded and motioned to Imatt. The special agent of the Galactic Bureau of Intelligence led Lon Pana's team around the rear of the residence, positioning them in case their quarry was home and would try to escape the coming trap. There were no lights on, although with the late hour, he hadn't expected anything else. A tall row of bushes covered one wall, blocking visual access to the windows arrayed there. Videre gave them a silent count of thirty seconds before he signaled for his team to move closer.

His team. He almost stopped in his tracks when the enormity of it hit him. If someone on the team was injured or killed, it would be on his shoulders. How did Arano deal with the pressure? He vowed to himself that, upon Arano's return, he would stop his endless game of distractions and jokes, which always seemed to irritate the veteran Daxia. Or at least, he thought with an inward chuckle, he wouldn't joke around quite as often.

It was random chance that had brought them to the house in the first place. The landlord for the rented residence had stopped by a Coalition military recruiting facility to pick up a few leaflets for his son, and happened to see a bulletin board featuring pictures of people wanted by the military and GBI. He immediately recognized one of them as the eccentric renter living at a small property he owned in Immok City's lower west side.

Videre stepped lightly on the front porch, and the wooden surface creaked slightly beneath his weight. His sharp Gatoan sense of smell picked up the odor of chemicals emanating from the house. He crinkled his nose in response, baring the long eye-teeth hidden behind his muzzle. With a wave of his pistol, he positioned the rest of the team around the front door.

From inside the house, a warning beacon sounded, breaking the stillness of the night. Videre swore and slapped the door release, throwing his bulk into the portal and snapping it from its hinges. They burst inside, weapons ready, and found the main room to be empty. Videre held one hand up, motioning for his team to stay in place, and activated the Comm while he dropped to one knee.

"Pana here."

"Front room is clear," Videre whispered tensely, eyes still searching for signs of movement. "We set off some type of motion sensing alarm in front of the house. I need you to spread out and cover every possible exit, front and back. We'll take care of the inside."

"Acknowledged."

Videre rose to his feet and surveyed the situation. There

were two possible ways in and out of the room: one a closed door, and the other an open hallway. He pointed at his eyes, then at the closed door, and finally at Kish and Pelos. The veteran soldiers knew what was expected, and they took up positions watching the door. Videre and Lain padded down the hall, the lights mounted on their pistols casting eerie shadows on the walls. A partially open door loomed ahead on his left, and he gestured toward it with his weapon. Lain padded forward and stood ready at Videre's side. The Gatoan kicked the door open and they rushed into the room, each covering one's own span—but they were alone.

Another door stood ajar, and through the opening a bed was plainly visible. Videre slipped closer, weapon held ready before him, and he examined the room as best he could without opening the door farther. Not only did it appear empty, but dust covered the wooden furniture, giving the appearance that no one had stayed in the room for quite some time. Lain nodded, and the two rushed inside. The bedroom was empty, and a quick search of the closet, drawers, and bathroom revealed nothing to indicate the house was even being lived in.

"This is Videre," he whispered into his wrist-mounted Comm unit. "The ground floor is clear. We're returning to the front of the house. There was a closed door in the main room, and I believe it leads to the basement."

"We copied that," Lon replied.

Videre tried the door, but it was locked. Since the element of surprise was long lost, he resorted to the simple expedient of kicking it open. The door hung crazily on one hinge, and splinters showered the stairway revealed beyond.

"I think you enjoy that too much," Lain noted dryly, proceeding carefully down the stairs. Videre grinned broadly in return.

There was a short hallway at the bottom of the stairwell, ending in a metal door. Videre tried it but found it secured from within. He glanced over at Lain and arched his eyebrows sharply, while the Kamling Avenger rolled his eyes in response. Videre stepped back and plunged into the door with all his weight. There was a solid *thump* from the impact, but the solid portal didn't budge. Videre stood to one side, rubbing his sore shoulder and trying to ignore the subdued laughter from his teammates.

"Any suggestions?" he asked.

"Yeah," Kish said, raising her pistol and firing. After the third hit, there was an explosion of sparks, and the ruptured door creaked slowly open amid a cloud of smoke. Videre dropped into a crouch and swung his light through the opening. The roiling haze obscured his vision, making it impossible to see more than a few feet into the room.

They found only one room beyond, a wide open space broken only by the pillars supporting the roof above them. The floor and walls were concrete, and the only furniture in the room was a scattering of utilitarian chairs. Two walls were fitted with shelves, which were covered with large metal containers. The remaining wall had been painted with an enormous depiction of the silhouette of a horizon just after sunrise. In one corner, a cot stood alone, with a simple bedroll and a small pillow perched askew and ready to fall off. Food wrappers littered the floor near an overflowing garbage can, and footprints carpeted the area. A careful search of the room revealed no sign of their quarry.

Videre contacted Lon Pana's team and called them inside, telling them the house was empty. A thorough check of the room revealed a total lack of traps left behind by the former resident. While Lain and Kish examined some of the devices on the workbenches, Videre prodded the piles of trash, looking for anything of value. Pelos read the manifests of the containers on the shelves, taking notes on what he had found. Imatt was deep in conversation with his superiors via his Comm, and Pana's team was riffling through the various drawers.

Lon Pana whistled in surprise. "This drawer is a disguise artist's dream: makeup, latex masks, and phony facial hair. He could look like anyone right now."

"He could *be* anyone right now," said Testa Marquis, a young Human who had recently joined Pana's team. She held up several ID cards. "There are enough identification papers in here to supply a small army. And this computer over here is capable of making more."

"These are definitely our missing containers from Darin Station," Pelos noted thoughtfully, tapping his finger against his beak. "These are some of the missing chemicals."

"This place appears to have been used as a bomb-making working workshop," Kish said, holding a small metallic device up to the light. "This would have been used as a timer."

Videre nodded. "Let's finish up here. We need to try to figure out his next move. Gomid is a very dangerous man, and I won't feel safe until he is dead or incarcerated."

The noise subsided, and Arano gingerly removed his hands from his ears. The ringing rattling through his head told him he should have tried to block out the sound of the explosions a bit sooner. At his side, Hawan chuckled softly.

"As I said, it's a bit overdone. When I was in the RLF, I didn't have to attend these shows, a luxury I no longer have."

Arano glanced out over the field in front of the stands. "Is it over?"

Hawan snorted. "Not by a long shot. Now they send the infantry troops on some maneuvers, where they'll murder more innocent targets. Are you thirsty?"

Arano nodded, and he followed Hawan back to the refreshment table. They were deep in the hangar, unable to see what show the Bromidian military was putting on, but Arano decided it must have involved a lot of troops. He could hear their shouted commands and heavy footfalls even from where he was standing. From the assembled forces, he heard the sounds of laser fire once more. His cup fell to the floor, and he spun to face the front of the building, dropping into a defensive crouch.

"What is it?" Hawan asked, his earlier show of indifference gone.

"Those rifles sound like they're being fired toward us. And my danger sense . . ." Belatedly, he cursed himself for not even thinking to hide a small pistol somewhere in the crisp folds of his dress uniform. From high overhead, he heard the screeching whistle of incoming artillery rounds.

Alyna stood with Lentin and Laron at the open entrance to their hangar, watching the ongoing display of raw firepower. After several minutes, the barrage subsided, and the military units regrouped. Lentin shifted impatiently from one foot to the other.

"Bored?" she asked with a smile.

He laughed. "If the truth was to be known, I'd rather be hunting padorsas with Viper."

"You're not the only one," Laron said, squinting from the Rystorian sunlight despite the dark glasses he wore. "How much longer will this go on?"

"It used to last for hours," Lentin said, folding his arms across his chest. "I have a feeling, though, that the new government can't afford to run this for too much longer."

Alyna's body tensed, and she realized something was wrong. The soldiers on the field had turned to face the wrong direction, as if they were going to march right up to the section of bleachers set aside for the distinguished guests seated in the main bleachers. The formation marched closer, stopping only about a hundred meters from the stands . . .

And opened fire. Alyna's mouth dropped in surprise, and she could only watch as the bodies of the new Bromidian government fell from the seats like rain. The execution-style firing continued unabated, even as those seated there scurried for cover. Alyna prayed that Arano had sensed the danger in time to escape, or at least to duck beneath the bleachers, where he would be a less likely target. Her hopes were dashed moments later when the first artillery round landed in the center of the bleachers, sending a shower of bodies and debris into the air.

CHAPTER
FOUR

VIDERE, ON HIS FUR-COVERED HANDS AND KNEES, poked through the garbage he had dumped onto the floor. The other members of the group were dutifully cataloguing everything they had found, in preparation for the local police to cart the items away to be stored as evidence.

He found several receipts from various restaurants and bars around Immok City, and while he did set them aside, he didn't think they would offer much help. In all likelihood, Treng Gomid would be leaving the system as soon as he possibly could. What Videre really wanted was something connecting their quarry with locations in another system.

A half-eaten meal consisting of something resembling chili had spilled near the bottom of the trash container, staining several sheets of paper almost beyond legibility. Forcing down the wave of revulsion he felt from handling the rotting food, he brushed away the worst of the mess and tried to decipher the writing.

It was a handwritten note, scribed in a foreign alphabet. Although he couldn't read it, he recognized the letters as Bromidian in origin. He frowned. Why would someone write a letter to a smuggler, using the Bromidian language? The most obvious answer would be that the author, or the intended audience, was a Bromidian. At the bottom of the letter was a likeness of the image on the wall, a newly risen sun over a barren landscape.

Videre set the note aside and pushed on.

He sorted through the rest of the garbage, and while the stench seemed embedded in his fur, he found nothing else of interest. He sat back on his haunches and retrieved the note he had found. He heard a light step behind him.

"Find something?" It was Imatt Deeps.

"I don't know. Maybe. It's a note written in Bromidian." He handed the note to the GBI Special Agent.

Imatt nodded slowly, meticulously examining every inch of the paper. "Let's hang onto this. The police would just lock it away somewhere. I think a translation of the contents might tell us something."

Lain walked carefully over to his acting team leader, several partially burnt pieces of paper in his cupped hands. "I found these images of Treng and several colleagues gathered in what looks like a meeting or something. In addition to the possibility of identifying some of his cohorts, we may have something else of value here. This photo was taken in the daytime, as you can see through the window behind them. With a little enhancement, we may be able to figure out where these pictures were taken."

Videre tossed the gray metal garbage can back where it had been, scowling when he heard the hollow sound it made as it impacted the floor. He stomped his booted foot and was rewarded by the echo he heard from beneath the concrete. Another hands-and-knees search was fruitless for several minutes, until Kish located a switch under the edge of the nearby workbench. She pressed the button, and a crack formed in the floor, forming a square roughly two feet on a side. The section of floor sank away into the darkness, then slid aside, allowing access to the underground passage.

Videre directed his team into the darkness, his weapon once

again throwing light ahead of them. He motioned for Lain to take the lead, and he fell back with the others. The passage, while winding, led in a general westerly direction from the house, with no side tunnels to confuse their search. Before they had gone a hundred meters, they came to a blank wall. This time, however, the switch operating the opening and closing of the hidden door was out in the open. While Lain, Kish, and Pelos took up firing positions, Videre flipped the toggle with a snap of his wrist, and the door grinded open.

The reek of raw, untreated sewage assailed them in a wave. The four Avengers from Team 5 cast their lights ahead, confirming what they already knew: the clandestine tunnel led directly into Immok City's sewer system. With all the branching tunnels and multiple access points to the surface, they had no way of following Treng Gomid.

Another shell detonated with ear-splitting efficiency, the concussion from the blast throwing Arano to the ground again. He staggered to his feet, blood from a cut to his forehead dripping into his eyes. The laser fire, which had stopped when the soldiers took cover from the incoming artillery fire, started anew. Arano vaulted from his hiding place behind an overturned table and started toward the mouth of the hangar. Hawan grabbed his arm from behind and spun him around.

"What are you doing, Viper? We must escape!"

"Alyna is in danger! I'm not going to leave her!"

He tried to pull free, but Hawan held him fast. "You can't help her right now. Look!" He gestured toward the ground in front of the hangar, which had become a killing field. Troops loyal to the government officials were scurrying about, searching for cover, but were being cut down by the troops in the field. Even the unarmed politicians, clearly marked by their light brown robes, were offered no quarter, and were being murdered with brutal, reckless abandon. To step into the open was suicide. Arano allowed some of the tension to leave his body and nodded his acquiescence.

"We can still escape," Hawan told him, a wave of edginess giving his guttural voice a nervous twitter. "Follow me."

He ran to a rear corner of the hangar, Arano close on his heels. The Bromidian soldier opened a closet door and pointed to a plain, black handle securely attached to the floor. He pulled it open to reveal a ladder leading down into the depths of a cellar. Arano dashed back to one of the tables and snatched up his backpack before returning to the closet. They scrambled down the rungs as quickly as their formal uniforms would allow. Three doors faced them from different walls, but Hawan chose one of them without hesitating.

"These tunnels have been around for a millennium," Hawan gasped as they jogged along. "Our people decided long ago to seek a way of moving from building to building without having to be out in the Rystorian sun any more than necessary. Many important buildings have access points to them; one just needs to know the layout in order to navigate them. The RLF used them extensively, and we even discovered a few that had been forgotten." He smiled. "Like the ones leading out of the capital."

"And then what?" Arano asked, his breathing more labored than Hawan's. While Arano was by far in better shape than his Bromidian counterpart, the thinner atmosphere of Rystoria 2 was wearing him down, and his body was starving for oxygen. His side was cramped, and his legs felt leaden.

"We have to contact people we trust and find out what happened. Obviously, there was some sort of coup d'etat, but by whom?"

"What about Alyna and the others?"

"We go after them," Hawan assured him, "when it's safe to do so. But right now, we're a bit pressed. We're on the run, we have no supplies, and we have no weapons. Not to mention," he gave Arano's uniform top a dark look, his bulbous, insectoid eyes narrowing in concern, "you are wounded."

Arano followed his friend's gaze, seeing the crimson stain darkening the jacket of his uniform. With that, he understood why his side ached so much; the piece of shrapnel protruding from between his ribs gave mute testimony to the source of his pain. He felt the onset of lightheadedness. From far to their rear, they heard the sounds of pursuit. He set his teeth together, grinding them against the pain, and pushed on.

It could have been another mile, or it could have been ten, but they staggered through a vine-draped cave opening to find themselves on the side of a wooded hill. The temperature had fallen farther, and his breath rolled away from him in white puffs of steam. They had slipped away from whoever was chasing them, and Hawan guided them to a sheltered little draw. He told Arano to rest for a moment, and he flitted away, disappearing into the trees. Arano panted heavily for several minutes, unable to catch enough oxygen to satisfy the needs of his battered body. He tried to stand but failed, so he lay back and closed his eyes.

Why hadn't he seen this coming? Shouldn't his danger sense have warned him of the peril long before the attack was launched? The only solution Arano could find was his time off from work. From the day he first attended Daxia training at Whelen Academy, he had scarcely taken more than a few days off in a row. However, with the birth of Nicole, he had stayed home with his wife and child for months. His convalescence may have dulled his senses.

Who had led the insurrection? Would they know who Alyna was and use her against Arano? In all likelihood, he believed they would. If, of course, they knew it was Arano who had escaped their carefully laid trap. He glanced down once more at the sharp-edged sliver of metal jutting out through his jacket and realized he hadn't escaped yet.

With startling suddenness, he remembered his backpack. It took an excruciating effort, but he managed to unstrap it from his back and bring it out where he could access the contents. There was a bottle of water, his chess computer, several datapads he had meant to read, and a portable light. He took a deep drink of water, the cooling liquid easing his pain slightly. An idea came to him with such clarity that he spilled water down the front of his uniform.

He picked up the chess game, skipped over the message he had received from Videre, and activated the communication function. *Videre, emergency situation. Revolution on Rystoria 2, rebel forces in control of the city, maybe the entire planet. I'm wounded; Alyna, Lentin, and Laron are missing and presumed captured. Send help.*

He pressed the send button, watching with satisfaction and relief as the FM radio indicated the successful transmission. He checked his watch, mentally counting forward through the hours until he could expect a reply from Videre. *Assuming the message got through at all.* The rebels might be blocking communication, at least on the subspace level. And even if they hadn't started scrambling the Comm channels yet, they probably would before Videre's message came back.

There was a slight crashing in the undergrowth, and Hawan

emerged from the trees carrying a small satchel under one arm. "I found one of our old supply dumps a short distance from here. The weapons were all removed a long time ago, but there was a scattering of things left. I found some water, so drink what you have left and I'll refill your bottle. There were also a few tools lying around." He pulled out a pair of forceps, resembling the pair of pliers Arano had in his tool kit back home. The Bromidian gave Arano a look of deep sympathy, pursing his lips. "This will hurt . . ."

Arano nodded and turned his head, not really wanting to watch the procedure, and felt the shrapnel moving inside his body when Hawan took hold. With a grunt, Hawan gave a fierce pull, drawing the fragment of metal out in a shower of blood. Arano doubled over in pain, biting his lip in an effort not to cry out. Hawan gently pressed him back, opened his bloodstained uniform, and examined the wound. Using water and a piece of cloth torn from the remnants of Arano's jacket, he cleansed the laceration, but blood continued to seep out.

Hawan retrieved a plastic can marked with spidery, indecipherable Bromidian letters. He removed the lid and produced a white cream, which he scooped out liberally with his fingers. "This is a special salve made from the roots of herbs," Hawan explained. "Since we often lacked formal medical facilities, the RLF had to come up with expedient means of treating the injured. It burns a little, but it will eliminate the possibility of infection and stop the bleeding."

Arano took several deep, labored breaths before nodding his consent, and Hawan gently wiped the cream onto the still-bleeding wound. The pain lanced through Arano's body once more, only much more intensely, and his body curled into a ball, convulsing with agony. The pain slowly subsided, and he lay gasping for several long moments.

Hawan gave him a sympathetic frown. "Maybe Padian physiology reacts differently to this treatment than ours does."

Arano gritted his teeth. "Gee, do you think?"

Alyna watched with horror as round after explosive round struck the bleachers with deadly accuracy, and even from a distance, she could see the destruction the attack had caused. The shelling finally subsided, but the infantry stationed nearby picked up where the artillery had left off. Survivors of the barrage ran about in confusion, only to be shot in cold blood. A group of Bromidians made a final stand, but they were cut down in a lethal barrage. The shooting subsided, and green-uniformed Bromidians dashed into the hangar beyond the bleachers.

A lone Bromidian, who had stood motionless up until then, suddenly leveled his rifle at Alyna's head, the muzzle only inches away. "You are under arrest," he said, "by order of—"

His impassioned speech was cut short by a sharp blow from her right forearm, knocking his rifle aside before he could react. Her next blow took him in the abdomen, then in the throat, and he dropped to his knees. She snatched the rifle from his feeble hands and fired once, knocking his lifeless body flat on the ground. She swung the rifle around, just in time to intercept two more green-uniformed soldiers who had entered the hangar. Her stolen weapon belched laser energy several times, and two more Bromidians lay lifeless in the hangar. Lentin and Laron each grabbed a rifle, ignoring the panicked crowd gathered behind them.

"Where do we go?" Alyna asked tensely, her eyes on their

Bromidian friend.

"The tunnels," he said without hesitation. He led them to a tool closet, kicked aside some debris, and opened a hatch in the floor. They descended a flight of metal stairs into a dank, well-lit corridor, and dashed away. Lentin counted corners and side passages, gesturing at the various landmarks and muttering to himself. Finally, he motioned them to a rickety wooden ladder on one side of the passage. Alyna reached it in a bound, landing halfway up and climbing the rest of the way two rungs at a time. The hatch above her was unlocked, and she carefully edged it up, just far enough to allow her to see into the room beyond.

She couldn't see anyone, so she pushed the hatch the rest of the way open and climbed up, finding herself in a maintenance garage, surrounded by a number of land vehicles, some wheeled and some hovercars. Her two companions climbed out behind her and surveyed the scene.

"Do we take a vehicle?" she asked breathlessly.

Laron nodded. "I think we need to get out of the city as quickly as possible, and those tunnels are a bit too well-used for my liking. Should we use a hovercar?"

Lentin shook his head. "The military would use an anti-graviton wave fluxor to disable the craft's hover generator." He made a face. "It's another of our former government's control efforts. They wanted to be able to disable vehicles in case of theft or insurrection. The flaw in our hovercars has never been removed."

Laron and Alyna climbed atop one of the wheeled vehicles, taking cover beneath an old tarp in the vehicle's rear compartment. Lentin donned a pair of coveralls he found nearby, dressing himself as a public works employee. The engine rumbled to life, the sudden noise shattering the silence of the open building. The vehicle shimmied and shook, then suddenly lurched forward when Lentin engaged the drive. Alyna lay under the canvas with Laron, trying to ignore the stench of grease and sweat permeating the fabric.

They bounced along for several minutes, and while the ride was uncomfortable, Alyna took solace in the fact that they were making progress. The hope was dashed when she was suddenly pressed to the rear of the vehicle, the engine roaring in protest. Through the noise of the vehicle and the barrier of the tarp, Alyna could hear Lentin cursing.

"We've been found!" he shouted. "Might as well stay under cover, since we're unarmed, but be prepared. We may have to run on foot!"

Alyna's heart raced, pounding heavily in her chest while she tried to stretch her stiff leg muscles. The solid hum of the paved roadway turned into a hollow echo. She lifted a corner of the tarp to peer out, and saw Lentin was driving them across a narrow chasm, crossing on a wooden bridge.

"Damn! They're in front of us, too! We're trapped." There was only a moment of silence, and Lentin's mind was made up. "Get ready to jump. I'm going to crash through the guardrails and dump us into the river. It's about a thirty-foot drop, so when we break through, brace for impact!"

Alyna felt a sudden lurch, unsettling her stomach and making her grab reflexively for a handhold. There was a deafening crash, and the vehicle slammed to a sudden stop. It teetered back and forth, balanced precariously on the edge of the bridge.

"What happened?" she asked, throwing back the tarp.

"We didn't get all the way through the rail. Can you get out? We'll have to jump. They'll be here momentarily."

She nodded briskly. "Go! We'll be right behind you!" Lentin spun, leaped from his seat, and dropped over the edge of the bridge, lost from sight. While Laron grabbed for a nearby tool kit and a water bottle, Alyna tried to flip the latch to open the door. It wouldn't budge. She pressed her hands to the glass of the window, and realized their time was almost up. She tried the latch once more, then threw her weight against the door. Laron joined her, retrieved a hammer from the tool kit, and smashed the glass. She reached through the window, released the locking mechanism which had somehow become jammed, and opened the door.

They were too late. Over a dozen Bromidians surrounded their transport, weapons leveled. They were prisoners of the revolution.

Lentin plummeted the ten or so meters to the rushing waters below, knifing into the water feet first. He swam to the surface, careful to only stick enough of his head above water to enable him to see what had happened. For some reason, Alyna and Laron hadn't emerged, and the Bromidians had encircled them. His fears were confirmed moments later, when the two Avengers stepped disconsolately from the vehicle, arms raised high in the air. There were at least two dozen enemy soldiers, all armed, holding his friends. He had no weapons, no supplies, and no help. He ground his teeth in frustration, twisting around and swimming downriver. He would find one of the old RLF weapons caches, and from there he would try to marshal what forces he could.

Arano found his strength rapidly returning. The medical oint-
ment Hawan had applied, while excruciatingly painful, had been
more than marginally successful. Hawan had made him drink
all of their remaining supply of water, then had taken their bottles to refill at the abandoned RLF depot. Arano passed the time
by rummaging through the tools Hawan had found and was
pleased to discover a hatchet and a knife. He had a rudimen-
tary plan, which would hopefully culminate in the rescue of his
friends and, ultimately, the defeat of those responsible for the
insurrection. They would need weapons, supplies, and soldiers.
He already had plans for obtaining weapons. Hawan would take
care of the supplies, and as for the soldiers . . .

Hawan's return broke his concentration. The Bromidian
carried the refilled water bottles, and he wore a long knife at
his hip. A pair of battered but serviceable rucksacks dangled at
odd angles from his back, one on each shoulder. Arano rose unsteadily to his feet, head swimming with vertigo. Hawan set his
burdens aside.

"Are you ready to travel, my friend?" he asked, the harsh,
guttural Bromidian voice somehow managing to transmit some
measure of concern.

Arano licked his lips and nodded. "We should be moving
along. Do you have any idea where we should go?"

"I've been scouting the area. There are no immediate signs of
pursuit, but we need to put more distance between us and the city."
He took a deep breath. "I'm going to suggest we take a gamble.
There are a number of secret meeting places the RLF maintained
during the war. If we could make our way to one of those hideouts, we could gain a tactical advantage. While there are probably
few, if any, weapons, there should be some equipment. But more
importantly, I don't believe anyone who knew about the hideouts

would've been involved in this insurrection. In all likelihood, if any of those people escaped the attack, they will try to follow the same strategy and reach one of the strongholds."

Arano gestured with an outstretched hand. "Lead on."

After a brief debate, Arano convinced Hawan he could carry one of the rucksacks. He placed the contents of his smaller pack into the rucksack, and then he slung the tattered pack across his shoulders. They plunged into the surrounding trees, pushing past the obstructing branches and losing themselves in the brown foliage. The sky dimmed noticeably, the brightness of the Bromidian day fading into night. In the hazy twilight, Arano pushed resolutely onward.

He wasn't certain how long he had been hearing the sound before he recognized it as running water. They pushed through a particularly dense patch of tall thorn bushes, and the swift, narrow river lay before them.

"There," Hawan whispered, "just ahead. There's a small skiff we could use."

"We're traveling by water?"

"The place I have in mind is less than a mile from the river, about ten miles downstream. We can save our strength by taking this boat."

Arano felt a wave of relief rush over him, allowing him to drop his "all's well" façade. His shoulders drooped wearily, and he shuffled forward to help Hawan pull the boat into the water. They boarded wordlessly, pushed off, and moments later the trees along the riverbank were rushing past.

CHAPTER FIVE

VIDERE TOSSED THE THREE EVIDENCE ENVELOPES onto the table and slipped easily into a conveniently located chair. Two of the envelopes contained photographs of Gomid and his colleagues, while the third held the letter written in the Bromidian tongue. The rest of Team 5 was still filing into the room, carrying other, less important items they had recovered.

"Lain, why don't you work on enhancing these pictures?" Videre rubbed his eyes wearily. "If you can't get anything from them, we'll let the boys at the crime lab have a shot at them."

Lain nodded his agreement. "And if that fails, there's always Alyna's nephew."

"Good idea. We'll talk to her when she gets back. In the meantime, I'm going to see about getting this letter translated."

Videre spent the next several minutes fruitlessly trying to arrange to have one of the Bromidians working in Avengers Headquarters sent to their planning room. Most were out on training missions, and one was on leave. A helpful administrator promised he would have a Bromidian meet with them within the next few hours, but said all of their resources were devoted to escorting key members of the Coalition Government to places of safety. Videre closed down the Comm line with the irritable flick of a finger.

"You would think they could at least spare us an interpreter, or something," he complained out loud to no one in particular. "This is a fairly crucial project we're working on."

"Why don't you call Arano?" Laron suggested. "I'm sure there are a few Bromidians with him on Rystoria 2."

Videre gave him a withering look. "Now I see what it is about *me* that irritates Arano so much." He spun his chair back to the control panel and opened a Comm line to the Bromidian homeworld. He sat lightly tapping his furry forefinger on the table, waiting for a response. His eyes narrowed suspiciously, glaring at the blinking light on the Comm panel.

"What's wrong?" Kish asked.

"There's a problem with the Comm system. I can't get through to anyone on Rystoria 2." He tapped several controls, trying a different transmission.

Almost immediately, the leathery face of a Tompiste soldier appeared on the screen. "This is Sergeant Shida, Niones 4 Comm Center."

Videre nodded in greeting. "Lieutenant Genoa, Avengers Team 5, calling from Immok City. Have you had any Comm failures?"

The slender soldier looked away from the screen, consulting an unseen assistant. "Negative. All systems are functioning normally."

"Can you try raising Rystoria 2 for me? We need to speak with our team leaders, but we're unable to raise anyone at our base there."

"Stand by." Sergeant Shida turned to face a panel to his right, tapping the controls with nimble fingers. His large, almond-shaped eyes blinked rapidly several times, and he leaned back in his chair. "We're having trouble, also. There must be some localized interference."

"Okay. Thanks for your help. We'll look into this further." He closed the Comm link with a slow tap of his finger. "I'll in-form command about the communications problem and let them deal with it. In the meantime, I have a document to translate."

"Stop here." The harsh, growling voice cut through the haze of darkness and pain.

The plastic bands securely holding Alyna's wrists behind her back were cutting into the soft skin, and she felt the first trickle of blood dripping down her hands. The blindfold her captors had wrapped around her head was also covering her nose, forcing her to breathe through her mouth.

There was the sound of a metal latch being drawn, followed by the heavy creak of corroded hinges, and Alyna was assailed by the dank odor of a damp room that had been closed up too long. She was taken by the arm, none too gently, and dragged a few steps to her left. Rough Bromidian hands groped across her body, conducting the third search of her captivity; then she was forced into a chair. The bonds on her hands were released, but her arms were immediately forced into leather restraints on the arms of her seat. After her legs were similarly secured, the blindfold was removed.

She stared painfully into a bright floodlight, preventing her from obtaining a clear view of the Bromidians standing around her. One of them stepped closer, leaning down so that his insectoid face was close to her, his fetid breath steaming in her nose.

"What is your name?" he hissed.

Alyna mentally appraised the situation. A darting glance told her that her nametag had become dislodged at some point, leaving her safely anonymous. She was certain, with Arano having been in the V.I.P. section, they would know who he was. If they learned she was Arano's wife, they would certainly try to exploit the situation, especially if her husband had escaped the attack. She considered telling them nothing, but decided otherwise. The rules of engagement were clear: she was required to give her name and rank, nothing else. But she wouldn't necessarily tell them everything . . .

"Captain Alyna Marquat."

"What is your function within the Coalition?"

"I'm a pilot."

The Bromidian grabbed her roughly by the throat, squeezing tightly enough to cut off her breathing. "Do not think you can lie to me. You are a prisoner of the new Bromidian Empire. We have no treaties with your government, so there are no restrictions on what I can do to you." He held his grip for a few moments longer, then released it, leaving her gasping and coughing for air. He struck her a stinging blow across the face, leaving a large welt beside her left eye.

"What is your function within the Coalition?"

Alyna fixed him with as calm a stare as she could muster, hoping her defiance might buy her some time. The Bromidian struck her another blow, this one splitting her lower lip. The blood ran freely down her chin and onto her dress uniform. He repeated the question yet again, but she met his gaze and refused to answer.

The Bromidian stepped back, folding his arms across his chest. Eventually, he placed his hands on his hips, turned his head toward a Bromidian by the door, and nodded wordlessly. The soldier disappeared, returning minutes later with a Human Coalition soldier. Although Alyna didn't recognize him, she saw by his uniform that he held the rank of lieutenant. He too had been beaten, his swollen and battered face almost unrecognizable. A knife blade protruded from his back, the handle from his chest. The blood staining his clothes was still wet, and she knew he hadn't been dead long.

"We have brought him to you as an object lesson. You have a few hours to reconsider. If you continue to refuse to cooperate, your situation will worsen."

In total darkness, Arano followed Hawan through the dense foliage. Fruit trees grew in abundance, threatening to choke out all passage. Adding to their troubles was a low but thick thorn bush, grabbing their clothing and scratching their legs. Arano was looking forward to sleeping in a more secure area, especially if he could get his hands on a medikit. In the morning, they would begin the process of trying to make contact with anyone who had escaped the purging at the ceremony, and then Arano would set about his first order of business: rescuing his friends.

Hawan held up a hand in silent warning, and they eased themselves into a crouch. The Bromidian glanced back and mouthed a message to Arano: someone was approaching on a path ahead of them. Arano cast about for a weapon, selecting a fist-sized rock. He hefted the stone, and Hawan nodded in agreement. Then Arano heard it too; someone was walking along a game trail to their front, making no attempt to hide the sounds of passage. Odd, but Arano's danger sense had failed to warn him once more.

The footsteps on the path fell silent. "Hawan, Viper, are you there?"

Arano exchanged a curious look with Hawan, then rose to his feet. Lentin stood before them, smiling his relief and excitement.

Arano's elation reached a new high, but another thought occurred to him.

"Alyna! Where is she?"

The smile fell from Lentin's face, and his hard-shelled face dropped to gaze at the ground. "I am sorry, Viper. I have failed you. She and Laron were taken captive." Unable to look Arano in the eyes, he related the incidents leading up to Alyna's capture.

Arano laced his fingers atop his head, directing his eyes up into the uncaring sky. "Lentin, I . . . at least she's alive, which we wouldn't know for sure if you hadn't been there to help. You gave it your best effort. I am in your debt once more." He extended his hand, took Lentin's in greeting, and shook it warmly.

Hawan stepped forward grimly. "Have you been to the stronghold yet?"

Lentin nodded, still unable to smile. "I have gathered a dozen former RLF soldiers. We have no weapons, but there is a good supply of field rations, radios, medical equipment, and other gear still stored there. Come."

Ament, the note began, *the mission is a go. Fifteen targets in the next twenty-four hours. The first two have priority and are a must. Attempt the others at your discretion. If you are compromised, return to Epsilon Center. We will have more assistance for you there. Luck to you.*

Khonsu

Videre ran a clawed finger through the short fur on his head, contemplating the letter's contents. The only items he couldn't elucidate in the entire body of the letter were Epsilon Center and Khonsu. The latter was likely to be Ament's point of contact within whatever organization had hired him. The former, however, could be just as useful: Epsilon Center would be an excellent starting point in the hunt for Treng Gomid, or 'Ament,' as the letter writer referred to him. The trick would be deciphering the two clues.

It had taken almost two hours to translate the Bromidian writing; not only was the handwriting hard to read, but the stains from the garbage that had been dumped on it served to confound his efforts.

"Are you finished already?" Imatt Deeps stood behind him, smiling, hands in his pockets.

Videre rolled his eyes. "Everyone's a comedian these days." He stood slowly, enjoying the feeling of stretching his legs. "Yeah, I'm finished. Here, smart guy, take a look for yourself." He handed the GBI special agent his copy of the translated note. Imatt immediately gave the words his full attention.

"I think I have these pictures modified as well as I'm able," Lain announced, not removing his eyes from the monitor. "Why don't you guys take a look at this, and we'll see if anyone sees anything familiar."

The shorthanded Avengers team and Imatt Deeps gathered around behind Lain and Pelos, grouping tightly together to get a better view. Videre saw nothing of note. Ament was pictured, certainly, along with two Kamlings and a Tompiste, but there was nothing in the photo to indicate where it had been taken. From below his bulky right shoulder, he heard Kish exhale sharply, setting down her mug.

"Look at the building in the right background, the one with the brown sides and black roof. It's a recital hall in Nomma City on Ladium 3. My niece played in a concert there about four years ago."

"Are you sure your memory is correct?" Imatt asked. "Four years is a long time."

Videre gave him a withering look. "Please, Imatt, don't get her started. She remembers. I think we're going to have to make some assumptions. Given the disguises and false identifications Treng had, I think it's safe to assume he could easily escape the planet."

Imatt nodded ruefully. "I'd say that's reasonable."

"We have only one clue where Epsilon Center might be, and that's this picture. If nothing else, maybe there will be something in that area to lead us in the right direction."

Lain stood and shrugged his indifference. "Sounds like it's time for a little trip."

Alyna took a shuddering, deep breath, held it in briefly, then let it out. She struggled against her bonds, but to no avail; the leather straps weren't all that thick or wide, but they were too strong for her to break, and they were too tightly secured for her to slip free. She absently continued working at them while she considered other options. There weren't many.

She let her eyes wander about the chamber, looking for anything she might use as a tool. On a table in the far corner, she saw several cutting implements, doubtless left there in plain sight in an effort to unnerve her. But she couldn't reach them and had no way to bring them to her.

Her gaze fell reluctantly on the body of the Coalition officer lying before her. The killing blade still protruded from his body, a pool of blood gathered around the hole in his uniform. It was a long blade, and, in fact, a few inches were still exposed above his back. On an impulse born of desperation, Alyna closed her eyes, set her jaw firmly, and threw her weight against the side of the chair.

It tipped up on two legs, then settled roughly back to the floor. She tried again, with the same results. Alyna refused to concede defeat, repeatedly slamming her body hard to the right. Finally, the chair hung suspended on the two legs, teetering uncertainly before crashing on its side. She struck with jarring force, and she lay there motionless, allowing her head a chance to clear.

Slowly, inches at a time, she nudged her chair over to the body lying inanimate before her. The edge of the blade was facing directly toward her approaching foot, and she eventually made contact. Luck was with her; the cutting edge of the blade was at the perfect height. With painstaking slowness, she sawed back and forth, pressing the soft leather of the restraint up against the knife. Her heart leaped into her throat at every noise in the hallway beyond her cell, and certainty of her discovery coursed through her veins like ice. Once, she angled her foot to one side, and the blade bit home into the flesh of her leg, but she kept working.

She was rewarded with a second incision in her leg when she finally cut completely through the bond, and Alyna stretched out her foot, taking the bloody knife between her toes. She worked the blade back and forth until it came free in her toes' grip then, using the limberness inherent in her athletic frame, she brought the knife up to her hand. Alyna grasped the slippery handle, reversed the blade, and placed the edge against the restraint holding her wrist in place. She cut through more quickly this time, and within a few more minutes she was free.

Free from what? She stood in the center of the room, the knife dangling uselessly at her side, blood still flowing down her leg.

How was she to escape the room? She had freed herself from the chair, but she had no way of disabling the lock on the door, which had been magnetically sealed from without. All she had managed to do was slice open her leg and get out of the chair. When they returned, they would put her back in the chair or worse.

She glanced down at the knife, the blood of the slain lieutenant mingling with hers, and held it up to the light. Alyna grasped the dead officer under the armpits, her skin cringing away from the warm, sticky mess on his shirt. She removed her uniform jacket and wrapped it around his body, then carefully placed the restraints around his wrists and ankles. It wouldn't hold up under a close examination, but a cursory look into the cell might fool someone. She crossed the small room to the door and stood off to one side, shivering in her thin undershirt.

Alyna screamed with every last ounce of energy she had remaining, shrieking until her throat hurt. There was the sound of the magnetic locks being released, and the door to her cell swung ponderously open. A lone Bromidian stepped into the cell, making Alyna pause with caution. He wouldn't be there alone; there must be another guard. The Bromidian walked up to the chair, seized the lieutenant by the hair, and pulled his head back. He shouted something in the harsh Bromidian tongue, and two more Bromidians rushed into the cell.

Alyna vaulted from her hiding place, slashing the knife across the back of the first guard's neck. The blade bit deeply between two sections of his hard-shelled Bromidian skin, and the black blood rushed down his back as he fell to his knees.

She buried the knife in the neck of the second, and he dropped with a deep, gurgling breath. Then she threw herself on the third guard, who was trying to draw his pistol. They toppled to the floor, and Alyna landed with a knee in his abdomen.

The air rushed from his lungs, and she ripped the utility knife from his belt, slicing it across his throat while he struggled to draw a breath. To be certain she wasn't discovered, she finished off the first Bromidian.

After pulling the bodies off to one side, she secured their pistols and left the cell, closing the door behind her. "That's why prison guards shouldn't carry weapons," she muttered to herself.

Videre led his team from the ramp of the *Intrepid* to the waiting transports. A pair of detectives from the local police agency were onboard waiting for them, promising to offer any assistance the Avengers needed. The trip to the Nomma City Police Headquarters went smoothly, and within the hour they were in a planning room with several intelligence officers.

"Welcome to Nomma City," a Tompiste police officer told them. "I am Detective Sergeant Warl Groth."

Videre shook his hand warmly. "I appreciate the help. These are my teammates." He introduced Pelos Marnian, Lain Baxter, and Kish Waukee, explaining their functions within the team. "And this is Special Agent Imatt Deeps, with the Galactic Bureau of Intelligence." Videre explained the various incidents that had ultimately resulted in the trip to Ladium 3.

"I don't speak Bromidian, but I have someone on our staff who can verify your work, if you'd like. I understand the Bromidian tongue to be . . . difficult, at best, when it comes to translations. Would you mind if I looked at your photograph?"

Videre opened a large brown envelope and withdrew two pictures: one was the original they recovered from Treng's residence, and the other, the enhanced version. Warl studied the two photos silently for several moments.

"You said you recovered this first picture from the house of this pirate?"

"Yes," Imatt replied, moving closer to the detective's side. "Treng Gomid, or 'Ament,' as he likes to be called. Kish here has a somewhat remarkable memory, and she believes the photograph was taken here in Nomma City, at—"

"Let me guess," the detective said with a smile, holding up one finger. "This building right here would be the Nomma Conservatory."

"That was my recollection," Kish said. She fixed Imatt with an amused grin. "Some people might be skeptical, but certain things do come to me, once in a while."

"Give me a moment." Warl pulled his Comm from his belt, issuing orders over the air.

"I have arranged transportation to the conservatory in an unmarked transport. Also, I called the Bromidian we have on staff. He's going to meet us at the site."

Something inside Videre's pack gave an urgent beep. Smiling, he opened the pack and retrieved the gaming computer. "Sorry, everyone. This won't take long. Captain Lakeland is probably letting me know he wants to surrender."

He casually tapped a few keys, and a garbled, incomprehensible message appeared on the screen. He frowned, rubbing his forehead, trying to decipher the cryptic message. "The interference on Rystoria 2 must be worse than we believed. I can't make any sense out of this message at all." He briefly typed a message to Arano requesting he resend the information, then put the computer back in his pack. "I'll work on it later."

It was a short ride to the conservatory, and no one mentioned the case. Videre and Kish hovered over the gaming computer, trying to clean up Arano's message.

Imatt turned his attention to Videre. "Hey, Vid, have you made any progress yet?"

Videre didn't look up, his attention riveted on the computer in his lap. "Some. The text isn't entirely in the same order it was when he sent it. I've managed to pick out a few words here and there, mostly just some assorted prepositions, but also the words 'control' and 'captured.' I have him backed into a corner, so he's probably trying to use a smokescreen to get out of it."

The transport rolled to a stop, and they stepped out onto the street then passed through the unusually light traffic to stand in front of the Nomma Conservatory. Videre took another look at the photograph, using it to orientate himself to the positions of not only the subjects themselves, but also the unseen photographer.

"Here's our contact," Warl announced, and Videre looked up from the picture to see a Bromidian in formal attire approaching them. "Ambassador, these are the people I spoke to you about. Everyone, this is Ambassador Voss, of the Bromidian government."

"Obviously," Videre muttered, and Lain suppressed a laugh.

"Can I see the note, please? The original, if at all possible."

Videre rummaged through his pack, finally locating the envelope containing the letter, which he handed to the ambassador. Voss studied it briefly, holding it up to the light to better see the writing through the smudges.

"You did an admirable job translating this letter, Lieutenant. However, I think I can help you out here. Toward the end, the writer uses a word which, quite literally, translates to 'Epsilon.' However, like all languages, ours has its little idiomatic quirks, and this is one of them. The Bromidian word used here can have two meanings. In this case, it can be broken down into two separate words, 'eps' and 'ilon,' which means 'red dragon.'"

"There's a hotel and casino about a block over from here," Warl told them, eyes wide in anticipation, "called the Red Dragon. It's owned by a group of Humans, and it's operated on a medieval Earth theme."

Videre grinned broadly, baring his sharply pointed teeth. "This just gets better and better!"

CHAPTER
SIX

ARANO AWOKE WITH A START, EYES STRUGGLING to focus in the early morning light. The medikit Lentin had used the night before had repaired the majority of his injuries, and he felt most of his strength returning to him. He arose silently, not wanting to disturb the still-sleeping Hawan, and he slipped out through the tent flap into a foggy morning.

The "stronghold" Hawan had spoken of was less than what Arano had expected. There was a narrow crack in a rock wedged against the side of a steep hill, and the crack led to a dank, wet cave. The supplies they had spoken about were stacked neatly inside. All that remained was for Arano to put the many tools at his disposal to good use.

Several Bromidians sat around a smokeless fire, eating their breakfast. Lentin had introduced them to Arano the night before, and while some nodded in greeting, a few eyed him suspiciously.

Arano was concerned about the state of affairs in their camp. If they were to succeed in building a strong resistance movement, they had to have trust, above all else.

He found a springy sapling with a diameter roughly equal to his wrist. Using his hatchet, he chopped off a section about five feet long and dragged it near the fire. While the Bromidians looked on with expressions ranging from amusement to curiosity, he methodically removed the smaller braches from the main portion of the sapling.

When he was satisfied, he set it aside and rummaged through a pile of discarded equipment, eventually settling on a long but thin strand of steel cable. He retrieved a set of wire cutters and added these items to his growing pile of odd assortments. When he hiked back to the river and returned with several small, flat, pointed rocks, his audience openly displayed astonishment, gathering closer to see what he was making. Lentin peered over Arano's shoulder at his work.

"Can you do me a favor?" Arano asked him. "I need several straight branches, smaller around than my smallest finger, and approximately two-thirds of a meter in length."

By the time Lentin returned, Arano had also found a paper-thin sheet of flexible plastic, along with an adhesive gel. He used short strands of a resilient vine to attach a single flat rock to each of the branches. After cutting half-oval pieces of plastic from the sheet, he used the adhesive to attach them to the other end of the branches.

Lentin laughed. "I think I see where you are going with this, Viper."

Arano smiled, without looking up from his work. "I was hoping you would."

With the help of two of his RLF soldiers, Lentin built a target made of an old tarp and stuffed it with discarded clothing. Hawan aided Arano in bending the sapling he had cut, and another Bromidian threaded the cable through deep slots in each end and secured them. Arano hefted his new longbow, drew it experimentally a few times, then grinned broadly.

"A child's toy?" a Bromidian growled.

Arano licked his lips, squinting into the morning sky. "A toy, you say?" He nocked an arrow, sighted, and fired, striking home in the immediate center of his target. There were a few mumbles of approval, but Arano knew he hadn't quite won them over. Glancing around the camp, he spied a decrepit transport, intact but obviously out of commission.

"Could a child's toy do this?"

He drew back his bow a second time, sighted in on the steel plating of the door, and fired. The arrow penetrated the metal, piercing completely through the side of the vehicle and entering the passenger compartment. The stunned silence that followed was gratifying.

"All right, people," Lentin announced firmly, hands on his hips. "Let's get busy."

Lentin and Hawan delegated the RLF soldiers into various work groups, each tasked with gathering the various implements by which Arano would arm their small contingent. They spent most of the day hard at work, and by the time they gathered for their evening meal, all the bows and most of the arrows were ready. The silence of their meal, however, was broken by a startling announcement from one of their sentries.

"Hawan," he hissed, "someone is coming. It looks like a single Bromidian, wearing a military uniform. He's heading straight for us."

They all scrambled for cover, most of them picking up Arano's improvised weapons. He listened intently but could hear nothing other than the chirping of birds and whisper of the wind in the trees.

Moments later, a breathless Bromidian dashed into the camp. He slowed to a stop when several RLF soldiers stepped into the open, pointing their bows at him. Hawan stepped cautiously forward, then motioned for the others to lower their weapons.

"It's okay," Hawan told them. "This is Edan, from my cell in the RLF." He extended his hand in greeting, and the two comrades greeted each other warmly.

"I was hoping I'd find you here," Edan said, gasping. "This is the third stronghold I've checked, and frankly, I was starting to lose my breath."

Hawan chuckled softly. "I'm glad you made it. What news from the capital?"

Edan bent over and rested his hands on his knees, taking several moments to catch his breath and regain his composure. "It's not clear yet exactly what happened. Friends of mine heard vague references to some 'supreme commander,' but we have nothing concrete. It looks like you and your Padian friend were the only people to escape the massacre at the bleachers. Every governmental official in a position of authority is either dead or in custody."

"There were . . . friends of mine in a nearby hangar," Arano said slowly, almost dreading the answer. "Do you have any idea what happened to them?"

"I didn't get the specifics, but they were captured."

"I was there for that part," Lentin said wryly. "Do you know where they were taken?"

"Although it's by no means certain, I heard all foreign prisoners were taken to Mosten Prison for interrogation. I'm sorry if these are close companions of yours, but they will not be treated well. I recognized the leaders of some of the detachments in the coup, and they were notorious for using torture in the old days. Some of them were rumored to be dead, and the others were all wanted men."

"How could this have happened?" Arano demanded, a bit more harshly than he had intended. "Your people relished their newfound freedom. I should know; I fought alongside you to help attain it. How could everyone just fall in line behind some uprising, when in all likelihood it will drag Rystoria back into the totalitarian state you just escaped?"

Hawan sighed, placing a sympathetic hand on Arano's shoulder. "The Bromidian population has spent centuries under the iron fist of a brutal dictatorship. While we only tasted freedom for a short time, some of us would die to keep it. The problem is, we have been ruled by fear and oppression for so long, we tend to fall in line with whatever power claims to run the government. In fact, if it had been orchestrated by a member of Gorst's family, the people would offer their support automatically. They've been following Gorsts' 'Divine Right' doctrine for too many generations. And as for the military, they seem to have placed a few officers loyal to the old government in places of authority in order to carry out this strike."

The glimmerings of a plan flickered around the edges of Arano's consciousness. "And if someone in a position of authority told a group of these rebellious Bromidians to help restore the rightful government in the name of freedom?"

Hawan nodded. "You might have to kill one or two of their leaders, but the front line soldiers would follow if you have a forceful public speaker for a leader."

"Can I make a suggestion?"

"By all means, Viper."

"We have enough supplies here to last us for a while. We need troops, and we need them armed. I think our first task should be acquiring a few weapons. These bows are nice in an ambush, but I'd like something with a little more kick. We arm ourselves, then raid the prison."

A Bromidian soldier threw his cup to the ground with an angry oath. "Why should we risk ourselves to free your friends?"

Lentin stepped in front of the angry soldier and struck him a solid blow, sending him reeling to the ground. "If it wasn't for Viper, and his friends, we would never have won the war the first time. We can win it again, with his help. Do not show him disrespect again." He looked around the stunned group. "That goes for all of you."

After several seconds of deathlike stillness, Arano extended a helping hand to the Bromidian on the ground, pulling him to his feet. "We won't just be rescuing my friends. There are going to be Bromidian dissidents imprisoned there as well. If we free them, they are certain to join us. We should also be able to gather more weapons and equipment from their supplies."

Hawan looked around the assemblage. "Edan, would you be willing to be my eyes and ears around the prison?"

Edan snapped to attention. "You have but to command me, Hawan."

"Okay. I need you to return here within one day. Go to the prison and determine who they have. We need to know their troop strengths and what their defenses are."

"I need to rest and get some food, and I will be on my way within the hour."

Alyna padded softly down the dimly lit hallway. Her captors had taken her boots from her, and the bare skin of her feet slapped faintly against the cold stone floors. She wondered if she was being held underground; the air was noticeably cool, and there was a chill dampness about the prison that almost set her teeth to chattering.

There were several cells on either side of the passage, but she had no way of opening them, so she passed them by. Her left eye had swollen shut, which was a mixed blessing; her vision in that eye was blurry, and she had felt disoriented from the double vision. With the eye closed, her vision was clearer, although she had lost her depth perception.

A boot scuffed against stone in a room ahead of her and to the right. She shifted the pistol to her left hand and drew the knife which had served her so well. Walking on the balls of her feet to minimize the sound of her approach, she stole a swift glimpse around the corner.

A short Bromidian stood in the center of the room, reading from a text sitting open on the desk before him. He wore the uniform of the Bromidian military, and a set of flexible handcuffs dangling from his belt confirmed his status as a member of the prison staff.

With agonizing slowness, Alyna stuffed the pistol into the waistband of her pants then stole into the room, grabbed the surprised guard from behind, and jammed the knife into his throat. Keeping a hand over his mouth to keep him from crying out, she eased him to the floor. With an effort, she pushed the body under his desk, placing his chair in the way to help hide the evidence.

A single door stood slightly ajar on the far side of the room. She peered through the crack of the opening and found the hallway beyond empty of guards. There were more side passages in that part of the prison, and Alyna had to trust blind luck.

Imatt activated a small datapad, tapped several keys with practiced agility, and tucked it back inside his jacket. "Okay, it's ready."

"Are you sure this'll work?" Videre couldn't hide the incredulity he felt over the GBI agent's plan.

"I know you've never seen anything like this, but trust me. If I stand at the counter for a few minutes, I'll be able to download their entire database. I don't actually need to have a physical connection. This datapad will scan the contents of their computer's memory and download everything we need."

Kish gnawed absently at a fingernail. "But will he use his real name?"

"I would be surprised if he did. But he would be required to submit to a thumb imprint and a DNA scan in order to bill the room to his line of credit. It's extremely rare on Ladium 3 to see someone who actually carries cash, and to do so draws attention. Unwanted attention, in his case. He'll use credit, and we'll have him."

Videre and Imatt strolled boldly through the lobby and stopped at the main desk. A Tompiste clerk was using a stylus to enter data from the day's itinerary. His double eyelids blinked rapidly several times, and he snorted his annoyance. Finally, he leaned back in his chair, folding his arms. "Can I help you?"

"We want to ask about a room," Videre said simply.

The clerk waved his hands at them imperiously in a gesture meant to tell them to leave. "We're full. Try another hotel. Or go play games in the casino." He returned to his work.

Videre shrugged his indifference to the clerk's attitude, which was working in their favor. The more time he wasted, the less creative Videre needed to be about keeping the clerk occupied. The two stood stoically, waiting for a reaction from the clerk.

"I said we're full. We can't give you a room."

"We want to make a reservation for a different night."

The clerk dropped his face into his hands, shook his head, and finally sighed heavily in disgust. He reached to one side and produced a portable thumbprint scanner, which he held out for Videre.

"Scan here."

"Not until I see a price," Videre told him firmly.

"How can I give you a price if I don't know whether or not you can afford the room?"

"Look. I want to rent three rooms here for a week next month. I would prefer this hotel, but if you don't want to cooperate, I'll take my business elsewhere."

"And your point is?" the clerk said with a sneer.

"I'll send a copy of the bill to your manager, along with an explanation of why I left."

The Tompiste's gray skin managed to turn a pasty white color, and he slowly rose to his feet. "Sir, I'm sorry if I offended you. Just give me a moment, and I'll bring you a price list."

He dashed away into a back room, momentarily lost from sight. Imatt laughed and shook his head. "I'll bet you annoy the daylights out of Arano."

"Are you kidding? He loves me."

They both laughed, and Videre ran through several cutting remarks intended for the Tompiste clerk. His fun was cut short by a beeping signal from inside Imatt's jacket.

"I'm finished," Imatt told him. "It's time to go."

Videre sighed in mock disappointment. "I guess you're right. And after all the bellhop did for us . . ." They briskly left the hotel, their laughter trailing along behind them.

Back at police headquarters, Imatt pulled out the small data-pad once more, activating it and setting it aside. He slid his chair to the computer workstation, and for several minutes he worked silently, culling the needed information from another computer, light-years away on Immok 2.

"Our man was here, all right. He spent last night at the hotel, and according to this data, someone stayed with him. This morning, he booked passage for two to the Eden System. I have his complete itinerary here, including where he will be staying and how long he'll be there."

Pelos clicked his beak. "Do we notify the authorities on Eden 2?"

Videre shook his head. "It's too easy for someone to monitor the transmission."

"Agreed," Kish said.

Lain rose to his feet, running his hand over the line of bumps on the green skin of his forehead. "I guess we're going to Eden."

Arano tried unsuccessfully to stretch his legs and remove a cramp from his calf. He had been hiding in the boughs of a massive tree for the better part of two hours, bow in hand, waiting for the expected Bromidian patrol to arrive. The sun was dropping closer to the horizon, casting eerie shadows across the wide dirt trail beneath him. The temperature was falling, adding to the stiffness in his muscles.

His fortitude paid off. The sound of feet wading through piles of fallen leaves came along the trail, and the Bromidians drew into sight. Their rifles, while not slung across their shoulders, weren't held at the ready either. They carried their weapons arrogantly, confidently, secure in their belief that they owned the forest.

The snap of Arano's bow echoed across the road, and his arrow buried itself in a Bromidian's chest. He cried out in warning, too late, and crumpled to his knees. Seven other bows snapped, their arrows racing into the cluster of soldiers. Three of the Bromidians fell victim to the barrage, slumping over in their death throes. The fourth staggered but retained his footing. He tried to run back the way they had come, his efforts hampered by the arrows protruding from his stomach and right thigh. Arano snatched another arrow from his quiver, drew, aimed, and fired, all in one motion. The killing shaft pierced its target, and the escaping soldier tumbled forward to lie, dying, in the dirt of the road. The RLF soldiers rushed forth to claim their equipment; then they disappeared into the trees, lost from sight.

The wailing of an alarm announced that Alyna's luck had run out. Several Bromidians scrambled into the hallway in front of her, stopping in surprise and shock when they saw the battered, disheveled figure before them. She fired her pistol repeatedly while dashing for cover, ducking down a side hallway. She risked a look behind her and saw three Bromidians lying motionless on the floor.

A shot buzzed past her head to strike the stone of the wall, sending fragments flying. Alyna whirled to face a nearby door, but found it locked. She fired at the control mechanism, and was satisfied with the clicking release of the magnetic lock. Slipping through the doorway, she dashed down the hallway beyond. She had managed to put some space between herself and her captors, but it wouldn't last.

Voices sounded from around the corner ahead of her, and she dropped to one knee in a recessed doorway. Two Bromidians appeared, weapons holstered, growling harshly in their guttural language. She sprang out, intending to take them at gunpoint and force them to lead her to the way out.

Both lowered into a fighting stance, reaching instinctively for their pistols. Her own weapon fired twice, and they fell away with smoking holes in their heads—dead before they hit the floor.

Alyna paused at the landing for a flight of stairs winding up into darkness. A sense of elation filled her, and she circled her way up, pistol held carefully before her. She came to the top of the stairs, another landing, and another unlocked door. Frowning, she considered the likelihood that she was being led into a trap. She had only found one unlocked door prior to reaching the stairwell, and suddenly she found doors unlocked at both the top and bottom of a staircase. Voices sounded in the hallway below her—several voices—drawing closer. She set her jaw and reached for the door, pushing it slowly open.

The corridor beyond was empty. She looked to the left and right, shrugged her indifference, and turned left. There were windows set in the walls of the hallway, too small for even her diminutive body to make egress, but giving her a tantalizing view of the outdoors and freedom.

A door clicked open in front of her, and she found herself face to face with a startled, unarmed Bromidian technician. He saw the weapon in her hands and froze in place, a small tool tumbling from his grasp and clattering hollowly on the floor.

"Show me the way out." She raised the pistol higher, pointing it directly at his head. The move had the desired effect, and he nodded his agreement, eyes wide with fear. He led her back the way she had come, past the stairwell, and farther along the corridor. They came to another unremarkable door, and he keyed a security code into the door's control panel. It swung obediently open, and she ordered him through the doorway ahead of her. She found herself in a motorpool, several transports lined up in neat, orderly rows. She was still considering what to do with her prisoner when a rifle butt struck the back of her head, and she fell into darkness.

Arano and his team reassembled in another RLF stronghold. Arano had insisted from the outset that, until their numbers grew significantly, they wouldn't spend two consecutive nights in the same location. It had been a successful venture; they had conducted two ambushes and captured eight laser rifles, along with a few radios and several grenades. But, more importantly, Arano had captured the respect of most of the Bromidians in their entourage.

Edan rushed into the camp, gasping for air as he staggered to a stop. "Hawan! I just came from the prison facility. They have captured several former RLF operatives, and they have Viper's two friends. They plan to start the executions in the morning!"

CHAPTER SEVEN

AN ICY CALM CAME OVER ARANO, AND THE TENSION drained from his body. "Are they going to execute your people, too, or just the Avengers?"

"Everyone! They are going to kill them one at a time, publicly."

"No," Arano corrected him, returning to his planning table, "they're not. All the prisoners will be freed. Tonight. We've drawn a rough model of the perimeter of the prison facility. I want you to look this over and make any additions or corrections you see fit."

One of the Bromidians lounging off to the side came to his feet. "Another chance for you to kill Bromidians, Viper. You must be very pleased."

Arano stood before his accuser. "That part of my life is behind me. What I do tonight, and in the days to come, I do to save our friends, and I do for vengeance against those who have captured my wife. Most importantly, I do this to restore the rightful government I fought to install." He looked around the room, catching everyone's attention. "Thousands of my fellow Coalition soldiers gave their lives to see the despot Zorlyn Gorst VIII and his evil empire brought to their knees and a free and democratic society installed for all Bromidians. This insurrection is an affront to all those, Bromidian and Coalition alike, who gave their lives to make your people free. I need all of you to stand with me."

Hawan joined Arano, and the two walked casually to the opposite end of the tent. "How are you able to stay so calm, Viper? They have your wife."

Arano nodded, the muscles in his jaw twitching slightly. "I can't explain it. I have this feeling of . . . certainty. Vengeance is still a powerful driving force within the Padian people, just as it is with yours. And vengeance is what I shall have. Not just by freeing the prisoners. But by bringing the entire insurrection to its knees."

Arano motioned to a log, and they both sat. "Hawan, my friend," Arano said with a grim smile, "we have a rescue to plan."

Videre checked the navigational computer, which showed him they still had almost an hour before they would exit their wormhole in the Eden System. Imatt entered the bridge of the *Intrepid*, nodding to Videre as he took a seat and slid a datapad to him. Videre downloaded the information to his computer and brought it up on his terminal.

"What do you have for us?" he asked.

"He is fairly sure of himself," Imatt said, frowning. "He booked his room under the same name, Treng Gomid. He's staying at the Grand Paradise Hotel on Mahalo Island."

Videre rubbed his fur-covered chin, staring at his computer screen. "We can't even be certain he'll come here at all. This could easily have been a false trail, especially with him going out of his way to oblige us by not even using an alias."

Imatt closed his eyes, leaning back in his chair. "I know, but we've been over this. We have no other leads on his location, so we have to use what we can."

"At least we'll enjoy the scenery." Videre shrugged, a wicked grin slowly spreading over his face. "And the Coalition is paying for it. If only Arano was here." He reached for his gaming computer. "Speaking of which, I still haven't been able to do much else with the message he sent. Once we drop back into normal space, I'm going to send him another message asking him to clarify."

When the computer beeped its mechanical warning of their exit from the wormhole, the entire team was assembled on the bridge. They landed, and a waiting transport carried them to the local police station. Towering palm trees flanked the sidewalk leading to the portico, interspersed with patches of small, brightly colored flowers. The front of the building was largely made of glass, giving the station an open, inviting quality. They entered the lobby, with its white walls and marble floor, where they met with a Tsimian detective named Toller Gnell. They presented him with their information, and he left the room to make arrangements for the continuance of their investigation. While they waited, Videre tapped out a brief message to his absent team leader.

"What game are you playing?" The voice, coming from behind Videre, startled him with its nearness. He looked over his shoulder to see a young Human, her arms laden with datapads. He raised one eyebrow quizzically.

"Your computer," she said, indicating his gaming computer with a nod of her head. "I've seen them used for a number of different games."

Videre gave her a disarming smile. "Chess. My friend couldn't come with us, so we're playing a game, long distance."

"Are you winning?"

"I think I was." He shrugged. "We've been having trouble getting communications opened with him for some time."

She looked up, as if she could see the sky through the tiled ceiling above them. "It's the interference in the atmosphere. When they terraformed the planet, they left behind a great amount of ionic interference. It causes havoc with communications from time to time. Here." She set her burden aside and pulled a small, black device from a nearby drawer and handed it to the big Gatoan. "If you attach this to your dataport, it will help clear some of the interference."

Videre eyed the gadget doubtfully. "Actually, we had this problem before we arrived, and we think the problem was at the source, back in the Rystoria System. Will this still help?"

"It should, I believe. But you are right about Rystoria. I heard from a friend of mine in the local government that the Rystoria System is under some sort of blockade. They are jamming all transmissions, and no ships are being allowed in or out."

"Can you do anything with what I have already received?"

She shook her head sadly. "Sorry, but the signal has to be cleaned up while it's being received. I wouldn't go so far as to say it can't be done, but I wouldn't have the faintest idea of how to do it." She bent to retrieve her datapads but stopped, her mouth hanging open. "I may be able to help you, after all. I have a friend who specializes in communications issues. If you leave me a copy of the transmission, I'll send it to him and see what he can come up with."

Videre docked his computer with one of her datapads, transferring the information with the press of a few keys. She promised to contact him as soon as she could and hustled from the room. Imatt rose to his feet and brought a datapad to Videre, grinning broadly.

"I think we just caught a break," he said. "I had a colleague of mine, Ric Lambus, conduct a thorough examination of Treng's facilities back on Immok 2. Ric found enough there to put together a complete DNA profile of our elusive Treng Gomid. Now, when we get to our hotel, we can check my computer and find out for certain if this person we're following is really him or not."

Kish rose from her chair, setting aside her work. "Can we put out a Coalition-wide search for him? Anytime he passes through security or checks into any major facility, we would know where he is."

"Unfortunately, the answer is only a qualified 'yes.' The problem is the complexity of a DNA molecule. It would be impossible for the computers to update DNA checks on a live basis, so they compile their information every four hours and provide the central computers on Immok 2 with the data they have collected. It takes about two more hours to process all the searches we need — sorry, but he isn't the only fugitive we're after."

The door slid open with a *hiss*, and Detective Gnell reentered the meeting room carrying two large duffel bags. "I have transportation ready for you. The driver is waiting by a side door, and he doesn't know where you'll be going."

Videre regarded the detective silently, eyebrows raised, so the police officer provided further explanation. "You mentioned mission security and information leaks, so I figured I would keep as many people out of the loop as I can. We can stop a few blocks away and finish the trip on foot." He tossed the bags on the floor. "I've taken the liberty of securing several bathing suits similar to those commonly worn here in the Eden System. I thought you might want to avoid attracting attention, so going into the hotel in full military gear would be slightly counterproductive."

Imatt Deeps slapped a friendly hand on the bulky Tsimian's shoulder. "Videre is probably getting tired of hearing my recruiting speech, but if you're looking for a job with the GBI . . ."

Videre dropped his head on the table with a dull *thud*, and Pelos chuckled heartily. Toller was laughing openly when he directed them to changing rooms, but Videre noticed that the detective did take a business card from the special agent of the Galactic Bureau of Intelligence.

They changed clothes quickly, hiding their smaller, concealable pistols among the folds of the loosely fitting garments. Videre and his team followed Detective Gnell through the boxy police station and out the side door to the waiting ground transport.

Alyna's world spun with nauseating efficiency, and she concentrated on keeping her stomach under control. She had been awake for a few minutes, but hadn't attempted to open her eyes. Her head throbbed with a dreadful intensity, compliments of the surprise blow that had left her unconscious. She didn't know how long she had been comatose, but judging by the sounds in the room, she wasn't alone. She was lying on her back on some type of table, and the tension against her waist, wrists, and ankles told her she was bound once again.

She heard the door behind her open, and at least two sets of footsteps marched into the room. One of her visitors stopped, as if waiting for something, but the other approached her. She decided to bide her time, continue to feign unconsciousness, and try to learn what was in store for her.

There was a blanket covering her body, providing her with some measure of warmth against the chill air. The blanket moved, and she felt a pair of soft hands examine the injuries to her legs. The hands were Human, and she puzzled over the apparent contradiction. What would a Human doctor be doing helping a group of Bromidian rebels?

She realized with a start that her blood-stained uniform had been replaced with some type of thin gown, possibly similar to the kind used in hospitals. She catalogued that information away; she would need to acquire clothing for her next escape attempt. All consideration of modesty aside, the nights were too cold to be without better clothing, and in the Rystorian sunlight, she would need better protection.

The hands finished their examination with a more thorough check of the back of her head. She could feel an enormous bulge where the hands were probing, and she wondered if she might have a concussion.

"Well?" The guttural voice came from across the room, likely from a Bromidian.

"Her injuries are not life-threatening. The bleeding from her leg wounds has stopped, and there doesn't appear to be any internal damage. If I was trying to heal her, I would be most concerned about the head injury. At the very least, she has a major concussion; at worst, she could have bleeding in her brain. If so, she'll be dead within the hour."

"Ah. We can't have that. Our commanders won't be happy if we don't get to execute her publicly. Do what you have to, but just make sure she lives through the night or we'll both be in trouble."

"We? You're the one who hit her. You could have just taken her at gunpoint, but you had to strike her. In the head, no less."

"She killed the guards. She had to be punished."

Her doctor snorted. "You're going to kill her. Isn't that punishment enough?"

"*I* have to be the one to deliver it. Those were my men she killed. If she was in better shape, I would ensure she regretted her actions before her execution."

The observer left the room, slamming the door behind him with a metallic echo. Alyna's doctor left the table briefly, rattled some equipment on a nearby table, then returned to her side. She heard a medical instrument hum to life, and the pain in her head eased.

The doctor shut down the instrument and walked away once more. When he returned, he pulled the blanket back from her lower extremities, and she felt a cold, wet cloth against her legs, cleaning the dried blood from her skin. He applied some type of salve, which felt soothing at first, but quickly built into a crescendo of pain. She couldn't suppress a gasp, and the doctor chuckled.

"I figured you were awake." He was silent while he applied more of the salve to another gash in her leg. "I also figured the Rimex cream would get a reaction out of you. It's not exactly intended for medical purposes, but it will keep your legs from bleeding. We want you to look your best tomorrow." She opened her eyes to see a thin, bald Human standing before her in a white laboratory coat, arms folded across his chest.

"So you approve of the execution? You're going to devote this much effort to patching me up just so they can kill me?"

He shrugged. "It's only fair. They should have killed you instead of capturing you anyway. I guess they wanted a bit of entertainment. Personally, I would advocate keeping you around for a week or two, but they want to execute all the prisoners on the same day."

Alyna forced herself to remain calm, her mind diligently searching for a means of escape. "How do they plan to do it? Hanging? Firing squad?"

He laughed, shaking his head and returning to his equipment table. "Actually, someone in our chain of command has a sense of humor. During the run-up to the war with the Coalition, Event Horizon forces used a small group of operatives to create a phony serial killer scenario. Do you remember the Disciples of Zhulac?" Alyna's face drained of color, and she tensed against her bonds. "Yes, I can see you do. As a tribute to our fallen brothers, you will all be executed in the manner of the Disciples."

Arano slipped through the underbrush, senses probing ahead for signs of trouble. According to their scouting report, there would be long-range listening posts along the way, approximately two kilometers from the prison's perimeter fence. He checked on his team, three Bromidian soldiers who had fought in the Rystorian Liberation Front, and examined the foliage in front of them again, longbow in hand.

Lentin was leading a similar team, as was Hawan, each group having its best archer carrying one of the handmade longbows. The listening posts were occupied by lone sentries, making the stealthy removal of the guards a bit easier. His intelligence report covered the perimeter of the prison and the surrounding lands but was very sketchy on the interior. He would have to trust a warrior's luck.

He slowed his pace, and the Bromidians shadowing his trail did likewise. A small stream, gurgling over shallow rocks, crossed the path in front of them, and Hawan's scout had told them the stream was less than one hundred yards from the outer limits of the listening posts. He nocked an arrow, briefly inspecting it to be certain the makeshift projectile was still firmly assembled. In the space of a dozen heartbeats, his target came into view.

The Bromidian, his camouflage uniform unbuttoned lazily and fluttering in the wind, was deep into his evening rations.

Arano froze, turned to his charges, and waited until he had their attention. He pointed to his eyes, held up a single finger, then pointed to the sentry. Arano adjusted his sunglasses, the bright Rystorian sun too powerful for his unprotected eyes even in the shady forest. Keeping his gaze fixed on his target, he motioned for the Bromidians to take up flanking positions in case something went awry.

He checked his watch. Part of their plan called for maintaining surveillance on the sentries until a set time. Not only would this mean a simultaneous attack against all three positions, but if their information was correct, the timing would allow the sentries to check in with their headquarters, maximizing the time they would have before they were missed. He sank lower into the weeds until he could barely make out the outline of the Bromidian in front of him.

The appointed time came, and Arano took up his firing stance with agonizing slowness. He was only about forty meters from his target, who had finished eating and was sitting with his back to Arano. After a deep, calming breath, Arano drew his bow, sighted along the wooden shaft, and released.

The sentry flinched at the snap of the bowstring, but the shot struck true. The arrow pierced his lower right abdomen, impaling the Bromidian's heart on the killing shaft. He cried out once, grasped the arrow protruding from his body, and fell to his knees. Arano raced forward, drew his blade on the run, and slashed the soldier's throat. After making sure the guard was dead, he motioned the others forward, and they made a brief search of the listening post, securing the dead Bromidian's rifle, which Arano gave to one of the soldiers under his command.

They resumed their trek to the prison, angling to Arano's left in order to meet up with the other teams. As expected, Lentin's team was the last to arrive, since they had the greatest distance to cover. Arano consulted with Hawan and Lentin, and they reported the success of their tasks. All three sentries had been successfully eliminated, and the prison guards were unaware. Arano motioned the group into a formation, and they set out on the final leg of their approach to the objective.

Fifteen minutes later, they reached the perimeter fence surrounding the prison. According to their most reliable information, cutting the fence would trigger an alarm, as would scaling the fence, or even bumping it. But there were no motion sensors, so if they could somehow get over the three-meter high barrier without touching it, they would have successfully penetrated the prison without alerting the enemy forces inside.

The prison perimeter was arranged in a perfect square, with guard turrets towering over the surrounding forest at each corner. The turrets were at least seven meters tall, with a covered fighting position at the top. From high atop each structure, two guards maintained a relaxed vigil on the lands surrounding their position. At the midpoint of each length of the fence, a shorter guard tower was posted, sporting a single Bromidian guard from a fighting position mounted at the height of the fence. Arano's strike team hunkered down into the brush, remaining invisible to the guards while they awaited the coming of nightfall.

Arano removed his sunglasses, eyes comfortable in the fading light. With the thinner Rystorian atmosphere, darkness came more quickly, without the gradual introduction to twilight found on other worlds. He watched the gathering gloom with a certain anticipation and realized he was actually looking forward to the coming violence.

Videre Genoa strolled along the white sand beach, admiring the breathtaking vista across emerald-colored seas. With exacting regularity, white-capped waves rolled in from the sea to crash upon the beach, the waters pushing forward until the call of the ocean pulled them back. Seashells dotted the beach, to the delight of the scattering of tourists who crawled about on all fours, selecting items for their collections. The sun shone brightly, a facet of paradise enjoyed more by the humanoids whose skin was not covered with fur. He and Lain Baxter were approaching their target from the south, while Kish Waukee approached from the north. Imatt Deeps was planning to enter from the front of the building with Pelos Marnian.

The hotel came into view, the ornate sign behind the building announcing the splendor of the Grand Paradise Hotel. It was a towering structure, at least thirty stories high, its glass sides reinforced by what appeared to be titanium steel. A series of swimming pools surrounded the hotel, connected by an intricate series of canals.

The Grand Paradise was immaculately landscaped, with lush tropical plants from a dozen different worlds decorating the scene. On the far side of the hotel grounds, Videre saw Kish approaching, right on time. His teammate was carrying a blanket, which she spread on the sand, strategically positioned near the hotel's rear exit. Videre and Lain proceeded inside, where they were supposed to meet with Imatt. Pelos would try to remain inconspicuous in front of the hotel, watching for their target to use that exit.

The area immediately behind the hotel was paved with interlocking, decorative bricks, their red color contrasting with the white of the surrounding sand. Tropical plants were placed at strategic locations, accenting the atmosphere the architects had worked to create. A circular pool shimmered to one side, its azure waters looking inviting in the steamy air. Mahalo Island was located near the equator on Eden 3, and the system's star shone brightly.

They passed through the breezeway into the hotel's sprawling lobby, an ostentatious room sheathed in white marble. Videre found the open-air atmosphere appealing, and he enjoyed the feel of the gentle breeze wafting through the hall, bringing with it the tangy scent of salt water. They passed down a wide, circular staircase to the lobby's main floor, crossing to the fountain in the room's exact center. While Lain pretended to examine the fountain's décor, Videre watched for Imatt's arrival, trying to observe both staircases servicing the hotel's front.

He spotted the GBI special agent, casually descending the stairs and waving to Videre. For his part, Videre tapped Lain on the shoulder, feigning excitement at the coming meeting as if rendezvousing with a long-lost acquaintance. They crossed the floor and met Imatt in the middle, shaking hands warmly and laughing heartily with artificial joy. They approached the counter and signaled for the attention of the Human standing behind the counter.

While Imatt surreptitiously used his special datapad to access the hotel's reservations computer, Videre arranged for a trio of connected rooms. He changed his mind on the details more than once, varying the size of the beds, then requesting accommodations in the tower. Imatt coughed deeply, the agreed upon signal that he had finished downloading the data. The clerk was obviously irate, but controlling his temper, by the time the transaction was completed.

Imatt accessed his datapad, reading through the data he had downloaded. He found it in fairly short order: Ament had checked into the hotel the night before, and was still registered as a guest. Videre considered their options, from waiting until Ament either returned to, or exited from, his hotel room; to forcing entry into the room and hoping to find the fugitive at home. After a whispered discussion, they decided to have Lain use the computer to gain access to Treng Gomid's room, thereby allowing them to apprehend him if he was there, but not show their presence if he wasn't.

They took the elevator to the fifth floor and, turning right, followed the lushly carpeted hallway to their destination. While Videre and Imatt kept watch, Lain tapped into the building's computer system. His skills were more than a match for the hotel's security features, and in short order he had unlocked the door. They drew their weapons, took up positions, and Videre shoved the door open.

They rushed into the room, sweeping the area before them for signs of their quarry. Videre could see no one but didn't relax. As a single unit, they glided across the floor, nerves on edge, waiting for some unseen danger to leap out at them. They passed an enormous, heavily cushioned couch, and Videre's eyes fell immediately to the floor, seeing the Human lying face-down on the carpet, a bloody knife protruding from his back and a thick, red stain surrounding the still form.

CHAPTER EIGHT

ALYNA'S DOCTOR SLID A COLLAR AROUND HER NECK, secured it in place with a snap, and activated it with a press of a button. The tiny device hummed to life, and Alyna felt a slight tingle on the back of her neck. "Shock collar?" she asked in an indifferent voice.

"We prefer to call it a 'behavior modification system.' This is to make sure you behave yourself when I release your bonds. We can't have you killing a bunch of people again, especially me." He chuckled softly while he continued his paperwork.

Alyna turned her attention once more to plans of escape, rolling her eyes back to the sterile ceiling. With the addition of the collar, her chances of escaping her fate were slim indeed. Even if she managed to get the activator for her collar away from the doctor, there was no guarantee she would have the only device. As a fail-safe, there was probably at least one other, maybe two. The collars she was familiar with could deliver a charge ranging in intensity from mildly uncomfortable to paralyzing. She shook off the mental picture, angry with herself for despairing. If there were more controllers for her collar, so be it; she would still go down fighting. Her first opportunity would come when he released the bonds, and she could only hope they would be alone when he did so.

For an hour she focused on relaxing her body and mentally preparing herself for the fight of her life. Her meditation was interrupted when the door to the infirmary opened and a Bromidian soldier entered carrying a plain duffel bag over one shoulder. He growled something unintelligible to the doctor, handed him the bag, and left the room. The doctor tossed the bag on the floor near Alyna's examination table, then retreated across the room to a control panel.

"I'm going to release the ties holding you in place," he said slowly, one hand firmly on the shock collar activation device. Alyna felt a touch of satisfaction when she saw the hand holding the controller trembling. "You will put on the uniform in the bag, and then you will lie back down on the table. Failure to comply with my instructions will result in behavior correction. Do you understand?"

"You want me to get dressed in front of you? Forget it."

He sighed heavily. "I've already seen what you're hiding. I'm your doctor. Now follow my instructions. Do you understand?"

Alyna glanced at him, her face expressionless, then looked back to the ceiling. "I said, 'do you understand me?'" This time, Alyna didn't respond at all, determined to test the man's resolution. She received her answer moments later in the form of a violent shock causing her body to convulse. Despite her best efforts to the contrary, she cried out in pain. "Do you understand me?"

She nodded slowly, seemingly cowed into submission by the demonstration of the collar's effectiveness. The doctor pulled a short lever on the control panel, and the tension on her arms, legs, and body vanished. Alyna was free.

She sat up slowly, careful to keep the loose hospital gown about her body, then swung her legs off the table, rubbing her limbs to restore some circulation. The doctor stood patiently in the corner, intently watching her ritual. Alyna decided he had expected her to be unable to jump right to her feet, so he was willing to give her this small concession. Then something occurred to her: she wasn't completely unarmed. There was one weapon in her arsenal that her captors couldn't take away, and she hoped she could use it to lure her captor within striking distance. She slid to her feet, stretched sensuously toward her toes, and fixed the doctor with a direct look.

The doctor actually laughed out loud. "Give it a rest. You're not my type anyway. I prefer my women to have a little more meat on their bones. Besides, if you did have something I wanted, I could have taken it while you were unconscious. Or restrained. And who knows? Maybe I already did. Now, are you going to change clothes, or do I need to set my behavior correction device to a higher setting?"

Alyna fixed him with a deadly stare, wishing she could have just half a minute alone with him and a knife. Without breaking eye contact, she reached for the back of her gown.

The Bromidian in the tower picked up his radio, spoke softly into it, then placed it back on the table behind him. He returned to the opening facing the forest, gazing disinterestedly out over the ocean of blackness surrounding the prison. Arano didn't bother checking on the soldiers behind him; he had to assume they were ready. With painstaking slowness, he nocked an arrow, drew back the bowstring, and sighted in on his target.

He slowed his breathing, putting every effort into making the first shot count. Alyna's life depended upon him breaching the walls without raising the alarm; if the Bromidians inside knew of a possible rescue attempt, they would likely kill her and the other prisoners rather than allow them to go free. He offered up a silent prayer to the Four Elementals, eyed his target once more, and released the most important bow shot of his life.

The arrow hissed through the darkness, and Arano was rewarded with a dull *thud* when the arrow struck home in his target's forehead. The only sound the sentry made was that of his body striking the concrete floor of his elevated bunker.

Immediately, three grappling hooks whistled out of the gloom, caught on the edge of the tower, and held securely when their ropes were drawn tight.

Bromidian forms scampered from the underbrush to climb the ropes, vault over the front ledge, and disappear into the turret. Arano followed them up, joining the frenzied search of the guard's compartment. They found one more laser rifle, a portable radio, and assorted field rations. Most importantly, the sentry had a security card attached to his belt, and Arano promptly relieved him of the burden.

Arano led the way down the stairs and into the compound. His team fell into formation beside him, the darkness providing enough anonymity to allow them to pass for soldiers posted at the prison.

They crossed the open ground separating them from the main prison complex, and Arano found himself up against the next barrier: a locked door. He retrieved the card key from his pocket and placed it against a protruding device on the wall. A small, glowing red light on the panel changed to green, and the door soared upward to reveal the hallway beyond. They ducked through hurriedly, and the door slammed shut behind them.

Arano slung his longbow, drew his pistol, and stalked deeper into the prison. He judged by the shimmering stone of the floors and walls, and the ornate signs offering directions to different areas, that they were in an administrative area. The prisoners would likely be held on a lower level, making escape more difficult should an attempt be made. His suspicions were confirmed at the next hallway junction, when Lentin indicated a sign on the wall and then led the way to a nearby staircase. They descended deeper into the bowels of the prison.

The walls were a dreary color of gray, and the floors were filthy. Exposed pipes ran the length of the ceiling, covered in layers of dust.

They came to a series of doors, all on the right side of the hallway, and Arano assumed they were up against the outside wall of the underground facility. A lone Bromidian rounded the corner in front of them, skidding to a startled halt at the sight of the Human amid a group of Bromidians.

Lentin shouted at him in their own tongue. Whatever he said, the other Bromidian relaxed somewhat and came closer. Before the doomed soldier could cry out, Hawan had his hands around his throat. They hid him in a supply closet and pressed on.

Arano was relieved when Lentin held up a finger and pointed to a solitary door on the right side of the hallway. Arano positioned two pairs of Bromidians in the hallway, watching for guards, and took the rest with him. He used his security card to open the door, and as soon as it raced upward he dashed through the opening, laser pistol held ready, Lentin and Hawan at his side, and the others close behind.

There were a dozen Bromidians in the room, gathered around three tables. Arano leveled his pistol, sweeping it across the room. "Hands in the air!" he shouted. "Now!"

There was a moment of stunned silence, while the twelve Bromidians considered their options against the intruders. But as more of Arano's soldiers filed into the room, the sense of futility was plainly visible in their sagging shoulders and empty eyes. Arano had counted on this; by avoiding bloodshed, he gained more than one advantage. Sparing the lives of the Bromidian guards would go a long way toward gaining the respect and support of the former Rystorian Liberation Front fighters who fought by his side. In addition, some of the Bromidians might still be loyal to Hawan and the legitimate government.

As if reading Arano's mind, one of the Bromidians gasped in surprise. "Hawan? You are alive!"

Hawan cocked his head slightly to the side. "Do I know you?"

"I was with you during the final battle. The parachute assault, the fight within the walls, I was there the whole way with you and . . ." He shifted his gaze to Arano. "Viper!"

Arano leaned closer to Hawan, not taking his eyes off the group gathered before him. "Send four of your men to free the prisoners. I'll leave it to you and Lentin to determine who among these men is trustworthy, and what to do with the ones who are not."

Hawan barked his orders, and four Bromidians surged forward, activated a computer panel, and released the locks on the prison cells. Three of them rushed down the corridor, pulling the doors open and releasing the prisoners held within.

Hawan returned his attention to the Bromidian who had recognized him. "What is your name?"

"Lordan."

"Why are you serving the rebellion?" Hawan regarded the young Bromidian sternly, fixing him with an inquiring gaze as a father would a troublesome child.

"They told us you were dead. We saw the bodies of the governmental leaders, so we didn't doubt it. The bleachers where you were sitting were completely destroyed. I . . . that is, we went along with them because refusal meant death."

"How many men are here with you?"

"I have thirty more men in the next room, sleeping. We have an arms depot in there with them. We don't have any heavy equipment, but plenty of personal weapons."

"Can you figure out who is loyal to our government, and who is loyal to the insurrection?"

Lordan's face brightened noticeably. "Give me ten minutes and you can lead an army out of here." Hawan nodded, and Lordan immediately and systematically went to work. Arano had to admire his efficiency. First, he designated four men he trusted and divided the remaining guards into four equal groups. The four designees became squad leaders. The process was repeated with the sleeping soldiers, and by the time the prisoners had been gathered, twenty-two more Bromidians had joined the cause. They secured the others in the prison block.

Arano found himself shaking hands with Laron Alstor, his grateful smile tempered by a look of grief, his eyes wide with despair. His face was battered and bruised, but proud. "I thought you were dead, my friend!" Laron told him.

"Not quite," Arano said. "Where's Alyna?"

Laron looked away, then down at the floor. "We were told she was captured in an escape attempt today. I'm not sure what they did with her."

Lordan looked up from his work. "The female Human?"

Arano nodded earnestly, grasping Lordan by his arms. "Where is she? What have they done . . . ?" He trailed off, unable to phrase the question.

"She was injured when they recaptured her. They weren't very gentle with her after she killed several guards. The last I heard, she was in the infirmary."

"Can you lead me there?"

"Yes, Viper. I would be honored."

Arano whirled around to face Hawan. "Get the prisoners and our little army out of the prison. Take them to the rendezvous point, but don't wait more than an hour for me before you go to the secondary location. I'm going after Alyna."

"I'll go with you," Lentin volunteered. "It can't hurt to have another Bromidian along."

"And you couldn't keep me away," Laron added, retrieving a small laser pistol from the growing pile of weapons the Bromidians were gathering.

Arano nodded his agreement. "All right. Hawan, get your people out of here." He set his jaw firmly then stepped toward the door without looking back. "Let's go."

The infirmary was only a short distance away, Lordan assured him. At the Bromidian's suggestion, Laron and Arano concealed their weapons in the waistbands of their pants, pretending to be prisoners of Lordan and Lentin. At each intersection, Lordan gave the directions, guiding them with simple efficiency. He called Arano and Laron to a halt in front of a plain black door, whispering that the infirmary lay beyond. Arano, unable to read the Bromidian writing on the wall, took his word for it.

Lordan keyed open the door, and he and Lentin escorted the two Avengers into the room.

Alyna was lying on a table, securely fastened by some type of mechanical bonds. Her face was swollen and bruised, but she bore her wounds with a proud defiance. Some measure of her stoic silence slipped away when she saw Arano, hands on his head, march to the center of the room.

"Who are they?" a Bromidian guard demanded, rising from his chair in annoyance.

"None of your concern," replied Lentin. With a sudden snap

of his wrist, he sent a knife spinning end over end, striking the guard in the throat. He stumbled back into a table, the breath gurgling from his body, and Lordan rushed in to finish the job.

Arano started to struggle with his wife's restraints, but she pointed out the release lever to him, and moments later Alyna was free. She flew into his arms, and he allowed himself a few heartbeats in her embrace before they both had to become Avengers once more.

Alyna's dress uniform had been replaced with some type of utilitarian garment that would suffice to protect her from the harsh Bromidian sunlight. Lentin recognized the collar she wore as a pain compliance device, and was able to remove it without difficulty. Arano handed her an extra knife and laser pistol and motioned toward the door, but she shook her head.

"The doctor who tended my wounds is in the next room, sleeping," she said in a grim voice, teeth clenched against a boiling rage within her. "I need to pay my bill before we leave."

Arano recognized the futility of trying to deny such forceful vengeance. "Go ahead. Just don't linger too long."

She examined the edge of her knife, and the expression on her face never changed. "Just long enough for him to know it's me."

She disappeared through the doorway, which slid closed, but not fastened, behind her. Arano heard a startled scream, followed by the sound of breaking furniture. The final cry of pain was cut off suddenly, and Alyna returned to the examination room, wiping blood from her knife. "Excellent blade. Nice and sharp. Shall we go?"

Lentin and Lordan led the way, always the first through doors and around corners, ensuring there were no Bromidians in the area. They could talk their way out of an encounter; the Humans and the Padian would have inestimably more difficulty.

They had barely gone any distance when four Bromidians emerged from an office, stopping in place when they saw the group. One of them placed his hand on his pistol, but no one drew any weapons.

"Who are you?" Lentin demanded forcefully. "What are you doing here?"

The Bromidians looked at each other uncertainly. Arano gained a measure of confidence when he saw the low rank insignia on all four of the soldiers accosting them. "We were about to ask you the same question," one of them said finally.

"I'm Doctor Videre," Lentin told him with a haughty sniff. He pointed to Hawan. "This is Doctor Pelos. And this is Doctor Lon," he added, with an imperious gesture at Arano. "We came up from the infirmary to find out what happened to the supplies we ordered."

Hawan picked up on the charade with a mentally agility that surprised Arano. "This Human woman is going to die if we don't get the supplies we ordered, and heads will roll. Starting with yours." Alyna struck a theatrically mournful pose.

The four Bromidians took an involuntary step backward, en masse. The soldier who spoke before sounded less sure of himself. "What . . . what was it you needed?"

Arano rolled his eyes. "Well, this is annoying. How many times will I have to place this order?" He sighed, looking down at the floor. "I'll tell you what. If you can get me about fifty yards of flight line, that will be a good start. I'll have someone else tend to the rest of my list."

"Flight line? Where do we find it?"

Arano placed his hands on his hips, rolling his eyes in despair. "Central Supply, of course."

"At once, sir! And I apologize for the delay." The four

Bromidians scurried off, leaving the Avengers and their cohorts alone in the hallway. When the door slammed behind the four soldiers, they all broke into hysterics.

"What is flight line?" Lentin asked. "I haven't heard of it."

Alyna smiled broadly. "It's a prank typically pulled on new soldiers. A true flight line is the outbound portion of an airborne transport runway. But new soldiers tend to react first and think later, so when we tell them to get flight line, they run to supply. Apparently they think it's some type of string."

They made their way to the exit, encountering no one else. Lentin cracked the door open, just far enough to see outside. The way was clear, so they slipped out the door and into the darkness. They were halfway across the open field when the alarm sounded.

Although he was certain the figure before him was dead, Videre pressed his hand to the neck to check for a pulse but found none. Imatt knelt close to the body, running a scanner over the inert form. He stood and walked to the open window, tapping away at the keys on his datapad. The rest of the team was called into the room, and the police were notified.

"How long will it take for a DNA confirmation?" Videre asked quietly, staring at the knife protruding from the ugly wound.

"Just a few minutes," Imatt responded. "Since I already had his DNA encoded in my datapad, it's a simple matter of matching it up. We won't have to wait for a response from our main databanks back on Immok 2."

Videre nodded numbly, stepping away from the body. To occupy their time, he had instructed his team to conduct a meticulous search of the room, looking for clues about either the killer's or Ament's connections. Only a few minutes later, Imatt's datapad beeped urgently, and the announcement came.

"It was him, Videre. Treng Gomid, or Ament, if you will, is dead."

"Now what?" Videre asked rhetorically, straightening to his full height and closing his eyes. "We're no closer to finding out who his employers were. The trail ends here."

Total silence permeated the room, everyone considering their options but no one making any suggestions. Videre stared at the floor for some time before he realized what he was seeing. Next to the legs of the end table were impressions in the carpet where the table's legs had sat for weeks, or even months. The furniture had been moved for some reason, and Videre wanted to know why. He knelt, taking a closer look at the carpet.

"This table was moved, too," Kish announced. Videre realized the ever-vigilant Tompiste had recognized the significance of the moved furniture.

Videre surveyed the room, realizing several items around the room had been displaced. "Not moved," observed Videre. "Knocked over. There was a fight here, a fight for Treng's life."

"And Treng lost," Lain said.

"The perpetrator must have cleaned up, to some extent," Pelos said, examining the pool of blood. "But why do that if you are going to leave the blood?"

"He was probably interrupted," Imatt said, thinking out loud. "I would guess he was in the process of cleaning up the crime scene when someone came in. He has been dead for only an hour or so. Someone probably spooked the killer, and he fled before the job was done."

"Okay," Videre said, thinking quickly. "Whoever he was

working for knew he was being chased, so they eliminated him before he could talk to us. The killer ambushed him, thinking it would be an easy kill. Ament put up a fight, damaging the room in the process. The killer tried to clean up the crime scene, but he was interrupted before he could finish, and he had to flee. That means—"

"There should still be evidence in here somewhere," Pelos finished for him.

"Sketchy and hypothetical," Imatt commented, "but probably fairly accurate." He pulled on a set of thin, flexible gloves and lifted Ament's hands, examining them closely.

"What are you looking for?" Kish asked, kneeling curiously beside him.

"Sometimes the old tricks are best. Typically, when someone is in a fight for their life, they will scratch their assailant with their fingernails. Do you see this material gathered under the nail of his right middle finger? In all likelihood, this is flesh from the killer. And flesh means DNA."

He scraped some of the substance from under Ament's fingernail, placing it in a plastic bag for protection. He scanned it with his DNA scanner, sending the data out to the main GBI computer. "We should have the results in a few hours," he said.

As Videre had expected, they found a large quantity of cash on Treng's person, in his luggage, and even under the mattress. Whoever his employer was, the shadowy figure was taking steps to prevent identification, and cash payments were common in the criminal world for just that reason. He had two pieces of paper in his pocket with the logo of the newly risen sun drawn on them, clumsy representations of the mural on the wall of his basement.

"Here's something," Pelos said, holding up a crumpled sheet of paper he had recovered from the inner lining of Treng's suitcase. Videre took it and examined the handwritten note, the penmanship almost too sloppy to read. Seeing his teammates had stopped their work and were waiting expectantly, he read the note aloud.

"'*Ament. The plan has been changed. Your transport to bring you back to Khonsu will not be leaving until tomorrow. Stay in your room and remain out of sight. Follow our instructions to the letter, and we'll double your payment. The name of your contact is Osiris.*' Osiris . . . now why is that name familiar?"

Imatt laced his fingers on top of his head, rolling his eyes in frustration. "Our infiltrators don't appear to be very creative when it comes to their names. I can't believe I didn't see this before. Ament, Khonsu, and Osiris are all names found in ancient Human mythology. The Egyptians worshipped them as gods, thousands of years ago. Osiris was the god of the dead, which dovetails nicely with Ament's choice of moniker. His namesake was the greeter of the dead, which suggests a certain subservience between the two. Khonsu is the curious one. He was the son of Amun, who was considered the king of the gods. Khonsu may be a person of some importance in their organization. Likely, he is their number two man."

"And Osiris is probably our killer," Kish said, nodding slowly. "Ament let him in, and once his back was turned, Osiris struck."

"Let's go back to the police station," Imatt suggested. "We can put our heads together with Detective Gnell and see what our next move should be."

They returned to the planning room at the police station, where the clerk who offered to try and clear up Arano's message waited breathlessly. "I was trying to contact you! A friend of mine managed to unscramble the text of your friend's transmission. Here is the transcript."

She handed Videre a sheet of paper, and he swiftly read through the contents then had to sit down, legs suddenly feeling leaden and unable to bear his weight. The letter slipped unnoticed from his hands, and he could only stare at the table, jaw agape. He looked up at his friends, eye wide with disbelief.

"Two days ago, I would have figured this was a prank, but it fits too neatly with recent unexplained events." He took a deep breath, bravely holding his head high. "There's been a military coup on Rystoria. Arano was wounded, and Laron, Alyna, and Lentin may have been captured. He's requesting help."

Absolute silence reigned in the confining space of the planning room. All thoughts of tracking down Ament's killer faded from Videre's mind; his entire being focused on saving his friend. He retrieved the fallen note, reading through it once more.

"Okay, people. We need a plan. Suggestions?"

Kish had buried her face in her hands, and she mumbled through her petite, leathery fingers. "Obviously, we have to do something to help our friends on Rystoria. But I can't shake the feeling that we need to follow through on this business. I really think passing it off to someone else would be a mistake."

"I agree with Kish," Imatt said softly. "We have the momentum going for us, and we shouldn't give it up. Remember: our first duty is to the Coalition, and these people declared war on us when they assassinated our leaders."

Lain nodded reluctantly. "He's right. There must be a way for us to do both."

Pelos growled his frustration, beak clicking angrily. "Maybe there is . . ."

CHAPTER
NINE

SHOTS RANG OUT FROM EVERY QUARTER AS THE guards in the towers opened fire. The four beleaguered warriors sprinted ahead, all of them instinctively running in a crouch, following a zigzag pattern. Arano realized how fortunate they were; had the alarm gone off thirty seconds earlier, they would have been in the middle of a killing field. As it was, a short sprint left them within the meager cover of a group of ground transports parked in an outdoor motorpool. They managed to return fire, although their shots were unaimed, at best.

"The short tower, fifty meters ahead, is where we came in!" Arano shouted over the din of battle. "If we get that far, we can make it to the woods and try to lose them there."

Laron grunted. "That's great. Any bright ideas on how to pull off that miracle?"

An explosion of stone answered Laron's question, leaving a pillar of smoke in its wake. Arano dared a brief glance from behind his cover and shouted his relief. "We've got company! The guards are taking fire from the woods!"

"Hawan must not have listened to you," Lentin observed dryly.

"We have friends out there?" Alyna asked, firing off several more shots.

"Yeah," Arano responded, trying to get a better idea of where their allies were. "About forty or fifty Bromidians, under the command of Hawan. They were supposed to head to the check-point, but for some reason they stuck around."

"I think we can overlook their transgression this time," Laron said, forcing a smile.

Arano rose to his feet, staying in a crouch. "Here's our chance! Follow me!"

With his friends at his heels, he made a desperate rush for the unmanned tower ahead of them. Although shots were still fired in their direction, the occurrence was lessened with the guards' shifting their fire to meet the external threat.

They gained entrance to the tower, climbed the short flight of stairs, and entered the observation room. Arano heaved a sigh of relief when he saw the grappling hooks still firmly attached to the ledge, their ropes dangling into the night. Without slowing, he bounded onto the ledge, grasped the nearest rope, and swung over the side. He slid lithely to the ground, sweeping the area around him for enemy troops.

At his signal, the others approached the ledge to follow him down. The small turret was taking fire from an enemy emplace-ment in the taller tower to the south. Arano leaned out from his place of cover, took careful aim with his pistol, and fired.

The blast from his pistol struck the exposed power pack for the heavy laser cannon, and the entire system exploded in a shower of metal and stone fragments. His companions dropped roughly to the ground, and he motioned them into the conceal-ment of the trees.

He stayed in place for several moments longer, firing off a few more shots before following his companions to the relative safety of the forest. From their hidden positions, Arano's allies also initiated their retreat, pulling back singly and in pairs while discouraging any immediate pursuit by continuing their suppressive fire.

Through the haze and smoke of battle, Arano saw Alyna's battered face, and the rage boiled up within him once again. He had to fight down the urge to go back and try to eliminate the entire garrison. There would be time for vengeance in the days ahead, but the time had not come.

It took them almost half an hour to reach the dry creek bed, and they stopped to rest while Arano tried to figure out whether they needed to go north or south to meet up with the others. He made his best guess and led them to the north.

Less than a kilometer away, they found the rock formation they were looking for. Arano assessed the area, decided it was safe, and brought the group in closer. Off in the distance, he could still hear the sounds of battle; Hawan's forces hadn't fully disengaged from the enemy troops. Hawan had rescued him, so perhaps he could return the favor . . .

Hawan's laser rifle barked twice, and another Bromidian soldier fell on his back, a smoking hole in his chest. He retreated farther up the ridge, firing back into the trees to keep their enemy from getting too close, and bit down on the hard shell of his lip in frustration. He wanted to change directions and not lead the rebel soldiers right to their meeting point, but his force was spread out too far to have effective communication.

An RLF soldier to Hawan's left screamed in agony, the gruesome wound in his head telling Hawan he had lost another man. He scooped up the fallen warrior's weapon and continued the retreat. Peering ahead in the darkness, he couldn't see more than fifty or sixty feet. They might be close to the creek bed, or they could be a mile away; he had no way of knowing.

Hawan felt tangible relief when his feet hit the small stones in the dry creek bed. To his right, he could barely make out a jumble of boulders, and he knew he had come out almost on top of their meeting place.

He had no intention of stopping, which could give his foe some idea that they were planning to meet more escapees. He started up the far bank—but stopped, taking a moment to study the formation of stones to his right.

It was twenty meters high, with a number of odd angles where an ambusher could hide. Hawan wouldn't have time to get anyone up to the top, where they could slaughter the enemy almost at will, but he could certainly hide people in some of the lower nooks and crannies. He shouted orders for his team to continue to the next rally point, grabbed two nearby Bromidians, and took cover in the rocks.

His wait was short, less than a minute, before the enemy came into view. It was eerie watching them fire at targets farther up the hill, and see the return fire striking trees, rocks, and, occasionally, flesh. He waited until the main body of enemy troops was directly across from his position and then signaled his hidden troops. He took careful aim at a rebel soldier who wore the rank of major . . .

The target's head exploded in a flash of laser light, and the decapitated body collapsed on itself. The rebel troops paused, shocked disbelief on their wide-mouthed faces, trying to determine how he had been shot. From above Hawan's head, a murderous hailstorm of laser blasts rained down on the hapless enemy, and they fell like rain.

Hawan recovered from his shock and opened fire, adding to the carnage. The rebels tried to find cover, but Hawan's troops had heard the intense firefight and returned, their carefully aimed shots adding to the pressure on the Bromidian soldiers. Several broke and ran for the safety of the prison, but only two managed to make it to safety.

Kish Waukee stepped off the transport and entered the *Intrepid*, Pelos Marnian and Imatt Deeps close behind. She almost laughed, thinking about how useful the frigate had become.

When he had first obtained the ship, it was difficult to pry Arano away from her. He had allowed Lon Pana to fly her in the final battle at Rystoria, but he knew *Intrepid* would be coming to his rescue if his mission was successful. Now he allowed his team to take it any time they needed it even if he wasn't there.

The sad irony was that Arano was fighting for his life on Rystoria again, but this time *Intrepid* wouldn't be charging in to save the day. Help was on the way, but in true Avenger fashion, there wasn't a lot of help to be had.

Kish closed her eyes and took a deep breath, lightly tapping her leathery fist against her head. She desperately wanted to be there to help her friend, but it would be impractical.

They entered the Captain's planning room, and she flopped into a chair, satisfied to be able to sit. They hadn't had much rest in the last few days, and it was wearing on her. She went over in her mind what they had turned up.

They were expecting a DNA response from Immok 2 at any time, which would likely identify Ament's killer. They were fairly certain, based upon the letter they had found, the shadowy assassin's code name was Osiris. With any luck, Imatt could use his resources to tap into the starport's computer, compare Osiris's

DNA against the database of passengers leaving the system, and determine where to go next.

One question still pestering Kish, however, was in regard to the mysterious Khonsu. Who or what was it? Another assassin? The leader of a group? Could Khonsu itself be a group?

Too many questions and not enough answers.

"I'm getting something now," Imatt said without looking up from his datapad. "The DNA comes from . . . oh, this is interesting. His name is Ustin Shiba, and he's a Bromidian! Ament must have scratched him in the face, because I don't know where else on a Bromidian's exoskeleton he could've dredged up much flesh under his nails. Anyway, Ustin is a former member of Rising Sun. He was one of their top operatives, and he was in a special elite group called Dark Knights. They served purposes similar to the Avengers. They also performed assassinations, counter-espionage, and kidnappings. They were feared, even among the regular Bromidian military." He tapped at his datapad. "I'm pulling up the spaceport's data right now, and we'll see if we can figure out where he's going."

Pelos frowned. "If we issue outstanding warrants for his arrest, his DNA profile should automatically produce an alert at spaceport security when he checks in."

Imatt shook his head sadly. "No. Once, it would have but, unfortunately, no longer. Our wonderful High Council found such a procedure to be invasive and a violation of its citizens' privacy rights. They can store the data on DNA scans, and if the police can produce a writ, they can obtain the data after the fact. But actually using it to catch people on the spot is considered illegal. GBI agents have received special dispensation to conduct on-the-spot checks, such as I've been doing, but only under exigent circumstances."

Kish threw up her hands in frustration. "I thought Arano cured the Council of its deficiency disease when he killed Grand High Councilor Balor Tient."

"It helped," Imatt said, smiling. "But let's face it: Tient was only a symptom of the disease infecting much of the Council."

"Well," Pelos said, "I guess we have to work with what we've got. Osiris is likely the killer, and he's the next link in the chain leading us to the source of the attack on our government. But the question remains: who is responsible and why?"

"Maybe there is a group of surviving Rising Sun terrorists who have banded together to strike back at the Coalition," Imatt theorized. "We know we didn't get them all, and they certainly have a grudge against us."

Kish leaned back farther in her chair. "One thing that bothers me is the timing. Several of our government leaders are assassinated by a man with ties to Rising Sun, and at the same time, it looks like we have an insurrection on Rystoria. I don't think a group made up of a few ragtag terrorists could pull off something on this scale."

"Maybe this is where Khonsu comes in," Imatt said. "Whoever Khonsu is, be it an individual or a group, they might be the unifying factor here. We need more information. We need Osiris."

He turned back to his datapad in response to a beeping alarm. "Okay, here we go. He checked into the spaceport four hours ago. He boarded a ship bound for the Radlon Orbital Platform at Tectos 5." He checked the time display on his datapad. "If we get started now, he'll only have a ninety-minute head start on us."

Pelos rose to his full, impressive height, pulling his lucky tollep's tooth from where it hung beneath his uniform shirt. "Let's go."

Arano shook hands with the Bromidian sentry who was relieving him at his guard post and staggered in an exhausted stupor
to his bedroll. He still hadn't fully recovered from his injuries
sustained during the initial hours of the revolt, and the days on
the run were grinding him down. It had been two full days since
they eliminated the immediate pursuit from the prison, but they
still weren't in the clear. They had spent the entire time dodging patrols and hiding from aerial search vehicles. Fortunately,
among the equipment they had removed from the prison was a
sensor-scrambling device, which was preventing their detection
by electronic means.

His eyes fell involuntarily on his pack, and he could see a
faint blinking light coming from inside. Looking askance at his
pack, Arano wondered what could be the source of the light.
Fearing he had somehow picked up a tracking device, or worse,
he gently opened the flap and peeked inside. He eased a few
items from the top and found his answer: the chess computer
was blinking its electronic announcement of an unread incoming
message. He pulled the computer from his pack and activated it
with the touch of a button.

Arano sat bolt upright in bed, accidentally waking his wife in
the process. He smiled apologetically and showed her the screen.

"You woke me up so you could play chess? Thanks a lot."
She lay back down and rolled her eyes.

"When we first escaped the attack, I sent a message to Videre.
I didn't think it made it to him, because that was days ago, but
now I'm receiving a response. He must have found a way to
break through whatever transmission dampening equipment the
rebels are using." He cleared his throat theatrically, and Alyna

groaned and jabbed him lightly in the side.

"*Viper, I couldn't help but notice you were placed in check recently. You probably have any number of ideas in your head for your next move, but I'd like to offer my help. I'd hate for this to fall into your opponent's hands, because he could counter you if he knew your next move. Why don't you send me a location where I can mail you my idea? My delivery system is fairly quick. I'd say I could have my package to you in a matter of hours.*

"*Confusion to Videre,*

"*Lain Baxter.*"

Arano licked his lips, chuckling softly at Lain's attempt at combining a coded message with humor. He performed several mathematical computations in his head before formulating his reply. "*I would never turn down an offer of help. For my next turn, I'll move my queen from quadrant 4436 to quadrant 8792. Hopefully you can evaluate it and give me some feedback before I'm due to send that move to Videre. I don't really want to risk any more of my pieces; I just need some food for thought. Maybe a few tools, too. I'll probably be okay if you can give me a response in the next three hours.*"

He sent the message, then packed the computer away. "Never believed a game could be so helpful," he mumbled, lying down again. He stared at the trees overhead, barely visible in the covering darkness. "If I'm reading Lain's message correctly, help is closer at hand than we thought. I encoded our location and sent it to him, so if he's as near as I believe he is, we should hear from him soon."

"What do you think he's planning to do?"

Arano sighed. "It's hard to say. I'm hoping they have a cache of weapons they can get to us somehow, maybe by parachute. We'll have to keep an eye out for just about anything."

She checked her watch. "I'm on guard duty in about thirty minutes, and my watch lasts until sunrise. I'll let my relief know to keep an eye on the skies, starting at first light."

Although he was still fatigued, Arano awoke shortly after the sun came up, when Alyna returned to pack away her blanket. He surprised her with a quick kiss and a mischievous smile before he climbed a nearby tree, reaching as high into the boughs as he dared. The harsh Bromidian environment made for hearty indigenous life, and the trees were no exception. Although the tree he ascended wasn't exceptionally thick, its branches were noticeably stronger than most tree varieties Arano had seen before. He didn't quite reach the apex but was high enough to have a relatively unobstructed view of the morning sky.

The Bromidian star climbed higher above the horizon, and Arano donned his protective glasses. He maintained his vigil, even when Alyna tempted him with a hot breakfast. He declined, and she made every effort to make sure he knew she was enjoying the meal. His stomach growled audibly, and he smiled at his predicament. There he was, stuck in a Rystorian tree, helping to protect a people he had once sworn to eliminate, and he was ignoring the beautiful woman below who was offering to feed him. The ironies of life never ceased to amaze him.

At first, he assumed there was a spot on his glasses. Squinting painfully, he removed them and cleaned the lenses, but when he put them back on, the black dot was still there. In fact, the more he concentrated on it, he realized there was actually more than one dot in the pale blue-green Rystorian sky. He frowned in frustration, watching as the dots grew almost imperceptibly larger, then whistled for Alyna's attention, telling her to have everyone pack up and prepare to move out.

The dots grudgingly drew into focus, and moments later

Arano realized what he was seeing. "Parachutes!" he shouted to Alyna, fifty feet below him. "It looks like they'll land about a kilometer north of here. Gather the troops!"

He bounced from branch to branch, descending as quickly as prudence allowed. Dropping to the hard-packed, leaf-covered forest floor, he gathered his gear and packed it away. Within a few minutes, his entire retinue was ready to leave. After considering his options, he motioned Hawan and Lentin to his side.

"Follow as soon as you can, but Alyna and I are going on ahead. I want to reach the landing site as quickly as possible. We'll be fairly easy to track through the underbrush, so meeting up shouldn't be a problem. We'll see you shortly."

Alyna gave him an amused look, lips pursed in a barely suppressed grin. "Both of us are going? I'm surprised you didn't say you were going alone."

Arano laughed, throwing his pack over his shoulder. "I know better. You wouldn't have let me go alone."

They dashed into the woods, leaping over fallen branches with the agility of a cat. Despite the shade provided by the sheltering boughs and the crisp air of the autumn morning, Arano felt his body heating up, and the first beads of perspiration appeared on his forehead. He pulled up short at the sight of a large snake slithering across their path, but it showed no interest in them, so he pressed on.

Minutes later, he slowed their pace to a cautious walk. Although he believed the parachutes likely carried supplies sent by his teammates, he wanted to be certain before exposing himself to potential danger. Additionally, there was always the possibility that an enemy patrol had seen the parachutes and would investigate.

Arano pushed ahead one painstaking step at a time, easing branches and foliage out of his way, then lowering them back into place to keep them from snapping back and hitting Alyna. Something appeared in the shadows ahead, so he eased himself into a crouch and brought up his rifle.

Several crates dangled precariously from their parachute risers, swinging ponderously back and forth like giant pendulums, hanging at least three meters off the ground.

Arano turned his attention to the surrounding foliage, searching for signs of the enemy. He saw nothing out of the ordinary, and to his great relief, there was no warning from his danger sense. He slowly rose and crept forward, Alyna following several feet behind to provide covering fire.

"Hello, Viper. How are things?"

Arano's head snapped around and up, and his shoulders sagged in exasperation when he saw Videre sitting primly on a tree branch, legs crossed comfortably, Gatoan teeth bared in a broad, feline grin. Behind him, Lain worked at releasing the risers from his harness, and Arano noticed that he looked a bit irritated.

"I thought I told you to send only supplies. I really didn't want anyone else from the team to be caught up in this."

Videre snapped his fingers in wonder, as if the same idea had just occurred to him. "So *that's* what you meant. Sorry. Well, too late now. I guess you'll have to share the fun, if you can get us down from here."

Arano looked back at the pale blue Bromidian sky. "How did you get here?"

"We jumped from the cargo bay of a freighter belonging to a new shipping company. The owner owed me a favor, and he decided to help. I think you've heard of the company before . . . Marnian Shipping. It's unmanned, so there won't be a loss of life when the ships forming the blockade catch up with it and destroy it."

Arano grinned, in spite of himself. "What did you bring with you?"

"Basically, what you asked for. Food—I assume that's what you meant by 'food for thought'—weapons, power packs, scanners, secure FM radios, compasses, and other gadgets."

Arano sighed and rubbed his eyes, slowly shaking his head. "And you just couldn't seem to stay away. Okay, let's get you two down from there."

Lain managed to swing his bulky form within reach of a man-sized tree branch and climbed atop it. After releasing his risers, he skittered down the tree to stand at Arano's side. He had his own pack with him, and there were two weapon containers strapped to his side. Arano eyed the gear curiously.

"Two weapons? You must be expecting trouble."

"Not really," Lain said, smiling in false modesty. "I brought you a present."

Arano's eyes lit up like a Rystorian sunset when he saw Lain remove Arano's prized sniper rifle from the second weapon pack.

The *Intrepid* lowered to the deck of the docking bay, releasing a hiss of steam in the process.

Kish was impressed with the size of the Radlon Orbital Platform, the largest station in orbit of Tectos 5. The platforms used specially modified tractor beams to extract various gasses from the planet's atmosphere. Tectos 5 was a massive gas giant, and many travelers who had visited the abandoned Earth System commented on the similarities between Tectos 5 and Earth 5, also known as Jupiter. The Tectos System's location was on the opposite side of Rystoria from the Coalition-held systems, adding further intrigue to the whole scenario.

The *Intrepid's* ramp lowered noisily to the floor, and Kish strode down into the cargo bay, her teammates close behind. The hangar wasn't well cared for, and greasy tools were scattered about along the walls. The floor was in need of sweeping, and the paint was peeling off the walls. The odor of engine fuels was thick in the air, and Kish found it irritated her eyes.

Right on schedule, Lon Pana was waiting for them with two of his teammates, a Gatoan lieutenant named Toshe Jorgan, and a Human lieutenant named Vic Dermak. The rest of Pana's team had been pulled for guard details, protecting some of the remaining high-ranking members of the Coalition government. Imatt Deeps had called in a few favors, and for the time being, Lon, Toshe, and Vic were assigned to Kish's team. Lon and his two lieutenants would form Squad A, with Lon acting as team leader, while Kish's squad would operate with Imatt Deeps rounding out their numbers.

Kish and Imatt had agreed upon the continued need for secrecy, so they hadn't alerted authorities at the station about their impending approach. The timing of their arrival was fortuitous; local time on the station was after midnight, and few people were about. Pelos was able to pry the lock open on a maintenance closet, and as Kish had hoped, inside was a number of spare uniforms, which they quickly donned.

Pelos and Imatt each carried a maintenance kit with them, slung by a strap over one shoulder. Imatt's kit, however, contained an added bonus: the GBI computer he had used to tap into the database at the hotel, and which he would use against the station's computer. Kish consulted a nearby map of the area, then took her team into the main corridor. A sleepy-eyed security guard strolled past them, yawning and barely acknowledging their presence. Kish turned her almond-shaped eyes briefly in his direction, but when he didn't deviate from his path, she shrugged indifferently and led her team down a corridor to the right.

A filth-encrusted computer sat at the end of the hall, some of the blinking lights on its panel almost invisible through the sludge. Imatt raised an eyebrow but said nothing, pulling his computer from his pack and accessing the station's information. He pulled a towel from his maintenance kit and wiped away some of the grime before tapping a few keys on the maintenance computer.

"This may take a few minutes longer," he warned without looking up. "Their computers leave something to be desired."

Kish issued a few brief orders, suggestions really, to her team-mates, and they made some pretense of cleaning the area around the computer. A door to her right slid open with a grinding metal-on-metal noise, and a pair of Human guards, a man and a woman, stepped into the corridor. Unlike the last guard, these two looked anything but sleepy, although their uniforms were somewhat rumpled. They froze in place when they saw the crew working at the end of the hall. Kish immediately saw the suspicion in their eyes, so she decided to take a chance.

"What were you doing in there?" she demanded harshly, stepping closer to the surprised guards. "There's nothing critical in there. You should be out walking your perimeter."

The two astonished guards looked at each other, eyes wide with fear, then back at Kish. It was the woman who spoke first.

"We . . . had a security alert in this sector. We were checking that room to be certain there were no intruders."

Kish sensed her advantage and pressed ahead. "How long does it take to search that room? We've been here for quite some time. I'd hate to think how long you two were in there."

"Look," the female guard's companion said, hands extended

palms upward in supplication. "We're supposed to be getting married in a few weeks, but with the manpower shortage, we don't have much time off together." Kish almost laughed when the female guard's eyebrows shot up at the proclamation, a sure sign the man's claim was mendacious. "I'd appreciate it if you could be discreet about this."

Kish looked around as if considering the matter, and was relieved to see Imatt putting away his computer. Apparently, things had gone better than he expected. "Okay," she said with an exaggerated sigh. "I guess I'm a romantic at heart. But next time, please be more careful. You wouldn't want someone walking in on you."

The guards needed no further prompting and raced away. Vic Dermak laughed heartily. "How did you know there was nothing beyond that door worth guarding?"

"I saw the map back in the hangar."

"But how could you remember such a trivial detail?"

Lon intervened, waving off Kish's response. "Don't get her started. Let's just say she has a very good memory."

Kish smiled, wrinkling her brown, leathery cheeks. "Imatt, did do you find him?"

The GBI agent smiled. "I have his room number right here."

CHAPTER TEN

ARANO LIFTED HIS SNIPER RIFLE FROM HIS FRIEND'S hands and sat down on a nearby tree stump. He pulled out his utility knife, carefully pruning away the protective packaging. Once the straps holding everything in place were cut, he eased the weapon out where he could take a closer look at it. He scrutinized every inch of his favorite rifle, but nothing seemed damaged. With a deep smile of satisfaction, Arano ran his hands along the wooden stock in a gentle caress.

"Do you two need a room?" Videre asked. They both laughed, and Arano set the rifle down rather ruefully.

"Okay, Videre, how did you get this out of my personal weapon safe? It has a very expensive security system on it."

Videre rolled his eye theatrically. "I think I've told you before that systems like that are a waste of money. There hasn't been a security protocol made that Lain and I can't defeat. And if we can beat it, I'm sure there are less scrupulous people out there who can beat it, too."

"Less scrupulous than you? I doubt that. Okay, what's the situation?"

Videre gave Arano an overview of the investigation into the identity and location of Ament, the man responsible for the deaths of several Coalition officials, ending with the mercenary's untimely demise. He also told him what he knew of Ament's suspected killer, but he admitted his knowledge in that area was limited.

"When I left Kish, she had taken command of the team. She had Imatt assigned to her squad, and Lon Pana had brought in his squad to complete the team. They were on their way to Tectos 5 to find Osiris. Hopefully, they'll get some answers at the Radlon Platform.

"I have another bonus for you, as far as our situation goes. I managed to contact the Latyrian who was inspecting coalition military sites. He left immediately for the Niones System. He is planning to round up about a platoon of Latyrians and bring them here. I told him how to contact us."

Arano lowered his rifle to his lap and leaned back against a large branch, locking his fingers behind his head. "I hadn't planned on bringing in any more outsiders, but they would be a definite advantage. I was wishing I had them the last time we were fighting on Rystoria 2."

"Maybe we should put a garrison of them here, so we'll have them for the next war."

They were joined by Hawan and Lentin, who had been overseeing the unloading of the rest of the supplies and the distribution of their new inventory to the soldiers who would be carrying it. Hawan seemed genuinely pleased by the upcoming addition of Latyrian troops.

"This is good, Viper. We'll be able to coordinate ambushes much more efficiently, without the risk of electronic detection by the enemy."

"Not to mention their tracking abilities," Arano added, looking up at the sky.

A Bromidian crashed through the underbrush to stand breathlessly before Hawan. "Our scouts just reported seeing two skimmers heading this way."

Arano was on his feet in the space of two heartbeats. "Are they coming directly here, or are they making a general sweep?"

"They are on a course directly toward our position. The skimmers are running just above the tops of the trees. They should be here in less than fifteen minutes! We have to get out of here!"

"Stay calm!" Arano said, a bit more sharply than he had intended. He took a deep breath and closed his eyes for a moment, then opened them to face the Bromidian messenger. "We can't outrun them. The skimmers move much faster than we can on foot. We need to fight." He grabbed his sniper rifle and strode deliberately to the middle of the camp. Hawan whistled for everyone's attention.

"My friends, the enemy is upon us! It is too late to hide or flee, so we will make our stand right here." He held his hand out and gestured to Arano. "Viper?"

Arano looked around the assembled troops, hands on hips as he assessed their combat readiness. "Our foes have tracked us down. The enemy of your new government and newfound freedoms. Most of you assembled here today fought hard for those freedoms less than two years ago, only to see them taken away in a cowardly attack against the symbols of your new government's power.

"But those freedoms are not lost; they are only misplaced. If you want them back, there is a price that must be paid, a promise to future generations that must be written in the blood of patriots like yourselves!"

A Bromidian near the front of the crowd snorted, crossing his arms in defiance. "That should please you to no end, Viper. No matter which side wins, many Bromidians will die."

An uncertain grumbling passed through the crowd, and Arano knew he needed to head off that line of thinking immediately. He strode forward until his face was mere inches from his detractor's. "Years ago, I would have had to agree with you." He stared directly into his antagonist's eyes and held the gaze until the Bromidian had to turn away. He stepped back to address the crowd again.

"If a group of Padian soldiers had kidnapped, tortured, and murdered your family and loved ones, at the behest of the Padian government, would you not feel animosity toward Padians in general? Especially if that was the only contact you'd ever had with Padians?" He looked around the crowd, letting the statement settle into the soldiers' consciousness, then took a deep breath to steady himself. "We don't have time for this discussion. After the battle is won, I will give everyone here the explanation you deserve. But right now, we need to prepare."

Nods of assent and uneasy glances rippled through the assembled Bromidians. Arano called the soldiers designated as squad leaders to his side and briefly outlined his plan.

Groups of RLF troops were set out in an arc, with the center based along what appeared to be the enemy's line of approach. Arano dispatched Videre and Lain to retrieve some of the equipment they had brought with them, while he, Alyna, and Lentin selected their own fighting position at the center of their defensive lines.

Hawan remained on the ground, where he could direct the battle more readily. The enemy moved into Arano's field of view, and he sighted in on the pilot of the nearest craft in case his Avengers failed in their mission.

The skimmers drew closer. The Bromidian flying the nearest of the two craft completely filled the view in Arano's scope, with the crosshairs sighted in on the center of his chest. Beside him, Lentin tapped him gently on the leg. "Viper, your men are in position."

Arano nodded his acknowledgement, keeping his eye on the approaching ships. They were a mere fifty meters from his position when he motioned to Hawan, who passed the signal along to Lain and Videre.

The anti-graviton fluxors hummed to life, the portable jamming devices creating an invisible field of energy in front of the unsuspecting enemy soldiers. When their skimmers entered the field, they shuddered violently for several seconds, the Bromidians clinging desperately to the sides, and then they dropped from the sky. Tree limbs snapped with loud reports, and the craft tumbled end over end as they fell. Both landed upside down, and barely a half dozen enemy soldiers managed to climb free of the wreckage.

Arano felt a great apprehension strike him, and he wondered if he had made the correct decision for the next phase of the battle plan. The simplest solution would have been to kill them all, thereby saving more of his troops for later battles. But there was another battle to be won: the battle for the hearts and minds of the RLF soldiers under his command. Brutally slaughtering an outnumbered and badly weakened foe would strengthen the widely held conviction that he only lived to kill Bromidians. Taking the survivors prisoner was risky, but the benefits in the long run made it worth taking a chance. He waited breathlessly while the RLF soldiers left their places of concealment and began the dangerous process of capturing the enemy soldiers . . .

Kish casually indicated a doorway on the group's left, and the others followed her through. She cast a quick look behind her, where Imatt Deeps followed in silence.

"Did you have time to implant the backup protocol in their computer system?"

"Yes. If Osiris attempts to leave the station by any of the normal means, the computer will alert us as soon as his DNA is scanned at a checkpoint. Of course, if he has another way to get off the station, he could leave us floundering around behind him."

Kish nodded her acceptance of the risk. They didn't have the manpower to watch every conceivable exit point in the station. They reached the quarters assigned to Ustin Shiba, the infamous Osiris. Kish checked the hallway in both directions but found it deserted. She drew her pistol, as did Pelos and Imatt, while Lon's squad stood to either side, facing out for security. Kish and Imatt took up positions on opposite sides of the door while Pelos worked to disable the security lock on Ustin's quarters.

A staccato double beep told Kish the way was clear, a fact confirmed when Pelos stepped back and crouched, weapon trained on the door. Kish reached across and keyed the entry command, and the door slid open.

The Avengers darted inside, weapons sweeping the interior of the room. Kish stood just inside the door, breathing heavily with anticipation, but felt a sharp sting of disappointment at seeing the empty room. A single door was on the far wall. Motioning with her free hand, she pulled her team inside and gestured her squad toward the other door.

The portal rose rapidly upward with a steely hiss, and laser fire erupted from the next room. Kish dove for cover, returning fire as soon as she was able. Lon kept his two Avengers monitoring the room's main door, while he crawled forward to assist in the firefight. Bright streaks of light ripped back and forth through the air, striking the steel bulkheads with an explosion of sound and sparks. Judging by the volume of fire, Kish estimated there were at least two, possibly three assailants in the next room, all with usable firing angles.

It was Pelos who provided the solution. He shifted his aim to the right, blazing away at a section of the bulkhead near a corner of the room. The metal in the wall proved to be no stronger than it appeared, and an explosion of metal fragments announced a rupture.

Lon Pana, anticipating Pelos's plan, slid closer to the hole and fired through it. He wasn't actually trying to hit anyone, but his attempt at distraction proved successful.

The volume of incoming fire from the doorway lessened noticeably, and return fire erupted through the new opening. Pelos and Kish dashed from cover to flank the doorway, while Imatt, Toshe, and Vic poured a murderous rain of fire through the open accessway, suddenly abating at Kish's signal.

Kish and Pelos leaped through the opening, firing madly into the room beyond. Although it was difficult to see through the swirling cloud of dust and debris, Kish was rewarded by hearing a sharp grunt of pain, followed by the sound of furniture turning over.

The shooting subsided, and the other Avengers swept into the room. They faced out in a semicircle, waiting for the smoke to clear, fingers held lightly against the triggers of their weapons.

Kish panted heavily, blinking back the perspiration from her eyes, watching for the forms of their attackers to appear out of the gloom. Moments later, the station's air purification system activated, and the room came grudgingly into view. They were alone.

Toshe Jorgan stood, gave a Gatoan howl of rage, and threw a nearby lamp into a corner. Kish swept through the room searching for another exit, but there was nothing to be found. The bulkhead was damaged in countless places from the impact of incoming Avengers' fire, but there were no holes large enough to see through, let alone to allow a grown humanoid to escape. There had to be another answer.

Kish studied the room carefully, shunting her anger aside. An unmade bed stood in one corner, while against the far wall, a dresser lay on its side. A streak of blood was smeared down one side, evidence of a hit from one of their lasers.

The entire room was a testament to disarray, with clothing scattered over the floor, a half-eaten meal left at a table, and a pair of boots thrown casually in the middle of the room.

She frowned, returning her attention to the dresser. There was something about its position, something unusual that caught Kish's keen eye. She mentally returned the dresser to its upright position and pictured the room; the placement of the dresser seemed out of balance. A check of the floor confirmed her suspicions: a series of scratches on the soft plastic floor showed the dresser had been dragged to its final resting place.

Kish showed Pelos her findings, and the powerfully muscled Tsimian easily righted the dresser to reveal a gaping aperture in the floor. Pelos activated his handheld light and dropped through the hole, landing in a squat. He shined his light in both directions, then crawled to the left and motioned for Kish to join him.

After telling Lon's squad to secure the room, Kish followed Pelos into the hole, as did Imatt, and they found themselves in a ventilation shaft. A thick layer of dust covered the inside of the duct, which wasn't quite large enough to allow Kish to stand upright. The other soldiers had to crawl on their hands and knees, while Kish was able to walk in a deep crouch. She swung her light back and forth, immediately spotting the marks in the dust indicating which way their assailants had gone.

She studied the footprints for a moment. There were two distinct sets of handprints, both seeming to be an average size for a Human, although the fingers of one hand seemed unnaturally long. Since there were no bodies, she concluded logically that there had only been two assailants all along.

Occasional spots of blood dotted the floor, evidence of the violence of their earlier firefight. She managed to keep her sense of direction and compared their course to the map she had studied earlier. There was no doubt in her mind: their destination was the shuttle docking bays located near the station's Docking Control Center.

She picked up the pace, pushing her teammates harder in their pursuit, knowing it was difficult for them to keep up since they were crawling, but she wanted to catch their quarries before they reached the shuttlecraft. The dust in the air made her choke, and she sneezed frequently.

A vent appeared in the darkness in front of them, and Kish immediately noticed the blood on the louvers. The imprints in the dust around the edges of the vent increased the likelihood that the vent had been tampered with. But both sets of footprints continued in the same direction, so she ignored the vent and maintained her pursuit. Whatever had been done in the room would have to be determined later.

"Can you make a guess where that vent leads?" Imatt asked with a cough.

Kish nodded. "I believe it goes into the Docking Command Facility. They could have been up to anything in there."

Pelos snorted, trying to clear dust from his beak. "The tractor beam. They probably stopped long enough to disable it, in
case we try to use it to haul them back to the station."

Kish nodded and picked up the trail once again, which led
a short distance farther before ending at a dislodged vent cover.
Her light flashed across the opening, revealing more blood and
imprints in the dust.

She peeked through the opening to see the yawning open-
ness of the shuttle docking bay. There was no sign of Osiris
or his accomplice, but Kish maintained her vigil while stepping
through the opening. She motioned for Pelos to follow the wall
to the right, while Imatt used the wall to the left. Kish stayed
back a short distance to avoid getting caught by friendly fire,
then stepped carefully down into the middle of the bay.

While there was an abundance of unloaded cargo and unattend-
ed crates of equipment, there was only one shuttle left in the bay.

The three companions stalked their prey, maintaining their
formation, ready to pour deadly laser fire on any who opposed
them. They activated their lights in short bursts, allowing them
to see the bay but not leaving them on long enough to give away
their position. Kish swept her light to the left and was startled
to see a pair of legs jutting out from behind a stack of crates. She
trained her weapon on the target and glided forward.

She was disappointed to see a diminutive Tompiste dockworker, sleeping, blissfully unaware of the armed force stalking
past him. Still, Kish could not risk this being another accomplice of Osiris; if he was, and if she walked past him, she might
get shot in the back.

She waved to Pelos and Imatt and signaled to them that she
had a prisoner. Staying at least ten feet back for safety, she kept
her weapon trained on the sleeping Tompiste until Imatt and

Pelos had finished their sweep.

"I didn't find anyone," Imatt said, his grime-streaked face showing obvious disappointment.

"Me either," Pelos added. "I did see a computer terminal on the other side of this stack of crates. You ought to be able to access it with your GBI equipment and see if any ships have left here recently."

Imatt nodded and trotted over to the terminal, already pulling his computer from his pack. "What do you have here?"

Kish shook her head. "I'm not sure, but I don't think he's involved. I've been standing over him for a few minutes, and he hasn't so much as flinched. I'd say he's a bystander. Let's not wake him until we know more from Imatt."

Pelos nodded his agreement, and the two Avengers counted the seconds, waiting for Imatt's return. He came back at a dead run.

"They left here not two minutes before our arrival! The *Intrepid* is on the other side of that wall, so if we hurry we might catch them before they activate their Rift Drives!"

Pelos scooped the surprised dockworker up over one shoulder, and they sprinted through the filth-covered shuttle bay. Kish keyed the entry code, and they pounded up the ramp of the *Intrepid*.

Imatt secured their prisoner in the mess hall while Kish and Pelos initiated the startup sequence. Arano's powerful ship drifted off the deck, rotated, and glided out of the bay and into open space.

Kish activated the ship's sensors and was rewarded by the appearance of the missing shuttle on the display. She scanned the ship for life-forms and found two. One of them was Bromidian, likely Ustin Shiba. She frowned in confusion when she saw the readout on the other life-form.

"I think I have Osiris on the shuttle, but I can't get a reading on the race of his companion. It's not registering as any of the known races."

Pelos called up the data on his own screen, shaking his head after studying it briefly. "I can't make sense of it either. Maybe we should—"

With a tremor that threw both Avengers from their seats, the *Intrepid* suddenly reeled laterally. Kish rolled to her feet, the vertigo in her head telling her the ship was spinning out of control, the rotational momentum overpowering the inertial dampers. She staggered back to the command chair.

"Report!"

"We were hit by a concentrated energy beam. Not a weapon, but something . . . I've got it! A tractor beam from Radlon Station, but someone altered it to work in reverse. Instead of pulling us in, it pushed us away."

Kish struggled to bring her sensors back online. "I'm trying to get a reading on our direction. We have to get this ship stabilized and get back into the chase."

Pelos stiffened in his seat. "Pressure on our hull is increasing rapidly. We're falling into the atmosphere of Tectos 5."

Kish whirled to face him. "How much time?"

Pelos set his beak and studied the data scrolling before him. "If we don't get her under control in the next three minutes, we won't be able to escape the planet's gravity well. The atmosphere will crush *Intrepid's* hull."

Arano looked up from his sniper rifle, setting aside the cleaning cloth at Hawan's approach. "How many converts did we pick up?"

Hawan shrugged. "About ten, I believe. Some were too

wounded to be of any use, and of course there were a few who were rabidly devoted to the new cause. I conducted the interviews myself. Just as we agreed, I scattered the new acquisitions around to different squads, making it difficult for them to collaborate if they somehow managed to deceive me. There were several who professed to have a change of heart but didn't totally convince me. I left them in charge of the wounded." He sat down, drew his dagger from its sheath, and conducted a meticulous examination of the blade.

"What about those who still oppose us? What did you do with them?" Hawan looked up at Arano wordlessly, held up his knife as if to better catch the light on its keen edge, and dragged a sharpening stone across it. Arano caught his meaning all too well and was surprised at the regret he felt for the demise of the prisoners. There was a step behind him, and he recognized Alyna by her subtle fragrance before she spoke.

"No casualties on our side," she reported. "Now we're just waiting on our troops to finish salvaging what they can from the wrecked skimmers. We'll be ready to leave within the hour."

Arano sniffed the air. "How did you manage to smell clean? We haven't had a bath in days."

She laughed, giving his arm a gentle squeeze. "No, *you* haven't had a bath in days. Videre brought some personal hygiene items with him. You might consider asking him if you can borrow them."

Arano gave her a withering look out of the corner of his eye, and Hawan chuckled. Laron and Lentin returned after conducting their examination of the wreckage from the skimmers, and Arano thought Laron definitely looked upbeat. He had an extra spring in his step, and he stood a little straighter.

"You must have some good news for me."

Laron smiled widely. "Very good news. We managed to salvage two heavy laser cannons, along with portable power supplies. They're bulky, and we'll have to disassemble them while we are on the move, but at least we'll have the advantage of their firepower for our next ambush."

At Arano's suggestion, Hawan and Lentin gathered the various squad leaders together for a briefing. When the last of them had arrived, Arano rose to his feet. "I wanted a chance to speak to you before we leave. In a bit, I'll be addressing a serious problem facing us, but I want to start with the good news. We now number sixty-five troops, and we have two heavy laser cannons to add to our arsenal."

"That should make you very happy, indeed," noted one of the Bromidians sitting in the middle of the group.

Arano crossed his arms and took a step closer to the source of the interruption. "You have just brought up my next point." He looked around at the assembled squad leaders, pointing a finger at each of them. "And this is a problem you'll need to help me address. Right now, our greatest enemy is a lack of trust.

"I'm sure you've all heard the stories of my quest to single-handedly depopulate this planet. Along with that, I would hope you heard of the reason behind my actions: the occupation of my home by Rising Sun, and the murders of my family and friends." He moved even closer to the soldier who had spoken and fixed him with his gaze, hands on his hips.

"For two days, I watched as my fiancé slowly died of exposure while her captors waited in ambush for my expected rescue attempt. Following her death, I launched my campaign to kill every Bromidian I could get my hands on.

"But Lentin helped me past the hatred when he saved my life. I realized what all the hatred was doing to me. And for those of you who fought by my side during the Coalition invasion that toppled the old government, you should know with certainty that I am on your side. What I need from all of you is to instill trust with your soldiers. Trust in me; trust in my dedication to our mission here."

The same Bromidian spoke, less sternly this time. "What, in your opinion, is our mission? So far, all we've done is dodge patrols until we're cornered and have to fight."

"Our mission is simple," Arano told him with a disarming smile. "What is your name?"

"Dartok."

"Well, Dartok, our first task is to create an army. That means we need a base of operations, we need soldiers, and we need equipment. But most of all, we need leaders. Leaders like you, who can guide our troops to victory. We will overthrow this insurrection and restore the rightful government to power."

"Why are you helping us? You have rescued your friends. Why not leave?"

"I have a vested interest in this. Far too many Coalition soldiers fought and died to free your people, for me to simply walk away and allow you to be pulled back into the grasp of a despot. Besides, if another aggressive dictator takes over, my government will have to be worried about war with your people once again. Not only that," Arano said menacingly, eyes going flat, "they attacked me, my friends, and my wife. I don't care who they are—Bromidian, Human, or otherwise—but they will pay."

He walked back a few steps, allowing his words to sink in. "All right, everyone. We have a war to plan. We move out in five minutes."

CHAPTER ELEVEN

KISH WAUKEE WORKED HER LEATHERY GRAY FIN-gers across the control panel in front of her in a desperate attempt to restore power to the ship's engines. Despite *Intrepid*'s impressive hull structure, she could feel the pressure on her ears building. If she could even get the shields back online, they would gain more time to pull the floundering ship out of danger before they all perished.

To her left, Pelos was only partially visible, with the top half of his body jammed into the narrow compartment under the engineering controls, trying to reroute some of the main functions through secondary pathways. Imatt, having taken extreme measures to tie their panicked prisoner to a chair in the mess hall, was attempting to restore communication. If they could call their companions on Radlon Station, maybe one of them could take over control of the tractor beam and pull them back to safety.

She closed her eyes in momentary relief when the red light under the shield system display turned yellow, then green. She activated the shields, and they hummed to life, allowing the environmental systems to restore the normal atmospheric pressure inside the ship.

"Shields are up," she announced, and Pelos grunted in response. "Engines and thrusters are still offline. With the added help of the shields, I give us"—she pursed her lips, looking over the feedback on her display—"at least five minutes. Maybe six."

"You're full of good news," Pelos mumbled, voice a little muffled in his cramped compartment. "I'm making progress in here, but slowly. I honestly don't know if I'll have it back up in time or not."

"I've done all I can here," Kish said, rubbing her chin while she worked through several options. "I'm going to run down to the engine room and make sure nothing down there was damaged too badly."

She trotted through the gray, metallic corridors of Arano's small frigate, a ship that had almost become a second home for their team. She wondered at their luck; had they been in their Assault Class Fighters, as most Avenger teams would have been, the reversed blast from the station's tractor beam would likely have knocked them too deeply into the atmosphere for the small craft to survive. As it was, their ship was only barely enduring, teetering on the edge of oblivion. She reached the engine room and keyed open the door.

Smoke filled the air, but to her great relief there were no working fires. The fire suppression system probably extinguished any open flames immediately. She noticed one panel, in particular, with telltale dark smudges indicating that at least a brief conflagration had erupted inside.

Kish grabbed a nearby tool kit from a wall-mounted holder and tried to open the panel. It was jammed shut, and her attempts to pry it open were in vain. Without hesitation, she drew her laser pistol and fired, searing the panel off at the hinges. It fell away with a clatter of metal, leaving a great plume of smoke in its wake. She waved the smoldering cloud aside and turned her light on the machinery inside.

"Imatt to Kish, can you hear me?" The voice came over the

ship's intercom.

Kish rose from her crouch and activated the communication port on a nearby wall. "Yes, I can hear you. Have you got the Comm system completely back up and running?"

"Not yet. The internal system seems to be the only part I have back online. But I'm close. I just wanted to test this part before I finished working on the main Comm lines. I was afraid these jury-rigged repairs might overload the whole system."

"How long before you have it working?"

"I'm not sure; maybe a few minutes."

"Okay. I'm leaving the line open on this end. Keep me posted."

She dropped back to the floor and stuck her head inside the opened compartment once more, her handheld light illuminating the interior. She could see more clearly, most of the smoke having dissipated.

Kish saw the problem at once: three power diodes had overloaded and burned out, their melted hulks still emitting small tendrils of black smoke. A check of her tool kit revealed only two diodes. There wasn't time to trace them back and try to determine which were the most critical, so she would have to simply trust her instincts.

One of the diodes was on the left side, while the other two were on the right, so she chose to repair the two that were side by side.

Kish tried to pull the nearest diode out with her bare hands but found it much too hot to touch. She breathed a sigh of relief when she found a pair of leather gloves in the tool kit, and it took her all of a minute to remove the two badly burned diodes, the electrical surge that destroyed them having fused them in place. Moving more quickly, she jammed two new diodes into place.

"Pelos to Kish! Shields are failing, and the hull is on the

verge of buckling. Pressure on the hull is critical!"

"I just replaced two burned-out diodes in the main engine power relay console, but there is one more I need to fix. The problem is I'm out of diodes."

"Can you see the Rift Drive power console from where you are? It should be to your left, about ten meters away. It's marked by a circular red and silver symbol."

Kish looked to her left, spying the console immediately. "I've got it. What now?"

"If you open it, you'll find several more diodes like the damaged one you need to replace. Use one of them."

Kish needed no further urging. The *Intrepid* was in the early stages of its death throes, and the hull creaked and groaned under the enormous pressures of the gas giant's swirling atmosphere. With the failing of her protective shields, time was short—perhaps less than a minute before the ship was lost. She pried open the protective panel, instantly spotting the bank of diodes attached to the left side of the compartment.

Selecting one at random, she pulled it loose, ignoring the mild electrical shock she knew she would receive since she hadn't disconnected the power; then the Tompiste soldier stumbled across the deck, struggling to keep her feet while the ship trembled violently around her. She steadied herself with one hand and snapped the diode firmly in place with the other.

Kish heard the engines hum to life, and the *Intrepid* resonated with the struggle to regain altitude. She managed to reach the wall-mounted Comm.

"Pelos, what's our status?"

"Engines are back online, and we have climbed a bit higher in the atmosphere. We're still not out of danger, but the engines aren't able to pull us any higher. They still aren't operating at full power, and it looks like they might overload in a few minutes!"

"Imatt, how are you doing with the Comm?"

"Just getting it running right now. I'll try to contact Pana's squad in a few moments."

Lon Pana circled slowly, not disturbing anything but carefully studying the room's contents. Somewhere in here was the key to finding who Ament, and ultimately Osiris, was working for. After that, it would be war, at least for the Avengers teams. Lon's two teammates maintained security and paid no attention to their leader's circuitous path.

Lon's Comm squawked, the static cutting out the transmission and making the words unintelligible. He pulled the Comm from its place at his hip, holding it up higher as if the simple act would clean up the signal. The static was repeated, again without any comprehensible words coming through. He activated the link.

"This is Pana. Your signal is broken, and I can't hear you. Say again, entire transmission."

There was a brief pause, and then the Comm clicked to life once more. "This is . . . We've been . . . into atmosphere . . . five. Need . . . beam to pull . . ."

Toshe Jorgan rose to his feet, feline lips pulled back in a snarl. "It sounds like they are falling into the atmosphere of Tectos 5."

Vic Dermak, guarding the room's main entrance, kept his eyes on the door. "If they can't break free, their only hope is the tractor beam mounted here on the station."

Lon licked his lips, running several options through his mind. "Toshe, you're with me. Vic, maintain security here.

We'll try to stay in contact."

Lon activated his computer, checked the map of the area, and dashed off through the halls of Radlon Station, Toshe close at his heels. Luckily, there weren't many turns, so he was able to navigate his way to the tractor beam control room from memory. At one point, a startled security officer stepped from a side door to confront them, but Lon pushed him aside without slowing. When the angry guard raised a hand in protest, Toshe ducked his shoulder and crashed into him from behind, leaving him gasping for air on the cold, metallic floor.

They reached the control room, and Lon gasped in surprise. The door was locked shut, and the locking controls had been destroyed. He stepped back, drew his pistol, and fired, but the laser blast scattered harmlessly off the reinforced metal warding the control room. Toshe threw his considerable strength against the door, but to no avail. The way was closed.

"We attack tonight," Arano told the surprised leaders of his make-shift army. He cast his gaze around the room, catching the eyes of each of his soldiers. "We will free the imprisoned leaders and any loyal soldiers we can find, and then we run like hell."

Dartok snorted, his textured, insectoid eyes narrowing suspiciously. "Why tonight? Why not take more time, plan this whole escapade a bit more thoroughly, and maybe have a few more soldiers to back us up?" There were grumbles of dissent echoed through the room, and Arano knew he needed to head off that train of thought.

"Because we don't know how much longer these men will be alive. Undoubtedly, they are being tortured for information in your old strongholds even as we speak, and you can be certain that at least one of them has provided some information. Not only will this compromise our ability to fight, but it will increase the likelihood that the uncooperative leaders might be executed. We need those men. The more members of the old Rystorian Liberation Front we have on our side, the more likely other Bromidians will be to join our cause. Then we can stop running and start fighting.

"Here's the plan. Lentin and Hawan will each lead a detachment of soldiers into the compound where the political prisoners are being held. Lentin's team will go after the prisoners, while Hawan's team will prepare a diversion as a contingency. I will lead a smaller group, consisting of my Avengers and a small force of Bromidians, to hit their armory. We will steal as many weapons and supplies as we can and meet you back at the rendezvous point.

"We will attack three hours after sunset. There will be bad weather tonight, which—"

Dartok snorted derisively. "And just how do you know that? Do you have some weather prediction equipment we aren't aware of? Or are you psychic?"

There were a few scattered laughs around the assembled group, and Arano saw the opportunity to silence at least a few of his critics. "Weather patterns here on Rystoria 2 are not all that different from those on any other populated world. The humidity and temperature are up, and there's a brisk wind coming in from the direction of the equator. I know it's late in the year for a strong storm, but we have one brewing." He looked up into the evening sky, which was turning from the dark blue of the Rystorian day to a darker hue with a hint of a very light shade of red. "Do you see those tall, thin clouds overhead? Those are developing thunderstorms in their earliest stages. Most will fade away, but a few will mature. Mark my words: we're going to get wet tonight."

Lentin laughed out loud. "Don't worry, Dartok. You won't melt." Dartok scowled grimly but said nothing.

They left their encampment shortly after sunset. The thinner ozone layer on Rystoria 2 produced colors in the sky which Arano wasn't accustomed to seeing. The daytime sky was a deep blue, almost navy blue, and the sunsets were brief. The scarlet glow of sunsets on Immok 2 were absent, the sparse ozone layer only being able to produce a light pink shade, at best. With the growing cloud cover obscuring the bright, glittering stars, the darkness was nearly complete.

They traveled in a widespread wedge formation, weapons held ready, following the lead of Lentin, who was positioned in front of their force.

They were still about a kilometer from the prison facility when Arano first heard the faint rumblings of thunder. He smiled into the darkness, knowing that somewhere in their formation, a Bromidian named Dartok was probably receiving some good-natured but subdued teasing from his companions.

The terrain around him became noticeably hilly, and the trees gave way to a tall, thick grass that clung to his pants as he walked. He made a mental note about the area; they would likely be escaping in that direction, and cover would be at a premium.

Arano glanced over his shoulder to check on the Avengers behind him. Alyna was to his right, and the others were behind her. Each gave him the thumbs-up, which he acknowledged with a nod.

By the time they crested a small ridge to find Lentin waiting for them, the rainfall had arrived. A strong, chill breeze was blowing, a harbinger of the inclement weather in store for them.

Arano found himself thinking how lucky he was that Videre had brought extra Coalition uniforms for them, especially since the new uniforms provided protection from rain. Lentin waved him in, and after he signaled for the group to halt, he slid easily to Lentin's side.

"What do you have?"

Lentin pointed into the rain and gloom before them. "The outer perimeter is directly ahead, about fifty meters. There is another draw right in front of us, and the sentries are posted in towers on the other side. If we stay on our side of this ridge, they won't see us. This will be as good a place as any for use to divide our forces."

Arano considered the matter, trying vainly to see into the night. Finally, he shrugged at the futility and slid back down the hill, motioning for Lentin to accompany him. They gathered with Hawan for a last-minute strategy meeting. "I've been thinking about the plans we made, and I'd like to propose a small change. Hawan, I still want your team to prepare a diversion if we should end up being compromised. But I think that instead of trying to sneak past the outer guards, we should eliminate the nearest post. We could all penetrate the perimeter in the same place, then separate for our different objectives." He paused, staring back toward the ridge line and the waiting Bromidian forces, rain spattering off the brim of his hat. "This rain is pretty decent cover, but I think we'd be asking for too much by trying to sneak two large groups into the camp at two different locations."

"I agree, Viper. Do you have something in mind to eliminate the guards without raising the alarm?"

Arano smiled, clapping his hand on the Bromidian's shoulder. "As a matter of fact, I do."

Toshe roared his frustration at their inability to open the door to the tractor beam control room. "Now what?"

Lon stalked a few steps away, snapping his pistol around and cursing under his breath. "We have to get in there before it's too late. Hell, it might be too late already." He fixed his gaze on the hard, gray metal floor, then up at the ceiling. A series of pipes and conduits ran overhead, giving the station the appearance of being unfinished. In fact, the structure of the metal overhead was weak, with corrosion plainly evident in several places. Mechanically, Lon raised his pistol and fired.

He was greeted with an explosion of sparks and debris, and steam and water hissed from two ruptured pipes. A gaping hole revealed itself through the murky air, and Lon exchanged a quick look with Toshe.

The Gatoan, almost seeming to read his team leader's mind, laced his fingers together and squatted. Lon placed a booted foot in his partner's hands, and with a heave of the Gatoan's powerful shoulders, Lon had secured a firm handhold near the opening in the ceiling. He pulled himself up and into the superstructure over the hallway, got his bearings, and crawled to the side. When he was in the area he guessed to be over the control room, he drew his pistol once more.

Taking a deep breath and closing his eyes, Lon fired another volley. The floor beneath him collapsed, the rupture too much for the supporting beams to hold, and he tumbled to the control room floor, landing solidly on his back beside the body of the tractor beam technician.

Lon staggered to his knees, trying vainly to draw breath back into his lungs. Gasping and coughing, he dragged himself to the tractor beam control panel. It took several moments for him to figure out how to manipulate the beam, but with the press of a button, the equipment hummed to life.

He scanned the nearby atmosphere of Tectos 5, and the computer abruptly signaled the discovery of the *Intrepid*. Lon smiled through his pain when the tractor beam locked onto the floundering ship and began the arduous process of pulling the ship back to safety.

Kish was almost back to the bridge when the *Intrepid* gave a violent lurch to the side, throwing her to the floor. She climbed to her feet and ran to the bridge, keying open the door and slipping inside. "What was that?"

Pelos grinned triumphantly, throwing his head back in relief. "Radlon Station's tractor beam just locked onto us, and they're pulling us in."

Kish let out a heavy sigh and flopped into the captain's chair. She could actually feel the air pressure inside the ship decreasing, and her ears popped several times in the process. She wondered briefly about decompression sickness—what was the archaic Human term for it, The Bends?— but she dismissed the matter. They hadn't been under the increased pressure long enough to have the heightened levels of nitrogen in their bloodstream which could lead to debilitating or even fatal injuries. She relaxed and allowed the tractor beam to pull them back to the station.

Once the *Intrepid* was securely docked with Radlon Orbital Station, Kish assigned the ship's various repair jobs to her teammates and met with Lon in the tractor beam control room.

In brief, Lon reviewed what his squad had discovered.

Someone had entered the control room, killed the guard, and preprogrammed the tractor beam to propel the Intrepid into the atmosphere of Tectos 5.

Kish followed Lon back to the room where the firefight had started, then dismissed Toshe Jorgan and Vic Dermak, sending them back to the ship where they could assist with the repairs.

While the quantity of evidence left behind by Osiris had been small, the possible advantages were immense. Several documents were emblazoned with the now-familiar emblem of a newly risen sun, most of which detailed transactions with unknown traders dealing in non-military supplies, such as food and medical equipment. One name in particular caught Kish's keen eye.

"Xuber Mining Company . . . I read a report about them last year."

Imatt's eyebrows shot up in surprise. "Last year? How do you remember— Never mind."

Kish allowed herself a brief chuckle. "They only formed about eighteen months ago, not too long after the end of hostilities with the Bromidians. It seems the Broms had settled on Menast 4, a very hostile planet incapable of supporting life as we know it. But there was some sort of new organism there; not intelligent life, but alive all the same. It was silicone-based, able to change its form from a solid rock-like formation to a more fluid, gel-like state, depending upon meteorological conditions. The Broms discovered the planet to be mineral rich, so they immediately began a program of strip mining. It wiped out the silicone life, of course, and they terraformed the planet until it was capable of supporting carbon-based life.

"At any rate, if these men were dealing with Xuber Mining, they might be heading to Menast 4."

"I thought their last projected route was toward the Solarian

System."

"It was, but I'm sure they were only jumping a short distance, just far enough to get out of scanner range. They'll drop out of the wormhole, change directions, and go to their real destination, which I'm hoping will be Menast."

Lon rubbed the palms of his hands together. "It'll take their Rift Drives a few hours to cool down. They won't have much of a head start on us when we get there."

Kish allowed a broad smile to slowly cross her leathery face. "That's what I'm hoping."

Her Comm gave a beep, and she activated the link. "Kish, here."

"This is Pelos. You might want to get back here. We are receiving a transmission from Rystoria. It's supposed to be whoever is responsible for the insurrection."

"We're finished here. On our way."

On the bridge, Kish passed the time by studying the meager information they had gathered regarding the pirates, and their likely relationship with Xuber Mining. She was so intent on her reading that she started slightly when the video screen hissed to life and, not surprisingly, the logo of the newly risen sun filled the screen. After a few moments, the emblem was replaced by a fairly young Bromidian dressed in the uniform of the old Bromidian Empire. His collar displayed a rank Kish didn't recognize, but based upon the number of medals he wore, she assumed he had been a fairly high-ranking member of the military at one time.

"The illegitimate government of the planet Vagorst has fallen, and the rightful rulers are once again in power. We have secured our hold on the Bromidian Empire. Let our enemies beware. There will be nowhere for the cowardly forces of the Coalition to hide.

"We have eliminated every member of the Coalition's puppet government. The people of Vagorst now stand united with the true government. A team of Coalition special forces was captured while trying to assassinate ranking members of our government who expressed views contrary to what the Coalition wanted. These soldiers were summarily executed."

Kish exchanged a concerned look with the others on the bridge. Obviously, Arano and his friends weren't there on a mission of political assassination, but it wouldn't be unusual for members of a successful uprising to use lies as an excuse to murder their enemies.

The Bromidian speaker indicated the logo behind him. "We are called New Dawn. We will usher in the dawn of a new era for Bromidians. I present to you the ruler of Vagorst and the future ruler of the galaxy, Zorlyn Gorst IX."

Kish whistled in surprise, leaning closer to the video monitor. Another Bromidian entered the viewscreen, and the first discreetly departed. The new speaker had a wicked scar running from his left eye to the base of his chin, and several weapons were plainly evident in various locations on his body. He stared harshly at his unseen audience for several long moments, and everyone on the bridge of the *Intrepid* sat quietly in rapt attention.

"I am Zorlyn Gorst IX, the son of our late, glorious emperor, Zorlyn Gorst VIII. I have risen at the call of history to take my rightful place as the ruler of Vagorst and the entire Bromidian Empire, wherever its reach may extend. I will tolerate no dissension.

"During the battle above Vagorst almost two years ago, I was commanding our forces from the Star Fortress orbiting Vagorst. I left the station to investigate anomalous ship readings on the edges of the field of battle, and in my absence, the fortress was destroyed. When the RLF-led insurrection destroyed the

Nebulatic Beacon, it soon became evident that our fleet would be defeated. My father ordered me to leave the system and seek refuge, building an army to one day retake our empire. That day is here.

"We retreated to the Menast System, settling on the fourth planet. For the first few months, small detachments of my followers made trips to Vagorst, where they acquired weapons, equipment, and supplies. I set up a government in exile, and I dubbed our group 'New Dawn.' In an effort to find more allies, I sent scouts to different systems. We located hundreds of survivors of the Bromidian military, Rising Sun, and even Event Horizon. These new soldiers formed the basis of my military and my intelligence service. They used their connections to acquire numerous ships, both military and freighter vessels.

"It was only fitting, then, that we should choose the anniversary of the establishment of the new Constitution to overthrow the illegitimate government and reestablish myself as the one true leader of Bromidians everywhere. We cut off the head of the snake by capturing or killing every member of the new government. The few who yet live are being interrogated, and they will be executed publicly. The last remnants of the illicit rulers of my world will have been dispatched, and my people will be united once more.

"Let all Bromidians rejoice, and let our enemies quail, because Zorlyn Gorst is once again in power. My father's one great failing was his kindness, his mercy. I do not have that weakness. Anyone questioning my right to rule will be dealt with harshly and immediately. The Tycon Mar has been reformed, and they have eyes and ears everywhere."

Zorlyn crashed his fist to his chest. "Long live the Bromidian

Empire!" he roared, and the screen went dark.

Kish hissed softly. The Tycon Mar was perhaps the most brutal secret police force in the history of the known galaxy. Their efficiency and cruelty had become legend. The few Coalition spies who lived to tell of being captured by Tycon Mar operatives brought back tales of torture and deprivation too horrible to contemplate.

It was Imatt Deeps who broke the stunned silence pervading the room. "I hate to say this, but I think his claims are legit. GBI has a rather lengthy file on the entire line of Gorsts. This one had yet to reproduce, so he is the youngest member of the family. I used to be attached to a special wing of GBI that studied the line of Bromidian rulers as part of our counterintelligence efforts, and I can tell you, if that man isn't Zorlyn Gorst IX, he is the best forgery that medical science can produce. Every detail about him, down to the personality, was right on."

Pelos ran a hand along his fur-covered cheek. "It also explains the choice of code names. Khonsu is the son of the king of the gods, and Gorst IX is the son of the former Bromidian emperor. Their *king,* if you will."

Kish leaned forward abruptly. "This certainly answers a number of our questions. New Dawn financed, planned, and executed the attacks on our leaders. They timed the events to coincide closely with their uprising, knowing we'd still be reeling from the assassination, and therefore unable to aid the Rystorian government."

"What's our next move?" Lon asked.

"I think going to Menast 4 would be a bad move at this point," Imatt said.

"I agree," Kish replied. "If Zorlyn set up his power base there,

I have a feeling the local population might not react well if members of the Coalition military showed up on their doorstep." She sighed and shook her head. "I think it's time to regroup. Let's head back to Immok City and see what we can come up with."

CHAPTER
TWELVE

ARANO PEERED THROUGH THE SCOPE OF HIS SNIPER rifle, watching for his target to appear. He had decided at the outset to forego the use of night vision goggles; at their close range from the target, one of the enemy sentries could have easily seen the soft glow put out by the equipment. As a result, he was looking through his standard scope at . . . nothing.

The rainfall increased noticeably, and thunder echoed through the rolling grasslands. With each flash of lightning, Arano studied his objective.

He had become convinced, early on, that there were only two guards in each tower. The roof over their heads provided them with relief from the inclement weather, but Arano knew that wouldn't hold. For the time being, they were content to walk around the interior of their observation room, but when the wind picked up with the intensity of the approaching storm, the rain would be driven horizontally, and they would seek cover behind the walls of their tower, occasionally poking their heads over the wall in a display of performing their duties. It would be their undoing.

The lightning flashed sporadically, and a great gust of wind tore at Arano's uniform. He squinted against the rain spattering off his prized weapon, trying to keep the splashing water from blinding him. Just as he had expected, with the wind blowing

hard enough to rattle the roof of the guard tower, the two Bromidian sentries hunkered down behind the wall. The next flash
of lightning showed their two heads barely above the level of the
wall as the guards pretended to watch the surrounding terrain.
Another flash, and they were gone. Arano motioned to Lentin,
who sent two of his soldiers scurrying ahead.

Arano gave them enough time to get in place next to the
tower, then sighted in once more. Several minutes passed with
no sign of the Bromidians in the tower, but Arano remained vigi-
lant. He lay on the hillside, unmoving, ignoring the driving rain
and biting wind which tore at his body, focusing every fiber of his
being on the restricted view through his scope.

Another flash of lightning showed the two Bromidians had
partially risen once more. He forced his breathing to slow and
become regular, and his finger was already squeezing the trigger.
He tried to remain detached from his emotions, waiting for the
next bolt of lightning to emerge from the fury of the storm.

Lightning tore through the Rystorian night, ripping the
shroud of darkness asunder like an old, ragged cloth. The rifle in
Arano's hands jumped, the report of the rifle muffled by the awkwardly weighted silencer attached to the muzzle. In his mind's
eye, Arano envisioned the second Bromidian sentry, stretching
his neck out to see what had happened to his partner.

Without a moment's hesitation, Arano chambered another
round, aimed where he believed the second Bromidian would be
standing, and fired again. Lentin whistled softly, and the two
Bromidians at the base of the guard towers stormed inside.

Arano wiped the rain from his eyes, trying vainly to see what
was happening in the tower. The seconds ticked by, with only
the crashing of thunder to break the silence. The signal they
wanted finally came, and Arano gathered his rifle into the cradle

of his arms and climbed to his feet. Lentin rushed up the stairs
to check on his scouts, and Arano took a knee outside the tower,
facing out into the darkness. After a few moments, Lentin reap-
peared, grinning broadly.

"Excellent shooting, Viper! Both guards are dead . . . two
head shots!" He leaned forward, whispering conspiratorially.
"I'd say you may have just gained a few more converts."

Arano gave a half-smile and motioned the two invading forces
forward. Once inside the perimeter, they separated, with Lentin
leading his detachment around the complex's left side, while Arano
took his to the right. He passed the guard tower and saw two of
his Bromidian soldiers donning the uniforms of the fallen guards.
The blood stains would give them away at close range, but at least
from a distance, all would appear normal. The rain had slackened
somewhat, but he scarcely noticed; he was too preoccupied with
the ad-lib planning of the next phase of the operation.

He led his group resolutely forward, paralleling the prison
building itself, using tall bushes and grassy patches for cover.
The muddy ground provided for an oily purchase beneath his
boots, and his feet slid constantly. Between the rain and the
thunder, there was enough background noise that he wasn't concerned about stealth, instead staying alert for roving patrols. He
doubted there would be many soldiers outside.

The main supply center was on the west side of the building, and Arano saw it illuminated for a moment before his vision
faded to a red haze in the lightning's aftermath. He held up his
hand, telling his soldiers to stop and take a knee.

Mind made up, he stepped deeper into the head-high foliage
and called everyone in closer. Alyna was already at his side, and
Lain stood nearby with Laron and Videre. There were a dozen
Bromidian soldiers with them as well, and they waited patiently

in the tempest of the storm, placing their full confidence in the Avenger leading them.

I should have insisted upon having a few of my detractors with me. A successful mission with minimal casualties would have gone a long way toward winning them over.

"We're about a hundred meters from the supply building right now," Arano told them, voice just loud enough to carry over the din of the weather. "We can close in to within about forty meters, but beyond there, they've taken to a scorched-earth policy to clear away all the brush. We'll be exposed out there, but I'm hoping there won't be anyone around there to see us. When the time comes, I'll go forward with Videre."

He nodded to his Gatoan friend, who understood the implication of the statement then rummaged through his pack, retrieving a compact computer device, small enough to conceal in the palm of his hand. "Videre can use this Logarithmic Destabilizer to defeat the locking mechanism and the alarm on the entrance to the supply room. Once the way is clear, I'll signal for the rest of you to come forward. We'll try to get in and out without being seen, but don't be afraid to defend yourselves if necessary. Just keep in mind that if you fire an energy weapon inside the compound, it will alert the entire garrison to our presence."

The impromptu meeting broke up, with everyone moving to the edge of their established defensive perimeter and watching for signs of the enemy. Arano kept a close eye on his watch, knowing that timing was crucial for the success of their mission. The rain slowed to a heavy drizzle, with the associated mist obscuring everything around them. The fog had an eerie feel about it, giving Arano a sense of foreboding.

The time for the assault came, and he brought his troops forward to the edge of the tall grass. Videre nodded his readiness, and with a quick check of the area, the two Avengers sprinted across the open ground to the wall of the supply building. Arano crouched low, checking back and forth for the approach of the enemy while Videre went to work on the lock. A low beep announced Videre's success, and Arano flashed the expected signal to Alyna. She brought the rest of their team forward, and they slipped through the doorway into the dark interior.

The door to the Avengers Team 5 planning room slid obediently open at Kish's touch, and her mismatched group of soldiers filed inside. They hadn't accomplished much during the return flight, having spent most of the trip resting and conducting repairs on the *Intrepid*. There was more work to be done on the stalwart ship, and Kish wanted as many systems online as possible, in case another task arose upon their return. She had requested and received an emergency maintenance crew when they landed, and the Coalition's finest were already at work repairing Arano's craft. She collapsed into her customary chair, leaning back and staring at the ceiling for several long moments while her team discarded various pieces of equipment.

Pelos heaved a great sigh, then rotated his chair to face his computer, his beak stretching wide with a mighty yawn. "I want to get started on those anomalous readings we picked up from Osiris's ship. With the primitive equipment they had on that orbital mining station, I couldn't put much effort into figuring out what we were seeing."

Imatt used his terminal to access the main GBI database, monotonously plodding through the extensive security protocols. "We need to find out what has been going on back here," he announced. "The Coalition government is still in a state of upheaval, so there's no telling what might have changed in the last week or so."

Kish tried to catch up on her own affairs, which were severely backlogged since she was acting leader of Team 5. There were several training missions she needed to cancel, because they wouldn't be available for anything of that sort for quite some time.

Somewhere in the back of her mind, she heard Lon announce that he was going to move his operation to the Team 5 planning room to facilitate the two groups working together. The door hissed open and closed, but Kish paid no attention. She shook her head slowly, biting her lip while she read the news headlines. The military was racing to finish repairs on a fleet still not fully recovered from the Second Bromidian War. The repairs were moving at a snail's pace because the decision had been made to upgrade the aging fleet while the repairs were underway, which, of necessity, had dragged out the process. In the meantime, Immok City was in a state of chaos, and new rules imposed following the series of bombings and assassinations had the city on the verge of martial law. A curfew had been imposed from one hour after sunset until thirty minutes before sunrise, and the police were randomly stopping citizens on the streets.

Imatt's computer beeped twice, and Kish diverted her attention to his screen. "What do you have?"

"Nothing major yet. Repairs are already underway in the areas of the city damaged during the attacks. To expedite the situation, the mayor put the various jobs out to bid individually. Xalan Contracting has the winning bid for rebuilding the structures themselves, Greenscape is handling the landscaping, Cyberwatch is installing new security systems at all Coalition facilities, and . . . oh, very nice, Pelos."

The Tsimian turned slowly in his seat, eyes still on the screen for a few more moments. "What did I do?"

"All the equipment and supplies needed for the repairs and upgrades are being shipped through one company. Let's see, what was that name? Oh, yes. Marnian Shipping."

A smile played at the corners of Pelos's sharp beak. "Really? I had no idea." He turned back to his work, whistling softly to himself.

"They are actually moving pretty fast with the work," Imatt continued, eyebrows raised in surprise. "Xalan has several crews out, working in three shifts daily. They are well over halfway finished, and Greenscape is only a bit behind them. Cyberwatch seems to be a bit more meticulous."

Pelos growled his frustration. "This can't be right," he complained.

"What is it?" Kish asked, rising to her feet and moving over to stand behind her teammate.

"The readings from Osiris's ship. I've tried every means I can think of to clean up the signal, and nothing has changed. I'm still reading an anomalous life-form inside his ship."

"Could the equipment on Radlon Station have been malfunctioning?"

Pelos shook his head, the shaggy, feather-like fur undulating briskly with the motion. "No. I ran a diagnostic on the readings, and everything checks out. In fact, there were several other life-forms aboard the ship, and they all checked out just fine. You will probably laugh me out of the room for saying this, but I think we're looking at a new life-form here."

Imatt rose from his seat and examined Pelos's findings. "Let's not be hasty with this. While you might be right, I think we need to keep this little discovery under wraps. I'll send your information to the GBI's Division of Xeno-Biological Investigations. They can examine it further." He started to return to his work but stopped, slumping his shoulders in defeat. "What I'm about to tell you is classified Above Top Secret. Other than Lon's people, and obviously Arano, no one else can hear of it." He waited until they nodded, their silence speaking volumes about the solemnity of what Imatt was telling them.

"GBI has had Xeno looking into the possibility of a new species for several years now. There have been scattered reports from the fringe systems, but nothing concrete yet. Each race in the Coalition, and probably the Bromidians, for that matter, has a history replete with stories of alien visitors. Most of this took place before the development of Rift Drives, because once the races found each other, the question about the existence of other intelligent life in the universe was settled.

"The problem is, those tales haven't completely gone away. We receive dozens of reports every year about contact with a new race. The vast majority have been debunked as either an error in observation or an outright fabrication. However, there have been a few accounts of these chance encounters that we haven't been able to dismiss. That's where the Xeno project steps in.

"The most recent unexplained event occurred during the Battle of Rystoria. While examining sensor readings made during the battle, we discovered a group of ships hovering outside the area of battle. They appeared to be monitoring the progress of the battle, but they made no move to join the fight. They were too far away for proper sensor readings, especially while the Nebulatic Beacon was functioning, but it certainly matches up with the story Gorst was telling about new ships. The life-sign readings were sketchy at best, although on the surface I think there might at least be some similarities between them and what you have here. Like I said, I'll get this sent to the folks over at Xeno and see what they can do."

The door slid open, and General Vines strode through the open portal. The Avengers scrambled to their feet, but he smiled and waved them back down. "Where's Pana and his squad?" he asked.

"They're trying to move their operation to our office, sir," Kish told him. "He should be back shortly."

"I convinced Avengers Command to leave you together as Team 5 for the time being. You have done a tremendous job so far, Avengers. The information you found connecting the raids by those pirates to the leader of the Bromidian uprising has been very revealing. But those pirates are the reason I'm here. We discovered a group of them raiding a hidden Rising Sun base in the Niones System. They were able to recover weapons, medical research supplies, and some bomb-making equipment." He paused, suppressing a grin with effort. "The High Council issued an emergency edict to the military. They want us to find and eliminate all remaining hidden bases belonging to Rising Sun and Event Horizon."

Kish's mouth fell wide open, and Pelos was the first to recover his voice. "How can we find hidden bases if they're hidden?"

"I brought that up, but the Council was adamant. They believe we have the resources to locate these caches and eliminate them."

Kish sighed in resignation. "Where do we begin, sir?"

General Vines retrieved a data disk from the pocket of his jacket. "This has some information for you on their whereabouts. Team 3 was already in the system when the pirates struck, and they were able to determine their likely destination. It looks like they are heading for the fourth planet of the Trum System."

Kish cocked her head to the side, eyes opening wide. "Trum 4? That sounds like a dangerous place to store munitions. Okay, sir, as soon as Lon's squad is ready, we'll be on our way."

Arano shoved several more grenades into his battered pack, pausing briefly to survey his team of Bromidians. The operation was running according to plan, with pairs of Bromidians teaming up to delve into separate areas of the supply room. He felt his spirits rise; with what they were acquiring, they would be a force to be reckoned with. Arano hoped Lentin's team was meeting with similar success. He managed to shove a few more pounds of explosives into the depths of his pack and then forced the cover closed. With a wink at Alyna, he shouldered his burden and moved to cover the exit, relieving the Bromidian at the door and allowing her to collect her own ammunition. After a brief but exhaustive effort, the team had gathered all they could carry. Videre attached a remote detonator to a large mound of explosives.

When Arano's team emerged from the darkened supply room, they found the rain coming down heavily once again. Arano shivered beneath the weight of his backpack, feeling the damp chill leeching the heat from his body. He shrugged his shoulders a few times, trying to settle them in beneath the oppressive weight of his burden. Already, the familiar soreness had crept into the muscles of his upper body, but he pushed his discomfort aside.

From across the compound, there came a shout of surprise, followed by the crackling fire of energy weapons. Moments later, Arano heard the urgent blaring of the warning klaxon, the piercing alarm echoing through the complex and rallying the forces guarding the prison. Arano had no need to give orders to Videre; he knew the combat-seasoned Gatoan was already retrieving the detonator from his belt.

The confirmation came seconds later, when an explosion ripped through the supply building, shattering windows all around and knocking the stunned team to the ground. Arano struggled back to his feet, ignoring the stuffy feeling in his head and the ringing in his ears.

"Let's go!" he shouted, and they needed no further urging. In a disorganized mob, they sprinted along a path through the covering foliage, reaching their entry point in a matter of minutes. From Hawan's defensive position, Arano saw covering fire pouring down on the hapless guards who had charged recklessly into the open. His Daxia instincts took over, and he studied the battlefield with a trained eye. Lentin's forces were under attack, but they were in no serious danger. He had reached the cover of a series of outbuildings and divided his detachment into three groups, with each providing covering fire for the others while they were falling back to the breach. Hawan's team was able to take more precise aim, since they were not taking direct fire, and they were keeping the guards from advancing.

Arano directed the Bromidians under his command into various firing positions, and they waited in stoic silence. He ordered them to hold their fire until he gave the word, keeping their presence a secret.

His preparations proved prescient when a dozen Bromidian guards attempted to cut off Lentin's fleeing team by sneaking in front of them. Arano allowed them to set up in ambush, hiding behind various barriers that would protect them from Lentin's team, then gave the order. A blinding array of fire from their energy rifles crackled across the intervening space, slaughtering the Bromidians where they lay waiting.

Lentin's group reached the perimeter, leading a battered mob of newly freed prisoners. When they passed through Arano's lines, Videre and Lain handed each a rifle from the spoils they had taken during their raid. Arano saw the fires of hope and freedom burning in their eyes, and many seemed eager to use the weapons they had been given. He made a mental note to integrate them into the teams he had already created, allowing them to partake in the raids he was planning. Arano had no doubts about where their loyalties lay.

Arano turned back to survey the prison one more time. Several buildings were engulfed in flames, and secondary explosions continued to rock the complex. Videre's charges had more than done their job, and Arano clapped him heartily on the back. They gathered their gear, shouldered their packs, and plunged deeper into the forest, walking briskly to the rally point, where they were met by Hawan's team. Arano allowed them a brief respite, with the soldiers greeting each other in the exuberance of their victory, and then his entire force moved out together. They had done well, and he had high hopes for the prisoners they had freed. He looked over the list of names once more, squinting occasionally while trying to read Lentin's handwriting.

Most of them were members of the military who had espoused certain opinions which were in disagreement with the new government. Others simply had the misfortune of being out of favor with Bromidians who were in the inner circle of the new leadership. He paused in his rumination, grinding his teeth in frustration. He had more pressing matters at the moment, such as what he should do with four particular individuals on the list. His thoughts briefly scattered under the pestering of a swarm of flying insects, but he swatted them away and moved on.

The four Bromidians in question were clerics, religious leaders who were held in high standing by the Bromidian citizenry.

Before the war against the Coalition had toppled the former re-gime, these four Bromidians, a man and three women, had held secret meetings where they preached of freedom and struggle against the government of Zorlyn Gorst VIII. While they had not been members of the Rystorian Liberation Front, they had certainly held to the same ideals.

Overhead, the stiff branches of the trees blanketing the land-scape swayed with the winds rushing out from the passing storm, but on the forest floor, Arano felt only a light breeze. He was grateful for the meager shelter, however, knowing from expe-rience how miserable they would be in their wet clothes under a strong gust of air. The wedge-shaped formation of soldiers marched resolutely onward, each dealing with the damp and cold in their own way.

Ahead, the forest cleared to reveal a wide, pale green lake. In the back of his mind, Arano thought absently about the sapphire blue color such a lake on his homeworld would have, which he knew to be an effect of the slightly different atmospheric make-up on Rystoria. They drew closer to the water's edge, and in the distance Arano could barely make out a dock jutting from the shoreline. There were several cabins located nearby, and in bet-ter times, vacationing Bromidians would likely have filled the lodge to overflowing. But on this night, it was abandoned to the elements. Videre, confidently leading the force, raised his hand to signal a halt.

Arano crept forward, easing into a crouch at Videre's side. He was joined by those who had naturally become his council of advisors: Alyna, Lain, Laron, Lentin, and Hawan. They had ten-tatively planned to ransack the site, removing any useful supplies and equipment before moving on. But the inclement weather was continuing longer than they had expected, and Arano was considering a deviation in their tactics.

"So far," he whispered, "our rear scouts have reported no signs of pursuit. I don't doubt they are looking for us, but for the moment we seem to have eluded them."

"What are you proposing?" Hawan asked, resting his rifle against a tree while he wiped rainwater from his eyes.

"That we give the troops a rest," he answered. "Let's give them a few hours in the cabins, where they can try to dry out from the storm. Sunrise is coming in about four hours, which I'll grant you isn't far off. But we can drop to 50 percent security, settle into the cabins, and allow them to rest in relative comfort. When the sun comes up, we can make a more complete inventory of what has been left behind, and then we'll move on."

"Sounds reasonable," Laron told him, rising to his feet. "I assume you're planning a recon first?"

Arano smiled. "I wouldn't think of doing it without you."

They sent runners to their various teams, informing them all of the change in plans. Arano and Alyna entered the camp first, moving slowly from one covering position to the next. Lain and Videre were close behind, deviating from their path to enter the easternmost cabin, while Lentin and Hawan started from the west. Laron was left at the head of the formation, awaiting the signal from Arano to bring the troops forward.

A shutter swung heavily back and forth in the robust wind gusting in from the lake, creaking eerily against its rusty hinges. The first time the shutter slammed against the wall of the cabin, the clamor brought Arano and Alyna around sharply, weapons leveled. They smiled sheepishly at each other, both of them trying to calm their racing hearts. Arano's feet came down softly on the muddy ground, and he padded vigilantly closer to a side door. He flanked the wooden portal to one side, allowing Alyna to position herself on the other. He raised his eyebrows questioningly, and she nodded slowly in response.

Arano reached one hand out to try the door and found it unlocked. Giving a silent three count, he shoved the door forcefully open, and he and Alyna rushed through, weapons sweeping the room beyond. It was completely shrouded in darkness, what little ambient light the Rystorian moons could have provided blocked out by the heavy cloud cover. Arano activated his night vision goggles, bringing the area into focus. The room was empty.

They finished their sweep of the lodge, finding no one in the building. By the time his other two teams had reported similar findings in the outlying cabins, Arano and Alyna had managed to complete a cursory inventory of the supplies left in the campsite's main facility. Laron led the other troops forward, marshalling them in the main courtyard. Lentin and Hawan assigned their soldiers to various cabins, while Lain and Videre established security around the camp. With the preparations in place, they settled in for a few hours' rest.

CHAPTER THIRTEEN

KISH GAZED PENSIVELY AT THE FORWARD VIEW-
screen of the *USCS Summerwind*, almost not seeing the
mesmerizing kaleidoscope of red and blue shapes swirling across
the surface of the black tunnel before her. The artificial wormholes had an innate beauty, and usually the view was not lost on
Kish. But with the rush of events running through her mind, she
was too distracted to pay attention to the scenery.

She was traveling in the Assault Class Fighter assigned to
Squad B, accompanied by Pelos and Imatt. She almost laughed
out loud at that picture: an agent with the Galactic Bureau of
Intelligence, the highest and most revered law enforcement position in the Coalition, somehow assigned to an Avengers special
forces unit. Granted, the interests of the GBI and the military
coincided in this case, with the connections between the piracy
ring and the assassinations of so many Coalition leaders, but the
uniqueness of the situation was not lost on her. To give her a
complete team, Lon Pana was piloting his Assault Class Fighter, the *USCS Grappler*, with the Gatoan Toshe Jorgan and the
Human Vic Dermak rounding out his squad.

They could have taken Arano's frigate, the *Intrepid*, which
would have been a tremendous boost if they had encountered
hostile craft, but Lon and Kish had ultimately decided against
the idea. The Trum System was located near the vertical mid-

point of the galaxy, putting it in the midst of a virtual sea of space debris. Meteors and comets passed through the system with alarming frequency, and the Trum planets experienced daily showers of meteorite impacts. The possibility of taking damage to their ships from meteors, rocks, and comets was all too real. With their smaller size and greater maneuverability, the Assault Class Fighters stood a greater chance of emerging from the system unscathed. And in the time since the end of the war with the Bromidians, the Avengers' ships had been upgraded with better shields, the new plasma torpedoes, and the improved Rift Drive engines originally equipped on the Firestorm Class Fighters. In the end, the advantages of the smaller ships vastly outweighed those offered by Arano's frigate.

Their intelligence reports had provided little in the way of information regarding what to expect upon their arrival. Reports dating back five years indicated a possible Rising Sun outpost on the Trum System's fourth planet, but subsequent missions had revealed nothing to indicate a permanent installation anywhere on the surface. Of course, Kish acknowledged with a sigh, the scans were conducted from high orbit, and with all the debris in the system, there was too much interference for the scan to have been totally accurate.

According to Team 3, the pirates' freighter was accompanied by four single-pilot fighters. The greatest danger lay in the possibility that the pirates might have reinforcements, either already at Trum 4 or on the way there. Kish had already told Pelos to calculate a safe jump to the Solarian System as soon as he could, and recalculate it every thirty seconds until they had safely reached the planet.

Pelos and Imatt returned to their seats, waiting silently for the final minutes of the flight. The computer beeped its warning,

Kish touched a few controls, and the ship dropped out of the wormhole, returning to normal space amidst a brilliant flash of red and blue light. Seconds later, the *Summerwind*'s systems came online and the sensors showed the *Grappler* on their wing. Kish opened a Comm channel on the secure FM frequency.

"*Summerwind* to *Grappler*. Our systems check out okay; ready for the mission."

Lon's face appeared on the screen. "*Grappler* here. Ditto for us. Let's get started."

"I'm picking up the freighter and the four fighters," Pelos announced. "It's hard to be certain through all the interference, but it looks like there is some type of large shuttle docking with the freighter."

Lon frowned, tapping his console. "We can't get a reading from here. Vic, try to clean that signal up some." From off-screen, Kish heard the sound of several heavy blows. "That's better. I still can't get a clear fix on them, but I'd have to agree with Pelos. Let's move in closer."

Using a field of large asteroids as limited cover, the two Avengers' crafts closed the distance with their target. The path Lon chose led them along the pirates' flank, each passing moment bringing them ever closer to their target. What had appeared to be a shuttle from his earlier scan turned out to be a low-orbit cargo drone, designed for carrying heavy payloads out of the atmosphere of planets, where freighters could pick up the freight. The fighters continued to hold their positions, using their docking thrusters to maintain their position relative to the freighter.

Pelos's computer chirped, and the heavily muscled Tsimian leaned closer to his display. "Kish, we've got trouble. The freighter has started an active scan sequence. Estimated time to detection is ten seconds."

Kish took a deep breath, letting it out slowly before answering. "Signal the *Grappler*. Full power to shields, arm plasma batteries, and ready the plasma torpedoes. We're going in."

The two craft lurched forward, and after a brief delay the four enemy fighters responded. Two disappeared immediately in balls of fire, victims of a plasma torpedo barrage. The remaining two ships separated, heading to opposite flanks of the attacking Avengers. Kish followed Lon's lead, ignoring one fighter while bearing down on the other. On her viewscreen, she watched the *Grappler* and the enemy ship engage in an intricate dance, Lon tracking his target with the deadly fire pouring out of his plasma batteries, while the pirate fighter in front of him slipped from side to side, staying just ahead of the lancing beams of energy.

"Track the other fighter," Kish said tersely. "I don't want it sneaking up on us."

"Already on it," Imatt replied, face illuminated by the dancing lights on his display. "It ran straight for the freighter. Looks like it's going to act as an escort. The freighter is powering up its weapons."

Kish looked back to the viewscreen, just in time to see the small ship finally slide in front of Lon's plasma battery, tumbling end over end before silently exploding into nothingness. The two Assault Class Fighters executed a smooth turn, reversing their course to make their first assault run on the freighter. Their pursuit of the wayward fighter had taken them far enough from the other two crafts to allow the use of torpedoes, but Kish was reluctant to give the order.

She opened the Comm link once more. "Lon, this is Kish. I think we need to be careful here. If we destroy that freighter completely, we lose whatever intelligence we can find onboard."

There were a few moments of contemplative silence. "No

torpedoes, then?"

"Right."

The two Avengers' ships spread out their formation, closed the distance, and opened fire. Kish had to fight hard at the controls, changing directions quickly in an effort to confuse the targeting systems on the freighter. While it was not heavily armed, its weapons were strong enough that several hits from them could penetrate Kish's shields. Imatt fired the plasma batteries at the fighter and was rewarded when the small craft's stabilizers exploded, sending it spinning out of control.

"The last fighter is disabled," Imatt announced. He paused, and Kish could sense something was wrong. "We've knocked out its main power. Life support is offline. The pilot will succumb to hypoxia in about ten minutes."

Kish winced, turning her eyes away from the screen in dismay. No one deserved a death like that, but for the time being, there was nothing she could do. Through unspoken agreement, both Avengers squads concentrated their fire on the freighter's armament, racing around the ship in elliptical paths designed to minimize the amount of time they spent in the freighter's line of fire.

The *Summerwind* rocked hard, throwing Kish firmly against the back of her seat. A second impact sent a shower of sparks over Pelos, but he ignored it and maintained his station.

"Shields at 50 percent," Pelos warned.

"Not a problem now," Imatt replied, easing back in his chair. "We just destroyed their last plasma battery."

"*Summerwind*, this is *Grappler*. The freighter is powering up its Rift Drives. We have to take out her engines now!"

Without answering, Kish turned the ship hard to port, and the inertial dampers hummed their exertion in response, the forces pressing Kish against her armrest telling her that the dampers were not quite capable of compensating for the maneuver. She deftly slipped the *Summerwind* behind her target, and Imatt opened fire on the engines.

"We're not going to make it," Pelos said. "Ten seconds to Rift Drive operation."

Kish jabbed a leathery finger at Imatt. "Give me one plasma torpedo, directly at the main starboard engine. The Rift Drive Quantum Matrix should be located directly behind it."

Imatt nodded, fingers dancing agilely across the firing controls. A single blue streak launched from the *Summerwind*'s main torpedo tube, homing in on the freighter's aft section. The telltale tunnel of darkness opened before the ship, reaching out to engulf the freighter as it entered its artificial wormhole. The torpedo impacted, detonating against the engines of the freighter and setting off several smaller explosions. The wormhole wavered, racing faster and faster but losing its symmetry. It snapped like the cracking of a whip, and the freighter buckled as if struck by an unseen force. The ship's hull broke apart at its midsection and spun out of control. The gravitational forces inside the shrinking wormhole pulled the doomed ship into the shadowy interior, and the wormhole collapsed, taking the freighter with it.

Arano's modest army was on the move again. The storm had abated, leaving cooler temperatures, but at least the rain had stopped and the wind was calm. The trees covering the rolling landscape were sparse, allowing the formation to spread wider than usual. The notable exception was Arano's command staff, clustered tightly in the center.

"Are you certain it is wise to risk them in the cities?" Hawan asked. "Wouldn't it be safer to have them in the smaller communities, finding support there?"

"I'll grant you," Arano told him, "the risk is greater in the cities, but so are the rewards. We need to hit this rebellious leadership before they have a chance to solidify their power base. If the transmission we received is correct, and it is indeed Gorst IX who has overthrown the legitimate government, he could easily have your entire population beaten into submission in less than a month."

"I agree," Lentin said. "Especially if he has reformed the Tycon Mar. Our people remember all to well what that group is capable of. Once the stories of a few new atrocities get out, no one will dare stand against them. In fact, it will be as I warned you: Gorst's rule will be established by Divine Right."

"So you think these clerics can raise an army?" Laron asked.

Arano nodded, ducking beneath a low-hanging branch. "All four were able to preach sedition under the very nose of the former regime, and they were never caught. If they can stir up resentment toward Gorst IX, we should be able to gain more converts. We might even pick up a few people in positions of trust within the new military. We have a lot to work out, though. We need a secure means of communication, probably using the FM radios. I would also venture a guess that we'll need to slip into the cities ourselves on occasion, attending rallies, lending credibility to the cause, that sort of thing."

"Too bad Kish isn't here," Videre said, with exaggerated regret in his eyes. "She does an excellent job of stirring the pot."

They walked for the better part of the morning through a countryside covered with thin, springy trees with spiny brown leaves. The sun climbed higher, providing a measure of relief from the chill in the air. Winter was approaching, and Arano knew it was only a matter of time before the first snowfall. With the coming of cooler weather, just as was the case on Arano's homeworld, the animals of the forest became more active. He looked wistfully to the west, where a herd of hoofed animals grazed passively beside a narrow stream. In better times, he could have stayed there for days, camping and living off the land.

They stopped that afternoon, when their lead scout reported sighting the lake Arano wanted to use as a reference point. Once again, he gathered his staff and spread the map out on the ground, weighting the ends down with a few fist-sized rocks.

"The lake is here, about a kilometer to the east of our current location. We need to divide our forces, taking up at least three different defensive positions."

Hawan's jaw dropped open in surprise. "Is that wise? We only have around two hundred soldiers under our command right now. I think we could do more damage as a cohesive group rather than several small teams."

"True," Arano conceded, "but we would also be more easily defeated. If we stay together, they could eliminate our entire movement with one assault. If we split up, it will be more difficult for them to get us all. The six of us will know the locations of all of our strongpoints, but the regular soldiers will only know the location of their own. That way, if one of them is captured, they can't reveal anything to the enemy."

"How many cells will you want for now?" Lentin asked without looking up from the map.

Arano smiled at his friend's use of the unconventional warfare terminology. "We can start with just the three. I'd like to have enough troops at each location to maintain reasonable security at all times, but still have raiding parties ready to strike."

Arano sat back on his haunches, brushing the dirt from his

hands. "I will take Alyna and Hawan with me. Lain and Videre can lead the second cell, and Laron and Lentin can have the third. We'll divide our remaining resources as evenly as we can." He stopped, licking his lips, an idea running through his head. "I want Dartok on my team. Let him pick a few of his close associates to come with him."

Hawan smiled his acceptance of the plan. "That's a very good idea, Viper. Dartok is your strongest detractor. By working closely with him, you may just win his trust."

"Not only that," Alyna added, "but it would probably be best to keep him at arm's length, where you can keep an eye on him."

They selected the locations for each of their cells, and then the meeting broke up. Lain set about devising a way to conceal an FM radio within simple devices, such as Rystorian datapads, so the four Bromidian clerics could communicate with the rest of the resistance group. In a moment of what Arano considered a typical Bromidian lack of creativity, Hawan had decided to name their movement the Rystorian Re-liberation Front, but Lentin talked him into reusing the RLF moniker. By sunset, the three cells departed and went their separate ways, en route to their new homes. Each group took one of the clerics with them, with the extra cleric accompanying Arano's force.

In the encroaching darkness, Arano's cell turned west, found a river flowing south from the lake, and shadowed it for several kilometers. The trees were taller and thicker, and the only undergrowth was an occasional patch of briars. Arano's diminished force of sixty Bromidians walked well into the night, stepping blindly over fallen logs and protruding roots. There was a definite bite to the chill evening air, and Arano noticed scattered bits of frost clinging to the forest floor. He decided to take the opportunity to try and bridge the chasm between him and Dartok.

"Cold night," he said quietly, strolling closer to his Bromidian antagonist. Dartok grunted in response.

Arano glanced skyward. "How much longer before the leaves fall?"

Dartok almost smiled. "The leaves on this species don't fall. They remain all year. They are similar, in that manner, to certain trees from the Coalition homeworld. Always-green trees?"

Arano laughed, in spite of himself. "Evergreen trees. They're called evergreens. They have green needles instead of leaves, and the needles stay on all year. They were transplanted from Earth 3."

Dartok flushed slightly, finally laughing at his embarrassment. "Evergreens. Got it."

They reached their destination about two hours before midnight, and Arano wasted no time in setting out his defenses. In addition to a perimeter of defensive firing positions, where he would emplace their stolen heavy weapons, he planned a set of regular patrols to sweep the area for enemy scouts. He and Alyna built their meager shelter near the center of the encampment, digging about four feet into the ground and covering it with a brown tarp. The hole was large enough to store their gear and still allow room for their bedrolls. They managed to grab a few hours of sleep before dawn.

The first day was spent in fevered activity. Firing positions needed to be built, camouflage made, and weapons dug in. Arano spent his time walking the perimeter, trying to spot the various foxholes and bunkers his soldiers had made, and pointing out flaws where he saw them. By supper, he was satisfied that the camp was ready. Improvements would continue to be made, but for the time being, he felt secure enough to begin their operations.

His first mission was planned for that very evening. He would lead a team with Hawan and Dartok, escorting the two clerics to the city of Notron, about twelve kilometers away. It was a fair-sized city, and Hawan said it had been a hotbed of RLF activity during the war. With the sympathetic atmosphere, Arano felt it would be a simple matter for the clerics to preach a number of converts out of the population. He emerged from the shelter he shared with Alyna, armed with his compact laser rifle, and he joined Hawan in the center of their team.

Removing his hat, Arano knelt and rested the butt of his rifle against the ground. "Okay, everyone, here's the story. Twelve of us, including Hawan, Alyna, and me, will escort these two ladies to Notron. I had a team construct a pair of rafts today, and we will use them to get within about two kilometers of the city. We'll disembark under cover of darkness, enter the city, and meet with our contact."

"And then?" Alyna asked.

Arano smiled slightly. "And then we run like hell."

Kish took another sip of coffee, trying to set the cup down gently and not break the spell Imatt was weaving. The Tsimian pilot of the fighter they had disabled was sitting, eyes wide and mouth agape, listening to the tale being spun by the GBI agent. Following the destruction of the freighter, Kish had reversed course and rescued the pilot, mere minutes before his life support system failed completely. The pilot's fine, featherlike fur was singed in several places, mute testimony to his close brush with death.

"Look, Abbas," Imatt said, familiarly using the pilot's first name. "We don't care about your petty little privateer operation. You don't rank very high in the big scheme of things."

Abbas swallowed hard. "Then what do you want from me?"

Imatt sat softly on the corner of the desk, folding his hands in his lap and leaning slightly closer to their prisoner. "We want you to help us rescue your friends. All I need you to do is tell me what your emergency escape route was, so we can track them down."

"Why? So you can throw all of us in some Coalition prison? No thanks. I won't sell out my friends like that." Abbas crossed his arms and stared defiantly at his interrogator.

"Look, Abbas," Imatt said, spreading his hands wide, "I won't lie to you. There will be charges filed against you and anyone else we find. But if you help us, we can make sure the courts will go easy on you, maybe even get you a suspended sentence. Of course, there's another reason you should help us. Did you see what happened to your friends in the freighter?"

Abbas shook his head. "I was a little busy at the time."

"Pelos, can you play back main viewscreen segment one-one-three, mark two?"

Pelos nodded silently, tapped lightly on his computer panel, and the display came to life, showing the doomed freighter's final moments. Abbas's beak quivered noticeably when the ship was broken in half by the violent tempest of the collapsing wormhole.

Imatt never took his eyes of their captive, carefully judging his response. "Again."

Pelos tapped his panel once more, and the viewscreen played the demise of the freighter a second time. Silence reigned in the *Summerwind*, to the point that Kish thought she could hear her own heartbeat. Abbas sat staring wordlessly at the blank screen.

"Now do you understand?" Imatt asked. "We have no way of knowing where they were going, so we wouldn't have a clue about where to begin a rescue operation. Even if you name the system that was supposed to be their destination, I can't guarantee we will find them in time—or at all, for that matter. They could have reached their destination, or be anywhere along the way—on the other side of this system or a thousand light years away. But we need a starting point."

Abbas maintained his reticence, not even blinking in the face of the enormity of events. Kish studied Imatt carefully, and she could see him working through several courses of action. At last, the GBI agent must have decided he had his prisoner on the run, and that the time had come to change tactics.

Imatt rose to his feet, crossed the short distance between them, and yanked Abbas's head around by the beak, staring directly into his eyes. He held the Tsimian pilot transfixed by his gaze, eyes boring into Abbas and stripping away his last measure of resolve. "Damn it, Abbas, your friends need you! Are you going to help them, or are you going to let them die? Slowly? Just like you almost did?"

The last line of approach broke the Tsimian's will, and his shoulders slumped in defeat. "Penac System," he said finally, eyes on the floor. "If we were compromised, we were to escape to the Penac System, then jump to our final destination as soon as our Rift Drives were capable of another trip. I won't reveal the other system to you."

Imatt chewed his lip, evaluating what Abbas had told them. "It's a start. Kish, can you find a way to secure him while we investigate matters on Trum 4?"

Kish nodded. "I'll talk to Pana. I think he still has some repairs to finish, so we should be able to transfer our prisoner to the *Grappler*, and they can watch him while we check things out down below."

The prisoner was moved to the other ship smoothly, and Kish wasted no time in piloting her own vessel to the surface of Trum 4. Twice on the way down, a large object struck *Summerwind's* shields, pounding home with jarring force. Pelos had examined the computer found in the remains of the damaged fighter, and while he was unable to locate the pirates' contingency plans, he had found a reference to a certain area of the planet. This was an amazing windfall because, with the limited scanning capacity in the Trum System, they would have been faced with a proverbial needle-in-a-haystack search. At Kish's command, Pelos adjusted their weakened shields, bringing more power to bear on the struggling rear shield generators. For her part, Kish tried using a split viewscreen to monitor meteor activity behind them, as well as keep a watch on what lay before them.

They reached the coordinates Pelos had found, and Kish managed to find a relatively large overhanging rock, its immensity enough to cover the Assault Class Fighter and protect it from incoming meteorites. She left the systems running, enabling a speedy departure if the need should arise, but she prudently deactivated the shields. The generator needed time to recharge, or they might find themselves with no shields at all.

Kish pulled on the heavy protective suit, snapping the seals and securing her helmet in place. Her tiny nose wrinkled in protest at the smell of recirculated air mixing with the lubricants keeping the suit operable. Her breathing echoed in her ears, not quite drowning out the hum of the oxygen scrubbers. She strapped her laser pistol to her side, then secured a scanner and a medical kit to her utility belt. Her teammates were similarly clad, the dull gray environmental suits shining slightly under the bright lights in the ship's main compartment.

Summerwind's ramp lowered to the rocky surface of Trum 4, steam rising around them with a hiss of escaping gasses. Kish was first down the ramp, pistol in one hand and a handheld scanner in the other. The bulky suit hindered her movements, and she had to shorten her stride to maintain her balance. Gravity was slightly weaker than the standard artificial gravity aboard starships, which helped reduce the strain of walking. The terrain ahead shimmered in and out of view, partially obscured by a blue-green miasma hanging in the air. The atmosphere contained a number of virulent elements, mainly fluorine, and was not only deadly to breathe, but the fusion of the different components made long-range vision difficult, if not impossible.

Kish pointed in three different directions, and the companions split up. Kish walked a short distance away before testing the communications system.

"Imatt, Pelos, can you read?"

The radio crackled to life, atmospheric interference partially obscuring the words. "Imatt here. I copy. Your transmission is broken up a bit."

"Pelos here. I copy also. Ditto for my reception."

"All right. I'm not sure how far apart these subspace Comms will work with all of this interference. Let's spread out to about a one hundred-meter interval, then sweep the area clockwise from the north."

They gradually widened their search, stopping every ten meters to check the radios. While the interference did increase, they were still able to communicate, even when at the full separation Kish had designated. The drawback, she discovered, was that Pelos and Imatt, to either side of her, could not cleanly communicate with each other directly.

"Okay, let's make this quick," she told them, voice echoing hollowly in the confines of her helmet. "I don't want to get too far from the ship. We would risk becoming separated, and we might have trouble finding our way back. And keep an eye out for meteorite impacts. If you're too close to one, the shrapnel could rupture your suit."

A strong wind was blowing, but all it did was provide tantalizing glimpses of what lay ahead, then snatch it away to hide it within the oddly colored tentacles of the swirling fog. She relied on the scanner more than her eyes, as it was able to detect even the rise and fall of the landscape ahead of her, warning of potentially hazardous rock slides and unseen pitfalls.

When her scanner first indicated a metallic presence ahead, it did so only momentarily, and she thought she might have imagined it. But the signal was soon repeated, and she was able to get a lock on it.

"I've got something," she announced in her Comm. "About forty meters ahead, slightly west of the line I'm following."

"I'm not reading anything," Pelos said, a measure of doubt in his voice.

"I've got it," Imatt said. "It doesn't appear very large."

"Let's check it out," Kish decided. She stayed in place until Pelos drew close enough to pick up the object on his own scanner, and then she slowly approached, laser pistol in hand. There was a reddish, powdery material covering the ground to a depth of several inches, and small clouds arose from beneath her booted feet with every step, passing sharply away in the strong winds. A low structure gradually materialized out of the murky fog, and Kish paused to study it from a distance. One side was elongated, sloping at a gentle angle and disappearing in the covering layer of dust. Imatt and Pelos appeared at her side, and together they moved in closer.

Pelos reached out to touch the metal surface, brushing away the accumulated debris to allow a clearer examination. His efforts revealed a locking mechanism blinking a steady azure glow and blocking access to whatever was hidden behind it. Even with the cumbersome gloves of his environmental suit, Pelos was able to disarm the lock and gain access. The door slid open with a grating rumble, the gears grinding hard against a layer of dust coating the machinery. Imatt shined his light into the opening behind the panel, and they saw a set of stairs leading down into the darkness.

CHAPTER FOURTEEN

ARANO PEERED AHEAD INTO THE GLOOMY RYSTO-rian night, his breath appearing before him in a steamy white cloud. The temperature had fallen rapidly, and the sparse grass covering the ground was coated with a layer of filmy frost. He blew on his hands and rubbed them together, fighting to ward off the chill. The raid on the prison had provided a generous supply of cold weather gear, but Arano hadn't brought much with him. It was a philosophy he had borrowed from the old days of Human special operations units: travel light, freeze at night.

He and Alyna were the first to enter the town, traveling with Derna, one of the Bromidian clerics, walking between them. Lentin had suggested they journey in small groups to avoid attracting attention, so they had split the team into four sections. Non-Bromidians were not as unusual as they once were; during the intervening months following the end of the war, thousands of people from all races had flocked to Rystoria, anxious to earn their share of what looked to be a number of lucrative business opportunities. While they were not expecting to be welcomed with any measure of enthusiasm, they would not be automatically accosted.

Arano pulled his hood up tightly about his face and thrust his hands deep into his pockets, head down but eyes scanning the area. He was thankful for the cold weather; it enabled him to be more readily anonymous, just another resident bundled up against the elements. His feet scuffed lightly on the concrete sidewalk, the sound almost lost in the wind swirling around them.

The buildings in the city of Notron were, for the most part, heavily deteriorated. The harsh climate only added to the decomposition of the wooden structures, already weakened by the unforgiving Rystorian sun, not to mention the ravages of war. With the Bromidian economy still struggling, little was spent on upkeep, especially outside the capital. Broken planks hung askew from many of the buildings, and some even had sizeable gaps between the windows and their frames.

Arano and his companions were in a commercial section of town, and with the late hour, most of the shops were closed. There were no warehouses in that part of town, and in fact, most of the space was used for offices. The only businesses appearing to be open were a handful of taverns and restaurants.

It was to one of the taverns that they were traveling. Their contact, a Bromidian named Remina, was an associate of Derna, so there would be no need for an intricate and complicated series of recognition passwords. Derna led the group on a circuitous path, hoping to arrive at their destination at relatively the same time as the other groups without being seen loitering in the area. Although there hadn't been a confrontation yet, Arano had seen at least three groups of New Dawn soldiers patrolling the streets. He was confident in their ability to bluff their way past common soldiers who were probably bored with their jobs, but if any of those groups were members of the Tycon Mar . . .

"Around the next corner," Derna whispered. Arano winced, but said nothing. Whispering would draw attention to the group, but he had to assume Derna knew what she was doing. She and her compatriots had survived years of clandestine operations under the very nose of the Gorst VIII regime, and she hadn't stayed alive for so long by making mistakes.

They entered a low building, which had a sign over the door announcing it as The Shrieking Raptor. Arano stepped forward and pulled the door open, holding it for his companions while surreptitiously checking their surroundings. As he had hoped, two pairs of their operatives had already slid into place, taking up surveillance positions around the tavern. He moved inside.

Most of the patrons were Bromidian, although there was a scattering of the other races. The smoke-filled interior was dimly lit, reminding Arano of virtually every other bar he had ever seen. Tables were arranged in a haphazard fashion, most occupied by people far gone with drink. A few disinterested-looking waitresses wandered through the assemblage, bringing food and drink orders to their waiting customers. The polished wooden bar ran the length of one wall, and two Bromidian bartenders hustled back and forth, bringing drinks to their more intoxicated patrons. Irrationally, Arano found himself wondering why the heaviest drinkers always seemed to sit at the bar, rather than finding a table.

The door opened once more, and Dartok was the first to enter. He spotted Arano's group, waved casually, and led Fennel and another Bromidian to the table. They made a show a greeting each other in the fashion common among Bromidians, grasping right forearms and holding the pose long enough to acknowledge each other. A waitress stepped up, took their order, and returned momentarily with six Bromidian ales.

Arano sipped the bitter drink, hiding his revulsion behind his mug. He had experienced more than his share of foul-tasting beverages, but he found Bromidian ale to be a new expedition into the realm of the putrid libation. Everyone in the establishment was talking in hushed tones, almost afraid someone might over-hear them. The fear wasn't unfounded if the Tycon Mar was functioning the way it had prior to the war. A seemingly harm-less comment overheard by one of their agents could send an innocent person to the torture chamber—or the gallows.

Arano heard a light step behind him, and he placed his mug on the table as he turned around. An aging Bromidian stood a few feet away, and she was flanked on either side by a pair of tall, cowled companions. Arano assessed them in a heartbeat: likely, the female was their contact, Remina, and the two accom-panying her were bodyguards. Although their faces were hidden behind their bulky gray cloaks, he could see from their exposed hands that they were Bromidian. Derna gestured to three empty chairs at one end of their long table, and the newcomers took their seats without comment. Arano shrugged, sipped his ale, and tried to ignore the outrageous cloak-and-dagger antics of the Bromidian underground.

Remina broke the silence. "Derna and Fennel." She gave an insectoid grin, folding her arms across her chest. "As I live and breathe. I didn't expect to see you two back around here again. Looks like you will be back to your old tricks."

Fennel leaned forward, resting her elbows on the table, and spoke quietly. "Can you put us up until we find a place to stage our operations?"

"I can." She looked around the group, seeming to assess each of them in turn. "Are all of you staying, or just Fennel and Derna?"

"Just the two of us," Derna said. "The others will check in on us from time to time, bringing us supplies, if we need them. This is—"

"Hush!" Remina cut her off, eyes going flat. "I want to know as little as possible. The Tycon Mar is thick in this town, and they are trying to root out any opposition to the new government. Anyone arrested for treason against Gorst IX will be interrogated. If I should be caught, what I don't know, I can't reveal."

Arano nodded his approval. "I can see you've done this before." Arano's eyes narrowed as he realized what he had just heard. "Is it true, then? Gorst VIII had a son survive the war, and he is the leader of this new government?"

Remina sipped her drink, pursing her lips as she set her cup down. "Yes. He has been on every news brief over the past few days, trying to get his face out there. It's definitely him." She stared at the contents of her mug for a few moments, then suddenly drained it in one long drink. "It's time to be going. We have work to do, and you shouldn't stay in town any longer than you have to."

Hawan paid the waitress for their drinks, and Remina rose from the table, followed by the two clerics and her companions. They left without another word, and Arano gave them several minutes' head start before leading Alyna, Dartok, and three other Bromidians back into the Rystorian night. A fog had rolled in while they were in the tavern, and while it was only a fine ephemeral mist, it seemed to be getting denser. He pulled his cloak tightly about his body, covering his face with the hood, and strode boldly into the darkness.

The pavement was shimmering with frost, and the wind had fallen to a barely noticeable breeze. The town had the feel of a graveyard; the deepening fog had them isolated in their own little pocket of reality. Arano heard, rather than saw, the passing of a large group of people, and he decided they were more likely to be soldiers than citizens. He had not seen any civilians traveling in groups of more than five or six and realized how wise Hawan had been when he suggested they travel in smaller groups. From within the concealing folds of his hood, he kept a sharp eye on the buildings around him, senses alert for the first sign of trouble. His danger sense had already moved into high gear, warning him of trouble all around them.

A sudden, sharp twinge of prescience came to him, and he immediately signaled for the group to turn down the next alley. They were deviating from their planned route, and he could see the distrust in Dartok's eyes, but there was nothing to be done about it. With unwavering certainty, he knew trouble lay ahead and was approaching swiftly. The alley they entered bent sharply to the left, then came to a sudden end. Arano bit off a string of silent curses, then looked back to see the accusation in Dartok's expression. Rubbing his eyes in fatigue, Arano led the group back in the direction of the mouth of the alley but stopped short ten meters from the main road. He concealed himself in the fog and shadows, hiding behind a rusty garbage dumpster and trying to ignore the foul reek wafting up to him. His companions similarly hid themselves, and they waited, holding their breath to keep the telltale steam from giving them away in the cool night air.

The delay didn't last long. They heard the faintly muffled tramp of marching feet on the pavement, and within moments, a group of black-clad Bromidians passed their alley. They carried no rifles, but pistols were openly displayed on their hips. Each carried a knife and a handheld Comm on the belt, and each of their left sleeves was adorned by a diamond-shaped patch with a translucent pyramid rising out of the center of a red background. Although they appeared to be actively searching for someone, they couldn't see Arano's group concealed in the alleyway. There were about a dozen of them, and while most of the group stayed in the road, three of them entered the narrow lane where the conspirators lay in hiding.

One Bromidian, apparently the group's leader, hissed a sharp command in the guttural Bromidian tongue, and the three who had entered the alley trotted back to join the others. After a brief conference that was scarcely above a whisper, they padded softly into the fog and were gone. Arano waited only a few moments and then, motioning for the others to stay where they were, stepped out of the alley and slinked along behind the Bromidians. Once Arano was certain they were not trying to lure his group into the open, he slipped back to where his friends lay hidden. Together, they hurried off into the night, determined to escape before they were trapped.

"They were looking for someone, probably us," Arano told them when he was able. "They went about a block back the way we came, and they all took cover in recessed doorways."

Dartok's eyes looked a bit wild, and his exoskeleton seemed a bit paler. "Those men were with the Tycon Mar," he warned them urgently. "We need to get out of here, as quickly as we can!"

"Wait," Alyna said, eyes wide with concern. "What about the others?"

"They were supposed to be following a few minutes behind us," Dartok said. "If they do take the same route . . ."

Arano never hesitated. He needed Hawan's continued presence to lend credibility to his position as one of the impromptu leaders of the counter-revolution, and to allow him to fall into enemy hands would be unacceptable.

"Alyna," he said briskly, "I want you to take everyone else with you to the rendezvous point, then continue back to the base camp. Don't wait for me; I'll be along when I can. I'm going to fall back and try to help the others." He drew his pistol, cutting short her protest before she could give it voice. "We can't all go back. I won't risk losing the entire group. We need your expertise back at the camp. Don't worry; I'll be careful."

"But you won't be alone." It was Dartok who stepped forward, his own pistol in his hand. "I'm going with you."

Arano was about to argue the point but thought better of it. He nodded curtly, gave Alyna's hand a solemn squeeze, and stalked back the way they had come, Dartok close behind him. He glanced over his shoulder and was just able to see Alyna departing in the opposite direction, disappearing into a curtain of mist. He turned his full attention back to the heavily shrouded streets before them.

They hadn't far to go. Minutes later, he heard harsh shouting in the Bromidian tongue, followed by the sounds of several people rushing out into the street. He and Dartok stepped briskly ahead, hiding behind a parked vehicle, and watched the scene playing out before them.

The twelve members of Tycon Mar had surrounded Hawan's group, and they had their weapons trained on the hapless RLF soldiers, whom they outnumbered two to one. The Tycon Mar leader stepped forward, picking out one of Hawan's group at random—Pennon was his name—pointing his weapon directly into Pennon's chest. Arano leveled his pistol, but Dartok restrained him, nodding toward Hawan. Arano realized what the Bromidian was suggesting: give Hawan a chance to bluff past them.

"What are you doing out here at this late hour?" the leader asked.

Refusing to show any signs of intimidation, Perron crossed his arms and stared at his accuser. "Since when is it illegal to be out in the streets at night? And who are you to be going about accosting Bromidian citizens?"

The Bromidian raised his pistol a bit higher, and the barrel hovered inches from Perron's forehead. "I am Lyot, and we are members of the Tycon Mar. We have been charged with maintaining order and assuring that there will be no insurrection against the rightful rulers of Vagorst, the seat of the Bromidian Empire. As such, I demand to know what business you are about. It is not a request."

Hawan stepped forward, hands raised in supplication. "I wish you the best of luck in your endeavors, good sir," he said obsequiously, "but I assure you we are up to nothing illegal. We met some friends for dinner, and we are trying to find a transport back to the city of Rasat."

Lyot's eyes narrowed dangerously. "Then you are heading in the wrong direction," he growled. "The transportation depot lies in the other direction."

"Could you possibly direct us there?" Hawan asked. "As I said, we're not from around here, and we have no idea where we are. We were given directions, but the Tsimian we got them from was far gone in drink. I should have known better than to trust an outlander." He spat angrily, hands on his hips.

His tirade had the desired effect on Lyot. He stared calculatingly at the assembled Bromidians in his trap, then nodded softly. The Tycon Mar operative scratched out some instructions on a sheet of paper, explaining them to Hawan as he went. The two clasped forearms, and Lyot motioned for his men to allow them to leave. Arano slowly let out the breath he didn't realize he had been holding, and he relaxed his grip on his weapon, the muscles in his hands almost cramped from the strain. Hawan's group filed out of the trap.

Suddenly, a Bromidian in Hawan's group stepped aside, raising his arms and pointing wildly at the RLF leader's unsuspecting back. "Right there," he shouted. "That man is Hawan!"

One word shrieked through Arano's brain: *Betrayed!*

Kish was the first to descend the stairs, her light illuminating the concealing darkness below them. Static crackled in her helmet, a wordless testimony to the ravages of the planet's atmosphere. They reached the bottom of the narrow, metallic stairwell and found themselves in a two-meter-wide corridor, carved from the bedrock and sealed against cave-ins, likely by a laser cutter. The floor was much smoother than Kish had anticipated, and there were no protruding snags to catch their feet and cause a fall. With her pistol in one hand and her scanner in the other, she plunged into the tunnel.

The passage they followed bent continuously to the left, preventing them from seeing any distance to their front. As it was, her light source, even combined with that of her companions, probably wouldn't throw light much farther ahead anyway, she conceded. Her eyes roamed around the tunnel's interior, studying the craftsmanship. The sides, while not as well-groomed as the floor, were still fairly smooth. The roof, however, was a different story. In a testament to what Kish considered a lack of work ethic, the roof of the warren still had the rough, uneven look of a first cut.

They were brought up short by the sudden appearance of a door, blocking the passageway before them. It was emblazoned with a Bromidian inscription, and while Kish couldn't read their writing, her perfect memory recalled having seen those particular words before.

"This is definitely a Rising Sun base," she told her companions. "Roughly translated, this reads, 'Death to the Infidels,' or some such thing. It was the slogan of one of the brigades in Rising Sun."

Imatt stepped forward, looking back and forth across the portal's surface. "I don't see a seam or an input panel. How does it operate?"

Pelos indicated the control box on the door's right edge, near the bottom. "I don't think it was intended for unrestricted access from the outside. This device powers the sliders opening the door, but there's nothing on this side to indicate it can be opened manually."

Kish almost laughed. "Maybe we should knock."

Imatt smiled and shrugged his shoulders. "Why not?" He reached out and pounded on the metal barrier with his gloved hand, the sound echoing hollowly in the room beyond.

There was a brief lull, giving no sign anyone on the other side could hear them. Finally, a voice came through the door.

"Who's there?" the deep voice demanded harshly.

Pelos keyed the intercom. "Who do you think it is, you idiot? Open the door."

The big Tsimian grinned broadly when the machinery hummed to life, and the door slid obediently to one side. They stepped through into a decontamination chamber, and the door clanged shut behind them. There was a hiss of escaping gasses, and the fog in the air cleared. A green light appeared on the heads-up display in Kish's helmet, indicating the air was safe to breathe. At the far end of the chamber, another door slid aside, revealing the main complex. A bald, grubby-looking Human stood in the passage beyond, still in his environmental suit but with his helmet removed. His jaw dropped in surprise when he saw the visitors, and he stood rooted in place, obviously taken aback by the turn of events.

"Hi," Imatt said as he stepped forward, laser pistol leveled at the man standing before them. "Mind if we come in?"

The GBI agent, flanked by his Avenger counterparts, strode out of the decontamination chamber and into a staging area for cargo entering and leaving the facility. Crates of supplies, weapons, and ammunition were stacked against three of the walls in sloppy, disorganized fashion, some of the piles looking ready to tip over and spill their contents onto the rocky floor. The man who opened the door had turned pale, and he stood silently, trembling, facing his captors awkwardly. Imatt pressed the advantage, holstering his weapons and seizing the scruffy man by the back of his neck.

"What is your name?"

"L . . . Larn."

"Okay, Larn, where is the rest of your crew?"

"They . . . they're all up in the ships."

Imatt squeezed harder, eliciting a squeal of panic from his captive. "Do you really expect me to believe they would leave a toad like you down here all alone? Where are the others?" Larn hung helpless in Imatt's crushing grip, eyes wide with panic. "Don't make me have my Tsimian friend ask you."

Picking up on Imatt's lead, Pelos stepped forward, hand resting threateningly on the hilt of his knife. The gesture was too much for Larn, who broke into hysterics.

"They're inside that passage!" he shouted, almost in tears. "There are only three others, and they're all gathering the rest of the supplies. Don't let him touch me!"

Imatt released Larn and stood before him, hands on hips, staring into their captive's eyes with an intimidating snarl. "You will take us to them. Are they armed?"

"I . . . I think one of them is. The others weren't the last time

I saw them. Who are you? What are you going to do with us?"

"All in good time. Take us to your friends." Imatt gestured into the passage.

Larn nodded shamefacedly and, with his downcast eyes on the floor, led them deeper into the complex. Larn reminded Kish of a schoolboy who had just been reprimanded by a gruff teacher. They followed a short sub-hallway to a cavernous room, which apparently Rising Sun had used as a warehouse, at least when the defunct organization was still active. Everything seemed to confirm their earlier theory, that the pirates were in fact gathering weapons and supplies for their shadowy employers in the new Bromidian government.

They found the other three brigands in one corner of the warehouse, arguing over several items on their inventory. They were so intent upon their heated discussion that they didn't see or hear the approach of the newcomers until Kish and her companions were almost on top of them. One, a Kamling with a burn scar covering the left side of his head, had a pistol holstered on his right hip. When he saw the Avengers, his hand went immediately to his weapon, but he changed his mind and raised his hands. Kish decided his change of heart might have had something to do with the three laser pistols pointed at his chest.

They herded their new captives into a tight circle, checked them for weapons, and used several strands of malleable wire to secure their hands behind their backs. The four privateers were instructed to sit, shoulder to shoulder, which they did with only a minimal amount of grumbling. Kish stood before them, her diminutive form still somehow presenting a commanding presence, and glared down at them. In addition to Larn, they had the one Kamling, who called himself Shallon, and two Tsimians named Reles and Wonal.

"You four are under arrest for piracy and weapons smuggling," she told them. "We are operating as part of a joint Avengers-GBI task force specifically targeting your group. The Coalition government is aware you have been supplying weapons to the Bromidian uprising, and this will stop. You will come back with us to our ships, and once we have located the freighter and rescued any survivors, you will be taken to Immok, where you will stand trial for your crimes against the Coalition."

Shallon spat at Kish's feet. "We aren't Coalition citizens, and we are not subject to its laws. I won't be intimidated by—"

Pelos grabbed him by the throat, lifting him forcefully to his feet. Shallon's eyes nearly bulged out of their sockets, and he cut his tirade short. "Didn't your mother teach you any manners?" Pelos asked him in an icy voice. "You should show the lady a little more respect."

Shallon, afraid to answer, nodded his head vigorously. Kish bit her lip, coming to a decision on their next step. "Stand up, all of you. Do not try to escape, or we'll be forced to shoot. I'd rather see you in jail than in the ground, but I will not let you run." The four pirates, cowed into submission by Pelos's demonstration, nodded but said nothing. They resealed their environmental suits and entered the decontamination chamber. Larn indicated a remote control device, which would allow them to access the facility from the outside.

Kish was reminded of a lock and dam system on a river. People passing into and out of the complex had to stop in this room, allowing the atmosphere to change to that of their destination; then the other door would open. The equipment hummed once more, and the familiar hissing signaled the siphoning of the breathable air being replaced by the noxious gasses from outside.

A faint thrumming reached Kish's ears. She hadn't heard it

on their way in, and it didn't really sound like it originated from anything mechanical. She saw concern mirrored on her friends' faces, and the three raised their pistols cautiously. The door to the outside slid open, and the thumping noise turned into a series of small explosions. Kish pressed forward, with her two companions trailing behind the prisoners, and climbed the long staircase leading to the surface.

They stepped from the cavern into a nightmare. Hellish streaks of light lit the murky sky, each ending with a fiery detonation. "Meteor shower!" Kish shouted through her helmet Comm. "Everyone back inside!"

Although their captives could not hear her transmission, they quite obviously understood the implications of their situation, and they allowed themselves to be corralled back into the cavern. But in a surprise move, Shallon dashed to the side and raced into the fog, hands somehow freed from the restraining wire. Kish motioned for the others to move inside the protective opening and then ran after the Kamling. Despite his advantage in size, his suit was much bulkier than those worn by the Avengers, and she soon had him in sight. In his blind flight, he hadn't thought to change directions, for which she was grateful.

She fired her pistol into the ground next to him to get his attention, and he spun to face her, hand reflexively hovering above his empty holster. Even through the face shield of his environmental suit, she could see the hatred and rage boiling in his eyes, and she raised her pistol and pointed it at him, gesturing with her free hand for him to come closer. For the span of several heartbeats, she feared he might run again. Kish tried to ignore the streaking red lines above her head, a silent attestation to the barrage of incoming meteorites, focusing on her captive's every move.

With a burst of light that burned her eyes before her face

shield could darken, a massive meteorite struck the ground about a kilometer behind Shallon. The concussion from the impact roared outward, ripping across the rocky landscape and throwing Kish and her prisoner to the ground. She tumbled hard down a steep slide and struck the bottom with jarring force, then lay there gasping and trying to draw a breath.

A rush of stones tumbled down the hill, some at least a meter across. In a move born of sheer desperation, she dug her hands into the loose soil and pulled, trying to drag her stunned body away from the path of the landslide. She thought she had succeeded until the largest rock hopped obliquely, deflected in her direction, and came to rest on her right leg, pinning her beneath its weight. Through the fog of pain enveloping her head, Kish heard her suit beep its warning, telling her its integrity had been breached. Her supply of oxygen would run out in minutes.

CHAPTER
FIFTEEN

HAWAN SPUN ABOUT, RAGE DISTORTING HIS INSEC-
toid face as he drew his pistol to face his adversaries. Arano's own
pistol snapped up, firing the first shot in the melee and taking
Lyot's life with a shot to the back. Blasts from laser pistols flashed
in all directions, and Bromidians from both sides fell writhing to
the street. The patrol closed to hand-to-hand fighting, and the
skirmish turned into a street brawl. Arano, fearing he would as
likely hit a friend as a foe, dropped his pistol and charged into the
fray, knife in hand, Dartok close behind him.

He drove his knife into the nearest soldier's neck, burying
the blade to the hilt, and pulling the inert form away from the
fighting. He wrenched his knife free with an oath, dropped the
body to the side, and chose another target. Only five Tycon Mar
agents were still standing, but none of the RLF soldiers had yet
fallen. The unexpected, traitorous announcement, followed by
Arano's timely counterattack, had thrown the enemy into disarray, and he had no intention of allowing them to regroup.

The nearest soldier threw himself at Arano, grasping the
Avenger's knife hand. Arano delivered a blow to the Bromidian's
abdomen with his knee, forced his opponent to the ground, and
held him there while pummeling him with his free hand. As the
battle continued to rage around him, Arano fought to free his weapon, finally managing to rip his right arm free and jam the blade

home through the exoskeleton covering the Bromidian's chest.

He surveyed the scene in a heartbeat: more Bromidians had fallen, Hawan and Dartok were each locked in a death embrace with an enemy soldier, and the three remaining members of Hawan's entourage had the final Tycon Mar operative on the ground. Rising to his feet once more, Arano looked over the fallen and located the Bromidian who had betrayed Hawan. The pair of knives protruding from his back showed the fate Hawan's loyal friends had given the traitor, and he lay unmoving on the pavement. Arano rushed to assist Dartok, who was nearest to him, but the Tycon Mar soldier was slain before Arano could help. Hawan forced his opponent to the ground, boot coming down sharply on the Bromidian neck. Even from where he stood, Arano could hear the snapping of bones. Hawan gave the body a contemptuous kick, then looked up, swaying dangerously.

Arano's heart quailed at the sight of his friend, the thick, black blood pouring down the front of his tunic from two gaping knife wounds. Hawan fell to one knee, and Arano rushed forward to catch him, trying to lower the wounded man gently to the street. Hawan motioned for him to lean closer.

"I'm sorry, Viper," he said in a hoarse whisper. "I think I have fought my last. You need to finish what we've started, for me, for you, and for Rystoria." He broke off, breath coming in short gasps.

"Hang in there," Arano told him, gripping the Bromidian's blood-slick hand tightly. "I'll get Alyna on the Comm, and she can bring the medkit—"

His plea was interrupted by the eruption of a laser blast striking Hawan's head and shattering it in Arano's lap. He followed the shot to its source, blind fury boiling over within him. Before he could react, Dartok's pistol sounded twice, and the assassin lay limp on the ground. Arano's mouth hung agape, the shock slowly registering in his mind: the traitorous RLF soldier was the one who had fired the fatal shot.

Arano rolled his head back, barely able to suppress a cry of grief and hatred. His hands clenched into fists so tightly that his fingernails dug into the palms of his hands, and tears stood unshed in his eyes. He felt a calming hand on his shoulder, and he looked up to see Dartok standing over him.

"I'm sorry, Viper, but we must go. There's nothing else we can do here."

Arano's gaze fell back to the limp form on the ground before him. "I won't leave him here."

Pennon shook his head. "We can't bring him with us. Carrying him would attract unwanted attention, and it would slow us down. Besides, while we appreciate the gesture, we Bromidians are not concerned about what happens to a body after death. We believe in an endless life cycle, and part of that includes the body returning to the soil. Whether that happens here, or in the forest, or at a stronghold, matters not to us."

Arano wiped his eyes, struggling to his knees. "It's not just that." He swallowed hard, regaining some of his composure. "If they discover who died here, they will use it as propaganda to discourage others from joining our cause. We can't let them find out he is dead."

Dartok nodded his agreement, looking around to get his bearings. "All right, we bring him. But we need to move quickly. More Tycon Mar might be on the way, so we have to be clear of the area. There's a bog about a kilometer from the south edge of town. We can dispose of the body there."

Arano winced at the seemingly indifferent attitude displayed by Hawan's followers, but he knew they meant no disrespect.

With Pennon's help, he gently lifted Hawan's body, draping it across his shoulders. The situation looked bleak: hunted by the Tycon Mar, carrying the body of their fallen leader, and with only four Bromidians to assist him. The other three surviving members of Hawan's party—Garda, Pennon, and Forle—holstered their weapons. Dartok handed Arano his pistol, which he had dropped during the fight, and the group left the street.

Dartok led them between two buildings, taking them down a narrow, putrid-smelling alley to avoid the main roads. The ground sparkled back at them, the layer of frost reflecting the sparse lighting and giving the entire scene a surreal appearance.

An initial feeling of numbness had passed, and Arano found himself awash in grief. Surprisingly, his senses were heightened, as though he had entered an altered state of consciousness. He watched the breath leave his body in roiling white clouds, mirroring the steam riding from Hawan's heinous wounds. Piles of trash lay abandoned against the buildings, some of it spilling out into the middle of the alley, where it crunched noisily underfoot. Dartok stalked ahead of them, pistol in hand but concealed within the folds of his cloak, somehow managing to maintain their route and still watch for hidden dangers. Pennon and Forle trailed behind, guarding against an ambush from the rear, while Garda stayed next to Arano, offering her assistance if Arano grew tired.

Arano's suppositions strayed to the near future as he wondered what the RLF would do in response to their leader's death. Although Arano made a significant number of the tactical decisions for the growing resistance group, it needed Bromidian leadership. There needed to be continuity in that leadership, with the RLF's leaders assuming prominent roles in the reforming of their legitimately elected government, should their efforts prove successful. By rights, that eliminated Arano as the choice to succeed Hawan, because he couldn't take command of the government on Rystoria following the cessation of hostilities.

Several choices ran through his head, but he immediately dismissed all but two of them. Dartok had demonstrated his worth in the fight against the Tycon Mar, not only his combat skills, but his ability to react quickly in a critical situation, taking control when it was necessary. But Arano knew there was only one real choice for the position, and that was Lentin. By his nature, Lentin would oppose such an appointment; he had made that clear already. But he had natural leadership skills, and he was already a renowned figure within the movement. In fact, his lack of desire for power was another bonus, in Arano's mind, because he would never be corrupted by his sudden rise in status. He would talk to his oldest Bromidian friend when they returned.

Of course, he knew their return was not assured. They were still deep in enemy territory, carrying their fallen leader, and hopelessly outnumbered. Dartok confidently directed them through the back alleys, his own familiarity with the layouts of the town proving invaluable to their continued survival. Arano almost failed to notice Dartok's sudden stop. The Bromidian motioned for the others to join him in a sheltered alcove, and Arano gratefully lowered his burden to the frozen ground.

Dartok leaned in close, one arm pointing to a soot-covered brick building ahead of them and to the east. "This building is a foundry. They have an incinerator in the basement, hot enough to melt tritanium. If you want, we can cremate Hawan's remains in there."

Arano eyed the building speculatively. "Good thinking," he whispered, shrugging his sore shoulders. "I think we're pressing our luck by carrying him any farther."

Their other companions shrugged their indifference, and Arano gestured to the door, stooping to lift his burden once more. Dartok crossed the street first, with Garda, Forle, and Pennon watching to their left and right for more Tycon Mar operatives. Arano felt the weight of Hawan's body pressing down upon him, and the muscles in his shoulders and upper back ached with the strain, but he steadfastly refused to share the burden. Adding to Arano's misery, a snowfall began, starting with small, icy beads, but rapidly escalating to large, feathery flakes, drifting silently to the frost-white ground. Pennon helped Arano pull his hood up more tightly about his face.

Dartok strolled casually across the street, hands in his pockets and head low, and entered the alley along the right side of the building. He agilely dashed up a short flight of stairs, bounded over a railing, and tried a door, finding it unlocked. He held up a single finger in warning then disappeared inside, reappearing several moments later and waving them in. Garda and Forle nodded, letting him know the way was clear, and he dashed across the street and into the foundry.

They entered a factory-like building, with hissing pipes winding across the ceiling in a maze-like pattern, the labyrinth of conduits too confusing for the eye to follow. The platforms they trod upon were little more than metal grates, with painted steel rods forming a handrail. An acrid odor filled the air, and Arano's eyes watered in response. His nose wrinkled in protest, but he followed Dartok along yet another platform overlooking the foundry floor. The door clanged shut behind him, and he heard the dissonant footfalls of the others following behind them. Arano felt lightheaded, likely from the fumes, and placed a steadying hand on the rail. He noticed that both the railings and the mesh of the platforms were layered in soot, the original color only visible in patches.

He was sweating freely, and the temperature continued to climb steadily the farther they went. When he looked out over the railing and saw the vats of molten metal glowing brightly below them, his skin recoiled sharply from the heat. He laid Hawan's body on the platform and waited until the other four Bromidians had gathered around.

"I know we're pressed for time, and you have told me that in your society, death is treated differently than the way my culture deals with it. Please, just allow me to say a few words before we leave." The others nodded solemnly, and Arano reverently arranged Hawan's hands atop the battered and bloody chest.

"Today, we have lost a good man. Hawan grew up in a brutal world, ruled by fear and the merciless application of violence to maintain order. But he was able to see beyond the totalitarian society enslaving his home. He was a visionary, and his vision of a free Rystoria came to pass, albeit all too briefly. Although the man has passed, his dream and his vision live on. The Rystorian Liberation Front will carry on the fight in his name, and we will not stop until those responsible for this insurrection have perished and order is restored.

"He will be sorely missed. He was a good man, a good soldier, and a great friend." Arano choked off the last few words, tears coming to his eyes. He saluted Hawan's supine form and, with the assistance of Dartok, respectfully rolled the body off the platform. Silhouetted against the glowing brightness below, Hawan struck the molten liquid, flaring brightly before disappearing forever.

Arano covered his eyes with one hand, head bowed in sorrow, until he felt a firm hand on his shoulder. He looked into Dartok's eyes and believed he actually saw compassion there.

Dartok pursed his lips, giving the semblance of a smile.

"Viper." He sighed. "Arano. Since this odyssey began, you have fought to gain the respect and trust of those who are in my inner circle. I refused to relent, thinking you were involved with us for selfish reasons. This evening, you have proved your worth. I am proud to call you brother."

He extended his hand in camaraderie, and Arano grasped his new friend's forearm warmly. A faint glimmer of hope rekindled his warrior's heart, lending him resolve and a newfound strength.

"Let's go," he said simply.

Kish pushed vainly against the boulder, pinning her leg to the rocky ground. She could roll the stone back a short distance, but the boot of her survival suit was wedged too tightly under the pinning rockfall to pull free. She lay back, gasping. All around her, the meteor storm continued, the occasional meteorite streaking overhead in a blinding flash of light that left its imprint on her retinas. She tried to remain calm, fighting against the rising wave of panic threatening to take away her ability to reason.

Her suit's external monitors picked up the sound of someone maniacally screaming for help. She shifted and rolled, putting herself in a better position to find the source of the commotion. A powerful wave of revulsion washed over her when she spied the suited figure of Shallon, arms flailing in a futile attempt to stave off the inevitable fate stalking him like an implacable hunter. He spun to face Kish, and she saw the origin of his distress: something, likely a fragment from a meteorite, had severely damaged the faceplate of his environmental helmet. The festering blisters covering his green, ravaged skin betrayed the savagery of the atmosphere that slowly killed him, the smallest amount of toxic air having seeped through his shielding. He spied Kish and immediately rushed to her side, falling twice in his haste but each time staggering back to his feet. He knelt at her side, whimpering in agony . . .

He wrenched at her helmet seal, thinking in his delirium that he could survive direct exposure to the harsh elements for the brief time it would take to trade helmets. Kish slapped and fought against his probing hands, looking for anything to use as a weapon. Her pistol lay a scant five meters away, but it might as well have been back in the tunnel. His reptilian face had lost all traces of underlying sanity, and he fought her with a single-mindedness that was nearly overwhelming. She heard the first safety seal release with a hiss and knew her options had run out.

Abandoning her attempts to fight his hands, she seized a fist-sized stone lying near her shoulder and smashed it with her remaining strength against the fractured faceshield on Shallon's suit. It imploded into the helmet, the fragments lashing into Shallon's face and ripping him to shreds. He gave an unearthly howl, and his fingers stiffened into claws, feet thrashing against the earth in unspeakable anguish. After several agonizing moments, he lay still.

Kish lay back against the unyielding ground, resetting her helmet seals and allowing herself a brief respite to gather her strength. After seeing the tortured death awaiting her if she stayed where she was, she made up her mind. Setting her jaw, she released the safety seals on her boot, lifted against the pinning boulder, and pulled her foot free, leaving the boot embedded beneath the stone's bulk. Immediately, the skin on her foot burned as if on fire, and she cried out in pain. But she was free! She hobbled to her feet, feeling sheets of pain racing up her leg. The leather of her boot was already deteriorating, so she knew she had little time to spare. Kish got her bearings from the landscape and set off at a brisk trot back the way she had come.

The sole of her boot gave way completely, and she was forced to walk on the toe of her wounded foot. The entrance to the pirates' underground lair came grudgingly into view. She thrust herself to the top of the stairs, hopping down them two at a time using the railing for support. Imatt monitored her approach and had the door to the vestibule open for her. She tumbled inside, cradling her foot and panting heavily. The door to the complex hissed open, and Pelos rushed to her side, medical kit in hand.

They spent the next hour with Imatt guarding the remaining prisoners while Pelos tended to Kish's condition. Her foot had suffered severe second-degree burns, but the tough, leathery skin common to the Tompiste had served her well, and her wounds responded favorably to her teammate's ministrations. By the time the meteor storm had passed, she was able to walk unaided, although she still carried herself with a noticeable limp. She refused Imatt's suggestion that she remain in the compound until they could bring the *Summerwind* to her, insisting she could make the trek successfully. She took another dose of pain suppressant, and the Avengers left the Rising Sun stronghold.

Despite her assurances to the contrary, Kish found the trip to the ship excruciating. Through sheer strength of will, she completed the hike unaided, injured foot throbbing inside the boot she had pilfered from the underground warehouse. Limping heavily, she practically threw herself into the pilot's chair, ensured the systems were still online, and sealed the doorway. While Pelos and Imatt secured the prisoners, she wasted no time launching the *Summerwind* into the darkening skies. They rendezvoused with the *Grappler*, both ships maintaining their course away from the planet while they spoke over the Comm.

Toshe Jorgan's dark, feline brow drew tightly together, the Gatoan soldier concentrating on a series of mathematical computations. Behind him, Vic Dermak peeked over his shoulder, alternately running a hand through his short, blond hair and pointing at the figures in front of Toshe, making suggestions for solving the puzzle.

"They should have a fairly accurate read on the location of the pirate freighter in a few minutes," Lon told them. "At least, if Toshe's theory holds water. No one has ever tried this before, so he's starting from scratch."

"I saw their preliminary formula," Kish said, thoughtfully swirling the water in her glass. "The hypothesis seems to be fairly sound."

"I couldn't make any sense of it myself," Imatt said with a short laugh. "Theoretical physics has never been my strong point."

Kish shrugged, setting her glass down. "They simply based their calculations on the time span the wormhole was open, compared to how long it should have been open. They integrated the ratio with the rate at which the wormhole collapsed, and took the derivative of—"

"Okay, I surrender," Imatt said, holding his hands over his head. "Let's just see what they come up with, and I'll take their word for it."

Pelos slipped out of his environmental suit, the last to do so after ensuring their prisoners were well-secured. His tollep's tooth dangled in front of his uniform, and Kish noticed him subconsciously pass a fur-covered hand over it. She doubted he was even aware he had done it.

"What are the chances of survival for the freighter's passengers?" Pelos asked.

"A wormhole collapse places catastrophic stresses upon a ship due to the astronomical gravimetric forces unleashed during the incident," Lon told him, looking up from the report he was reading. "Not only will those forces rip a ship apart, but everything inside is also subject to the same forces, and there's no way for the inertial dampers to compensate. I doubt anyone could survive such an event."

Kish removed a burn treatment regenerator from the ship's medikit, and she applied more medication to her foot while adding to Lon's commentary. "And even if someone should somehow survive the crushing forces acting on the freighter, remember what condition their ship will be in. It was broken into at least two major pieces before it disappeared, so there will be multiple hull breaches in every section of the ship. Main power will be offline, and their engines will be down. Without power to the life support system, anyone who lived through the jump wouldn't last long afterward." She gave a sympathetic look to Pelos. "I think this will be a recovery mission, not a rescue."

Pelos nodded silently, beak twitching in frustration. He averted his eyes, and judging by the grim set to his features, Kish knew he wanted to change the topic. "What about the anomalous readings on that ship in the Menast System?" he asked suddenly. "Is there anything new from GBI?"

"Nothing yet," Lon replied, frowning and tapping several controls on the panel next to his chair. "The indigenous background radiation has increased, possibly due to the composition of the meteors passing through. Meteor activity is up 50 percent since our arrival. Due to the interference, we haven't been able to raise anyone on the subspace frequencies. Once we make our jump, we call Immok from our destination."

"We've got it!" Toshe said, receiving an excited slap on the back from Vic. "If our information about their planned destination was correct, I believe they will be found in this area." He called up a tactical map of the Penac System and its surrounding sectors. A small area between the freighter's destination and the Avengers' position lit up, blinking in a red circle. "They should be in open space, about fifteen light years from Penac."

Lon stepped closer, squinting at the screen. "I think I'm getting too old for this," he complained, half under his breath. "Okay, Kish, are you ready for this?"

Kish smiled. The dual rulership continued. "I believe we are."

"Then I'll send you the coordinates, and let's be on our way."

Alyna stepped grimly into the circle of firelight, leading her re-maining charges back to the safety of RLF-controlled territory. She was greeted by an anxious Lentin, who looked over her shoul-der as if searching for someone.

"The others were delayed," she said simply. "Arano and Dar-tok stayed behind to help Hawan out of an ambush. We waited about a half-kilometer outside of town, but they never showed up. Of course, they may have come out by a different route and missed us altogether." She stopped, jaw dropping open in sur-prise. "Where did we get the extra soldiers?"

Lentin gave her a sympathetic smile. "Do not worry, Alyna. Viper will return. And as for our new help," he said, gesturing around the camp, "they are not entirely what they appeared to be." He whistled sharply and motioned to one of his soldiers, who nodded and trotted off. He returned moments later, bring-ing a few vaguely familiar Bromidian faces with him.

"Greetings, Alyna, wife of Viper."

Alyna peered more closely, finally recognizing the man

addressing her. "Lord King Mendan?" The Latyrian before her grinned broadly, obviously pleased she had remembered him. "This is a great surprise, sir!"

He held up a hand. "I am king no longer," he told her solemnly. "In light of the current situation, I have abdicated my title, allowing my eldest son to take the position. I am now the leader of the First Latyrian Expeditionary Force. We have come, at the request of another of your soldiers, to aid you in your battle. The Son of the Great Evil must not be allowed to retain his throne. Such an event would be a catastrophe for Latyrians and the Coalition alike."

Alyna gave a curt nod. "You may no longer be a king, but you are still wise, my friend. How many of your countrymen did you bring?"

"There are two hundred Latyrian soldiers, all handpicked by Vantir, Enton, and myself. We have spread them out, dividing them among each of your enclaves. With any luck, we will soon take the battle to the enemy."

"Are Vantir and Enton in this camp?"

"Yes. We separated the group by tribes. All Latyrians here are with the Finlen Tribe. The other groups are headed by their tribal chieftain. Ultimately, they all answer to me."

Alyna smiled warmly, placing a soft hand on the hard shell of Mendan's upper arm. "I look forward to reuniting with old comrades. Right now, however, I need to help organize a search party. Viper has yet to return from his mission, and I fear he may be in trouble."

Mendan's face clouded, brow tightening. "This must not be. Allow me to take a dozen or so of my men. We can move silently if necessary, and our acute sense of smell should help us locate him more readily."

Videre had water and food brought for Alyna, and she ate as quickly as she could. Her mind fairly swam while she mentally walked through the possibilities. Having Latyrians on their side would provide a tremendous tactical advantage. Their resemblance to Bromidians was striking, and while it was not as complete as the similarities between Humans and Padians, it was close enough to allow them to pass as Bromidians. They could penetrate Bromidian cities, gather intelligence, and rescue stranded operatives. They had other advantages, as well, but her thoughts scattered when Mendan returned, a group of his warriors close behind. Alyna exchanged a brief look with Lain and Videre, and the three rose to their feet. Alyna extended a hand to Mendan. "We'll be coming with you."

CHAPTER SIXTEEN

ARANO COULD STILL SMELL THE SULPHUROUS reek of the foundry, even though they had left it behind over an hour earlier. An instructor of his at the Whelen Academy, the ancient Padian school where the formidable Daxia received their training, had once told Arano to try and make something good come of any situation. The Humans had a saying, Arano knew—something about storm clouds and a silver lining—but it all meant the same thing. He had escaped with Dartok and most of the Bromidians, which had never been a guarantee.

He felt a twinge from his danger sense, nothing strong, but enough to send him into a crouch. His companions froze in place, unsure what he was doing. He peered back the way they had come; seeing nothing, he called them in closer.

"I think we're being followed. We need to move more quickly, put some distance between us so I can begin disguising our trail."

Pennon glanced over his shoulder, frowning in confusion. "I've heard nothing."

"Nor I," Garda echoed.

Arano licked his lips, trying to decide how best to explain the situation to them. "Are you aware that I'm not actually Human?" Other than Dartok, his companions shook their heads. "I'm Padian, and I was trained as a Daxia. We have the ability to . . ." He crinkled his nose, fumbling for the right words, but deciding to simply say what came to mind. "We can sense danger and hostility. This ability has saved my life more than once. The greater the danger, and the more imminent the danger, the stronger the feeling and the earlier we can detect it."

"We've heard of the Daxia," Forle said. He rolled his eyes. "The leaders of the old government told us you were all dangerous assassins."

Arano shrugged. "We are. I am. But we are much more than that. But the important thing for us is that someone is close enough to set off my danger sense. We have a lead on them right now, but they're definitely tracking us. Let's pick up the pace a little. We're trying not to leave a trail, which isn't working and is only slowing us down. If we can put a little more space between them and us, we can slow down and allow me to take the time to hide our trail until we lose them."

Dartok took the lead, walking briskly across the carpet of leaves on the forest floor. The dead foliage crunched noisily underfoot, but there was nothing to be done about it. They had to duck frequently, dodging the low-hanging branches of the wiry dahala trees, and Arano felt tiny pinpricks from the spiny leaves brushing against his clothes. The air was still frigid, and tendrils of steam rose from his exposed skin, appearing oddly ghostlike in the darkness of the Rystorian night. Despite their quickened pace, Arano felt the sense of danger growing stronger.

Arano stopped, whistling for the others to do likewise, and he trained his ears behind him. In the distance, he could barely make out the sound of approaching hovercars. "They must be tracking us with some type of portable scanners. I think we need another plan."

Dartok motioned to Garda, growling a single word in the harsh Bromidian tongue. She immediately dashed off into the trees, skittering down a hillside to a gurgling creek. "She will pick up some delvonite. The creeks hereabout are full of it. It's slightly radioactive, but nothing you'll get sick from. The interference should keep them from tracking us."

"Should?" Arano asked, his eyes wide. "What if it doesn't?"

"It's true," Dartok conceded, "we may have to fight this group. But at least no one else will be able to find us so readily. The delvonite is less effective when blocking a more directed scan, like this closest group is probably using. So after we've dealt with this situation, they should have more trouble tracking us down."

Garda returned a few minutes later and distributed several fist-sized rocks. Arano found the stone to be warm to the touch, despite having been in the chill waters of the stream. He hoped the temperature didn't correlate to the lethality of the radiation. Bromidians were more resistant to radiation than Padians, and he wasn't certain just how much Dartok knew about Padian physiology. Just to be on the safe side, Arano placed his rocks in the outer pocket of his pack, placing as much distance as possible between his body and the delvonite.

For several minutes, the sound of the distant hovercars grew gradually quieter until it became inaudible, and Arano hoped the delvonite had succeeded in defeating the Bromidian scanners. They pushed ahead, not slowing their pace, eager to widen the distance from their pursuers. With Dartok in the lead, they covered another kilometer of forested, rolling hills before finding their path crossed by a wide, gurgling stream. While it wasn't more than a foot deep in most places, the rocky bottom gave Arano an idea.

"I want you all to wait here," he told them suddenly, stepping to the front of the group. "Rest for a bit, and I'll be back in a few minutes. I'm going to lay down a little false trail for our friends to follow."

Using rocks protruding from the water as stepping stones, Arano agilely hopped across the stream. When he reached the underbrush on the far side, he made exaggerated efforts at pushing twigs and branches aside, taking more steps than were necessary. He continued this for some distance, not stopping until he reached the summit of the ridge he had been climbing. He looked back with satisfaction when he saw his trail; it looked like more than one person had passed that way. He gradually reduced his trailblazing endeavors, hoping to make it appear to their pursuers that the little group was making a conscious effort to hide its trail.

After about fifteen minutes, he decided he had left as long a false trail as he dared, and backtracked to the stream, picking his way carefully this time to avoid leaving evidence of someone's passage back in the opposite direction. He emerged from the tree line near the water's edge, where Dartok and the others were waiting for him. Without explanation, he sat down and removed his boots and socks.

"I hate to do this, but we're going to have to get wet. I left about a click of false trail for them to follow, but now we need to disguise our true path. This stream will work, but as cold as it is, we can't afford to get our shoes wet." While his incredulous Bromidian allies removed their footwear, Arano tied his shoes to the top of his pack and waded into the middle of the stream. The icy waters bit into his legs with a numbing chill, freezing him to the bone. Dartok and Pennon soon joined him, and Garda and Forle were close behind.

Arano followed the frigid trail downstream, trying to step carefully so as not to disturb the rock-covered bottom.

Fortunately, the stones were rounded, allowing him to avoid stepping on a sharply pointed rock and injuring his foot. By the time they had traveled to a point where Arano felt safe leaving the water, his toes were numb with the cold. He knew his counterparts, with their Bromidian physiology, would not be as dramatically affected by the temperature. He found a sheltered bend where the low water levels had exposed a flat gravel barge and set his pack down on the dry, frozen ground. Wiping the water from his feet with his hands, he put his footwear back on and waited for the others.

The sun was brightening the eastern sky when they set out again. They pushed back into the cover of the trees, sacrificing speed for stealth. Twice in the next hour, they heard the resonating hum of passing hovercars, their sleek silver forms all but invisible through the canopy of the shrouding trees. Dartok calmly explained to his companions that the delvonite had likely done what they'd expected, and the Bromidians following them were no longer able to track them.

About an hour past sunrise, with fatigue taking its toll, Arano felt the first indications of trouble from his danger sense. It grew stronger with each passing step, so he lightly tapped Dartok on the shoulder. More quickly than many of Arano's comrades-in-arms, Dartok had learned to recognize the warning signs indicating Arano was perceiving a threat. At a signal from Arano, the Bromidian guided the group in another direction, angling southward from their westerly path. Dartok only took the group about a hundred meters before stopping and checking with Arano. The Padian shook his head grimly, telling his friend that the direction he had chosen was no better. Twice more in the next ten minutes, Dartok altered their heading, but to no avail; Arano could still sense the noose tightening around them. In frustration, Dartok called the group to a halt to discuss their options.

In a whispered conference, Arano explained his understanding of their situation. "I now believe the earlier fly-bys to have been more than simple reconnaissance. They must have been dropping off troops at various intervals, and those soldiers are searching the woods for us. I'm afraid we're going to need to find a defensible position in the next few minutes."

Garda looked back over her shoulder. "I think I saw a stone cabin in a deep draw about two hundred meters back. It ought to provide us with some usable firing positions."

Arano and Dartok exchanged a look, and Arano nodded. "Take us there."

Following Garda, the group topped a ridgeline and descended into a veritable warren of trees, low bushes, and briar patches. They picked their way through as best they could, ignoring the stinging strikes from the thorns grasping at them as they passed. The cabin stood in the center of a clearing, with just enough land around the modest structure cleared of the choking vegetation to allow for a garden. The compact chalet had been constructed from roughly hacked logs, tied securely together and sealed with mud. There were windows on each side, and through them Arano could see the thickness of the walls. He bit lightly on his lip in anticipation of a possible firefight; the foot-thick walls would provide more than ample cover and concealment for what he had in mind.

With their laser pistols in hand, the group stepped cautiously into the clearing. Taking a few darting steps, they reached the cabin and stood with their backs against the south wall. Garda and Forle were closest to the cabin's door, and they edged closer to the aging wooden portal.

Forle reached out a hard-shelled hand and shoved the door.

It swung wide raggedly, the hinges creaking in protest against the bulk of its burden. The two Bromidians walked forward slowly, pistols leading the way, and turned to face the darkened interior. They inched their way inside, rapidly swinging their pistols from one side of the room to the other.

Arano saw the frown on Dartok's face and knew the RLF soldier saw the same problem Arano did. They followed their companions inside, Pennon close at their heels, and stood in a rather plain sitting room, with dirt floors covered in places by the skins of fur-bearing animals. The interior walls were constructed of thinner logs than those used for the exterior, probably designed for privacy more than security. The roof was made of stone, with a rather complicated geometric pattern engraved across the surface. A couch and two chairs stood along one edge of the room, and the sofa was fronted by a long, low wooden table. Two doors flanked the far wall, and Garda and Forle had already entered the room beyond one of them. Arano and Dartok moved into position at the other doorway, waiting until their friends returned to the main room before advancing. At a nod from Arano, the two burst into the room, pistols covering the space beyond, but no enemy was to be found. The cabin was empty.

Holstering his pistol, Arano returned to the main room and called the others over. "I hate to be critical, but I don't want to lose anyone. I can't take a chance on losing you because I was afraid to hurt your feelings.

"When you clear a room, you can't hang in the doorway like that. You have the door frame on both sides of you, so you can't go anywhere but forward or back, which makes you a promising target for anyone on the other side. We call the narrow space inside a doorway the 'funnel of death,' because that's what it really is. When I clear a room with my Avenger teammates, we go through in teams of three, and we all have a portion of the room to cover. You ignore the rest, and only look at your sector. After you have cleared your area of responsibility, then you can engage targets in someone else's zone."

Arano was pleased to see how well they took the rebuke, and he even noticed Garda, Forle, and Pennon practicing the maneuver together, taking turns leading the way into the room. While Arano could sense the danger all around them, there was no immediate threat, so he was content to allow the group to relax for a time. He established a watch, maintaining at least two of them awake at all times, and allowed them to get some sleep for the long journey ahead.

In the vast emptiness of interstellar space, two swirling tubes of blackness suddenly emerged and thrust forward, the dark cylinders spinning rapidly, their surfaces covered with a racing maelstrom of red and blue shapes. From the mouth of the dark funnels, two Assault Class Fighters emerged into space, dropping into formation side by side. With a final lurch and a flash of light, the ebony tunnels of light disappeared, and the ships were alone.

The *UPCS Summerwind* swung gracefully about, matched in the maneuver by the *UPCS Grappler*, and the two ships came to a simultaneous halt. Kish activated the Comm, acknowledged the other ship, and had her crew initiate a scan of the sector. This was the fourth possible location for the missing freighter, with their previous efforts having been in vain. The only successful accomplishment had been the arrival of a Coalition Battle Class Light Cruiser, the *UPCS Molokai,* which had taken custody of their prisoners and allowed them to continue the mission un-impeded. Kish watched emotionlessly as the screen before her scrolled with useless data acquired by the ship's sensors.

The Comm beeped to life, and Kish tapped a button, bringing Lon's familiar face onto the screen. "You find anything yet?"

"Not a thing," Kish answered, shaking her head. "I'm afraid we may end up having to separate and search different coordinates on our own. It's more dangerous, but we could cover ground twice as fast."

Lon nodded glumly. "I'd rather avoid it, but you're probably right."

Imatt sat up stiffly in his seat. "I have an incoming message from GBI Headquarters. Stand by, and I'll see if they'll give me authority to put this on our Comm channels so you can all hear it firsthand."

Kish could barely make out the words, but a brief conversation followed, and in short order, a well-dressed Kamling stood before them on the screen, her green skin offset by the brown of her crisp suit. Kish manipulated her panel, and the screen split to include both Lon's group and the GBI agent.

"I am Special Agent Arlon Damis with the Galactic Bureau of Intelligence. You have been granted special clearance, based upon your position and your need to know, to be exposed to the following information. It is classified Top Secret Encrypted and is not for dissemination.

"We have completed our examination of your sensor records from the Tectos System. There was an anomalous life-form onboard the escaping shuttle, just as you surmised. Our final analysis bears out what Project Xeno had theorized: we are dealing with a new, as yet unnamed race. About all we can provide you are some likely characteristics for them, based upon detailed reports gathered during other encounters with them. They are bipedal, approximately Human-sized. They have ears resembling the wingspan of old-Earth bats, with points protruding both up and down. Their skin is scaly, and while we can't be certain of the color, certain algorithms have indicated brown skin. They have thick hair on their heads, and again, we can say with a degree of certainty the color appears to be predominantly white."

"Do we have any theories about where they're from or what they want?" Kish asked.

"Nothing, yet, but we're working on it. We believe their homeworld is out beyond the Rystoria System, somewhere in the unexplored regions beyond. That's probably why they made contact with the Bromidians first. Prior to the end of the war, Coalition ships hadn't been able to bypass the Rystoria System, so our knowledge of that region is sketchy, at best."

"I don't like seeing them coordinating with Ustin Shiba and his band of pirates," Lon said. "Especially since Ustin was ultimately working for Gorst IX."

Pelos absently rubbed a fur-covered hand across his beak, continuing Lon's line of thinking. "Maybe the conspiracy was bigger than we believed. There's a possibility of a connection between the new race and the Bromidian insurrection, at least by transitive reasoning. We know the pirates were helping the rebels, and we know the new race was at least associating with the pirates. But there's a possibility of another relationship in this mess."

"I think I see where you're going with this one, Pelos," Kish told him, her almond-shaped eyes going wide. "What if the new race was in collusion with Gorst's forces, helping to overthrow the new Bromidian government?"

Agent Damis watched the entire exchange with growing interest, and more than once, Kish saw her scribbling furiously on a notepad. "Imatt," Arlon said finally, you have an incredible group of people with you."

Imatt laughed heartily. "I think I've told you this before. You should have seen them on the Disciples case. They were nothing short of truly amazing."

"I hate to cut the party short," Vic said, standing behind Lon, "but we have some work ahead of us. My sensors just located the missing freighter, about five thousand kilometers from our position."

Lon swung about in his chair. "Heading?"

Vic leaned over his controls, running a finger along the screen until he found what he wanted. "The heading is three-three-two mark one-five."

Toshe Jorgan, his heavy Gatoan frame shifting slightly in his seat, looked up at his captain. "Course laid in, Lon."

"Ditto, here," Pelos answered.

"Okay, Imatt," Arlon said. "I'll take what information we know, and our theories, and see what else we can uncover from our end. Stay in touch."

Kish watched the GBI agent's face fade from her screen, and she returned Lon's picture to the normal full-screen mode. "We're all set here, Lon."

Lon nodded. "Let's see what we can find."

Arano peeked around the edge of the windowsill, trying to get a better view of the enemy approach. With all the patrols set against them, he knew it was inevitable that someone would eventually explore the little abandoned cabin. He waited, motionless, for signs of movement. His patience was rewarded soon enough, when a group of five New Dawn soldiers slipped through the woods from tree to tree, tactically approaching their shelter. Without looking away, Arano motioned to his companions, and he heard the whispered reply.

Dartok slipped to his side, as silent as smoke, nearly startling Arano with his approach. "There seems to be no one else around us—just the group you're seeing out there. What do you think?"

Pennon knelt in the doorway to the room, where he could watch the front door and still talk to his companions. "Should we shoot them right after they step out of the woods?"

Arano shook his head. "No," he hissed. "The killing zone is too small. If we try it, odds are one of them will make it back to the trees, and we'll have a serious fight on our hands."

"And we need to prevent them from calling for help," Dartok said, understanding.

"What we need to do is take tactical advantage of the situation," Arano said. "Are you certain there are no other troops in the immediate area?"

Garda nodded, double-checking the data on his scanner. "Absolutely."

"Okay. We send one person out the back door. The roof is made of clay and stone, so it should be easy to climb around on it without alerting the enemy."

"I'll do it," Garda said, leaning into the doorway. "I'm the lightest, anyway."

"Get into position, but stay back to the center of the roof. Allow them to pass on their way in. If any of them run back out, take them down, but just be sure of your targets before you fire." He continued monitoring the approach of the Bromidians outside, patiently allowing them to come closer. "We will allow them into the cabin, and we'll deal with them in here. Don't let anyone escape, Garda. You have the most important function here."

"You're going to let them come in uncontested?" Pennon asked.

Arano smiled and held up one finger. "In order to check this cabin, they will have to come closer, but closer is not always better. In this case, the defender has the element of surprise. Allowing them inside takes away their ability to seek shelter in the trees. By the time they realize we are here, at least two of them will be dead, and the others will have nowhere to go. If they try to run, Garda can cut them to pieces."

Garda nodded, and with Forle's help, slipped out a rear window and climbed onto the roof. Arano positioned his remaining soldiers in strategically hidden positions, placing himself in the most dangerous position at the base of their defense. He would be the one to initiate fire, drawing the enemy's attention to himself. From there, he would have to depend upon Dartok and the others.

A thump on the cabin's outside wall told Arano the group had arrived. The supposition was confirmed when the rusty hinges once again creaked their protests against the opening of the main door. Light footsteps echoed in the hall outside, coming closer in a measured cadence and stopping just outside the door to Arano's room. He slid down behind the bed, exposing just enough of his body to allow him to see the approaching boots of his hunters as they neared the room. One stepped over the threshold, while the next two stood side by side in the open doorway. The afternoon sunlight, pouring in through the open window, glinted dully off their pistols and set small reflections dancing on the walls.

Arano brought his weapon to bear and thrust out into the open. His first shot took the lead Bromidian squarely in the chest, knocking him back into his companions. Smoke rose from the gaping wound as his body fell limply to the floor. The next two Bromidians, frozen in a moment of startled panic, were trapped in the open doorway, where they were immediately cut down by a vicious barrage. The remaining two dove for cover, returning fire and trying to coordinate a retreat. Arano slipped from his place of cover and set up behind the doorjamb, allowing him a better field of fire. From the rapidly evolving firefight, he knew his companions were doing the same.

A sharp cry of pain from Arano's right had him biting off an angry curse. He couldn't take the time or the risk to check on Pennon; they must deal with the immediate threat first. With the cessation of incoming fire from that side, the two attackers saw their opening. They dodged to Arano's right, making it safely to the entryway in a hail of laser fire. In a burst, they dashed out the open door, sprinting for the cover of the trees. They only made the first two steps to freedom before Garda cut one of them down, her shot taking him full in the back. When the other spun and took aim on Garda, Arano's pistol barked once more, and the last soldier fell.

Arano dashed around the corner, shouting to Dartok as he went, telling him to check on the Bromidian soldiers and make certain they were dead. He found Pennon in a crumpled heap behind a low stone half-wall, a deep, charred hole in the center of his chest. His breath was coming in short, labored gasps, and Arano knew he didn't have long.

"I'm . . . sorry, Viper. I . . . I exposed myself too much . . . wanted to take the shot—" He broke off, wheezing sharply and unable to draw enough breath to speak.

"It's okay," Arano told him, taking the dying man's blood-soaked hand in his. "You killed him. With your help, we killed them all."

Pennon managed a weak smile, and Arano leaned closer. "I guess we did all right," Pennon whispered. "Lanala will be

proud . . ." His hand slid limply from Arano's grasp, and his eyes
went blank. Arano gently closed the soldier's eyelids, composed the
body on the floor, and stood up, grimly facing his companions.

"Pennon didn't make it," he said softly.

Dartok stepped past Arano, taking in the situation at a
glance. "You've done all you can here, Viper. We won't be able
to do anything with the body this time. We must leave, as soon
as we can."

Arano nodded, turning his gaze back to the lifeless form at
his feet. "Let's gather whatever equipment we can salvage from
their team, and we'll get going."

Arano returned to the first soldier he had shot, thinking he
recognized a certain pouch on the man's pistol belt. He was rewarded when he found a small gray pack, the Bromidian rune
for explosives embroidered on the outside. He retrieved the contents and laid them on the floor, telling Dartok and the others to
drag the enemy bodies over near the door. Arano's trained eye
scanned the items before him, and he decided upon the manual
detonator to perform his task. With the detonator and the explosives in hand, Arano rejoined his friends at the doorway.

While the Bromidians looked on curiously, Arano placed the
explosives in the midst of the pile of bodies. He connected one
end of the detonator cord to an igniter cap, and attached the
other end to the detonator. The mechanism of activation was
simple: pull the ring at the top of the detonator, and a charge
would be sent to the igniter, setting off the explosion. All he
needed was a way to activate the detonator.

His gaze fell upon the boots the dead Bromidians were wearing. With a little help, Arano removed their bootlaces and strung
them together into a long cord. He attached one end to the detonator, ran it across the floor and around the leg of a heavy chair,

and brought it back to the door. He made a loop with the free end of the bootlace chain, securing it into a self-tightening knot and hooking it around the inside door latch. After motioning the others outside, Arano joined them, pulling the door most of the way shut. He stretched his fingers through the opening, gingerly tugged until the string was taut, and pulled the door shut, grimacing as if he expected the bomb to explode.

He released the door and stood frozen in place for several beats of his racing heart, his hands hovering inches from the latch. Turning to his companions, he motioned for Dartok to take the point position once more. They continued their original westerly course, and while Dartok frequently looked to Arano for signs of danger, he held their steady pace toward safety.

About an hour later, the echoing rumble of a distant explosion reached their ears, rolling endlessly over the forested hills. Arano smiled grimly, knowing there was one less patrol looking for them. He hitched his pack a little higher, trying to relieve the stress of the added weight. They had recovered a number of important items, not the least of which was in Garda's hands. She had the military radio up to her ear, keeping the volume low but monitoring the progress of the enemy's search. She caught Arano's eye and nodded reassuringly; the enemy was no closer to locating them.

Alyna followed the bulky form of Videre, prowling through the tall weeds along the riverbank. Mendan was just ahead of Videre, helping guide the patrol in their efforts to locate their missing friends. A small ditch, about a meter deep and two across, blocked their path, and they had to scramble through it, struggling for a firm foothold on terrain still slick with the previous night's melted frost.

They emerged from the ditch, passed through a stubborn hedgerow of thorny trees, and found themselves in a farmer's field. The crops had been recently harvested, and the tilled ground made for difficult walking. By the time they had crossed the kilometer-wide field, Alyna was panting heavily with the effort. When Mendan offered to take a rest break, however, she immediately declined. She was fatigued, to be sure, between the all-night mission and the forced march they had undergone thus far, but she wouldn't allow herself to stop. Arano might need her, and every second could mean the difference between life and death.

A few minutes later, Mendan called the column to a halt. "Alyna, we must rest. You will do Viper no good if you collapse on the way, and we have to carry both of you out of here. My troops will scout the area, and we can decide on a course of action when they return."

She nodded glumly, seeing the wisdom of his words. Lain flopped onto a fallen tree beside her, offering her a drink of water. She accepted gratefully, and the two of them sat together, silently awaiting the return of Mendan's Latyrians. Videre had, of course, volunteered to reconnoiter the area with them, and he had left immediately.

"I think I need a drink," Alyna complained, massaging some feeling into her legs.

Lain smiled. "I think I'm ready for another of Arano's parties." He saw the halfhearted smile in her eyes, and he placed a green, reassuring hand on her arm. "We're going to find him, Alyna. That's a promise."

Alyna's lower lip trembled lightly. "Thank you, Lain." She

looked to the sky, gathering her strength for what was to come.

A powerful explosion rocked the afternoon, far away but echoing dully across the rolling countryside. Alyna and Lain dove for cover, their pistols jumping reflexively into their hands. Mendan and his rear guard joined them, forming a defensive perimeter and watching the encompassing landscape. They were still surrounded by the tall weeds, which Lentin had once called nala grass, and it limited their field of view. Alyna kept a watchful eye on Mendan, who was coordinating the return of his scouts.

As each Latyrian neared their camp, they used their unique ability to make and hear sounds outside the normal range of hearing of the other races, and they guided each other to safety. Videre's return, however, prompted a different response. He was unable to communicate with the Latyrians guarding the perimeter, and he materialized from the weeds to find himself staring down the barrels of several laser rifles. They lowered their weapons with relief, and the Gatoan Avenger joined Alyna and Lain.

"Before you ask, Alyna, I had nothing to do with it!" he said, holding out his hands in protest. "I was just as surprised as you. I can tell you, though, those were Bromidian military explosives."

Mendan slipped to their side. "My scouts have a fix on the general direction of the blast. It appears to be due east of our location."

Alyna managed a weak smile. "Lead on."

CHAPTER
SEVENTEEN

THEY SKULKED THROUGH THE TREES IN A TENSE, wordless trek, their enemy left behind but still on the hunt. The trees had thinned out, and what had been forested hills was giving way to an open prairie. Instead of a continuous cover of blanketing canopy, Arano's group was reduced to patches of trees separated by lands open to the sky. During those interludes between parcels of woods, where they had nothing to hide in but the waist-high weeds, Arano felt naked, vulnerable. Each time, he listened intently for the expected sound of approaching hovercars, but the afternoon passed without sight of the enemy.

They reached yet another open field, this one wider than the others had been. The nala grass was much thicker than he expected; apparently, the farmer had allowed the field to lie fallow. Dartok had warned them to expect wide open spaces, since their initial blind flight had taken them too far south and they were leaving the heart of the forest behind them. Backtracking and moving farther north, however, was out of the question. They had initially tried doing just that, but they had gone less than half a kilometer when Arano felt the prickling sensation which could only mean one thing. They decided to trust their luck where they were, sticking to the trees when possible. Obviously, their hunters expected Arano to keep his group in the sheltering cover of the trees, so they weren't checking this far south.

As he had each time before, Dartok paused at the edge of the trees, sweeping the field before him with a pair of binoculars. Apparently, he was satisfied and tucked the binoculars safely away in his pack. They moved from the woodland into the soft, muddy field, holding their weapons ready while nervously traversing the meadowland. To an observer, they would appear almost paranoid, the way all four of them constantly looked over their shoulders, to their sides, and even overhead. He shifted his pack, trying to keep the laser rifle strapped to the top from jabbing him in the back of the head.

The warning from his danger sense came much more quickly than it usually did, and in the back of Arano's mind he surmised that a chance event had placed them in harm's way. They had shifted direction slightly, angling more to their right in an effort to reenter the cover of the trees about fifty meters sooner. Perhaps something so simple had caused a problem.

Arano hissed his warning, and the group stopped. They knelt, trying to disturb the weeds around them as little as possible. Of course, if the threat was from skimmers, they would be spotted anyway. He listened intently, but could hear nothing other than the normal sounds of the countryside: the cry of a lonely bird of prey circling overhead, the endless chittering of small furry creatures racing to store their supply of food before the onset of winter. No, it had to be something on the ground.

The minutes ticked away, and while the feeling of danger eased somewhat, it didn't entirely pass. He caught Dartok's eye and shrugged, indicating his complete confusion. The threat was still there, but lying in the middle of a field wouldn't solve the problem. They needed to move, and they needed to do so rapidly, to reach the relative safety of the trees. Following Dartok's lead, they rose to their feet and, staying in a low crouch, glided across the meadow, weapons sweeping back and forth across the countryside. Arano's sense of danger grew ever stronger.

It was Forle who cried out a sharp warning, stopping them all in mid-stride. A long, black snake had arisen from the grass, fixing Forle with a baleful stare. The mouth opened wide, and a low, warning hiss emerged. It bared a pair of long, curved fangs, dripping with venom, and a pink forked tongue flickered in and out of sight. Forle was frozen in place, unable to move, transfixed by the spectacle before him. Arano shouted, trying to break the spell, and rushed forward to get a clear shot at the snake.

"Cantha snake!" Dartok shouted, taking aim and firing. His shots went wide, the narrow body of the snake proving a difficult target to hit. Arano drew within ten feet and saw the hideously long body concealed in the grasses of the plain. Fully two meters of the cantha snake reared above the ground, but there were easily another four meters of its length on the ground. It swayed threateningly to and fro, and Forle managed to bring his weapon to bear. His pistol fired once, then fell from his fingers when the snake struck, fangs biting deeply through his hard exoskeleton. He staggered back, falling to his knees, breathing in rapid, labored gasps.

Dartok's aim was the first to prove true, and the snake writhed in pain. It twisted around to face its new assailant, and Dartok was forced to give ground. Arano saw his chance to make a mad dash for Forle's side and pull him to safety. Somehow, Dartok saw Arano's plan and shouted his warning.

"Arano, no! Canthas are pack hunters, and their bite is deadly. If this one is here, there are likely at least four or five more in our area. Forle is lost to us! We have to get out of here!"

Arano felt a cold pit in his stomach, and one look at Forle told him Dartok was right. He fired into the grass just beyond the hissing and spitting snake, and two more canthas reared their scaly heads. Dartok fired on them, trying to keep them at bay until Arano and Garda could circle behind him. Once they were together, the three of them sprinted away from the melee, leaving their less fortunate comrade in his death throes at the mercy of the hissing reptiles.

They reached the relative safety of the trees, not slowing until they had covered another two hundred yards. Arano allowed them to rest for a few minutes, dropping their weighty packs and stretching their legs. Sensing Arano's questions, Dartok volunteered the answers.

"The cantha snake has a powerful neurotoxin in its venom. Their usual hunting method is for one snake to reveal itself, attack its prey, and wait. If anything challenges the lone snake, there are typically several others waiting to help out. Many Bromidians have died trying to rescue friends who have been bitten, only to be attacked themselves."

Arano stared at the ground and swallowed hard. "How long does it take?"

"Several minutes, usually. Their poison attacks the autonomic systems of the body last, which allows the heartbeat and breathing to continue. It first prevents the victim from fighting or running, rendering them completely helpless. As a side-effect, the person bitten lies on the ground thrashing, which tends to draw companions in to try and help. They themselves usually end up getting bitten, at that point."

"That's a nasty snake," Arano said, shaking his head. "With enough intelligence to coordinate their attacks with other snakes, that is a dangerous creature, indeed." He stared at his pack, shrugging the pain from his shoulders and trying to focus his thoughts.

"Is there something else, Viper?"

Arano managed a weak smile. "Yes. Before he died, Pennon told me he hoped Lanala would be pleased. Do you know who she is? If she's family, I'd like to be there to break the news to her about his death."

Dartok chuckled softly, the laughter seeming odd coming from his guttural voice. "Lanala is the closest thing we Bromidians have to a deity. All the known races trace their ancient ancestry to various members of the animal kingdom: Humans and Padians go back to primates, Gatoans to feline predators, and Kamlings to swamp-dwelling amphibians. Bromidians come from a large insect-like creature, originally crawling about on six legs, evolving to become bipedal, and eventually losing the extra pair of arms. As such, we have a hive mentality ingrained in our consciousness. Hives are always headed by a queen, and ours was no exception. In our religion, Lanala is our symbolic queen.

"Religion has faded into the background for most Bromidians. We rarely talk about it, and there are few remaining houses of worship. Maybe that's part of our problem. We became too secularized, and we've lost our way."

Arano shrugged, not sure how to phrase an answer. "It's possible, I suppose. If we all got back to basics, and were more concerned with protecting what is ours than taking what belongs to someone else, there would no longer be a need for such as you and me."

They pressed deeper into the woods, maintaining their westerly track but trying to stay well back from the edge of the trees. Arano couldn't erase the image of Forle thrashing about in agony, the deadly snakes closing in for the kill. A somber mood settled over him, and he struggled to maintain his mental edge. There were but three of them now, so he had to stay sharp and try to ensure they all survived. In a moment of blunt realization, he concluded how important it was for Dartok to return to the camp alive. Arano had Dartok's unwavering support, and when the others who still distrusted him saw Dartok's change of heart, it would likely make all the difference in the world.

They marched for another hour before Arano once again became aware of an unknown threat. He snapped his fingers and knelt, craning his neck to see if anyone was approaching from behind. He could hear nothing, but he knew the enemy was out there. A part of him felt relief; he had worried, at the outset of the insurrection, that his ability to sense danger had been dulled by months spent in an office environment. This mission had proved, however, just how sharp his senses remained.

The distant hum of hovercars came to his ears, approaching rapidly from the west. He lay flat and crawled closer to the others. "They can't have found us by sensors. The delvonite is still scrambling their readings. There must be something else."

Garda looked around sharply, trying to see the approaching threat. "It could be anything. A scout, motion sensors—anything could be alerting them."

"Or the fight with the cantha snakes," Dartok added. "We fired our weapons at them, for whatever good it did. I'm sure the shots were picked up by their sensors, with or without the delvonite."

Arano surveyed the lands around them, deciding on a course of action. "Follow me," he ordered tersely, staying low to the ground and crawling up the slope of the ridge to their right. On his hands and knees, pistol safely tucked back into its holster, he made the torturous climb, stopping just below the summit. The trees near the top of the ridge had thicker trunks, providing excellent cover should they have to fight their way to safety, while the boughs of brown leaves swaying gently overhead would conceal them from the rapidly approaching airships. Telling the others to stay where they were, Arano completed the climb and peered into the draw on the north side of the ridge.

He saw more of the same: endless trees and a more gradual slope than on the side they had just ascended. Judging by the tops of the trees, the wind seemed stronger on the northern side of the hill, giving the chilly air a definite bite. He spotted another defensible position and returned to Dartok's side. Garda slid over next to them.

"I think we're surrounded," Arano told them. "The airships are circling the area, trying to pinpoint exactly where we are."

Garda frowned, stress evident in her wrinkled brow. "They're maintaining radio silence. I can't hear a thing."

Arano nodded in acknowledgement, biting his lip, eyes darting around the hillside. "About fifty yards west of here, there's a narrow ravine running from the top of the ridge down the south slope. It's deep enough to provide safe defensive positions, so I want you two fighting from there. I'll watch the approach from the north. Try to keep out of sight, because it would be nice if they would just pass on by. But with that in mind, don't be afraid to fire first if discovery seems inevitable."

Keeping below the top of the ridgeline in order to avoid silhouetting himself against the late afternoon sky, Arano crawled west along the hillside. It was a painstaking process, having to lift each hand and foot carefully so as not to dislodge leaves and other deadfall, but still moving hastily enough to be in position before the enemy arrived. They reached the ravine, and Arano surveyed the southern slope from their new vantage point. He scrutinized the terrain, pointing out to his two Bromidian companions what the enemy's likely avenue of approach would be, and warning them of areas below that would provide their foes with cover.

Arano left Dartok and Garda and crossed the top of the ridge once again. Luckily, he found a convenient tree almost immediately. He guessed the diameter at two meters, and the irregularity of its circumference served his needs perfectly. He could step inside several different depressions in the trunk, affording him a decent amount of cover without restricting his view or line of fire. He dropped his pack from his weary shoulders and removed his rifle. The waiting began anew.

The agonizing seconds ticked past, and still there was no sign of their hunters. Gradually, like the steady rise in ambient light from a Leguin sunrise on a sultry summer day, his perception of danger grew in intensity. He wished they had a way to communicate with each other. Even though they were only about thirty meters apart, if would be extremely difficult to talk to each other loudly enough to be heard yet quietly enough to avoid giving away their location.

The waiting came to a sudden end with an eruption of laser rifle fire on the other side of the ridge. Furious volleys blasted away, and Arano swore in frustration at not being able to help his friends. He risked a better look from behind his tree, sticking his head out into full view of anyone who might be approaching but saw nothing. He ducked back into his shelter and made up his mind. There might be an enemy on his side, but they still hadn't joined the fight. Those to the south of his location had, and his friends needed help.

Arano shifted his weight to leap out of his shelter and cross the ridge to join the fight, but he received a jolting warning from his danger sense. He pulled back against the trunk, just in time to avoid a deadly blast of laser fire that ripped into the hillside where he had been standing. Tossing his hat to the left, he drew their fire again, then jumped to the right, rolled, and came up firing from his knees. Two Bromidians were shooting from a position about fifty meters away, visible only due to the bursts of energy coming from their rifles. Arano opened fire on them, and one of them dropped his weapon to fall, unmoving, on the forest floor.

They were joined by over a dozen other Bromidians, some of them firing on Arano and others maneuvering for a better angle. Arano kept them guessing about where he would appear next, rushing from one side of the tree to the other, sometimes firing from a prone position and sometimes climbing into the tree's lowest branches, always trying his best to keep them from flanking him. Three more fell victim to his barrage, but then the others formed into two separate groups, each covering for the other and allowing one another to move closer with greater ease. He did what he could to slow them down but knew it was only a matter of time before he was overrun.

From the other side of the hill, a cornucopia of laser fire rang out, followed by disconcerted shouting and screams of pain and terror. He couldn't take the time, or the risk, to see what had happened, and he knew he had to depend on Dartok and Garda to hold successfully. The shooting increased in intensity, followed by a sudden silence. Arano gave a low snarl, certain his friends had been killed or captured. If that was true, then his defeat was inevitable. He prepared to sell himself as dearly as possible, knowing what regimes like those under Gorst IX did to prisoners, and vowed not to be taken alive just to be tortured and executed. He dodged to the right, firing from ground level and taking a surprised Bromidian in the center of his chest. He didn't even watch his enemy fall, instead shifting his fire farther to the right.

A movement caught his eye, someone moving atop the ridge.

He spun around, weapon leveled, and was shocked to see Dartok roll over the top of the hill and tumble down to Arano's side. He stood, insectoid face split by a broad grin. Arano's eyebrows shot up, and he regarded his friend silently for a brief moment, trying to catch his breath.

The moment passed, and a new force entered the battle. At least a dozen Bromidians swept over the ridge, some to Arano's east and some to his west, and they engaged the New Dawn forces in an ambush, catching several of them in the open. The surprised enemy pulled back, trying to regroup and avoid the trap closing in around them. Garda led a charge from Arano's left, and some of the enemy rose from hiding to run in panic but were cut to pieces by the merciless rain of fire from the other group. Arano looked back to the first squad, just in time to see Garda dart from behind a tree. She raised her rifle, but a brilliant laser beam ripped through her abdomen, knocking her to her knees, and she slid limply to the ground.

Arano and Dartok rushed to her side, but they were too late. Life had fled her crumpled body, and she lay in a pool of thick, black blood. Some distant part of Arano's mind casually noted how the laser had failed to cauterize her lower left abdominal artery. The bleeding had stopped, however, with the beating of her heart. Dartok took Arano firmly by the arm and led him back to the top of the ridge.

"We can't help her, my friend. It's time to go. There are some people waiting for you."

Numbly, Arano retrieved his pack and crested the hill a final time. The sounds of the firefight to the north faded into the distance as the government troops fled, pursued by those who had just rescued him. He dropped back into the ravine and was smothered in hugs from his wife.

"Alyna! What are you—"

"Saving your hide, it looks like," she said, squeezing him all the more tightly.

"No charge." Arano knew it was Videre's comment before the proud Gatoan extended a firm handshake. "I think we have it cleared on this side. Our Latyrian friends shot down two hovercars, and the third one found a pressing reason to be somewhere else."

Arano gave Videre a double take, eyes going wide. "What? Latyrians? What are they doing here?"

"Killing Bromidians, it looks like," Videre said, shading his eyes as if he were looking over the hilltop into the battleground beyond.

Lain Baxter smiled, running one hand over the row of bumps on his amphibian-like head. "We found some old friends. Mendan, Vantir, and Enton are all here, and they brought about two hundred warriors with them. We've divided them up between the camps, and we're working on adding their unique abilities to our battle plans."

Videre bowed grandly. "With your kind permission, of course."

The two Assault Class Fighters slowed to a stop, using their tractor beams to hold their position relative to the freighter. While it had appeared, back in the Trum System, that the freighter had been ripped in two by the intense gravimetric forces of the collapsing wormhole, it had, in fact, remained in one piece.

Of course, that's only if you consider this mess to be one piece.

The ship was divided across its midsection, and only a few twisted lengths of metal kept the two halves from drifting apart.

"Pelos," Kish said quietly, "scan for life-signs." The silent

Tsimian turned to his panel, pressed a few controls, and sat back in his chair, awaiting a response. He stared at the screen, shaking his head slowly back and forth, doubtful that anyone was left alive. Finally, the computer in front of him emitted three staccato beeps, and he spun slowly in his chair.

"Nothing," he told her solemnly. "There's no one left alive on the entire ship."

Kish swallowed hard, regarding the crushed, buckled mess before them on the viewscreen. To die in ship-to-ship combat was one thing. That was a risk they all understood, whether they were soldiers, terrorists, or pirates. But to die in a gravimetric field run amok . . . The agony of such a death was nearly unthinkable. She slapped the activator switch on her Comm, opening the channel to the *Grappler*. The picture on the viewscreen dissolved from the wreckage of the freighter into the grim face of Lon Pana.

"Lon, we're not picking up any signs of survivors."

"Same here," he replied. "Do you think it's safe to send boarders?"

"We're about to find out," she said. "Why don't you have your squad stay on the *Grappler* as an emergency response team? I'll take Pelos and Imatt and see what we can find."

"Do you have an extra environmental suit? You lost a boot back in the Trum System, as I recall."

Kish sighed, a rueful smile appearing on one side of her mouth. "Yes, we do. It's a little big for me, but it'll work. We'll stay in contact with you the entire time. Let us know if you pick up anything we should know about."

She turned off the Comm, swiveling deftly around in her seat to find that Imatt had already retrieved the environmental suits. They donned the bulky equipment, checked each other for safety, and waddled awkwardly to the airlock. Once inside, Kish activated the controls to seal the airlock from the rest of the ship. A warning klaxon sounded, accompanied by a flashing red light, and she heard the hiss from the life support system as it removed the air from the dark, confined chamber. The trio activated the magnetic function in their boots, and Kish felt her foot being pulled sharply against the metallic deck. Once the air had been removed from the vestibule, the light flashed again, and the outer airlock doors crawled silently open.

She reached toward the panel on the right thigh of her environmental suit and activated the Comm. "Lon, can you hear me?"

"Loud and clear, Kish. You ready to go?"

"Airlock is open, preparing to disengage magnetics."

They shuffled heavily to the threshold of the ship, and Kish felt somewhat disoriented by the vast emptiness before them. The *Summerwind* vibrated noticeably, and the blue nimbus surrounding the ship told Kish that the *Grappler* was using its tractor beam to guide them closer to the derelict freighter. Distances in open space were extremely difficult to judge, given the lack of perspective, so she had to rely on Lon to pull them in close, but not to the point they risked a collision. Several anxious heartbeats later, the vibrating stopped, and Lon's voice came over the Comm.

"Okay, Kish. It's all yours. Keeping the Comm line open."

Kish and her teammates joined hands, leaned forward, and pushed off sharply. They drifted closer to the freighter, their slight rotation telling Kish someone had either pushed earlier or harder than the other two. Nonetheless, after drifting across the chasm, they reached the wrecked outer hull of the ship. They reactivated their magnetic boots, and Kish pointed in the general direction of the breach and began the arduous process of walking on the outer hull of a ship, an act complicated as much by the irregular surface as by the unwieldy motion with the foot required to deactivate a boot and allow that foot to move forward. Kish had the added handicap of the large boot on her injured foot but endured the situation without complaining.

With practice, the trek became easier, and they reached the gaping hole in what used to be the ship's midsection. Kish found herself wishing they practiced more often in zero-gravity environments, which would help to eliminate some of their clumsiness. Climbing inside proved to be a challenge as well, not only from trying to climb across the twisted metal but also protecting their suits from snagging and tearing on some sharp protrusion. They managed to clamber through the opening without mishap and activated their portable scanners.

Kish waited patiently, watching the display on her scanner repeat what her ship's scanner had already told her: no one was left alive. They padded maladroitly into the ship's interior, prudently avoiding areas where the bulkhead or decking had buckled under the tremendous strain from the wormhole's collapse. The Comm hissed in her ear, and Lon's static-filled voice came over her helmet speaker.

"We're not able to detect any independent power sources in there. We have three life-signs, obviously yours, and the energy signature from your environmental suits. You find anything yet?"

"Nothing, and we're not even reading any residual power sources. I'd say this ship was dead in space before it even came out of the wormhole."

"Should we split up?" Imatt asked. "We could cover the ship much more quickly that way."

Kish shook her head. "I don't want to take the chance. If one of us gets in trouble, we'll need help there ASAP. Let's take our time on this. Lon, can you get a readout on the schematics?"

"Stand by."

After a few moments of near silence during which all Kish could hear was her own breathing, Vic Dermak answered her question. "I've got it here, Kish. What are you looking for?"

Kish licked her lips, dehydrated by the dry air in her suit. "Let's start with the bridge. From there, if we don't find anything, we can check the engineering section and maybe even the engines. We'll save the hold for last."

"Okay. The hold is in the other half of the ship, so getting there will be tricky. As for the bridge . . ." She heard him tapping his control panel, and the computer beeping in response. "Straight ahead about twenty meters; then turn left. You'll have to climb up two levels on the maintenance ladder since the power for the lifts is out. If you can get the doors open at the top, you'll be on the bridge."

"Got it." She increased the brightness setting on her helmet-mounted light, and with an effort they tottered along the hallway. Reaching the lift doors, they tried vainly to pry them open. Pelos set his impressive strength against the sealed portals, trying to pry the doors apart with a discarded metal shaft, but Imatt put up a restraining hand.

"Hold on, Pelos. Look over here." Kish followed the GBI agent's pointing finger, and her gaze fell upon the buckled wall beside the doors. The forces that had destroyed the ship had also ensured the doors would never open again.

"There's another way," Pelos grumbled, panting a little from exertion. While Kish and Imatt stepped a few paces back, Pelos drew his laser pistol and set it for its highest output level. They lowered the filters over their face masks, which were normally used to protect their faces from the severe and potentially deadly rays of a nearby star. Pelos activated the trigger, and an intense beam of light struck the doors. Even with the filter in place, Kish squinted, her eyes not prepared for the intense light. After a few seconds, she found she could watch the procedure without discomfort and saw the cut Pelos had made in the door. Using his metal rod as a ram, Pelos knocked aside the barrier and exposed the lift shaft. The cutaway section of the door drifted ponderously aside, gently rebounding from the wall to drift eerily about in the narrow shaft.

Kish poked her head through the opening, looking first up to the bridge area, then down below them. Luckily, the lift car was near the bottom of the shaft and wouldn't be an obstruction. She climbed through the opening with painstaking care, not wanting to chance a suit rupture from the glowing hot metal where Pelos had cut through. Once she reached the ladder, she deactivated her magnetic boots, gave a gentle push, and floated gracefully to the top level.

"Nice," Imatt said admiringly. He and Pelos followed her up, and the three floated together outside the entrance to the bridge. The doors at the top of the shaft were jammed open, eliminating the necessity of cutting through again. Kish pushed off the back wall and floated onto the bridge, activating her boots and alighting with a metallic *clank* that reverberated through her suit. Imatt and Pelos landed beside her, and together they surveyed the bridge.

Computers lay smashed on the floor, the ceiling bent askew and coming within a meter of the deck on the far side of the room. The captain's chair had been smashed nearly flat, still connected by a few unbroken conduits. Kish checked her scanner, and as she had expected, it indicated the complete lack of an atmosphere. She swung her light back and forth, trying without success to find an undamaged panel. She felt the rhythmic vibrations in the deck from her teammates as they moved about the bridge, inspecting the ruined equipment.

"Kish, over here." Imatt's voice was low, almost inaudible.

She moved awkwardly to his side and looked down where his helmet light was shining. Dried blood covered the floor, and small chunks of flesh and bone dotted the stain. They panned their lights around, finding several similar stains, some on the floor, others on the walls, and even one on the ceiling.

She sighed. "Pelos, can you find any memory crystals or datachips we can take with us? Maybe we can analyze them on our ship, or even back at headquarters."

She watched dispassionately while Pelos used the tools from his pack to access the various computer panels. Some he was able to pry open; others he had to cut with a small torch. He managed to recover three datachips from the wreckage of the bridge, and they retreated to the lift shaft. Duplicating their method of ascension, Kish deactivated her boots, inverted herself, and pushed herself down the shaft. She debated that for a moment, amused by the duality of the definitions of "up" and "down." In a null-gravity environment, "up" could mean just about any direction, as long as it was away from her feet. She shrugged off the distracting physics of the situation, caught herself by the access to the main level, and swung through the opening.

They had no success in reaching the engine compartment. The crushing forces of the wormhole appeared to have been concentrated there, and the aft areas of the freighter had been compressed to the point of inaccessability. They were forced to leave the engines to the recovery team already enroute from Immok and made their way to Engineering. It was more readily accessible, but the computer terminals had been smashed with a ferocity that left no doubt as to the survivability of the data they had once held. Three more piles of remains were found near the main engineering station. Pelos conducted a brief, inefficacious search, and they returned to their entry point.

"Lon, this is Kish. We're at the breach, preparing to access the other section."

"I copy that. Give me a moment to increase power to the tractor beam. I want to make the two pieces as immobile as possible while your squad is crossing between them." There were a few seconds of silence, during which Kish could hear Lon's muffled instructions to his crew; then the Comm crackled back to life. "Okay, Kish, it's all yours."

She studied the gap sundering the ship, the two halves separated by about forty meters of vacuum. There were three metal beams still connected to both sections, but two of them appeared not only unstable but peppered with protruding chunks of jagged metal. She dismissed those as routes; it would only require a single misstep for one of them to rip an environmental suit, with potentially fatal results.

The third beam, however, was the main beam along the keel of the vessel and looked to be relatively intact. There were few obstructions, and it seemed to be the safest method for crossing the opening. Kish deactivated her magnetic boots and pulled herself along the edge of the breach, meticulously avoiding the jagged metal. She reached the keel beam safely, and magnetized her boots to its broad expanse.

It was a dizzying spectacle, and Kish found the entire experience to be quite disorienting. While her footwear was being pulled firmly against the metallic surface, the rest of her body was free-floating. She looked down to confirm her footing on the meter-wide beam, gauged the distance left to the other side, and checked on her squadmates. Glancing to the right, she gazed into the vast desolation of space, and suddenly wished she hadn't. She became dizzy, head spinning with vertigo, and forced herself to concentrate her vision on the beam beneath her feet.

Kish reached the far side, then carefully climbed through an aperture in front of her, opening the path to the ship's cargo hold.

CHAPTER EIGHTEEN

ARANO AWOKE WITH THE SUN, LYING ON HIS BACK for a time and relaxing. The tent he shared with his wife glowed with the pale morning light, framing Alyna's face with an angelic halo. The heater kept the tent's interior at a comfortable temperature, eliminating the need for heavy blankets. He traced a finger lightly along Alyna's hairline, and her eyes fluttered open.

"Don't you ever sleep?" she asked with an impish grin, rising sensually from beneath their covers.

Arano was about to respond when the tent flap whispered open and Videre's head poked through, sending Alyna diving back undercover with a startled *whoop!*

Arano smiled at his wife's modesty. "Didn't anyone ever teach you to knock?" he asked with a laugh.

Videre feigned innocence. "On what? This is a canvas tent. Besides, I didn't see much. By the way, before I forget, we just had a visitor from Notron. The Tycon Mar has compromised one of our clerics, so we need to plan a rescue. She's in hiding, but we don't know how long she has before they locate her. As secret police forces go, they seem to be fairly efficient, so we'll need to move quickly."

Arano pursed his lips and nodded. "I'd hoped to get some rest today, but it looks like that won't be happening." He gave Alyna a studied glance, then faced Videre again. "We'll be out in a few minutes."

Videre gave a short laugh. "We will anxiously await your arrival." He pulled back from the tent but thrust his head back inside. "Alyna, you need to get out in the sun more. Your tan lines are really fading." He darted away from the tent, just in time to avoid her boot as it hurtled toward the opening.

Later that morning, they gathered in a council. Representatives of each RLF cell were present, as well as the entire membership of Arano's resistance coterie. More importantly, several influential Bromidians were in attendance. These were men and women who had not yet joined the RLF, but were considering it, and who were in a position to bring great numbers of people with them, bolstering the size of the resistance movement. He hated what he was about to do to a man he considered to be a friend, but he knew there was no way to avoid the inevitable.

Arano grimly faced the assemblage. "My friends, we are gathered here on a somber occasion. Hawan, the leader of the Rystorian Liberation Front, has fallen in battle. He died on the streets of Notron, betrayed by one of his own, but loyal to the Rystorian Liberation Front, to the bitter end. He believed in the cause, and he would want the fight to go on.

"I know there are some among you who may wonder if the fight is truly worth it. I've heard the calls for capitulation, for negotiation, and for settlements. I say to you now, if you want freedom, true freedom, you must be strong, you must stand up, and you must fight! Freedom comes at a great cost, and its tale is written in the blood of those who thirst for it.

"Centuries ago, one of the greatest Human military commanders in their history stated that anyone who thinks nothing is worth fighting for, who values nothing over their own personal safety, is a miserable creature with no chance of being free unless made and kept so by his betters. Well, I stand before you today, and I say your freedom is something I value more than my safety, and I am here to fight to recover your freedom. I hope there are those among you today who cherish liberty enough to stand at my side."

A great roar went up from the assemblage, with hundreds of Bromidian fists thrust into the morning sky. A chant of "Viper, Viper!" arose from the throng, ending in a thunderous shout, shaking the platform upon which Arano stood. He let their zeal build, listening to the steadily rising crescendo of the boisterous crowd, then raised his hands for silence.

"Gladly will I continue my role as the primary advisor to the RLF, but I cannot take Hawan's place. His shoes need to be filled by one of his own people, another Bromidian. Whoever leads our group will likely end up in a position of authority in the interim government, and will probably be voted into office when the time comes. The person who takes over the leadership of the RLF needs to be a talented tactician, an experienced veteran, and yet someone without a lust for power. This is a rare person, indeed, but fortunately, I have someone in mind."

With a grand gesture, he slowly pivoted and held out his hand to Lentin. Arano's Bromidian friend managed to turn pale, and he shrank away for a moment. But, as Arano had predicted, Lentin's sense of duty overcame his reluctance, and he stepped resolutely forward.

"I don't believe I'll ever thank you for this, my friend," Lentin said quietly. "I'll eventually forgive you, but I will never thank you."

They clasped forearms, and Arano gave a firm shake. "That's all I can ask, my friend. Rystoria needs you, now more than ever. I'm glad you chose to answer the call."

Lentin managed a weak smile. "At least you could've warned me."

"You would probably be halfway to Immok already."

"True."

Once the ceremonies were over, and those from outside the camp had returned to their respective homes, Arano met privately with the leaders of his cell. He noticed with satisfaction how expeditiously Lentin was adapting to his new role. Already, he was leading the discussion for the rescue of Derna, the Bromidian cleric who was trapped in the city of Notron.

"I want to continue our scheduled raids against New Dawn targets, so the rescue team will have to be made up of whoever we can spare."

"But not you," Arano warned him. "I want you back here, getting things organized. I'll go get her. I can take a few of our Latyrian friends with me and be back before you know it."

"What about us?" Videre asked.

Lentin smiled, although he still had a wild look in his eyes. "I think I know what Arano has in mind. If I'm right, you, Alyna, and Laron will be forming a task force to assault the main New Dawn garrison at Notron. All you will be doing is making a brief but heavy strike on their perimeter before you fall back. We'll put you in position, and if Arano's team is compromised, he can signal you from inside the city. When you make your diversionary attack, fewer soldiers will be available to go after Arano."

Arano clapped a hand on Lentin's broad shoulder. "I couldn't have said it better myself."

Kish slowly circled the shattered hold, letting the light from her helmet spill across the interior and illuminate all that remained of the privateers' cargo. Containers, rated for extreme weights and pressures, lay in ruins, their contents spilled and floating aimlessly about the room. She explored the entire expanse of the cargo area, looking for anything intact which might provide some insight into the activities of the pirates and, ultimately, New Dawn. Some of the debris she readily recognized, such as pieces of energy pistols and rifles. Fortunately, the damage to them was so severe that they would never function again.

"Kish, do you have anything to report?"

"Nothing yet, Lon. We're still conducting our search of the cargo."

"I copy that. We have Avengers HQ on the Comm, requesting an update. They said the salvage team will be here within the hour."

Kish checked the time on her suit's readout. "Okay, we should be done by then anyway."

"I have information about New Dawn, but it can wait until you get back to the ship. Enjoy your stroll."

Kish acknowledged the comment with a short laugh, pushing aside a cargo lid which was floating in front of her helmet. The three of them had been examining the cargo for over thirty minutes, with nothing to show for their efforts. Looking around at the debris field, she realized the cargo was almost immobile. She frowned, kneeling for a different view. For the items to have slowed almost to the point of stopping, they would have to have spent some time ricocheting around the hold, losing speed each time they contacted the ship. It was possible for the remains of different cargo containers to be segregated into separate quadrants of the room. Her team had examined the entire floor without results . . .

She leaned back, affording herself a view of the hold's ceiling, movements hampered by the bulky suit. At first, she could see nothing definite, but after increasing her light's intensity, the ceiling appeared through the debris field, less than ten meters over her head. Without looking away, she found the control pad on her leg and deactivated the magnetic boots, thrusting herself up through the wreckage. She used her arms to stop her ascent when she reached the roof, rolled over, and activated her boots. She stood once more, reorienting her sense of perspective. She methodically searched through the upper levels of the hold, finding the press of debris to be much tighter. Imatt and Pelos joined her, and together they continued their hunt.

It was Imatt who ultimately found what they wanted. He called excitedly to Kish and Pelos, then used his helmet light as a beacon to guide them to him. He held up a sheaf of papers, bundled together in a plastic pouch.

"It's a list of the items they were looking for at the facility on Trum," Imatt told them. "For some reason, they used a handwritten list instead of putting the info on a datapad."

Kish accepted some of the papers from Imatt, examining them under her light. "The datapads they had were small, with closely configured input buttons. It would have been difficult to use them with their environmental suits on, and some of the storage at the Trum facility was out in the elements."

"This is an interesting, if eclectic, list they have," Pelos said softly, paging through the papers in his gloved hands. "Weapons, foodstuffs, raw materials . . . looks like they're stocking up for an army."

"Or a war," Imatt added ominously.

Kish held one page closer to her helmeted face, trying to read the inscriber's handwriting. "This appears to be a medical list, but most of these items are used more for research and experiments than for treating the sick or wounded. I'm not sure why they would need them."

"Perhaps they were researching new biological weapons," Pelos suggested.

"I'm not sure," Kish said, shaking her head in confusion. She handed the papers back to Pelos, who tucked them away in a pack at his waist. "Most of this info appears genetic research." She looked up at her teammates, her double-lidded eyes blinking rapidly. "Let's finish the sweep and get out of here."

With a bit of assistance from Lon's tractor beam, Kish and her squad returned to the *Summerwind*. They doffed the bulky suits, laid out the sheets of paper, and transmitted copies to the *Grappler* before consulting with Lon's squad by a secure FM link.

"Before we delve too deeply into what you found," Lon told them, "let me fill you in on what Command told us. After reviewing the evidence we've uncovered thus far, the High Council ordered a response from both the government and the military. Several teams of Avengers, coordinating with investigations by GBI agents, added more fuel to the fire, so to speak. We have definitely made a connection between the pirates and the emerging group called New Dawn, which apparently is controlled by Gorst IX. Command believes, at best, the attacks against our officials were meant to throw our government into chaos, preventing us from interfering in the coup d'état. Eliminating powerful politicians who supported the war effort could be an effort to keep us sidelined until it's too late for us to act."

Kish leaned forward, resting her elbows on the table in front of her. "What's our response going to be?"

Lon's face darkened. "We aren't exactly declaring war, but

we're close. As soon as the salvage team arrives, we are to join a task force in the Niones System. From there, we're going to launch a strike against the New Dawn forces gathered at Menast 4."

"And what about the new race?" Imatt added, biting his lip in apprehension. "Have they said anything official about them?"

Lon scowled. "Not in an open fashion. They issued an order to report 'anomalous situations,' which is probably a reference to the new race. They won't acknowledge it until they have one to put on display."

Simultaneous warning beeps were emitted from the computers in both ships, and a glance at the controls told Kish there were ships emerging from their wormholes. In the distant darkness of space, several points of light flared briefly and disappeared. Pelos immediately returned to his controls and scanned the incoming vessels.

"It looks like the salvage team," he announced. "There are two freighters, a trio of Tug Class Cruisers, and a fighter escort. Looks like they're not taking any chances." He bent closer to his screen, beak agape in disbelief. "They brought a Raptor Class Frigate with them." He tapped several controls, and Kish could see the ship's identification information scrolling across his screen. Pelos sat back and laughed.

"It's the *Intrepid*," he told them. "They brought us the *Intrepid*."

The subspace Comm squawked to life, and Kish brought the viewscreen online. A furry-skinned Gatoan appeared on the screen, her rank designating her as a captain. "This is Lieutenant Kish Waukee of the *USCS Summerwind*."

The figure on the screen nodded in greeting. "I'm Captain Malona. My task force is here to secure the remains of the freighter." She rolled her eyes and gave a half-smile. "The data you sent showed us two Tug Class Cruisers would be enough to tractor the vessel back to Immok, but Command made us bring three. You know how they can be."

"Do I ever!"

"Anyway, when General Vines learned how many Tugs we were bringing, he had us bring you a gift, this Raptor Class Frigate. He said to let you take it with you, wherever you're going, and we are to tow your assault ships back to Immok with us. Whenever you're finished with that freighter, your ship awaits."

Kish grinned broadly. "We're ready any time you are."

Arano trudged through the ankle-deep snow in apparent disconsolation, hands shoved deeply into his pockets and hood pulled up tightly to ward off the chill. His toes were actually feeling cold, even though the rest of his body was warm. The snow crunched steadily underfoot, echoed by the boots of his five Latyrian companions. They marched on in a chaotic mob, a group of companions out for an evening stroll. The blond hair from the wig Arano wore dangled outside his hood, blowing in the gentle evening breeze. He kept his head down, stealing an occasional glance at where they were going.

They entered a darkened restaurant, choosing seats in the corner and waiting. They ordered an evening meal and chatted quietly among themselves while they waited for their food to arrive. At irregular intervals, customers walked past their table, none of them so much as acknowledging the existence of Arano and his friends. He chewed his food without tasting it, concentrating on surreptitiously discerning the identity of their liaison.

Enton, the Latyrian whose son fought against Arano in the Judgment of Denabin, rose from his seat and approached the bar, ordering a round of drinks for everyone and casually prattling with a tall, thin Bromidian beside him. When the drinks arrived, Enton shook hands with his companion, and Arano noticed he put the hand in his pocket before picking up the tray full of drinks and returning to their table. Their rambling conversation continued for several minutes before Enton retrieved a sheet of paper from the pocket of his cloak and tried to read it inconspicuously. Arano drained his glass to cover his anxiety. Enton finished his note, folded it, and returned it to his pocket.

Enton pushed away from the table and stood up. Arano and the others followed his lead, and they filed out the door into the snow-covered streets. The snow was falling once again, drifting lazily on the gentle evening winds to float feather-like to the ground. It looked like another inch had fallen just while they had been inside, and there was no end in sight. Arano sighed his frustration, watching his breath curl away from him in white tendrils of vapor. Ordinarily, he would have called the mission off. If they were compromised and pursued, the snow would give them away by their footprints. But they were on a strict timetable. Derna had to be rescued as soon as possible.

Enton took several deep breaths, seeming to enjoy the crisp evening air. He slowly spun in a circle, breathing deeply but not saying a word. Finally, he straightened, thrust his hands into his pockets, and motioned with his head for the others to follow him. He walked off to the west, setting a brisk pace and forcing Arano to work to catch up to him. At each intersection, at the entrance to every alley, Enton slowed, breathing deeply once again, before choosing their route. At last, Arano gained a glimmer of understanding. The Latyrians had another ability the Bromidians didn't possess, and that was their ability to deploy a special stinger hormone. While it was completely odorless to the other races, a Latyrian could follow the scent as easily as if someone had drawn him a road map. One of their Latyrian agents must have left a trail of the hormone, from the safe house where Derna was hiding, to the restaurant where they were waiting. Arano smiled at the intricacy of the Latyrians' deception, thinking that the note the other Latyrian had passed him probably told him to follow the trail.

The snowfall increased in intensity, blocking out everything beyond twenty meters. Arano found it to be a mixed blessing; on the one hand, the fresh snowfall would cover the tracks in short order, but the enemy could be following them at a relatively short distance and not be visible. He relaxed, working on regular breathing patterns, and reached out with his senses, trying to find trouble around them. Not detecting any danger, he shrugged and pushed on, following Enton along a narrow street.

They entered a shabbier area of town, with dilapidated buildings and deserted transports. Street signs hung askew from their posts, crumbling in disrepair. Although the ground was blanketed with newly fallen snow, Arano could still tell the sidewalks were decaying, his feet stumbling over unseen cracks and furrows.

Enton slowed his pace, finally stopping before a short flight of stairs descending beneath the sidewalk. He walked carefully down the stairs, hanging onto the handrail for fear of falling on the icy pavement. Arano and the others followed him down to stand in front of a rusty iron door, and Enton stepped up swiftly, pounding on the door in a series of measured strokes. He repeated the pattern, and Arano heard the sound of stirring from beyond the door. Several locks and chains were drawn back; then the door creaked open, the hinges squeaking in protest. No one was visible beyond the open doorway, but Arano assumed there were several armed guards hiding beyond the threshold, alert for signs of deception. He followed Enton inside, and the door swung noisily shut behind him.

The lights slowly came up, and Arano became aware of his surroundings. They were standing in an entryway, a square room approximately ten meters on a side, with no decorations or accoutrements. The room was shrouded in shadows, and in the darkness, Arano could barely discern the shapes of several Bromidian guards. Their weapons were drawn, but held low, not trained directly upon the new arrivals. The lighting gradually intensified, and the bare walls came into focus. There was no furniture in the dour little room, as it appeared to serve more as a redoubt for the defenders than as a place of greeting.

One of the guards holstered his pistol and stepped forward, taking Enton's hand in greeting. "Welcome. I am called Renlon. You have come for the cleric?"

Enton nodded slowly. Renlon glanced at each of them in turn, then spun on his heel wordlessly and opened a small door behind him. They followed him into a narrow but well-lit corridor, which took them to what apparently served as guest quarters. He selected the third door on the right, knocked softly, and entered. Arano and Enton walked in behind him, leaving the door ajar. Derna rose to her feet, harsh Bromidian features seeming slightly pale.

"Viper! I knew you would come. You are a man of your word."

Arano inclined his head, acknowledging her compliment. "If you can gather your possessions, we'll be on our way. The weather is worsening, so you will want to dress warmly."

"It shall be as you say, Viper. Renlon has been kind enough to supply me with the cold weather gear I'll need. If you can give me a moment, I'll be ready to go."

Derna bundled up in a bulky travel cloak, gloves, and a hood, and the entourage stepped back into the snowy night. The wind still wasn't a factor, but the heavy snowfall definitely impeded their progress. They took a different route, fearing someone might have been following their trail in the snow and run right into them. Arano walked close to Derna, explaining to her in a low voice what their plan of action was to leave the city.

Eventually, Arano felt a sense of unease come over him. He ramped up his efforts to watch the surrounding buildings, paying close attention to the darkened windows and shadowy recesses. Enton noticed his dismay and held up one hand to stop the group.

"What is it, Viper?" he asked quietly.

"I don't know. Something threatens us, but it isn't close. I feel . . . danger . . . pressing in around us."

Enton's eyes went flat. "Spread out," he ordered in a harsh whisper, moving closer to Arano. In response to his command, the other Latyrians widened the space between them, covering both sides of the street. Derna, her hands nervously clenching and unclenching, looked first to Arano, then Enton, eyes wide with worry.

"Do not worry, good lady." Enton gave her a reassuring smile. "We are simply being cautious, at this point. Let's keep moving."

The little group moved out once more, everyone keeping a nervous eye on the snowy terrain around them. Arano felt his unease grow and change to a sense of impending peril, and he hissed a warning to the others, pointing them into areas of cover. With a gentle hand, he guided Derna behind him and pointed her to the corner of a nearby shed.

Laser fire pierced the darkness, striking metal and stone targets with explosive eruptions of fire and snow. Arano shoved Derna to the ground, shouting for her to crawl to safety, then rolled behind a broken light pole and assessed the threat. Two

Latyrians lay unmoving in the snow, bodies almost concealed by the fluffy whiteness. Most of the incoming fire seemed to be originating from a single building in front of them. Enemy troops were firing from four different windows, two on the bottom floor and two on the top. An idea came to Arano, and he shouted for Enton's attention.

"Enton! I'm going to try to flank them! Give me some cover fire; then get Derna out of here. Don't wait more than ten minutes at the transport. If I don't make it, go on without me."

He could see Enton frowning at the idea, but Arano had no intention of allowing the Latyrian soldier to lodge a protest. He sprang to his feet and dashed across the street, hearing the intensive fire the Latyrians laid down for him. Although a few shots narrowly missed him, he made it to the structure across the street unscathed. Pressing his back to the wall, he tried the door and found it unlocked. With the sounds of battle raging all around him, he thrust the door open and rushed inside, laser pistol in hand. The room was empty.

He was in a small office building. With the true military penchant for making everything look the same, all the buildings in that sector of town were two stories tall. This particular one was outfitted much more extravagantly than the others, however. Well-cushioned seats stood behind dark stained wooden desks. Intricately carved sculptures decorated the corners of the room, and the floor was covered with a thick carpet. A brief tour of the ground floor revealed a set of stairs leading up to the second level. Arano climbed the staircase, weapon in hand, peering sharply up into the darkness.

The top floor was dedicated to a single office, with an open floor plan. Most of the room seemed to be wasted space, a monument to the frugality of the company's senior executive. Arano saw the benefits immediately, however; it was a simple to task to ensure he was alone. He checked several closets along one wall, at last locating the door concealing a narrow, dank staircase to the roof. He stepped lightly on the stairs, found the roof hatch unlocked, and eased it open. A cascade of snow tumbled down upon him, some of it slipping icily down the back of his shirt. He shrugged it off and pushed the hatch ajar.

He emerged from the relative warmth of the office to find himself back in the frigid snowstorm. Getting his bearings from the firefight raging on the streets below, Arano found the building where their enemies lay hidden. He gauged the distance between the two premises and set his lips together in firm resolve. Arano prudently wiped the snow from the ledge surmounting the roof and moved back several meters. Climbing atop the low wall, he ran directly to the edge of the precipice, throwing himself into the air at the last moment. He hurtled through the snowy air, alighting on the icy roof. His feet slid out from under him, and he landed flat on his back, ears ringing as his head bounced off the concrete. He lay still for several moments, waiting for his world to stop spinning, then climbed unsteadily to his feet.

The entrance to the edifice was only a few meters away, and while it was locked, Arano found it simple enough to force the door open. From below, he heard the New Dawn soldiers shouting to each other, accompanied by the crackle of energy weapons, and the occasional scream as a well-aimed shot found its mark. He hurried to the bottom of the staircase, held his weapon before him, and stepped out into the hallway.

CHAPTER
NINETEEN

AMID A SWIRLING BLACK CYLINDER, THE *INTREPID* emerged from its artificial wormhole, and Kish guided the powerful frigate into formation with the rest of the fleet. The Avengers' craft docked with the *USCS Ranger*, an assault carrier, the flagship of the task force. Following instructions from a newly minted ensign, the five Avengers and their GBI attaché found their way to the meeting room, where the coming battle was being planned.

They entered wordlessly and were motioned to an empty row of seats. The commanders of the ships from the battle group were all present, along with their advisors. One section of seats on the far side of the room held the entire squad of fighter pilots, who seemed engrossed in some type of jocularity instead of the planning session. The leaders of the ground forces were also present, lending their expert advice regarding their participation in the coming battle.

Three enormous screens dominated one wall of the room, and the chairs faced them from a gradually upward sloping floor. The screen on the left depicted the positions of the planets in the Menast System as they would be when the task force arrived, including the orbital weapons platform. The second screen showed the various points where the task force would emerge from their wormholes, along with their planned routes for the assault. The third screen was divided into several smaller sections, and displayed a number of ground targets, along with the defenses arrayed to protect them. A Tsimian, who held the rank of major, stepped to the podium at the center of the room. His fine, bristly fur was surprisingly light-colored, more so than any Tsimian's Kish had seen.

"Greetings, all. I am Major Celert, and I will be leading the task force on this mission." There was an unsettling amount of grumbling around the room, and it took some time for the major to restore order. "Colonel Winert was injured in an unfortunate hovercar incident, so I have been placed in command.

"As you can see here," he said, indicating the second of the three screens, "we will divide the task force into five smaller groups. This will force New Dawn to split their defenses in an effort to counter all of our wings, and the chaos in their ranks will be their undoing. We will meet their ships out here," he told them, pointing at a red line ringing the fourth planet, "where we are beyond the range of their planetary defenses. After we have dealt with their mobile forces, we can destroy the orbital weapons platform before we start the ground invasion. You will each be given a data card containing your assignments in the coming battle. Any questions?"

Kish was seething in helpless frustration and finally rose to her feet. "Begging the major's pardon, but what do you think you are doing?" Major Celert's beak dropped open in surprise, and he stood speechless before them. "You call that a battle plan?"

Major Celert recovered his composure and crossed his arms defiantly. "I suppose you could do better?"

"You've been to schools, but how much combat have you seen?"

The major looked to his aides for assistance, but found none forthcoming. "Well, none, yet . . ."

Kish shook her head in disgust. "My first question would have to do with their fleet. What makes you think they will pursue you outside the range of their orbital platform? That would be very obliging of them, but for some reason I don't think gross stupidity is taught at their academies." The room was filled with soft chuckles, and Celert showed his discomfort by standing first on one foot, and then the other, unable to bring his eyes up to meet Kish's.

"You've split your forces evenly between the five groups," Kish continued. "This is another mistake. You need one main wing, which will lead the assault against the weapons platform. But before they arrive, you want two of those other, smaller groups to show up, engaging the enemy ships and pulling them out of position for your main strike. The final two groups will serve as a blocking force, and should include your Thief Class Cruisers to prevent any ships from escaping."

Major Celert sighed theatrically and rolled his eyes. "Anything else?"

"Actually, yes," Lon said. "Your battle plan shows us attacking the orbital weapons station from all sides. This is the most foolish decision you could make, short of going in one ship at a time with shields down." The polite chuckles turned to outright laughter. "By attacking from every direction, you allow the station to employ its entire weaponry. If we hit it from one side, in a series of successive waves, we concentrate all our firepower in one location while allowing the enemy to use less than half of their weapons."

The protests from the crowd rose in volume, and it took several officers to restore the room to order. During the mayhem, Imatt had left his seat and spoke to Major Celert quietly, off to one side. The major looked unhappy, but then his beak dropped open in surprise; he nodded his agreement and left the room. When he returned, his beak was contorted into an unhappy scowl. He returned to the podium.

"I have just spoken with General Vines. At his suggestion, command of the fleet is hereby turned over to Major Tinmar. He has chosen to be assisted by Captain Pana and Lieutenant Waukee."

Kish's narrow mouth dropped open, and she stared at Lon in wordless amazement. Major Celert must have sensed her reluctance, because he seized the moment. "I was as opposed to this as you seem to be, Lieutenant. But the general has made his decision."

Lon recovered his wits first. "Very well. Obviously, we appreciate the confidence General Vines is showing in us. Prepare the fleet for departure. The finalized battle plan will be ready within two hours. We'll be helping to command the fleet from the *Intrepid*."

Kish took a certain amount of delight in the bug-eyed expression on the furry countenance of the flabbergasted major. There were several hearty congratulations from the attendees who knew the two Avengers; then they set to work on their strategy. Pelos pulled up as much intelligence information about the enemy fleet as he could find, and the team put their heads together. They constructed what Kish considered to be a workable plan of action, ran through a few contingency situations, and submitted their final product to the fleet.

Once aboard the *Intrepid*, Kish took her place in the command chair. At her order, Pelos radioed the fleet, and in return, each ship signaled its readiness. "Pelos," Kish said confidently, "take us there." The burly Tsimian agilely danced his fingers across the controls, and the ship's Rift Drives hummed to life.

Through the front viewscreen, Kish watched the wormhole form in front of them. From a tiny flash of light, it swirled into an immense tunnel of solid darkness, with various hues of red and blue chasing around its surface. It extended to engulf the *Intrepid*, and they disappeared into the wormhole.

Kish could restrain herself no longer. "Imatt, what did you say to Major Celert to get him to put us in charge?"

"Yes, Imatt," Toshe Jorgan said, Gatoan fangs bared in a broad grin. "That overstuffed bootlicker would have gotten a lot of people killed, but I didn't think he would relinquish command so easily."

"I simply suggested he give General Vines a call on subspace. Since the general knows us all and trusts us implicitly, I figured he would put someone else in charge if Celert proposed the idea. I don't know for certain why he went along with the idea. All I did was drop a hint about calling some friends of mine in the Bureau of Taxation and having him audited."

Kish laughed out loud, covering her face with her hands. "You blackmailed an officer in the Coalition military and got him to give up command of a task force?"

Imatt pursed his lips in feigned thought. "Yeah, I guess I did. Is that illegal?"

Arano prowled slowly along the wood-trimmed hallway, one hand holding his weapon in front of him, eyes and ears alert for signs of the enemy. A harsh Bromidian voice brought him up short, and he pressed his back against the wall to minimize his silhouette. After a deep breath, he allowed a little space between himself and the elaborate furnishings along the side of the hallway, and glided forward on soft feet. The next door stood slightly open, and the Bromidian voice he had heard sounded once again from within the room.

With a steely calm that came with the confidence of a trained veteran, Arano drew closer to the narrowly open doorway and sank to his knees. He leaned out with painstaking slowness, each heartbeat exposing another area of the room as, bit by bit, he tiptoed forward. Through the narrow gap between the door and the frame, he saw the two Bromidians inside the room almost immediately, kneeling side by side. They had their backs to him, and they were laughing out loud while they fired upon the hapless team below them. Arano considered his options. He was basically faced with either shooting both of them or charging in with his knives drawn and taking them into hand-to-hand combat. He checked the hallway in both directions, made sure he was clear, and stepped lightly away from the wall. He mentally pictured the locations of his two foes and brought up his pistol.

In a flash, he had kicked the door open and leveled his weapon. The deceptively small laser pistol hummed twice, and he shifted his aim before the first body had hit the floor. The second Bromidian barely had time to turn, surprise etched in his widened eyes, before Arano's pistol fired again, and he fell next to his companion. Arano spun around, checking the room for unseen hazards, but he was alone. He briefly considered taking the weapons from the lifeless guards but discarded the idea. Time was of the essence, so he settled for firing on the rifles, rendering them useless.

He located the stairs to the bottom floor and descended them with as much haste as stealth allowed. He kept his attention focused, not on the steps themselves, but on potential danger lurking below. Arano stalked the corridors like death incarnate, an unstoppable force bent on destroying any who stood against him. Voices came to him, somehow carried on the still air over the din of the battle.

He took his pistol in a two-handed grip, trotting forward on the balls of his feet until he was close to his target. The door to the room was pushed nearly shut, so he had no chance to survey the space ahead of his rapid entry. In his mind's eye, he pictured the room's likely layout. While he had no way of predicting the types and locations of pieces of furniture, he knew the windows would be against the far wall, and he would find his targets there. They weren't likely to be protecting their backs, believing their greatest threat came from outside the building. Arano hoped it would prove their downfall. He skulked into position, took another calming breath, and kicked the door open.

The wooden portal swung about with a crash, bouncing off the far wall and rebounding on its hinges. Arano dove across the open threshold, rolled to his knees, and fired. One Bromidian fell screaming to the floor, clutching the gaping wound in his shoulder in agony. The other swung his rifle about, desperately searching for the shooter who had just fired upon his companion. As Arano had hoped, the hapless Bromidian tracked the motion of the still swinging door, and before he realized his mistake, Arano's pistol had burned two searing holes in his chest. The wounded Bromidian rolled onto his side, weakly lifting his rifle in a frantic attempt to return fire. Arano, left with no choice, shot the nearly incapacitated soldier in the head, and he sprawled lifelessly beneath the window.

Arano kicked his body aside, holstered his pistol, and seized the fallen man's rifle. He surveyed the scene in the street beyond the building, and was satisfied to see Lentin rallying what remained of his troops. From somewhere back in the city, a tremendous explosion shook the building to its very foundation, sending streamers of dust down on his shoulders. He assumed it was due to Alyna's strike team, which meant Lentin had sent the distress signal. Arano slipped to the other side of the window and fired on the New Dawn soldiers who were assaulting Lentin's unprotected rear flank. He launched an intense barrage, but was dismayed when the weapon stopped firing; he had used up the last of its charge. He retrieved the other rifle, checked on Lentin's progress, and made his own retreat to safety.

Arano had last seen Lentin's team heading north from the ambush site, so he tried to shadow their movements from inside the building. It took a bit of searching, but he located a door on the north wall. But before he could reach it, the door burst open, and several Bromidians poured through, raining fire in all directions. Arano dove back into another hallway, not even bothering to return fire, and rolled to his feet. In a mad rush, he tried to drop back to the building's south side, but yet another door opened, and more enemy troops charged in. He changed directions once more, found the staircase, and took the steps two at a time as he charged to the top floor.

He had just opened the door to the roof when he heard feet pounding on the stairs, pursuing a prey they thought would be trapped. He pushed the door closed behind him, breath steaming in the night air, and fired the rifle at the doorjamb. The metal frame hissed loudly, sealing itself against the sturdy door. Snow was falling heavily, and he plowed through foot-high drifts in a frenzied search for a way to safely reach the street below. The building to the north was slightly shorter than the one on which he stood, and he figured he could easily make the two-meter leap across the empty chasm before him. His mind was made up for him when he heard the pounding attempts to open the door to the roof.

He stepped onto the wide ledge, bent into a deep crouch, and leaped. He placed a steadying hand behind him, and was able to catch himself when he landed, avoiding the nearly debilitating landing he had suffered the last time he'd jumped onto a roof-top. He scrambled to his feet just before the door on the other roof gave way, and a dozen Bromidians emptied onto the roof, spreading out and searching for their quarry. Arano didn't need to look back to know he had been discovered, the fresh pursuit given away by the triumphant shouts and sporadic shots fired in his direction.

He knew he couldn't hope to escape by heading directly to the street. His hunters would be on him too quickly, and he would be pinned down and either captured or killed. Running in a crouch, he sprinted across the rooftop to the next ledge and jumped without hesitating. The next building was farther away, but he caromed off the ledge to land flat on his face. Bleeding from numerous scrapes, he ran off once more, dodging the ven-tilation equipment atop the concrete structure, energy weapon fire crackling all around him. He discarded the unwieldy rifle, knowing speed, not firepower, would free him from the trap.

The next precipice was easier to cross without the rifle to slow him down, although he still found staying on his feet to be impossible. The surface of the rooftops was simply too slick from ice and snow to afford a tenable purchase, so he had to settle for a graceful fall and an easy impact. He was breathing hard, the exertion amplified by the repeated rough landings. Perhaps that was why on his next leap, his feet fell short of the ledge. He crashed into the building with stunning force and tumbled limply down the wall.

It was the metal staircase affixed to the outside of the building that saved him. He alighted on the grated landing and, with senses slowly returning, crawled lethargically to the ladder descending into the snowy darkness. With an effort, he swung his body over the edge, planted his feet firmly on the rungs of the ladder, and painstakingly descended. He was halfway down when the Bromidians above him reached the ledge.

To his surprise, they hurtled across the gap between the buildings, and several moments later he heard their startled shouts. He continued his descent, cursing the ill luck of the snow. If not for the smooth, unbroken icy drifts on the roof above, his pursuers might not have known he hadn't actually reached the roof. Within moments, beams of light were cascading down, illuminating the alley and giving away Arano's location. He released the ladder, fell the final three meters, and landed in a deep snowdrift. Arano rose to his feet yet again and pressed as close to the building as he could, forcing the Bromidians above him to take shots from an awkward angle. He reached the mouth of the alley, looked around for signs of other New Dawn soldiers, and sprinted away from the trap which had been slowly closing about him.

Scattered beams of laser fire struck the snow around him, erupting in bursts of steam where they hit. Arano's lungs and throat burned as if on fire, and he knew he was nearing the end of his strength. The cold air was testing his endurance that much more, adding to the problems caused by his numerous falls and injuries. He slowed his pace, trying to stick to smaller roads and avoid the major thoroughfares. With the snow, he knew speed wouldn't work, and he wouldn't be able to elude them by hiding.

The best idea he could think of was a disguise. He wasn't likely to find any clothing lying around in the cold, so he would probably have to steal new attire. Arano found the idea of mugging an innocent bystander distasteful, so he elected to find a shop where such items could be bought. In the next block, he found the store he was looking for and slowed to a panting walk and stepped into the alley, looking for a side door. In his exhaustion, he failed to notice the warning screaming from his danger sense until it was too late.

"Going somewhere?"

The voice came from behind him, but before he could swing his pistol about, a heavy stun blast struck him in the back, and he fell into darkness, not even feeling the blows that descended upon his unconscious form.

The computer beeped its warning that the trip through the wormhole was nearing its end, and Pelos guided the ship back into real space. The wormhole retreated to a small point of light before disappearing, while the ships of the fleet appeared around them in a breathtaking panorama of swirling colors. Their systems came online, and Imatt opened a channel to the fleet.

"This is Captain Pana, aboard the *Intrepid*. All ships, form up. The first two waves appear to have arrived on time, and they have already engaged the enemy. We're going in."

The task force raced forward, Firestorm Class Fighters taking the lead and engaging the few remaining enemy fighters emerging from the orbital station. Kish watched her display with satisfaction, seeing a few New Dawn ships attempt to disengage from the pressing Coalition ships in order to battle the new threat, only to be cut down when Coalition plasma torpedoes struck their more vulnerable aft shields. From behind her, Vic Dermak's computer sounded a warning.

"Enemy ships emerging from Menast 4's second moon. They weren't on the intelligence briefing. If we had come in, as Celert suggested, and were tied up fighting the entire fleet and that space station at the same time . . ." He trailed off meaningfully, and his words were lost on no one.

Kish checked the tactical display. "When the blocking groups arrive, order Wing 5 to assist us, and have Wing 4 maintain their position." She keyed the channel, speaking to the fleet again. "New Dawn is bringing thirty fighters, five frigates, and three light cruisers against us. We have to hit them now, while they are far enough away from the weapons platform that it won't be able to assist them. 'A' Group and 'B' Group, take up flanking positions, and don't let their fighters get in behind us. Move into point-blank range, and open fire. Once we're that close, even if we do move within range of the station, they won't be able to shoot, for fear of hitting their own ships."

The *Intrepid's* weapons fired, and the plasma torpedoes slammed into the first frigate. It listed helplessly, but Imatt gave them no respite. Three more torpedoes struck home, and the ship was rocked by internal explosions, finally erupting in a blinding fireball. A pair of frigates, with fighter escort, tried to close with the *Intrepid*, but a wing of Assault Class Fighters streaked ahead, cutting off the attack and forcing them into a defensive formation.

Kish frowned, reading a report on her display. "Five wings of enemy fighters just broke off the attack and headed spinward around the planet's second moon. Lon, what can you offer me?"

He rubbed his eyes, squinted at his readout, then activated his Comm. "Fighter Wings 2, 4, and 6, with . . ." He trailed off, and Kish guessed he was selecting a light cruiser. Her speculation was confirmed moments later. "*Pacific*, I want you to go around the planet anti-spinward and intercept the group of fighters that's trying to flank us. Dispatch them as expeditiously as possible, and return when you can. We need you here."

"*Daytona*, *Mercury*, and *Luna*, I want you farther out on our right flank," Kish announced. "If the enemy gets in between us, you'll be too close to use torpedoes."

The *Intrepid* rocked hard to the port side, struck by some weapon's impact, but its flight stabilized. A second tremor blasted through the ship, and a shower of sparks rained down upon Pelos. The Tsimian was thrown from his chair, the hair around his face singed, but he dragged himself back to his seat and regained control of his station. Two more hits struck the stout vessel, but with less devastating effect.

"Fighter Wing One," Kish called out. "There are two fighters on our upper port side. Chase them out of there." She glanced back to Vic's post. "Status report."

"Shields at 85 percent. That shot got lucky somehow. It shouldn't have managed to get through our shields so easily. All systems are functioning normally. Hull damage on level two, but no breach."

"*USCS Dulles* calling *Intrepid*."

"Go ahead, Dulles."

"We've reached our objective. Ready to launch fighters on your mark."

"I copy. Stand by." Kish called up another tactical display, studying the readout. She saw the flashing indicator showing ships emerging from their wormholes, and was relieved to see it was Flight 5, arriving right on schedule. "Wing 5, this is *Intrepid*. The tactical situation has changed. I need you to join the *Dulles* in their mission. We've had to redeploy the ships I intended to use for their escort, so it's up to you."

"This is Major Celert, Wing 5, we copy. Moving in."

"Intrepid to *Dulles,* begin your assault."

"Dulles copies, out."

Kish checked her station once again, and watched the tiny blips of light representing her reserve force of fighters come pouring out of the launching bays on the *USCS Dulles,* the task force's Assault Class Carrier. The fighters split into small groups and made strafing runs against the weapons platform, which was firing its weapons madly in an attempt to stave off the storm. Kish looked back to the main screen, and slammed her fist down when she saw two Coalition Light Cruisers spinning out of control, small eruptions bursting through their hulls. One of the cruisers split slowly in half, rocked by a massive explosion amidships, and was consumed in a fireball. The other drifted out of control, defenseless against the two destroyers menacing it.

"I'm going to take us closer to the *Lockhart.* We need to provide them cover until they can get their engines repaired and get out of harm's way."

Pelos set his beak firmly, fingers dancing across the controls with a deceptively light touch, coordinating with other ships while Kish guided the agile ship through the battle, taking up a position roughly a hundred meters astern from the *Lockhart.* Lon and Toshe, firing the plasma cannons, concentrated their fire on one of the destroyers, while Imatt fired plasma torpedoes into the other at nearly point-blank range. Kish watched the GBI agent's tactics curiously; from this range, they couldn't obtain a computer targeting lock, so Imatt was aiming the torpedoes manually. The first two went wide of their mark, but the destroyer's weapons fell silent. Obviously, Imatt had their attention. The next torpedo was true, impacting just behind the bridge with a violent explosion that rocked the ship from bow to stern.

Kish allowed the computer to obtain a lock and fired the Disruptor Beam repeatedly, each strike sending a brilliant blue-white halo of energy shimmering out in nearly concentric circles. The combination of plasma torpedoes and Disruptor hits took their toll, and the lights on the destroyer went dark. Imatt prudently fired two more torpedoes and was rewarded with a major hull breach. Kish turned her attention to the other destroyer, but found it unnecessary. Lon and Toshe, working in tandem, had just disabled the ship, and the *Lockhart* was safe for the time being.

She checked on the progress of the *Dulles* and its contingent of fighters, and was surprised to see they had already disabled an entire bank of beam weapons on the hapless weapons platform. This allowed the fighters to circle in a relatively small area, safe from the station's damaged weapons, and fire with impunity. The Assault Class Carrier, along with the ships Kish had dispatched to help, were holding New Dawn's ships at bay, preventing them from coming to the rescue of their doomed weapons platform. At last, it tilted crazily on its axis, ruptured in multiple locations, and exploded, the remains falling through the moon's nearly non-existent atmosphere for an inevitable crash on the surface.

The battle turned swiftly. Without the protection of the impressive armament on the weapons platform, and with their contingent of fighters destroyed before they could flank the Coalition fleet, the remaining ships were in a hopeless situation. Kish was ready to accept their surrender, but she would not offer until they requested quarter. Her task force encircled the enemy, collapsing inexorably around them, destroying their ships one by one. To Kish's chagrin, there was no communication from the enemy ships, and they never quit firing. They were forced to destroy every last ship, even after the situation for New Dawn's fleet had become beyond hopeless. The taste of victory was bitter in her mouth, and she sat stoically watching the final New Dawn ship, a heavy cruiser, disappear in a fiery conflagration.

She shook her head sadly, staring down at her lap, before she spoke to the fleet once again. "*Intrepid* to all ships. Take up blockade formations. Firestorm and Assault Class Fighters, conduct your strafing runs and destroy your assigned ground targets. Transport ships, bring in your troops."

Kish slowly rotated her chair to face Pelos. "Take us in."

CHAPTER TWENTY

ARANO PAINFULLY OPENED HIS SWOLLEN, BLOOD-shot eyes, and his blurry vision came grudgingly into focus. He was lying facedown in what appeared to be a stone cell. He managed to get his arms beneath his chest and pushed himself off the cold, hard floor. There was no furniture in the tiny room, which was barely two meters wide by three meters long. Only a single door opened to the world beyond his cell, and he assumed it was locked. It would be a few minutes before he could test the theory, however. He lay back down, waves of nausea rushing over him from the effort. Arano retched uncontrollably and lay helplessly in the foul-smelling pool, darkness overcoming him once more.

He had no idea how much time passed before he awoke once more, this time to the sound of a heavy latch being thrown. He feigned unconsciousness, keeping his eyes closed but trying to gather what he could with his ears. There were two definite sets of booted footsteps, and judging by the heavy footfalls, they were bulky individuals. This was not unexpected, given that he was in a prison. The guards seized him roughly by the arms and dragged him, facedown, out of the cell. Arano allowed his head to dangle jauntily between his shoulders, which afforded him a view, through slightly parted eyelids, of the feet of his captors. Unfortunately, they were wearing boots and long pants, preventing him from learning even their race. He tossed his head casually to the side and caught a glimpse of a hand covered in a rough brown exoskeleton.

Bromidians. But then, who else could it be?

Apparently convinced Arano's comatose state was genuine, the two burly ruffians engaged in casual conversation.

"Carraf will not be pleased when she finds out he's still not awake."

"Not our fault, Denle," the other replied. "All we're doing is bringing him to her."

"That's true, Worel, but she sometimes likes to take these little problems out on the messenger."

Denle gave a snickering laugh. "Maybe we should stop by the stream and wake him up."

Worel chortled at the thought. "Let's just be careful not to drown him."

They turned sharply to the right, dragging him down a long ramp. Arano continued to feign unconsciousness, not sure what was coming next. Gradually, the sound of running water came to his ears. He guessed that a stream coming out of the sharply rolling hills to the west of Notron must pass through the prison, and they likely used it for fresh water. If he could escape the prison and find his way back to the stream, he could use it to guide him back to familiar territory. Unfortunately, the water would likely be incredibly frigid.

His fears were confirmed when the two guards threw him into a shallow pool of water. With a startled gasp, he rose up, the icy waters biting him deeply. His Bromidian captives stood before him, arms folded across their chest, laughing uproariously. Gasping for breath, Arano tried to climb out of the pool, but one of them—Denle, he believed—thrust him back in. The air *whooshed* from his lungs, and he rose to his hands and knees, breathing coming in sharp, ragged bursts. The two Bromidians grabbed him by the arms again and dragged him from the water.

Since there was no longer any point in keeping his eyes shut, Arano decided to study his surroundings, trying to memorize the layout. The floors and ceiling were made of plain stone blocks, seated tightly together with mortar and left unpainted. The floor was made of a seamless, hard substance that appeared to be concrete. Metal doors were spaced at regular intervals, giving no landmarks to the battered Avenger, should he get the chance to make a break for freedom. Other than the ramp leading to the pool of water, the floors seemed to be level, so Arano assumed either there were stairs hidden behind certain doors, or some type of lift system. *Or perhaps both.*

Worel pulled a key ring from his pocket, selected a key, and fitted it to the lock in a door. Arano filed that interesting tidbit away; when he escaped, he would have to kill Worel and grab his keys. He made the deliberate change in his line of thinking, from wondering if he could escape to knowing he would. His cognitive functions were still returning to him piecemeal, and as his mind came into focus, he accepted his situation and planned to abscond from their prison. Till that point, he had seen no technological barriers: no shields, no scanning devices, no electronic fields needing to be disabled before entering certain areas. He would use the flaw against them, when the time came.

The door yielded to Worel's key, and Arano found himself in a lift. His stomach lurched, and he knew the elevator was rising sharply. His stomach heaved once more, but he managed to keep it under control. They slowed to a stop, and Denle muscled the doors open. They passed from the lift to enter a wide hall, with fires burning brightly in several tall urns around the room. Shackles dangled from the walls, along with tongs, clubs, and cutting implements, giving the room a decidedly medieval aura. The Bromidians lifted Arano into the air, slamming him down on his back atop a stone table. A sticky wetness clung to his back through the tattered remains of his shirt, and he assumed it was fresh blood. He lay helplessly while the guards restrained his hands and legs. Then they left the room, talking quietly between themselves.

Another door clanked open, and a lighter set of footsteps came his way. A female face appeared above him, peering down with a cold, evil gaze. Her sharply drawn features showed not even a glimmer of compassion. She was Human, Arano realized with a start. Her fine, blond hair was pulled tightly behind her head, held in place by a black leather band. She wore tight-fitting black leather garments, which accented her athletic figure. She ran her fingers through the blood beneath him, licked it sensually, then regarded him with a calculating eye.

"I am Carraf," she anounced simply. "I will ask questions, and you shall answer them truthfully. Cooperate, and you will be treated with mercy." She emphasized her point by sensually tracing a finger along the line of his bruised jaw. "Lie, or refuse to answer, and things will become most unpleasant." As if to emphasize her point, she drew a wickedly curved knife from a shelf and used it to remove Arano's shirt, slicing into the skin of his chest in the process.

"What is your name?" Arano met her gaze, unflinching. From another table, she drew forth a leather glove, placing it on her right hand. "What is your name?" she asked again, more firmly this time. When he still refused to answer, she delivered a stunning blow with the glove, adding to the swelling on his battered face and cutting the inside of his lip.

She brought her face down close to his, breath hot against

his ear. "Your name, Avenger." He turned his head toward her, then spat bloody saliva into her eyes. She screamed a curse, in a language Arano knew all too well. The next blow caught him on the temple, sending him spinning into a vortex of pain, but he scarcely noticed. She had cursed at him in his native tongue. She was a Padian!

Alyna's Comm flashed an urgent warning, and she read the scrolling message before climbing to her feet. "That's the signal," she said. "Let's go. They're in the third quadrant, taking heavy fire. We need to hit our target soon."

Flanked by Videre and Lain, she tramped through the loosely packed snow, surrounded by fifty Bromidians interspersed with a scattering of Latyrians. At pre-planned locations, groups of ten Bromidians and a single Latyrian split off from her force, the smaller groups moving into position on their own while she led the main body of troops.

Alyna knelt along the edge of a ridgeline, slowly lifting her head higher until she could see the outskirts of the town of No-tron. Scanning the buildings, she found her primary target, then slipped back below the hill, out of sight of any New Dawn soldiers who might be patrolling the area. A check of her watch told her she had to wait but five more minutes. Their battle plan didn't allow much time between arriving and attacking, but then, with its implicit purpose, time had to be of the essence. If any of the elements of her band weren't in place at the prescribed time, they would simply have to attack whenever they could. She leaned back into the frozen snow and watched the seconds tick by, trying unsuccessfully not to worry about Arano.

When the appointed time arrived, Alyna eased back onto the top of the ridge, her white and gray combat fatigues concealing her within the snow's folds, rendering her nearly indistinguishable from the surrounding terrain. Her rifle had been similarly wrapped, minimizing its visibility. Around her prowled twenty Bromidians and Latyrians, passing through the wooded land like smoke on a summer breeze. Lain and Videre were on her immediate flanks, staying close at hand in case of trouble. Somewhere in the snow-filled darkness, three other similar, albeit smaller, teams were also approaching the city. She drew as close to the guard shack as she dared, then took a knee, and the others followed suit. Raising her rifle, she sighted in on a Bromidian guard, his head and torso visible through a brightly lit window.

Her first shot was true, sending the New Dawn soldier spinning away with a gaping head wound. Chaos reigned as the others in her group also fired on their targets, and small explosions rocked the tower. One of her soldiers sat up, shoulder-fired missile held at the ready. He launched the rocket, and it streaked across the night sky, leaving behind a scarlet trail and striking the guard tower. The explosion shook snow from the branches over Alyna's head, and the tower collapsed upon itself. A cheer went up from her ranks, and they charged into the city.

To her left and right, Alyna saw fires burning along the edge of town. She found her spirits lifted significantly, knowing the diversionary attack was proceeding well. Arano would escape easily, once the troops pursuing him were called away to repel the invading army. She trotted out of the wood line and into the smoky streets, slowing occasionally to fire on maneuvering enemy troops. With the crossfire coming from her smaller RLF detachments, the soldiers of New Dawn found it impossible to attack from her flank. However, with a stubbornness born of leaderless desperation, the defenders continued executing the same maneuvers, apparently hoping strength of numbers would eventually succeed.

Their failure to repel the RLF invasion in the opening minutes of the battle proved decisive. Alyna took advantage of their errors, driving directly to her objective. Ten minutes after breaching their lines, she stood outside the munitions warehouse. Whistling sharply, she gestured to several defensible locations, and teams of two Bromidians from her group established fighting positions to protect the next phase of the operation. While they lay down suppressing fire, a dozen of her soldiers, handpicked for their strength and endurance, forced entry into the building. For several long minutes, she faced scattered resistance from the city's defenders. All the while, her team was inside the warehouse, loading their bulky packs with as much weaponry, ammunition, and explosives as they could carry.

A shot shattered against the wall behind Alyna, and she reflexively fired a couple of blasts in return. She spotted her adversary, a Tsimian mercenary creeping along the roof across the street. She steadied herself, took careful aim, and fired. He tumbled lifelessly against the rooftop ventilation apparatus, sliding down and out of sight. She checked her watch once more, knowing they were pressing their luck by staying so long. She whistled twice, and three more of her team ran inside to plant explosives around the facility. The Bromidians serving as porters for the mission emerged, heavily laden with equipment jutting out of their packs at odd angles. They bore their burdens aloofly, and by appearances it seemed they hardly knew the weight was on their backs. They took cover behind vehicles and concrete walls, waiting for the order to retreat.

The demolition team emerged, and the leader held up her

thumb, telling Alyna she had accomplished her task. "Fall back!" Alyna shouted, and the entire group rose into a low crouch, backing away from the encroaching enemy troops. The forces of New Dawn had taken up firing positions on several more rooftops, and they had a deadly advantage over Alyna's troops. Their high-angle assault claimed several RLF soldiers almost immediately. She activated her two smoke grenades and threw them into the heart of her formation, obscuring their exact positions.

"Run! Everyone back to the rally point!"

They needed no further urging. At an all-out sprint, they turned and fled, some of them firing over their shoulders as they ran. Without waiting for the order, the Bromidian who had led the demolitions team activated her remote detonator. With an ear-splitting clap of thunder, the weapons warehouse exploded, sending billowing clouds of smoke and fire belching into the night sky. Secondary explosions rocked the area, as more of the munitions not caught in the initial fulmination succumbed to the hungry flames. Alyna's ears were ringing, and her head felt stuffy from the concussion of the blast, but at least it would slow the ground pursuit. Her primary concern was those firing from the roofs.

Beams of energy struck the pavement all around, but two of her sergeants were throwing smoke grenades ahead of the retreating force, allowing them to stay under cover that much longer. After they had covered a dozen city blocks, she slowed their pace. The race to the safety of the deep woods might be a long one, so she wanted to save the group's strength, especially those burdened with weapons.

They reached the edge of the city, somehow managing to find their way back to the same point they had entered, despite all that had happened. While her soldiers filed past her into the sheltering trees, Alyna stopped and looked back. The burning warehouse was plainly visible, lighting the city's skyline like a beacon. Another explosion erupted from the bowels of Notron, and she smiled grimly. New Dawn would not soon forget the evening's events.

For the next hour, they continued in a generally westerly direction, although they made frequent course changes in an attempt at deception, in case they were followed. The snow was falling more heavily and should cover their tracks in relatively short order, but Alyna had further precautions in mind. They would locate the wide, shallow stream rushing down from the steeper hills and into the city. By walking in the middle of the stream, she hoped to lose anyone tracking them, and their boots had sufficient waterproofing to prevent cold-related injuries to her soldiers. She loosened the cap on her head, moved her rifle into a more comfortable position, and marched into the swirling snow.

A group of figures materialized out of the darkness. The leader of the new group was flashing a light in a prearranged sequence, alerting Alyna's group to the presence of friendly forces. She hurried over to them, eyes scanning the faces in the low light, desperately searching for one man. When she had passed deeper into the group and still couldn't find Arano, her heart sank to her toes, anxiety gnawing at her like some insidious beast. She found Lentin, and the look of apprehension he wore told her what she didn't want to know: Arano was missing.

The *Intrepid* settled gracefully onto a landing pad on Menast 4. The ramp opened with a *hiss* of gasses, and Kish stepped briskly down the ramp, feeling the bite of the cool air. Menast 4 was a temperate planet, tending to the colder end of planets of its classification. In the distance, scrubby plants dotted the rocky terrain. The air felt thin, and Kish was breathing hard after only a short walk. While they crossed the tarmac to the assembly area, she allowed her ruminations to go back to the events of the past few hours.

The ground forces of New Dawn had been easily routed by the Coalition air strikes, and they had offered only token resistance. Kish hoped the relatively easy victory had stiffened the weak spines of the Coalition leadership, who had been tentative about the operation. Considering what New Dawn had done during their widespread attacks on Coalition governmental officials, she felt there should have been an immediate declaration of war. Instead, there was the piecemeal approach, consisting of investigations, covert operations, and finally the strike on Menast 4. It was a step in the right direction, she felt, but the Coalition still had a long way to go.

Odd news had come from the salvage team studying the wreckage of their captured pirate freighter. They had managed to locate several documents labeling what had been carried in their containers prior to the disastrous collapse of their wormhole. Chief among these items had been biological laboratory equipment taken from the defunct company called Biomek. Strange, how a group indirectly owned by Event Horizon was resurfacing. She also wondered what the pirates or their New Dawn allies had in mind for the equipment. Most of Biomek's research had been in the field of inter-species live organ transplant technology, which was fairly archaic. She thought back to what Pelos had learned about the company when researching them for Arano's investment portfolio.

While Biomek's primary thrust had been in the area of transplants, they had a few other areas of interest—mainly inoculations, retro-virus studies, cloning, biological weapons defense, and genetic disorder prevention. She considered each facet of their business, but none seemed to fit the priorities of New Dawn. The closest she could get was the biological weapon defense systems. Perhaps they were looking for ways to circumvent Coalition defenses against such weapons. But even that didn't seem right. Such technology would be years behind the new preventative measures the Coalition was employing. The answer had to be something else.

She and her team entered a large hangar, which was being used to house a planning session for the military leadership. A makeshift tactical display had been set up, showing the Menast System and including the positions of the various components of the conquering fleet. General Vines stood in the center of a raised platform, speaking with other command level officers. She heard he had arrived aboard one of the troop transports, and that he had personally led the assault. The crowd milled around for several minutes before taking their seats, and General Vines called the meeting to order.

"Excellent job, soldiers! We routed them so quickly, their collective heads are still spinning. I have good news for you. The Coalition High Council has voted to allow the fleet to blockade the Rystoria System."

Triumphant shouts rang from the rafters, and the general allowed the celebration to run its course. "We will not be allowed to invade yet, but we have permission to defend ourselves, subject to certain rules of engagement. If you have to violate these rules to complete my objective, then I will stand beside you at the court martial."

Kish felt the pride swelling in her chest, pride at serving under such a leader. The general retrieved another datapad. "One concession we did wring out of our worthless Council was the use of our Avengers teams. We can continue using them to infiltrate New Dawn facilities in an effort to determine their plans for the future. We need to find out what their objectives are, and the Avengers teams are the answer. Immediately following this meeting, I need to meet with the team leaders for a briefing on their next missions."

He summarized the losses suffered by each side, told what types of hardware and numbers of personnel had been captured, and concluded by offering more congratulations. He led Kish and the other team leaders to another area of the hangar and briefed them on their assigned tasks.

"Lieutenant Waukee, I understand your team is incomplete right now. You are operating with only one squad?"

Kish pursed her lips. "Well, sir, it's actually rather complicated. Yes, it's true that one of our squads is . . . trapped on Rystoria 2, behind enemy lines, along with my squad leader."

General Vines laughed sharply. "Trapped? I heard about the parachute insertion of the rest of Lakeland's squad. I can't imagine the kind of havoc he's causing right about now."

Kish smiled. "We have joined with Captain Pana's team for the interim. He had three team members out also, and it seemed logical to join up. To complete my squad, we have a member of GBI working with us. His resources have proven useful on more than one occasion."

"So, in essence, you have a functional team. And you are acting as team leader?"

"Yes, sir. Of course, in the practical application of things, Captain Pana and I share the leadership duties. It's not a typical military operation, but then, among the Avengers, what is?"

General Vines nodded slowly. "All right. I'll give you the

mission. Xuber Mining Company, located here on Menast 4, is actually a front for New Dawn. We haven't moved to pacify them yet because they are acting as noncombatants. However, they have some data there we really need, and if we charge in with guns blazing, they will likely destroy their computers rather than let us have the information. Your mission will be to infiltrate the headquarters, gather all the intelligence you can, and destroy the place." He crossed his arms, grimly. "We have confirmed this to be a military target, and the employees have been proven to be members of New Dawn. Do not hesitate to fire on any threat if you feel it is necessary."

"I understand, sir. We'll take care of it."

"Good. Get it done as quickly as you can. We leave in twenty-four hours to initiate the blockade, and I want that little ship of yours there with us."

"You can count on us, General."

"One other thing. We haven't located Ustin Shiba, or Osiris, as he likes to be called. It's quite possible he's hiding somewhere in their facility. I want him."

"So do we, General. So do we."

A Padian! How could a Padian find herself in league with the very sect of Bromidians who had so brutally oppressed her people only a few short years before? Arano blinked away the pain in his head, trying to make sense of the scene around him. Carraf had stalked away a few paces, but she returned with a vengeance and struck another stinging blow to his head, drawing a trail of blood from his mouth.

"Answer me! Are you the Avenger who was with Hawan on

the day of the uprising, or are you one of those who parachuted in, days later? You think we aren't aware of what's going on? I know much, but I want to know more. And you are going to help me."

Setting aside the glove, she crossed the floor, the wooden heels of her boots clicking hollowly on the stone floor. She bent down, and when she stood up, she carried a metal rod, the end glowing red with heat from the fire. Carraf approached Arano slowly, weaving intricate designs in the air with the incandescent rod. She stopped at his side, the tip of the rod hanging precariously close to his uncovered abdomen. His skin recoiled from the radiating heat he could already feel, and he steeled himself for what was to come.

"Have you remembered your name, my love?" When he didn't answer, she lowered the rod. Arano's howl of pain filled the room, and Carraf's eyes rolled back as if in ecstasy. She lifted the tip from his damaged skin, and the smell of burning flesh assailed his nostrils. He lay there, panting heavily, not wanting to give her the satisfaction of continuing to call out his pain. She looked down at him once more.

"My, I can see you're a tough one. Wait—maybe that's it. The problem is that you, too, can still see." She brought the still-glowing tip up to Arano's face, where it hung suspended mere inches from his eyes. He refused to give her the satisfaction of quailing.

She suddenly took the rod away, smiling. "I have a better idea. If you don't respond to pain in your own body, perhaps you will when the pain you cause is someone else's." She spun on her heel and marched smartly from the room, the door slamming shut behind her.

Arano let out his breath. Part of his Daxia training had been in the area of resistance to torture, but he had hoped he would never have to put it to practical use. He felt despair washing over him but pushed it aside. His body could only take so much abuse, and he was no good to his captors if he died. They would make sure he was alive when the session was over, and as long as he lived, he would work on his escape. His break from her torture ended much too quickly, and her return to the room brought him a great sense of apprehension.

She moved back to his side, smiling sweetly, once again caressing his face as if they were lovers. "Don't worry, my friend. Your pain is done this day. It may return, but for now, you can rest easy." The door opened, and two Bromidians dragged a struggling captive into the room. The Gatoan seemed to be in worse shape than Arano, with one arm obviously broken.

"This young man is from your intelligence service. He was recently captured and injured in the process. His fate isn't sealed, however. Tell me what I need to know, and he will be released. Refuse, and he will die. Now. In front of your eyes."

The guards bound the prisoner's hands behind his back, ignoring his screams of protest. Carraf spent several minutes inflicting lingering tortures on her new subject, and Arano felt every blow. Obstinacy in the face of his own torture was one thing, but when it caused the pain of another . . . Arano found this torture much harder to endure. The look of pain in the young Gatoan's eyes. His howls of pain. Arano found himself ready to break, but his eyes met those of the other captive. The Gatoan's anguished features were proud, and he gave a barely perceptible shake of his head. Arano drew strength from his companion's display.

Carraf grew more irritable. In a fit of rage, she seized the Gatoan by the fur on the back of his head and hauled him to Arano's side. She drew her knife and set the blade against the Gatoan's throat.

"Either you talk, or he dies. Slowly." She drew the knife

across his throat, and blood flowed freely. The cut wasn't deep enough to be life threatening, but the message was clear. Arano met the other's eyes one more time, then looked back at Carraf and shook his head. A member of the intelligence service should be too valuable to kill, even more so than Arano.

To his shocked disbelief, Carraf ripped the knife across the fur-covered throat, severing the arteries in his neck. Blood fountained out to cover the three of them, and Carraf seemed to bask in the warm stickiness. The Gatoan slumped forward, every exhaled breath spraying a fine mist of blood over Arano's body. It took the Avenger a few moments to realize what the other was doing: he was lubricating Arano's arms with his own lifeblood. He collapsed against Carraf's grip, and she allowed him to fall limply to the floor.

"You know, I think I almost had you there," she said happily. "We have a few more prisoners just like him. Perhaps I'll bring in another."

Humming softly to herself, she strolled casually to the door, disappearing once more into the prison beyond. Arano immediately worked his arms against the leather restraints, the blood making his skin slippery and more maneuverable within their bonds. Setting his teeth, he pulled sharply with his right arm, and it came free. He repeated with his left, untied his leg restraints, and was free from his bonds. His eyes searched the room, finding what he wanted: a long-bladed knife hung from a peg on the far wall. He grabbed it from its perch, tested the weight, and found it to his liking. Lying back upon his bier, he carefully placed the straps atop his arms and legs, giving the illusion he was still in a helpless state.

Carraf's moment of reckoning was imminent.

CHAPTER
TWENTY-ONE

THE SNOWFALL HAD SLOWED NOTICEABLY, AND the wind had lost its bite, but Alyna scarcely noticed. Her limbs felt leaden, but somehow she managed to keep putting one foot in front of the other, following the hulking form of Videre Genoa as they wound their way through the forest to their base of operations. This wasn't the first time Arano's life had been in grave peril. For that matter, it wasn't the first time he had been left behind. Hadn't he come out unscathed when left behind in the midst of an Event Horizon stronghold in the Selpan System?

But Selpan was different. He had been left behind enemy lines, but safely anonymous, and while he'd had a few hair-raising adventures, he had escaped without falling into enemy hands. But Lentin's contacts had confirmed what Alyna feared: New Dawn operatives, specifically the Tycon Mar, had captured an Avenger, a Human by their reports. Once they determined their captive was Padian, it wouldn't take Gorst's people long to figure out who they had. After all, it was common knowledge that Arano had escaped the insurrection at Hawan's side, and there weren't any other Padians around at the time.

What frightened Alyna the most was who his captors were. If Event Horizon, or even one of the smuggler bands, had captured him, they would probably interrogate him, maybe rough him up a little, and then try to exchange him for a ransom. But if half of what she had heard about the Tycon Mar was true, he could be in store for tortures so severe they would make medieval interrogators ashamed. She could not permit him to remain in their hands, yet here she was, trudging through the calf-deep snow in the opposite direction from where her husband was being held captive.

It was dawn by the time they returned, and Alyna was exhausted. Despite her protestations to the contrary, Videre and Laron insisted she needed sleep, so she lay down. She allowed her eyes to close briefly, and when they opened, it was noon. She clambered out of her tent, still wearing her jacket, and pushed her hair under a winter cap. The footing was treacherous in their camp; the booted feet of the soldiers had tramped the snow down, and the night's temperatures had frozen it solid. She slipped and slid her way across the compound to the ruins of an ancient temple, which they were using as a planning room. Lentin, Videre, Lain, and Laron were gathered there, along with Mendan, who represented the Latyrians. They looked up wordlessly when she entered.

It was Mendan who found his voice first. "Alyna, you have our sympathy. Rest assured, we will see to it that Viper will soon be freed."

Alyna bravely fought back the unshed tears standing in her eyes. "Thank you, Mendan."

Videre stood beside her, enveloping her shoulders in one of his massive, fur-covered arms. "Like the man said, we're going to get him out. We have a plan laid out, and—"

"What are we doing, and when do we leave?" she asked briskly.

Laron gave a halfhearted smile. "We're going to move in small bands. Each group will have a Latyrian, in order to facilitate short-range communications. Non-Bromidians are still moving about freely in Notron, so we'll be able to accompany the teams without jeopardizing the mission. You and I will go with Enton and three Bromidians on the first team. The second group will be Videre, Lain, and Vantir with another three Bromidians. We'll have a few other teams consisting of Bromidians and a single Latyrian.

"We won't be able to raid the prison right away, because they'll be looking for a rescue attempt. Instead, we're going to hit them where it hurts. We'll be planting bombs around the city at numerous sites: bridges, power stations, weapons depots, command and control centers, military housing areas, and so on. When we set off a few of these bombs every hour, the Tycon Mar will have to respond. While we have them racing around the city trying to find us, Mendan will lead a band of Latyrians into the prison, and they will rescue Arano."

Alyna drew herself up, hands on her hips in protest. "I want to be on the team that goes into the prison!"

"Sorry, Alyna," Lain said, holding up a green-skinned amphibian-like hand. "They are going to enter through the ventilation system, which isn't big enough for you to squeeze through. Remember, Latyrians can fold themselves into impossibly small areas. They'll have to leave another way, but they should have the element of surprise when they enter."

Alyna nodded, eyes dropping to her feet. "When do we leave?"

"In two hours, our team will head out first," Laron told her. "We should arrive at the city shortly after sunset, which will make it more difficult for them to determine we are more than what we'll seem to be."

Alyna dropped into a chair, pulling out a packet of field rations. "I'll be ready."

Kish scanned the perimeter of their target building, but no one could be seen. She gave a sharp cutting motion with her free hand, and Vic sprinted from his place of shelter. Running in a low crouch, he reached the entry doors and checked their status. His signal to Kish, not unexpectedly, indicated that the door was secured and protected by an alarm. Following their established protocol, Toshe ran up to join Vic, and together they attached several electronic leads to the panel controlling the door. Kish waited breathlessly while they worked, watching the streets and alleys around her for signs of movement. She shifted the un-wieldy short-barreled rifle in her hands, not used to the extra weight of a projectile weapon.

It had been Arano's idea, originally. One of the dangers Avenger teams faced on covert raids was detection by internal sensors when firing energy weapons. Perhaps it was due in part to Arano's affinity for his sniper rifle, which fired a large projectile round at incredible distances, but he had suggested projectile rifles as an alternative weapon. The obvious drawback of the loud report from such weapons was dealt with rather easily by attaching silencers to the ends of their barrels. That left the other two shortcomings, those being the added weight and the necessity to carry ammunition. However, Kish had decided to give the idea a try. The length of the rifles was almost identical to that of the compact laser rifles they carried for the same purpose, long enough to provide accuracy, but short enough to be efficient in the cramped quarters of a building's interior.

With a mechanical hum, the doors slid open, and Kish was the first through the opening, Pelos at her side. The corridor beyond was empty, so Kish motioned the others forward. With leveled weapons, the Avengers team peered down their sights, prowling the corridors and searching for signs of the enemy. Kish kept a close eye on her wrist-mounted scanner as well, checking for electronic surveillance equipment. The hallways were ornately decorated, and Kish decided it may have been a place of learning at some point. The floors were made of something akin to marble, sectioned into square tiles and polished to a high sheen. The walls were covered with decorative paper, and there was a wooden railing running the length of the wall on both sides of the hallway, fixed at about waist level.

They moved in pairs, Kish and Pelos in the lead, Imatt and Lon in the middle, and Vic and Toshe acting as a rear guard. Kish wasn't certain what they were looking for, but since the rooms appeared to be labeled in the standard language of the Coalition, she counted on finding some type of computerized data storage area using the signs as a guide.

The wing they were in was devoted to offices for lesser functionaries. On a whim, Kish called the group to a halt and inspected one of the offices at random. They found nothing of interest, discovering only bills of lading and shipping orders, so they moved on. After checking three more similar offices, she decided to try another section of the building.

Pelos located a staircase, and they filed inside. They climbed the stairs one teammate at a time, trying to keep from bunching up in the confined quarters of the stairwell, and wound their way to the top floor. Kish reasoned that the ten floors between her and ground level were less likely an area to store sensitive information. Such data would either be in a basement, a hidden area, or an executive suite, such as those they were about to inspect.

The hallway on the top level was even more immaculate than the one on the ground level had been. The floor had been polished to mirror-brightness, and the doors had ornate handles.

On tables interspersed along the hallway stood intricately carved statues of various gods, heroes, and beasts which seemed to hail from the various mythos of every race.

The doors on the top level were dispersed at greater distances, likely an indicator of how much larger the executive offices would be. She gathered her team around the first door and placed them into position. She gave a silent three-count and burst through the door, Pelos and Imatt at her side. The office was empty, and they called the all-clear to their teammates.

Kish ordered the team inside, and they secured the door behind them. As a security precaution, Toshe volunteered to continue watching the door while the others made their search. A sprawling wooden desk dominated the far wall, topped with a pair of wire baskets and piles of datapads. Pictures of landscapes dotted the walls, and there were several hanging plants. A lush carpet covered the floor, except a small area around the executive bar, which had more of the marble-like tile. Kish went to a tall metal filing cabinet in one corner of the room, pulled open the top drawer, and rummaged about inside. Not finding anything of interest, she moved on, checking the other three drawers in the cabinet.

"Aha!" The triumphant shout came from Imatt, who had physically removed the main drawer in the massive desk and stuck his arm into the opening up to his shoulder. He pulled out a folder containing a sheaf of papers, and from where Kish was standing, she could plainly see the New Dawn logo at the top of the first page. She returned to her own exploration of the filing cabinet, figuring Imatt would tell her if he found anything useful.

"Well, I suppose this is helpful," Imatt said reluctantly. "About all it does is confirm what we already believed: Xuber Mining Company is owned by New Dawn. These papers express the exact relationship between the two entities. I guess, in the grand scheme of things, it could be important at some later date, but for now, there isn't a whole lot here."

"At least we know our intelligence reports were correct, and there is a link between the two," Vic said, holding a piece of paper up to the light for a closer inspection.

They completed their search of the office without turning up anything else of interest and moved back into the hallway. The other doors proved to open on bare walls and floors, showing rooms in total disuse. They were halfway back to the stairs when the door to the stairwell opened, and a sleepy-eyed guard stepped, yawning, into the hallway. The young Bromidian was startled by the appearance of so many people who were not supposed to be there, and he hesitated for a moment before reaching for his weapon. The delay proved fatal when both Kish and Pelos opened fire. Their silenced rifles hissed and clanked, but Kish was amazed by how quiet the weapons were overall. With a grim detachment, she watched the guard's body slam back against the door and slide limply to the ground, blood dripping from his mouth.

"That was messy," Vic said with understated aplomb, admiring the spattered blood dotting the door and wall. The thick black Bromidian blood was pooling on the floor around the guard, and Kish wondered how they could hide it.

Lon supplied the answer in expedient fashion. He returned to the office they had inspected, where he retrieved a towel from the bar and a rug from behind the desk. He used the towel to wipe the blood from the door as best he could, and the rug covered the mess on the floor rather handily. Using the towel to prevent the blood from dripping on the floor, they carried the Bromidian back to the office and hid the body in a closet.

Once again they entered the stairwell, this time descending

to the basement level. The construction was more utilitarian than decorative, and Kish's intuition told her it was a good sign. Perhaps in such an area, New Dawn might house the computers holding the data they so desperately craved. Their feet shuffled and scratched against the bare concrete floors, and the cinder block walls were covered with a light layer of dust. Rooms were set aside by plain metal doors, each having a window near the top, but the windows had been blacked out.

The short corridor had no outlets other than the six doors, three in each wall, but none of the doors were labeled. She posted Lon and Imatt as security at the base of the stairs and sent Vic and Toshe into the rooms on the left side of the hall. She and Pelos would handle the other rooms. She flicked a switch on her rifle, activating the barrel-mounted light, and Pelos did likewise.

They burst into the first room, finding it unoccupied. There were several short stacks of boxes on one side of the room, while the other was bare. She grabbed the nearest box, dumping its contents on the floor. After pawing through the mess and finding nothing of interest, she moved on to the next box.

They finished searching the room, but with nothing to show for their efforts but a tremendous mess. Both Avengers reactivated their lights, kicking their way into the second room. Again, with no one inside, they slung their rifles and surveyed the contents. This room was more organized than the previous, with filing cabinets lining two walls. Most of them were empty, but a few contained files bursting with papers. In the next fifteen minutes, Kish located three different files containing financial transactions between Xuber Mining and New Dawn. With the minerals Xuber Mining had been providing New Dawn, they could fuel their Rift Drive engines and manufacture torpedoes and plasma cannons. She tucked those files safely away in her pack.

She was about to close the drawer and move onto the next, when a reflection of light caught her eye. There was something at the back of the cabinet. She removed the entire drawer and set it aside, then aimed the light from her rifle into the void left by the drawer. It was a data disk, secured to the back of the cabinet by an adhesive. She tugged gently on the disk, and it came free with little resistance. She had no way of reading it until they returned to the *Intrepid*, but whatever was on there had to be important, having been hidden so well. She placed it in a small, well-protected pouch in her jacket.

They found no other major items, just a few references to the relationship between New Dawn and Xuber Mining. She joined Lon and Imatt in providing security, while Pelos, Toshe, and Vic circled the basement, placing their explosives and attaching the detonator devices. Although she heard footsteps on the floor above, and occasional muffled voices, no one came down the stairs to challenge them. When Pelos returned, she opened the door and motioned Lon and Imatt through. On a whim, she removed the silencer from her rifle, signaling her comrades to do likewise. The need for stealth was over, especially with the imminent destruction of the entire building. She wondered what effect the loud crack of the report from a projectile round would have on enemy morale, especially in such closed quarters.

They reentered the main floor hallway, still traveling in pairs. When the group was only halfway to the exit, a door opened right next to Kish, and a surprised Bromidian soldier stood towering over the diminutive Kish, insectoid mouth open in surprise. Too slow, his hand tracked in the direction of his holstered pistol, but Kish's rifle was already in position. She fired three shots in rapid succession, sending the Bromidian tumbling back in a spray of blood. Kish dropped to one knee, anticipating further resistance from within the room. She wasn't disappointed, and three more Bromidians took up firing positions. Kish fired off a few shots before diving for cover.

The firefight raged in the hallway, the piercing shots of the Bromidian laser rifles contrasting sharply with the deafening blasts from the projectile weapons of the Avengers. Lon shouted a curse, stepped back, and fired point-blank into the wall separating the hallway from the room beyond. He emptied his entire magazine, spraying bullets randomly through the room, suppressing the returning fire coming from within. Vic and Toshe, by the unspoken agreement that comes from years of working closely together, dove through the doorway, rolling in opposite directions and peppering the furniture the Bromidians were using as cover. The bullet-riddled insectoid bodies tumbled into view, their black, viscous blood spilling across the floor.

"Everyone out!" Kish shouted, and climbed to her feet. The six soldiers scampered for the exit, pouring through the door and into the alley beyond. She felt her strength fading rapidly, an expected side effect of the thin atmosphere. They had barely gone a block when she beckoned to Pelos. He raised a shaggy eyebrow, but shrugged and reached for his detonator. The explosion rocked the city, knocking them staggering to their knees and shattering windows all around them. Kish paused only long enough to check everyone for injuries before she had them off and running again.

She was gasping for air by the time they teetered up the ramp into the *Intrepid*. She wasted no time increasing the air pressure and, as an added measure of protection, also temporarily increased the oxygen levels in the ship. With the tap of a few controls, the ship's engines fired up in preparation for takeoff. Kish looked around the bridge at her team, their shoulders heaving with exhaustion, and burst out laughing.

"Wow," she said, rubbing her leathery hands over her ears. "I had no idea how loud those rifles would be inside."

"What?" Pelos shouted, cupping one hand behind his ear.

"I said . . ." Kish started to say, louder, then caught the impudent grin on Pelos's face and erupted with laughter once again.

The *Intrepid* launched from the planet's surface, meeting no resistance on the way into planetary orbit. Kish hadn't expected any problems; the entire fleet had been destroyed, along with New Dawn's only known remaining facility, but she raised the ship's shields, just in case. She programmed the automatic pilot to guide the ship to the rendezvous point with the rest of the fleet and then opened her pack.

She rummaged through the contents, locating the data disk in its protected pocket. Tapping the disk gently against her hand, she ambled across the bridge to a dataport and inserted the disk before sitting down. She stared absently at the screen for several moments while the computer analyzed the data contained on the disk. The computer flashed a warning that the data contained therein was inscribed in the Bromidian tongue, and asked if it should translate. Kish slapped a button irritably, and the computer processed the translation in short order.

Reading the data scrolling across her screen, she frowned sharply, trying to decipher what she was seeing. "This makes no sense," she complained bitterly.

Imatt stepped lightly behind her, one hand on the back of her chair. "What's that?"

She gestured irritably at the screen. "The information on this disk. It has no coherence at all. There are a number of files, but they seem totally unrelated to each other. Look at this. The first file is a list of the names of all the victims of the Disciples of

Zhulac, including the dates and times of their attacks. Another one contains info about the efficiency of various ion engine models. Others contain such vital information as weather reports from Rystoria 2, a complete genealogical listing of the names, DNA, and dates of birth of all descendants of the Bromidian emperors from Gorst VI to the present, and the schematics for a prototype fighter they seem to have been working on. I can't make any sense of it." She scrolled farther down the screen. "Here's a complete recording of sensor data from the final battle over Rystoria 2."

"I'd like to see that," Imatt said. "We are always looking for more data on the battle, especially with the unknown alien ships we found there."

"We still have several hours before the fleet leaves for the Rystoria System, so you should have time to look it all over," Lon replied, peeling off his body armor.

"I hope we can make some sense of all this," Pelos said, shaking his head darkly.

Arano lay unmoving on his back, the cold steel of his newly acquired blade pressing uncomfortably against his bare skin. He didn't like the idea of lying on what amounted to a short-bladed sword, but he had nowhere else he could hide it and still have easy access to the weapon. His skin recoiled in revulsion from the sticky wetness under him, remnants of the murdered Gatoan's final, terrifying moments. He closed his eyes, concentrated on his breathing, and tried to slow his racing heart. Arano's entire body ached from the beating it had taken over the past twelve hours which, added to the fatigue he was facing, would have incapacitated most people. But his spark of life had been re-kindled by the violent death he had witnessed, and he knew one fact with a dreadful certainty: Carraf would pay for what she had done, whether Arano escaped or not.

The heavy lock slid open, and the moment he had waited for arrived. Through half-closed eyelids, he watched the lithe form of Carraf strut across the floor.

"Good news, my friend!" she said cheerfully. "We have an-other Coalition spy on her way here—a Tsimian. I have some extra special treatments in store for her." She ran her fingers lux-uriously through her hair. "I really think you'll enjoy them."

"Why don't you go to Martok," Arano hissed, invoking the name of the Padian god of evil. Her jaw dropped in surprise, and then her face flushed red with anger. "That's right," he contin-ued. "I know you're a Padian. You can't hide it from me because I'm one, too."

She stopped mid-stride, rolled her eyes, and licked her lips with the tip of her tongue. "So our suspicions were correct. We are holding the infamous Captain Arano Lakeland, the man who is single-handedly trying to exterminate the Bromidian race. I think my friends will be excited to know who we have." She moved to his side, reaching out a hand to stroke his face, then froze, a premo-nition of danger evident on her suddenly scowling features.

Arano sat upright with the speed of a cat, bringing the blade around and down sharply across her forearm. The short sword bit deeply and continued through, severing her left arm just below the elbow. She grasped the stump of her ruined arm, blood spurting through her fingers, and raised her eyes to his, unable to form a coherent phrase. With grim determination, Arano rose from the platform and inexorably stalked his former tormentor, who was backing away from him on unsteady feet.

"Scream," he said coldly, no expression on his swollen and bloody face. "Scream as loud as you can. I want to hear you scream before you die."

She regained her composure and made a sudden leap for freedom, jumping past Arano's outstretched hand and bolting for the locked door. Arano gave chase, deliberately allowing her to reach the metal portal, where she pounded and screamed for the guards' attention. From directly behind her, Arano looked through the small window and saw two Bromidians responding to her cries. He seized her by a shoulder, spun her around, and slashed her diagonally from shoulder to hip. Her entrails came boiling out from between her fingers, and she dropped to her knees, forlornly trying to push the dangling organs back inside her dying body.

Arano left her sprawled in front of the entryway, limp body blocking the door from opening, and stood to one side against the wall. The guards unlocked the door and pushed their way inside, attention focused on the crumpled figure in front of them. Arano slashed one across the back of the neck, nearly severing his head, and plunged the blade into the body of the other. They both tumbled to the floor, piling on top of Carraf's still-thrashing body. Arano used his sword again, making sure the two guards were dead. He had planned to leave Carraf to die slowly, but changed his mind. His anger at his treatment was fading fast with the taste of freedom, and his barbaric streak didn't run all that deep.

He rolled her over to face him, and she stared up with wide, frightened eyes. "Captain Arano Lakeland," he said. "USC Avengers. I'm here on a covert mission to overthrow the illegitimate government of Gorst IX. Or, 'Vagorst,' as we like to call him. Anything else you want to know? I didn't think so." He drove the blade home once more.

Arano checked the hall outside the door, saw it was clear, and returned to the bodies. One at a time, he rolled them over, going through their pockets and equipment belts for anything of value, although he was a bit standoffish about touching Carraf, with her intestines arranged across her hips. Knowing what the weather was like outside, he wrapped his tattered shirt around his torso, then covered it with a guard's plain brown jacket before continuing his inventory. His efforts rewarded him with two laser pistols, a set of encrypted key cards, a key ring similar to the one carried by his original guards, a radio, and a decent knife in a sheath he could conceal inside his sleeve.

He returned to the doorway, checked the other side, and slipped through. Although he didn't know the way out, he wasted no time in rushing through the complex. Freedom was his for the taking, but he must be swift. His most logical location was below ground; for some reason, every culture in the known galaxy liked to put its torture chambers underground. Maybe it was from having too many captives escape through windows. For whatever reason, if he was right, he needed to find stairs going up.

He heard a voice ahead of him, around the next corner. Walking as softly as he could, he sidled forward to the intersection and holstered his pistol. He smiled grimly at his foresight of bringing not only the knife, concealed in his sleeve, but also the short sword, which dangled from his belt. He drew both weapons, firmed his jaw, and crouched low against the wall.

Two Bromidians turned the corner, dragging a limp form between them. Arano exploded into violence, leaping to his feet while plunging the knife into the chest of the first soldier and slashing at the second. He delivered three devastating blows in lightning-quick succession, and his foe was dead before he hit the ground. Arano wiped his blades clean, replaced them in his clothing, and checked on the Tsimian who had dropped, almost unnoticed, to the floor during the scuffle. Her breathing was shallow and ragged, and judging by the wounds to her abdomen and chest, she was dying. Her eyelids fluttered and opened, and she coughed, a thin rivulet of blood trickling down along the edge of her beak.

"Who . . . are you?" she asked quietly, chest heaving with the effort.

"I'm with the Avengers," he said. "I'm getting you out of here."

She shook her head slowly, closing her eyes in pain. "I can't walk, and I'm too heavy for you to carry. There's something more important you must do." Her voice dropped to a near-whisper, and Arano leaned closer to hear her words. "Just south of the Town Square is a baker's shop. In the back, beneath a storage room, is the entrance to an underground lab. My friends and I had just found it when we were captured. The Tycon Mar agents were furious about its discovery. You must find out what is down there."

Arano nodded, and said under his breath, "I will."

"You must! I overheard them talking after they thought they had beaten me unconscious. Whatever is down there could destroy New Dawn and restore the rightful government to power. Now, you must go. My time is short."

Arano looked up at the ceiling, firming his resolve for what he knew he must do. The Tsimian was right: in Arano's condition, there was no way for him to carry her out. He handed her one of the pistols he had taken from the guards in his cell, took her hand in reassurance, and dashed away. Based on the rank worn by the two he had just killed, they were not stationed in the prison complex's lower levels, and he was guessing either stairs or a lift would be nearby.

His speculation was proven correct. Not too far from where he had slain the guards, he found the lift he expected they had used. Pulling out the key ring he had taken, he tried placing them, one at a time, into a slot in the wall. The fourth key brought the lift to life, and it rose smoothly upward. Although he had no idea how many floors it climbed, he was satisfied when it finally lurched to a stop, sending his stomach reeling for a moment. He leveled his pistol, and the doors hissed open. He was alone.

At the end of a short hallway stood a set of double doors. He tried his key cards, this time getting lucky on the first try. The doors slid open, and Arano was momentarily blinded by the bright Rystorian sunlight streaming through the towering opening at the far end of the motorpool. Hovercars lined the walls, and one was even running. There were a few technicians scattered through the sprawling structure, but none had noticed his entry. He casually crossed the floor and climbed aboard the working hovercar. A Bromidian, who was cleaning the driver's area, turned in shock, and Arano struck him sharply across the head with his pistol. His eyes rolled back in his head, and he fell limply against the front seat. Arano tossed him over the side and moved to the front of his new vehicle.

Good luck was with him. Not only were the controls not locked out, but the hovercar actually had front- and rear-mounted laser cannons, controlled remotely from the pilot's seat. His familiarity with Bromidian technology paid off, and in moments the hovercar was gliding for the exit. There was a startled exclamation, and several technicians ran to block his way. He accelerated sharply, sending them diving aside. Another tried to close the doors, but Arano would not be denied. He fired the cannon, blasting the doors from their tracks, and sped off into the bright sunshine. He was free.

CHAPTER TWENTY-TWO

ALYNA LINGERED OVER HER TEA, CASTING OCCA-
sional surreptitious glances at her watch. *Less than a minute to go,*
she told herself. With one leg crossed daintily over the other, she
chatted casually about the weather, noting Laron's rolling eyes
and almost laughed in amusement. Lentin and two Latyrians
joined them, sitting down a bit quickly, and picking up menus
in an attempt to look nonchalant. Alyna rechecked her watch.
Five, four, three, two, one . . .

Right on time, a tremendous explosion ripped through the
wall of the police station down the street, throwing vehicles and
people in all directions and belching a plume of smoke into the
morning sky. A second explosion, echoing the first, detonated
a block farther north; and then a third. People were screaming
in panic, not sure where to run for safety. Alyna shrugged her
indifference, winked at Videre, and screamed in apparent panic,
running into the stirring crowd with her companions close behind her. Sirens shrieked through city, with emergency crews
struggling to respond through the uncontrollable masses.

After several minutes of utter chaos, military forces arrived.
With brutal efficiency, they clubbed those people who wouldn't
move for the crews trying to extinguish the roaring flames.

"Time to be going," Alyna muttered. "We have other havoc
to cause. I do so hate to be late for a party."

They joined the crowd in its generally westward retreat, escaping both the incendiary aftereffects of their bombings and the dangers posed by the Bromidian soldiers who were pummeling the citizens of Notron. After several more blocks, they managed to work their way clear of the crush of people. Lentin got his bearings and directed them to their next safe house, where they would pick up more bombs for use that afternoon. The military forces of New Dawn were reeling in chaos, and Alyna intended to keep it that way.

She hadn't heard from Vantir's group, but it was probably too early. They were trying to infiltrate the lower ranks of New Dawn's military, concentrating on the establishments they frequented while off-duty, in an attempt to learn where they might be keeping Arano. In all likelihood, he would still be alive, but only for as long as his captors felt he could provide the Tycon Mar with information to use against the Coalition. And with Arano's stubborn streak, his usefulness would decline repidly.

They walked through the arched doorway of a bookstore, the six companions selecting novels at random from the shelves and pretending to read them. With her back turned, Alyna heard Lentin ringing the bell at the desk and an employee responding.

"Yes, sir. Can I help you?"

"I'm looking for something by Pletare," Lentin answered. "Preferably his early works."

"Pletare's first contributions to the literary world were less than stellar. It may be quite difficult to locate them."

"I'm a patient man. In the meantime, perhaps some poetry by Garas?"

Alyna heard the final lines of the ritualistic recognition passwords, dropped the tome she was perusing, and joined Lentin. The employee made a casual show of checking the sidewalks in front of the store, and was apparently satisfied by what he saw.

"Come with me," he said shortly, leading them into the area restricted to employees. He reached beneath an ancient, hand-carved chair, manipulated some unseen release, and a panel in the floor slid aside, revealing a rickety ladder descending into darkness. The clerk went first, swinging his legs over the edge and disappearing into the hole. Alyna followed, nervously climbing down the quivering ladder, and reaching the bottom just as the lights came up. Her companions joined them, and she heard the panel slide shut overhead.

The unnamed Bromidian beckoned for them to follow and led them to an earth-walled room, which had wooden beams supporting a dangerously sagging ceiling. Clods of dirt dotted the floor, a testament to the validity of Alyna's fears about the roof collapsing while they stood there. The walls were adorned with wooden shelves, which were covered with explosives, timers, and detonators. Videre spent several minutes assembling three more bombs, stashing them in their packs when he was finished. Their reticent host returned to the ladder but, instead of climbing out, checked a small scanner lying nearby.

"Two New Dawn soldiers have entered the store," he said. "We can't leave just yet." The minutes ticked by anxiously, and Alyna unsnapped the holster for her pistol in anticipation of the coming fight. The Bromidian continued to monitor the situation upstairs, occasionally giving his head a barely perceptible shake, trying unsuccessfully to hide his frustration.

"They just left, but I think the store is still being watched," he reported. "There is another exit in a nearby building, but none of our operatives are working today at the other end of the tunnel."

"I'd say we take our chances with the tunnel," Lon said.

The Bromidian seemed to consider the idea. "Agreed."

With casual disregard for the fragility of technology, he tossed the monitor back to the clay floor and entered another corridor. The ceiling was low, and Alyna frequently had to stoop over to keep from banging her head against the supporting beams. She lost track of how far they had walked but guessed it to be about two city blocks. The employee stopped before another home-made ladder.

"The monitor here no longer works," he cautioned them.

I wonder why, Alyna wondered dryly.

"Give me a moment to see if the way is clear."

He climbed the ladder, chunks of dirt falling from his shoes, and reached the top. With one hand braced against the roof for balance, he flipped a corroded metal switch and slid the covering hatch aside. From above, Alyna heard a startled gasp. Their escort darted out of the hole, and sounds of a scuffle ensued. Before the Avengers could react, a body tumbled back through the opening.

"Let's go," came a voice from above. Lain was the first onto the ladder, climbing with pistol in hand. Alyna followed, entering the storeroom for what was likely a restaurant. The rest of her team emerged, and the Bromidian motioned them to silence. He cracked open the door, then stepped aside and opened it farther.

"Go," he said simply. "I will deal with the body."

Before she stepped through the doorway, Alyna chanced a look back, just as the Bromidian slipped through the opening and the panel slid back into place, edges blending in perfectly with the decorative lines on the floor. Fortunately, business was slow, and there were no customers waiting to be seated. They left, emerging into the brightly sunlit streets, which were just being restored to some semblance of order following the bombings.

Alyna was doggedly determined to make sure the sense of order didn't last. The more chaos they created, the more soldiers

New Dawn would have to place out on the streets, and the fewer would be left to guard Arano.

She tried to regain her sense of direction while they briskly left the area of the restaurant. Next door was a store carrying various brands of outdoor clothing, and next to that, a baker's shop. Lentin set a northerly course, leading them to a large marketplace covering an entire city square block. In the center was a gazebo, made of wood and painted a light shade of blue. It was surrounded by a small park, with a close-cropped lawn and well-manicured bushes. Along the edges of the square, several merchants had set up temporary shops with wheeled carts, selling everything from souvenir trinkets to quick lunches. Alyna's team stopped at one such cart, ordered their food, and ate it on the move.

The bustling galleria offered a nearly irresistible target for a bombing, knowing the chaos and panic it would create, but Alyna decided against it. Most of the civilians were innocent members of Bromidian society, who were simply trying to live their lives in peace. They followed Gorst IX blindly, believing he had Divine Right, and because to oppose him meant death. They didn't deserve to be blown away in a senseless act of terrorism.

She decided they should try to find another target, near enough to have the desired effect on the patrons at the square, but without the needless death. She was still shaken by the casual way the Bromidian from the bookstore had disposed of the employee from the restaurant, but there was nothing to be done about it. She whispered her incendiary plans to Lentin, who stood up straight, peering over the heads of the crowd, before setting off across the square.

He took them to another eatery—this one with outdoor tables—which seemed to be frequented almost exclusively by members of the military. The two Latyrians peeled off from the group and sat at one of the tables, earning hardly a glance from the aloof soldiers dining around them. Alyna and Laron stopped near an office used as a military outpost, watching Lentin, Videre, and Lain disappear into the mingling crowd. She tried to act casual, chatting with Laron as if nothing were amiss.

"Who are you?" asked a harsh voice.

She spun to face two Bromidian soldiers, their arms bearing the New Dawn patch. "Us?" she asked, trying to sound indignant.

"Yes, you," one soldier sneered, coming closer. "I want to know what business you Humans have here. More than likely, you're Coalition spies."

"Now, Garlis," the other said in a deceptively calm manner, "we don't know that for sure. I'm certain they have a perfectly legitimate reason for being here." He gave them a menacing look, the gray shells of his eyelids narrowing dangerously. "Don't you?"

"We're looking to set up a business here," Laron lied smoothly. "We thought we'd check the main square, where everyone else seems to have a shop, and see what's missing. It wouldn't do to start a shoe store if there were already four shoe stores running, now, would it?"

Some of the suspicion drained out of Garlis's eyes. "Well, you shouldn't be loitering. There have been some bombings today, and we have orders to arrest anyone suspicious." He looked at his companion. "Do you want to run them in?"

He seemed to consider the matter. "No, not this time." He thrust a hard, bony finger in Laron's face. "Don't let me catch you so much as spitting on the sidewalk, Outlander."

Alyna followed Laron's lead, turning swiftly away from the soldiers. They wasted no time in scurrying away from the outpost, putting distance between them and the suspicious Bromidians. So intent was Alyna on their hurried pace that they had gone two full blocks before she realized Laron no longer carried his satchel. He noticed her puzzled look and arched his eyebrows, face split by an evil grin.

"Oops," he said simply.

Alyna flinched at the sound of the explosion rocking the street and sending Bromidian citizens scrambling for safety once again. Another detonation rocked the café where they had left the two Latyrians, and yet a third from the direction where Lentin had gone. Joining the clamoring throng, Alyna and Laron rushed away from the direction of the first explosion, trying to stay side by side in the juxtaposing mass.

"How did you. . . ?" Alyna asked, trying unsuccessfully to phrase the question.

"When they looked away, I dropped it in the garbage can," he explained. "Let's get to the rendezvous site."

Arano cursed, slamming his fist on the console in front of him. He turned his hovercar to the left, being as nonchalant as he could about the sudden change in direction. Bromidian soldiers ringed the main road to Notron, stopping and thoroughly inspecting each vehicle as it left the city. Obviously, something was amiss, possibly more than a simple prison break. He wondered if the heightened alert status might be related to the series of explosions he had heard from deeper in the city. He turned down another side street, hoping the explosions were a result of RLF activities.

Obviously, he needed another way out of the city. Perhaps he could find somewhere near the town's outskirts where he could leave the hovercar, and set off some type of explosion to distract any New Dawn operatives in the area. He would escape on foot and make the long trek back to safety. One thing was certain, he assured himself, the resolve strengthening within him had set his blood boiling. He would not be captured again.

For several minutes, he followed a meandering course to the northwest, taking him within two hundred meters of the edge of the city. In the distance, he saw New Dawn soldiers encircling the city, not only on the roads, but in the unpaved terrain as well. He frowned, turned his hovercar down an alley, and headed deeper into the city. The plan he had in mind would not succeed easily. There were too many soldiers out there for one exploding vehicle to clear a path for him in broad daylight. Perhaps he should wait for nightfall and take his chances under cover of darkness.

A lone Bromidian stepped from behind a dumpster, blocking his progress. Arano almost pressed the accelerator, giving the man a choice—move or die—but hesitated, wondering why he had received no warning from his danger sense. It was possible for this to be something other than what it seemed, so he decided to allow the scenario to play itself out. He surreptitiously felt for the pistol he had found in the vehicle, which he had conveniently stowed away under the dash, and slowed the hovercar to a stop. With casual slowness, he powered up the forward laser cannon.

"What do you need?" Arano asked, crossing his arms, irritation coming to the surface since the other hadn't said a word.

"We need your hovercar," the Bromidian said simply.

"We?"

Several figures detached themselves from the shadows, rifles leveled, and surrounded him. Arano hesitated, instinct telling him to go for his weapons and try to get the hovercar away, but wondering why he still felt no danger. He set the vehicle to idle and rested his elbows on the console.

"And just who might you be?"

"No one you need to know. Get down from there, and you won't get hurt."

Arano never found out what he would have done next. He heard a startled gasp, and glanced to his left to see another Bromidian, weapon lowering, jaw hanging open in dumbfounded stupefaction. The other finally found his voice.

"Viper?"

Then it was Arano's turn to be rendered speechless. He nodded, not knowing what else to do. He hadn't believed these Broms posed a threat to him, but he also didn't know how they could recognize him. Unless . . .

"My name is Xalen. I believe you know my father." He extended his right hand, pulled back the sleeve, and a retractable claw flipped into view. He was a Latyrian! "Enton is my father. We're here with Vantir, and we've come to rescue you."

There was a low but triumphant shout from the group, and several more emerged from hiding to extend a hand in greeting. Arano felt a wave of relief rush over him, finding himself once more among friends. He was taken along the filthy, trash-laden alley to a smudged, cracked wooden door. One of the Latyrians knocked twice, and the door slid open with a loud creak. He was ushered inside, and two of the Latyrians rushed back down the alleyway.

"My friends will move your hovercar into hiding," Xalen said. "It may yet prove useful, but we wouldn't want the Broms finding it and starting a search in the area. In the meantime, my father will be happy to see you. He was just planning how we were going to break into the prison unnoticed, and when we saw the hovercar with the prison logo on the side we figured we'd found the means. Looks like now we don't need to."

"Viper! You're alive! By Xaxil, I didn't think we'd ever see you again!" Vantir rushed out of a small room, embracing Arano in a rough bear hug. Arano freed himself, hands firmly gripping his friend's shoulders.

"Thank you for coming after me. I managed to escape the prison, but I don't know how much farther I'd have gotten without your help."

"We'll find your wife and the others, and figure out a way to get you out of here. I think the time is coming when only Bromidian and Latyrian operatives should be in town. They're starting to get suspicious of the Coalition races, even with all the pirates and mercenaries working for them."

Arano rubbed one hand over his stubble-covered face, wincing in pain when his hand found the marks left by Carraf. "Actually, I think there's something more important we can do. An agent with Coalition Intelligence told me about a clandestine lab New Dawn has hidden beneath a bakery here in town. She said the lab holds a secret that could bring down the entire insurrection."

"Okay. Why don't you rest for a bit and have someone tend to your wounds. We'll get your wife and her teams in here and get something together. We'll have you in that lab tonight."

Alyna hunched over her drink, Laron on one side and Videre on the other. With their entire strike force, they had gathered in a tavern, eating an evening meal and waiting for the clamor outside to settle down. Alyna had agreed with Laron's assessment that things were heating up in Notron, and the military was reacting at a greater level than they had anticipated. In a way, it was good news, because they had hoped for an overreaction in order to facilitate Arano's rescue. But it also provided an added element of danger to their continued operations in the city because, as they had already seen, non-Bromidians were going to be accosted regularly and for no particular reason. They had to be cautious.

The tavern owner entered the eating area, adjusting the volume level on the various monitors hanging from the walls. "His Imperial Majesty, Gorst IX, is about to speak," he announced by way of explanation. Alyna exchanged concerned looks with her companions, and then the monitor sounded a long, monotone alarm, catching everyone's attention.

The screen went blank for several seconds, replaced by a patch Alyna had seen on Tycon Mar uniforms: a red diamond, overlaid by a silver pyramid. Soon, Gorst's hate-filled countenance appeared, features drawn back in a perpetual sneer.

"Attention, people of Vagorst. I am your rightful ruler, Gorst IX, son of Gorst VIII, and I come before you with tidings this evening.

"First, I wish to address today's madness in the city of Notron. Forces loyal to the Coalition-installed puppet government have infiltrated Notron, planting explosives in foul acts of cowardly terrorism. Afraid of facing the might of the Bromidian army on the field of battle, they instead cower among the populace and choose to destroy public facilities. Thousands of civilians of all races have died in the wake of their carnage. These are the people who would claim to act in your interests. Remember, my people, only one who is of the bloodline of Gorst has the Divine Right to rule the Bromidian people.

"I also come before you bringing good news. For too long

have we stood alone against the aggression and might of the Coalition. We have new friends now in our struggles, allies who will help bring about the destruction of the Coalition and all its stands for, ushering in an unprecedented period of peace and prosperity for our people.

"But I speak in haste. They are only close friends, not allies, although the time for alliance is not far off. We will join forces and crush our enemies. They will rue the day they stood against us in battle. I give you my friend, Zirof, ambassador for his people. I give you . . . the Chrysarthi!"

Another figure appeared on the screen, grinning grotesquely, baleful smirk revealing a row of sharply pointed teeth, with protruding canines on both jaws. His ears obtruded distinctly, both up and down, ending in well-defined points. Vertically slitted pupils glared out from green eyes, and a long, thin, forked tongue snaked in and out of his mouth. Brown skin was covered with scales, face lined with long grooves and deep pockmarks. The only hair Alyna could see was on his head, a great, white tuft protruding at insane angles from his scalp. He spoke with a dry, husky voice.

"I, Zirof of the Chrysarthi, do hereby pledge by my life's blood to make every effort to bring about a never-ending period of friendship with the Bromidians and their rightful ruler, Gorst IX. We recognize only his government, and any pretenders to the throne will feel our wrath, as surely as they will feel the wrath of Gorst himself. Someday soon, I hope to sign articles of alliance, forever cementing our relationship." He thrust a scaly fist into the air. "Death to the Coalition!"

Gorst prattled on about the state of affairs, but Alyna had quit listening. She caught Videre's curious gaze and followed it to where the Latyrians in their group sat. Both were sitting bolt upright, ears cocked as if listening. One pursed his lips, appearing to whistle but making no sound, and Alyna finally understood. They were communicating using the sounds they were able to make and hear, but which were above the audible spectrum for other races. The muted conversation went on for a brief time, and then one of the Latyrians sent a meaningful look in the direction of the door. Alyna drained her glass and stood. Her team followed her back into the oppressive sunlight, and one of the Latyrians moved immediately to her side. They followed the broad avenue before them, walking briskly to blend in with the gradually calming crowd.

"What do you have?" she asked.

"We just received word from Vantir. We have good news. Viper has escaped from New Dawn's prisons, and he is with Vantir even as we speak. We must join them as soon as possible for a critical mission."

Alyna's knees buckled, and tears of joy stood out in her eyes. Unable to speak, she gestured forward with an open hand, palm up, telling her Latyrian escort to lead the way.

CHAPTER TWENTY-THREE

ARANO TRIED ONCE AGAIN, UNSUCCESSFULLY, TO disentangle himself from his wife's arms. She smothered him in kisses, careful to avoid the remaining unhealed contusions on his face. While his Latyrian medic had been thorough, the equipment they had simply couldn't deal with the extent of the wounds Arano had received. All the same, with a bath and a change of clothes, he felt rejuvenated, and was ready to undertake his next mission. He squeezed his wife a bit more tightly, trying to find a way to gracefully sit back down while enfolded in her embrace.

His entire team stood assembled. *No*, he corrected himself, *not the* entire *team. Kish and Pelos are still on the* Intrepid *somewhere, doing who knows what. Maybe Commander Alstor has more information on what is happening off-world.*

It was Laron, naturally, who took charge of the meeting. "We just received an encoded message from the Coalition fleet. They have moved against a New Dawn stronghold in the Menast System, and they won an overwhelming victory. Coalition losses were light, and the relief force has already arrived to take care of occupation. The fleet is en route here."

There was an excited buzz in the room, and Laron had to wait for the assembled soldiers to calm down before he could continue. "Unfortunately, this is not a declaration of war." He placed a datapad firmly on the table in front of him, clearly expressing his displeasure with the turn of events. "Even though New Dawn has openly attacked Coalition targets, including government officials, the High Council was afraid to make the big call. Elections are coming, and it appears too many of the councilors feared for their political careers, thinking a vote for a declaration of war would be the end of their tenure on the Council. So they settled for a halfway measure. They are going to blockade the system.

"I know this isn't much, but it's a start. Once the blockade is in place, we can communicate directly with Coalition forces. They plan on dropping in more Avenger teams, hoping to wreak some havoc and maybe uncover something to get the Council to grow a backbone. There are even unconfirmed rumors that the Tsimians are sending a few Kian assassins to retaliate for the murders of some Tsimian officials within the Coalition government.

"This is where we stand. We are going to continue our covert missions against New Dawn, although we will have to minimize the daytime exposure of non-Bromidians while we're here . . . Latyrians notwithstanding, of course. The Tycon Mar has begun hassling outlanders at random, and there have even been reports of kidnappings. We must be cautious.

"Before I forget, I'm going to offer a word of advice. Based on the experiences Viper had while in their custody, do not expect humane treatment if captured by the enemy. Apparently, they will stop at nothing to extract information. Do not surrender to them, no matter what they might offer you. The tortures they are willing to mete out to their prisoners are beyond description.

"Arano, we need to get to this lab your contact spoke of. Are you sure she was both lucid and honest with you?"

Arano nodded firmly. "I have no doubt. She was fully aware of her surroundings, and she was deadly serious. Whatever is in that lab, we need to find it. We might just end up saving Coalition ships and lives in the process."

"What news did Kish have?" Alyna asked, leaning her head against Arano's shoulder. He arched his shoulder sharply, but she elbowed him in the ribs and laid her head on his shoulder. Arano sighed theatrically.

"I'll let you read her report in a moment. They've been quite busy. Your ship is still in one piece, if you're concerned at all."

"Okay," Arano said, ignoring Laron's attempt at humor. "The important question right now is this: how do we get into that bakery? It's going to be difficult enough to get through town at all. Walking right up to our target wouldn't be the brightest idea we could come up with."

Alyna raised her head long enough to offer a suggestion. "Were you referring to a bakery just south of the town square?" Seeing Arano nod his confirmation, she continued. "When we were using the tunnels made by the RLF operatives stationed here in Notron, one of them came out just a couple of buildings away from a bakery in that area. If it's the right one, we could use tunnels to end up right by our objective. Let the Latyrians act as our lookouts, and when it's clear, we can move the whole team into the bakery."

"What about the bakery employees?" Videre asked. "I doubt they will let us simply stroll through their store and open a hole in the ground."

"They'll have to be neutralized," Laron said, running his fingers through his hair. "I don't see any other way around it. We'll capture them if possible, but we can't let them raise the alarm."

"I'd hate to hurt innocent civilians if there's another way around it," Lain said.

"We've been planting bombs all afternoon," Vantir pointed

out. "We were targeting military subjects, but it was possible for innoncents to be hurt, either directly, by the explosion, or indirectly, in the aftermath. I don't see the difference."

"The difference," Laron replied, offering a half-smile, "is that we won't deliberately target civilians. We can't always avoid them getting hurt in the fallout from our actions, but we try to avoid inflicting intentional harm on them."

"It's a moot point anyway," Arano said. "In all likelihood, the Tycon Mar won't risk a chance discovery of their lab by someone working at the bakery. I would bet you the people working in there are going to be military at the least, but Tycon Mar in all likelihood."

"Okay," Videre said, "we go in through the tunnels. How do we get to the entrance? We're pretty far from the safe house where we were picking up bomb parts."

"I think that's where we come in," Enton replied. "My son and I can move through the populace undetected. We'll check with the RLF agents at the safe house and see if there are any other tunnels we could use to get closer. We might have to follow several tunnels, with short trips aboveground, but it would be less risky than openly walking all the way to the safe house."

Enton and Xalen left minutes later, dressed in the cloaks common to the Bromidian residents of Notron, enroute to the RLF safe house. Arano and his friends passed the time by reading Kish's reports, catching up on the information they had discovered in the intervening time since the insurrection. There was a puzzle before him, Arano knew, and he felt the pieces would all fit together at some point. He studied the data, but the answer eluded him, floating tantalizingly out of reach, like a hunter's prey in a dense fog.

It was dinnertime before the pair of Latyrians returned. They entered with a steely look in their eyes, and Arano wondered what news they brought with them. Enton waved everyone over.

"My friends, the way is open. We have a contact in the RLF who will meet us in a building only about a block away from where we now sit. We will follow two tunnels to get to the stronghold, and another to arrive at the building near the bakery.

"But the agent at the stronghold warned us in the strongest terms about using caution when we arrive. She said four agents have disappeared near that bakery in the last two days. I'd say there is something going on in there, something New Dawn would kill to cover up."

Videre shrugged indifferently as he finished cleaning his pistol. "Sounds like the place to be."

"When do they want to meet?" Lain asked.

"Right after dark. We want to minimize the chances of discovery, after all. She suggested we get into the tunnels and stop at the end of the one near our target. We could wait until the bakery is closed and go in while the employees are closing up."

Arano gnawed absently on a fingernail. "I think I'd like to get in as soon after closing as possible. If we wait too long, they'll be activating alarms and such. In fact, if the lab is so important, there may be a protocol about what time the alarms are supposed to be activated. We could end up finding what we want, only to discover a platoon of soldiers waiting for us when we come out."

The evening passed quickly, and night fell. The group pulled their cloaks tightly about their bodies and pulled their hoods up to cover their faces. Luck was on their side, and a light rain was falling. Arano fully expected it to turn to snow before the evening was over, but at least they had an excuse for keeping their hoods up, and with the combination of the rain and the near-freezing temperatures, there should be a concealing fog bank rising from the snow on the ground. The less attention they drew to themselves, the better.

They moved into the alley, plodding through a snowbank before reaching the center of the alley, which had been cleared. Two shadowy figures materialized near the mouth of the alley, and with only a brief check of Arano's team, stepped out onto the sidewalk and vanished into the mist. Arano and his companions hurried to catch up to them, trying to keep their contacts in sight. The two figures entered an abandoned building near the next corner.

Enton walked right past the door, stopping at the corner and checking the area. He clasped his hands behind his back, a prearranged signal telling the others it was safe to proceed. They filed inside, and Enton soon followed. Their escorts were waiting for them, guiding them through the darkened building without the aid of any illumination. They stopped before a cobweb-covered door, ignoring the ages of dust on the latch.

"This tunnel hasn't been accessed in quite some time," one of them said in a quiet, gravelly voice. "I can't guarantee you it will go all the way through. If it does, someone will meet you there. You'll find the access panel beneath a dresser in the far corner." Without another word, they left the Avengers alone in the empty building.

Arano reached out a gloved hand to gently open the door, disturbing the dust as little as possible. They could do nothing about the footprints they had left behind, but he would still do what he could to make tracking them difficult. Just as their guide had promised, there was a wooden dresser in the far corner. The only other furniture in the room was a heavy desk. In the center of the floor was the skin of some enormous Rystorian animal, which was being used as a decorative rug. Enton and Videre moved the dresser aside, and Alyna easily opened the trapdoor. Lain dropped through the opening first, waving his light around to ensure he was alone, and the others followed. Arano went last, choosing to drag the rug around the room, all but eliminating the dust from the floor. While it would be obvious someone had entered, it would be next to impossible to see how they had left.

Arano dropped through the trapdoor into a tunnel almost two meters high and a meter wide. He slid the panel in place overhead, drew his pistol, and followed his wife down the dark passageway. He tried using a pace count to track the distance they traveled, but even such a simple act was complicated by sudden turns and places where rocks, jutting downward from overhead, forced them to crawl. Eventually, he had no idea in which direction they were heading, nor how far they had come.

Lain announced the sighting of the tunnel's terminus, and they approached cautiously. The Latyrians moved to the fore, ready to be the first to emerge and assess the situation. The release for the hatchway above them wasn't hidden, and when Enton was in position, Lain pulled the latch. Enton climbed out first, followed closely by Xalen. After a few tense moments, Xalen's whispered voice called to them, telling them everything was okay.

When Arano stood above ground once more, there was another Bromidian waiting by the door. They seemed to be in a small warehouse, with crates stacked in orderly rows along the four walls. One corner was obscured by piles of pallets, which was where the tunnel access point had been located. Their guide, as taciturn as the two had been on the first leg of their journey, led them to another warehouse directly across the street. He took them into a janitorial closet, moved aside a garbage can, and activated the hidden release. They took to the tunnels again, arriving in the basement of the safe house at the end.

The Bromidian waiting for them at the next tunnel's end was a bit more forthcoming. "I've been stepping outside on occasion, trying to find out what they know about the bombings today. The odd thing is, I would have expected more soldiers on the streets. Very few of them have patrolled here, and none in the last hour." He paused, almost seeming to look through the front wall of the building to the street beyond. "I suppose it's possible they are concentrating their forces on the city's perimeter, trying to keep you from escaping."

They gathered near the tunnel's exit, settling into semi-comfortable nooks to await the next phase of the operation. Arano dozed off, finding the rest to be a welcome respite from the demands he had placed upon his body over the past several days. He awoke feeling refreshed when Alyna gently squeezed his arm.

"It's time," she said softly.

He pulled on his boots, gathered his gear, and joined the others. Their guide from the RLF, who had been keeping watch from aboveground in the bookstore, gave a prearranged tap on the access panel before opening it. His head appeared in the opening, a worried frown creasing his features.

"I don't like this. I've still only seen two small groups pass within sight of the shop. Something is wrong."

Alyna gave Arano a questioning look. "Well?"

He shook his head uncertainly. "It's difficult to say. We've been in danger since we started this mission, but I don't think we're any worse off now than we were before."

"I say we press on," Lain said. "Even if the Broms are planning something, it doesn't mean we can't outwit them."

"I agree," Laron added. "Let's go."

Their new escort took them out to the streets, turned left, and followed the sidewalk for about half a block. The streets were dark, the artificial lighting provided by the light poles too dim and too spread out to be effective. Long shadows lined the walkway, deepening in the scattered alleys. The rain had picked up, pattering noisily off the thick fabric of his hood, and the cold dampness in the air left his breath roiling in steamy clouds. Arano walked with hands buried deep in the pockets of his cloak, but his hand firmly wrapped around the hilt of his pistol. It was a trick he had learned long before, in his Daxia training. He had cut a slit in the cloak pocket, which prevented him from carrying anything but allowed him to reach through and lay hands on his weapons. His unease grew, and he released the snap on his holster.

In the dark haze of rain and mist, a shoe store appeared from the gloom. Their Bromidian escort stopped in a doorway, hands reaching from the depths of his cloak to place a keycard against a magnetic strip. From somewhere within the darkened structure, a lock audibly clicked its release, and the door swung silently open. The RLF agent stepped through the doorway and held it ajar while the others followed him inside. He locked the door behind them, and turned on a very dim light held in the palm of his hand. By that scarcely glowing beacon, he led them past racks of shoes to the back of the store.

Everything seemed well ordered in the store, the employees likely having cleaned up before going home for the evening. Arano caught the scent of freshly oiled shoes, and he wondered absently what type of animal the Bromidians used to make their leather. They passed through a doorway obstructed by several overlapping, hanging plastic straps and entering the area restricted to employees, where they stopped before the garbage chute. The Bromidian knelt, found a hidden release, and slid a panel aside. Laron thrust his light inside the darkened passage beyond and activated it, illuminating a steeply sloping incline leading to a rough chamber. The team slid down the rugged terrain into what was more of a large hollow than a room. There were several boxes lining one wall, and a check revealed them to be empty. A single passage led to what Arano believed to be the north, which was the way they needed to go. He heard the panel being secured behind them.

There was a water leak overhead, somewhere in the darkness, and the rain falling above ran in steady streams down the walls to collect in puddles on the floor. Arano feared a cave-in if the rains continued, but he hoped they would be well away from the tunnel before it became an issue. Their feet splashed through the pooling rainwater, and they passed on into the darkness. The path they followed joined another on two different occasions, but the RLF agent guided them with confidence. They made it to the end of the line, and Arano reached for the monitor lying in a mud puddle near the wall.

"Don't bother," Alyna said with a smirk. "It's broken. We've been this way before."

Laron triggered the release, and the panel slid aside. Enton scaled a rusty ladder and poked his head into the room above, pistol in hand. After a few tense moments, he clambered off the ladder and into the restaurant, Arano close behind. The odor of cleaning chemicals was quite pungent, and it made Arano's eyes water. They passed into the kitchen, where cooking utensils were neatly arranged on the grill, waiting for the next day's business. Beyond that was the dining room, containing row upon row of tables, wiped down and covered with placemats.

"Should we enter the bakery through the front or the rear?" Lain asked.

"I don't think it matters," Laron answered, setting his fingertips lightly against the wall while trying to get a look outside.

"If the building is being watched, they'll have both entrances covered."

"There's one way to find out," Arano announced. He grasped the latch for the front door, eased it open, and applied pressure to open the door. Immediately, the sense of danger was nearly overwhelming. He pursed his lips, secured the latch, and crossed the floor, trying the rear door. Once he began to push it open, he found the same results as with the front. They were at an impasse.

He returned to the others. "They definitely have the bakery under surveillance—maybe this entire block. I don't feel any particular danger from remaining in here, so I'd speculate they know our objective, but not our route. They probably don't know our time on target, either, although they could make an educated guess easily enough."

Enton scowled darkly. "How could they know about this? The only people who were aware of the mission were our escorts, but they could have just as easily led us right into the arms of the Tycon Mar."

"He's right," Videre said, pulling out a chair and taking a seat. "Who else could have known? We sent no transmissions, left no written record."

"I know how," Arano said, placing his hands over his face in anguish. "If I'm right, this is my fault. The agent who told me about this place was still alive when I left her. I gave her a pistol to defend herself with, but she must have somehow been captured. I'll bet they tortured her until she told them what she told me."

Alyna placed her hands about his waist. "Arano, there was nothing you could have done. In your condition, you could barely have carried your own weight, let alone that of a Tsimian weighing almost half as much as you. She had broken legs, so she couldn't help herself. What were you to do—kill her?"

"No, Viper," Xalen added, "the blame is not yours. Your wife is correct. You are not barbaric enough to kill your own, not when there is a chance for them to fight on."

"The question is," Laron said, "what do we do about it now?"

"Let's use some of this logic you Humans are so famous for," Xalen said. "We can't approach the building undetected by walking straight to it, no matter how careful we are. We don't know of an underground approach to the lab, so we can't attack from below. In my mind, we are left with only one direction. The roof."

Kish guided the *Intrepid* into position with the rest of the fleet, establishing the blockade ordered by the Coalition High Council. She opened the subspace Comm, awaiting the announcement by Admiral Aradle to the Bromidian people. With the perimeter ships in place, including several contingents of Thief Class Cruisers, the main body of the task force set a course for Rystoria 2. The planet grew in size until it nearly filled Kish's viewscreen.

Barely visible above the planet was the superstructure of the new orbital star fortress being built to defend Rystoria 2. With the old Bromidian government's defeat, the Coalition had abdicated certain aspects of the treaty, such as the restrictions on their military forces, in the spirit of friendship. Fortunately, the fortress was not operational, and in fact had not even had the weapons installed, let alone a reactor core to power them. They wouldn't have to deal with the starbase's devastating firepower this time.

A fleet of Bromidian warships emerged from behind the

third moon of Rystoria 2, placing itself in a defensive posture where they could protect the planet. The message Kish had been expecting finally came through. The admiral's leathery, wizened face appeared on the screen, her Tompiste form appearing somehow menacing despite her size.

"This is Admiral Aradle, commander of the United Systems Coalition's Fifth Fleet. We are here in response to acts of interstellar terrorism committed by agents of Gorst IX, who has unlawfully placed himself as the head of the Bromidian state. Since, at the time of the acts, he had no official authority within the legitimate Bromidian government, our quarrel is with him and him alone. For this reason, our fleet is enacting a blockade on your star system, until such time as Gorst steps down from his position of authority and makes reparations for his crimes. During the time of this blockade, no ship will be permitted to enter or leave the system. Any ship attempting to do so will be dealt with harshly."

Kish's viewscreen split in half, and a second face appeared, this one Bromidian. From the dispatches they had received, she recognized him as Gorst IX himself.

"Coalition forces, this is Emperor Gorst of the Bromidian Empire. I have restored the righteous government to power, and I will not step aside. My forefathers carved this empire out of the chaos of war, and the rulership belongs to me and my descendants. All who oppose me shall perish, as this illegitimate expeditionary force shall soon see, if it remains. Flee now, or face my wrath. And that of my friends!" With that, he laughed maniacally, ending his transmission with a sneer and a flick of his wrist.

The admiral addressed the fleet once again. "All ships, hold your position. We will not attack unless they fire upon us first. For now, we shall hold the line and maintain the blockade."

The screen returned to a panoramic view of Rystoria 2, and Kish let out the breath she hadn't realized she was holding. Imatt leaned back in his chair, swinging around to face the room. "Anyone bring a deck of cards?"

While Videre held the hatch ajar, Arano rolled out onto the roof. His cloak immediately soaked up copious amounts of water, and he felt the chill seeping through his clothing and into his body. The flattop roof was sealed with tar, which rendered the building below virtually waterproof, but caused the rainwater to pool annoyingly. His wet uniform clung tenaciously to his skin, but he tried to ignore it, cautiously approaching the edge of the roof. Most of the previous day's snow had melted, but some of the larger drifts stubbornly remained, mostly clustered along the south edge of the building.

Strangled curses from his teammates told Arano they had found the wet surface to be as unappealing as he had. He reached into his pouch and withdrew a set of night vision goggles. Without taking his eyes off the streets two stories below, he thumbed a switch on the side of the goggles, and they obediently lit up with a soft glow. Arano swept the sidewalks, roadways, and buildings around them, but he couldn't find anyone, even with the night vision. He knew he couldn't activate a scanner to try to locate the Tycon Mar operatives he was certain were out there; just as soon as he tried to sweep the area, his foes would detect him with *their* scanners.

"I think it's clear, at least to the next building," Arano reported. "Beyond that, I can't say."

Without waiting any longer, Enton sprinted across the roof

and leaped across the gap between the buildings. He landed well beyond the ledge, rolled, and came to his feet. His son, Xalen, followed him, and the two Latyrians prowled the rooftop. Arano shrugged, backed up several meters, and jumped over to the next building. Once his entire team was across, he approached the ledge on the far side of the roof, and with night vision in hand, once again checked for enemy surveillance.

He immediately spotted a group of four Bromidians in the building across the street from the bakery, weapons ready, hiding in the tenebrous recesses of the darkened front hallway of a computer outlet. The building next door also had a contingent of Bromidians waiting, this group hiding behind an abandoned hovercar. Arano reported his findings to the others.

"I have to assume the rear entrance is similarly covered. They're definitely waiting on us."

"Did you see anyone on the roof of the bakery?" Laron asked.

"No. I'd say we should stick to the rooftops. Coming in from above seems to be the only unguarded entrance."

They discovered the flaw to their plan once they had crossed to the roof of the bakery. The building had no roof access hatch from inside the building, instead relying upon a rickety metal framework running up the side of the building in a series of ladders and platforms. Arano knew they obviously couldn't descend the ladders, but they needed to find a way in.

"I hope they don't mind this in the morning," Videre said, mopping rainwater from his furry visage. "They have a small leak here already anyhow. You can feel the roof sagging in a small area, where the wood is rotting from exposure to water." He plunged his knife into the roof, and it easily penetrated the surface. "The hole won't be huge, but we can get in."

He and Lain went to work with their blades, patiently sawing away at the decomposing lumber. For the better part of a half hour they worked in silence, while the others kept a stoic vigil in case the enemy should somehow appear. Arano heard his two friends whispering to each other, coordinating the final stage of their efforts in an effort to prevent the section of roof from falling when they finished making their cuts. Finally, with Lain holding one edge of their cutout, Videre made the last slice, and the way was open.

CHAPTER
TWENTY-FOUR

KISH WAS SHOCKED TO SEE THE BROMIDIAN FLEET launch a coordinated assault against the blockade. One moment, all was calm and the ships in the Coalition task force were simply holding their position, and in the next they were under attack. Fortunately, Admiral Aradle had the foresight to order the ships to maintain active shields and charged weapons. Eventually, they would have eased back their vigilance, but without knowing how the Bromidians would react, they would err on the side of caution. Their discretion saved the fleet from tremendous losses at the battle's onset.

The Coalition fleet had numerical superiority, but the Bromidians had the advantage of initiative on their side. Before the Coalition ships were able to acquire targeting computer locks, Bromidian torpedoes were already racing to their targets. Staccato points of light erupted from the lead ships when those torpedoes found their mark.

"Taking evasive maneuvers!" Kish shouted, securing a hold on the captain's chair to keep from being thrown. Her crew scrambled to their stations, finding their weapons still ready, and the *Intrepid* entered the fray. "All weapons, fire at will!"

Kish stayed generally in formation with the more agile ships assigned to her wing, veering sharply from side to side. She chanced a look at the tactical display, and saw the first salvo of plasma torpedoes slam into a Bromidian frigate, completely disabling it on the third impact. With the fourth, the frigate disappeared from her scope. She turned her attention back to the viewscreen, fascinated by the sharp flashes of light and brief detonations when a weapon struck home.

"Wing 5, this is the *Intrepid*. We have a Scimitar Class Heavy Cruiser with fighter escort trying to flank our Assault Class Carriers. Follow me in. I want the Firestorms to go after their fighters, and the Assault Class ships to go after the cruiser with me."

Her wing acknowledged the orders, and the *Intrepid* raced ahead. The big cruiser was slow to react, swinging about ponderously in an effort to bring its heavier forward weaponry to bear against the encroaching attackers. The Bromidian fighters were engaged by the more agile Firestorms, and the Coalition ships gained the advantage in rapid fashion. Kish saw the duel between fighters going in the Coalition's favor, so she concentrated on the cruiser. Three pairs of Assault Class Fighters made the first run on the massive ship, wreaking havoc but without destroying it. In the process, one Coalition ship was destroyed and two damaged.

Then the *Intrepid* entered the fray. While her gunners assaulted the ship with torpedoes and plasma batteries, Kish fired the forward-mounted Disruptor Beam, not disabling the ship but scrambling some of its systems. With the crew of the enemy vessel hurrying to both repair the damage inflicted upon it and still respond to the Raptor Class Frigate menacing it, the remaining assault ships swung around for another pass. A barrage of torpedoes struck the shielding, and a brilliant explosion in the aft section announced the destruction of the shield generator. Blast after blast from Coalition plasma cannon rocked the ship, which suffered hull breaches in at least a dozen locations. The cruiser drifted askew on its path, its helmsman no longer able to control the hulking ship. With another barrage of plasma torpedoes, the vessel succumbed to the damage inflicted upon it and exploded.

Kish scanned the area, selected another likely target, and set a course for it, the assault ships formed up behind her. Before they could engage, however, a warning beep sounded from Pelos's station.

"We've got another fleet emerging from their wormholes. Fifteen capital ships, eight wings of fighters. They . . ."

"Pelos, tell me what you've got," Kish implored.

"I . . . don't really know what we have. I've never seen ships of these types before."

Imatt spun his chair to face Kish. "Chrysarthi?"

Kish's eyes flew wide, and she checked her own tactical display. The battle had been one-sided, with the Coalition decimating their foes. But the addition of the new ships shifted the fortunes of both sides. A ship Kish could only classify as a frigate fired a lancing beam of blue into the closest Coalition ship, a light cruiser. It passed through the cruiser's shields as if they weren't even there, to detonate against the unprotected hull. A fiery explosion burst from the cruiser's starboard flank, and its lights flickered before stabilizing once more. The cruiser returned fire, but the new ship remained undamaged.

The Comm squawked to life. "All ships, this is Admiral Aradle! Fall back and regroup! Try to avoid the new ships if possible!"

Kish reversed course, following the preprogrammed flight plan to the first fallback position. She didn't know what the fleet could do against such technology, but the Coalition capital ships' Rift Drive engines wouldn't have cooled down enough to risk jumping out of the system for at least another hour. They would have to hold out until then.

Arano was the first to drop inside the bakery, checking the area and finding it empty. The others joined him, and they found their way to the staircase. The scent of baked goods greeted him before he had even begun the descent to the first floor of the bakery. By the time he reached the bottom of the stairs, the aroma of pies, cakes, and fresh bread was so strong that his mouth was watering and his stomach was growling. He glanced to his rear and chuckled at the sight of Videre reaching into a display to grab a small pastry and cram the entire thing into his mouth. Videre made a half-hearted attempt at wiping the frosting from the damp fur around his mouth, but it only made the matter worse. Arano was laughing openly when he turned back around.

They passed through a hallway lined with shelves, which were topped with white statues bearing a marked resemblance to creatures from the Humans' adopted homeworld at Subac 3 Prime. Curious, he picked one up and examined it, finding it was indeed from Subac, according to the inscription on the bottom, and seemed to be made of porcelain. Replacing the statue, he traversed the length of the hallway to find himself standing in front of a locked door. There was a large glass window, framed in ornate wood, centered in the door's upper half. He leaned forward and peered through the glass. There was another hallway, this one unpainted but with a thickly carpeted floor, leading away to his left. Arano could barely discern the top of a staircase several meters beyond the door. The locking mechanism seemed to be operated through a palm print identification system. Arano stepped aside and gestured to Videre, who knelt and examined the lock.

Videre let out a long breath. "This will take some time, Arano. If someone would open the door from the other side, we'd be fine. But there are several redundant failsafe alarms on this side, all protecting each other in addition to the lock itself. If I'm not careful, I could end up letting them know we're here."

"Hang on." Arano moved back down the hallway and retrieved one of the porcelain figurines. He returned to Videre's side, placed the figurine on the floor, and by gradually increasing pressure from the heel of his boot, crushed the fragile porcelain into tiny pieces. With a deliberately impudent grin, Arano gave an imperious wave of his hand, motioning for Videre to step back. Seizing a handful of the porcelain fragments, Arano tossed them against the glass.

In a soundless detonation, the window fractured into countless pieces, collapsing to the carpeted floor with a dull *thump*. He gave a shamefaced smile to his friends. "I wasn't always a law-abiding citizen in my youth. I guess I picked up a few bad habits."

Videre's head snapped back and forth between the pile of broken glass and his gloating team commander. "How—?"

Arano shrugged. "I don't understand all the physics involved. All I know is porcelain fragments, when tossed against glass, will set up a violent resonance, and the window will shake itself apart. We always liked the low noise levels. That way, the owner of the hovercar didn't find out what we'd done until we were well out of sight."

Arano reached through the empty frame, unlocked the door, and swung it open. He took a step through, but froze in place, his danger sense racing. Something wasn't what it seemed. He knelt, trying to determine the source of the warning.

Videre leaned next to him and whispered, "My turn." He

disappeared back into the restaurant, and when he returned, he carried a sieve filled with baking flour. Carefully, moving forward inches at a time, Videre turned the crank on the sieve, sending a cascade of flour drifting to the floor. Only a meter past where Arano knelt, his sifted flour lit up when it passed through a previously invisible beam of light. Videre used his knife to carve a mark in the wall, denoting the location of the beam for the others. He found two more beams before they reached the stairs.

Arano checked the stairs to be certain they were unguarded, then faced his teammate. "Videre, you have the soul of a thief."

"Why, thank you, Captain!"

Arano knelt and pulled up his pants leg to reveal a concealed holster carrying another pistol, this one a projectile weapon, which he fitted with a silencer. The report he had received on these weapons from Kish was favorable, with the primary drawback being the mess. He drew the weapon, secured it in a two-handed firing grip, and descended the stairs. They reached the landing, where the hallway made a sharp curve to the left. Peering around the edge of the wall, he saw two Bromidians in a foyer who appeared to be guarding the entrance to another room. Their military garb was decorated with the familiar red diamond-shaped patch bearing a silver pyramid in its center. He stepped back under cover and motioned his team closer.

"I think we've found the lab. There are two Broms wearing the official Tycon Mar uniform, and it looks like they're guarding whatever is beyond the door. With this long hallway, we'll never get close enough to kill them both before they sound the alarm. We need some ideas."

"I have one, Viper," Xalen offered. He sketched his plan, and with only a slight modification to the idea, Arano conceded it was their best chance.

With Xalen on his left and Enton on his right, Arano walked around the corner and approached the guards, hands behind his back as if secured in arm restraints. The two Bromidians looked at each other, mouths slightly agape, and stepped in to block their progress.

"Where do you think you are taking him?" one of them asked.

"We caught this Human trying to break in through the rear entrance," Enton said, stepping into the foyer. "We thought you might want to deal with him."

The Bromidian who spoke first smiled, eyes narrowing. "Indeed, we would."

"Wait—" the other said, "how did you get past the security system? I don't even know who you are." He reached for his weapon.

Arano's hands snapped around, right one tracking to the unfortunate Bromidian's head. The silenced pistol fired once, and the Tycon Mar operative's head shattered, the body lurching back to collapse on the floor without a protest. The remaining guard froze in a moment of shocked panic, and Enton seized him by the throat before he could react. Xalen stepped close, placed his own pistol to the soldier's head, and pulled the trigger. The way to the lab was secure.

Kish piloted the *Intrepid* through a hailstorm of enemy fighters. One of the capital ships, which an enemy transmission had confirmed to belong to the Chrysarthi, had opened a fighter bay and unleashed at least fifty Bromidian fighters. It appeared the Bromidians and the Chrysarthi had planned for the contingency of a Coalition attack, and considering the timing of the arrival of the additional ship, she guessed they knew the task force was coming. She wondered why they hadn't sent the Chrysarthi ships to the Menast System for the battle there but decided the move wouldn't have been as effective. Not only did the Coalition stand to lose more ships in the battle over Rystoria than at Menast, but the earlier victory had given the Coalition leadership a case of overconfidence.

To her left, Vic worked alongside Imatt and Toshe to blaze away at the foes around their ship, wreaking a deadly toll. Enemy fire struck the *Intrepid's* shields, and occasionally a blast struck with enough force to rock the ship, but the shields held firm. Kish studied the tactical display, frowning in confusion at the enemy tactics. She established a Comm link with the admiral.

"This is Lieutenant Waukee. Admiral, with the way the Chrysarthi ships swept through us on their first pass, why are they holding back and allowing the Bromidians to take the brunt of the attack? Those new ships could be tearing us apart right now."

Several moments of silence told Kish the admiral was as surprised as she. "I'm not sure, Lieutenant. It looks like they want the Bromidians to soften us up first, before they come in to finish us off."

Kish remembered the initial engagement when their new foe had first arrived. "It seemed to me, our plasma torpedoes had better luck damaging their ships than our beam weapons. Maybe they're waiting for us to exhaust our supply of torps before they engage us."

"You may be right." There was a pause while the admiral switched her Comm channel to address the entire fleet. "This is Admiral Aradle. The Chrysarthi ships are holding back, and they may be waiting for the Bromidians to thin out our numbers before they fully engage. Let's take out the Broms, keeping clear of the Chrysarthi when possible. And save as many torps as you can. We believe they have a better chance of penetrating Chrysarthi shields."

Kish shut down her Comm. "Okay, everyone, you heard the admiral. Go easy on the torpedoes, but let's see what we can do to remove a few ships from New Dawn's inventory."

The next door Arano found was slightly ajar. The room was vividly lit, and a beam of light shone brightly into the darkened hallway. Arano seized upon the advantage of the difference in lighting levels to get a glimpse into the room, knowing the occupants' eyes would be adjusted to the room and wouldn't be readily able to see clearly in the darkened passage. He found his brief view to be quite revealing.

It had to be the laboratory they were seeking. Banks of computers lined one wall, and the center of the lab was dominated by a table which formed an island, and was being used as a workstation. Several vials of varicolored liquids bubbled over tightly controlled flames, giving off a faint white vapor. A screen on another wall listed a series of chemical equations involving some sort of biological compounds, if he remembered his chemistry classes correctly. Two Bromidians stood with their backs to him; judging by their white-robed garments, he believed they were scientists. There were also three Chrysarthi with the Bromidians, two of them armed with pistols on their hips, but the other garbed like the Bromidians.

Arano reached into his pack and removed the thin, snake-like tube used by military and law enforcement alike for surveillance.

One end contained a recording device, the other a lens and a microphone. The diameter was only one millimeter, making the instrument inconspicuous, and allowing the user to see and hear conversations beyond doors and around corners. Arano slipped the end of the recorder into the lab, plugged in the earpiece, and sat back to listen.

" . . . what is causing this degradation," a voice said with a strange accent. Arano decided the speaker was a Chrysarthi, most likely the scientist.

"Look," another said. "The whole cloning process has never been perfected. Sure, we can make a clone of just about anyone, grow them to any age in around a year, and have them able to function as well as you or me. But no one has been able to work around the DNA degradation problems. In lower animals, we've been able to achieve a life expectancy very near that of the sample donor. But with humanoid species, there are simply too many other factors involved."

A third voice joined in. "The intricacy of the operations within the humanoid brain require a very exacting structure. When we grow the clone to adult age in such a short time period, the neuropathways aren't able to fully develop. The brain is placed under such stress that it will eventually shut down and fail."

The Chrysarthi scientist growled. "What can you do to postpone his demise?"

"We have several formulas we are working on, some showing more promise than others. But my best guess is that you will need to replace him within three months."

"This is not good. Will you be able to transfer the memories of the current clone into a new one?"

"No. It would help if you have the current clone keep extensive personal logs. His successor can read from them to establish the image of him being the same man."

The Chrysarthi sighed heavily, dropping into a chair. "Do you have any idea how hard this man is to work with? His ego is beyond anything I've ever seen. Sometimes, I find myself wishing we had never started this scheme. He knows he's a clone, but he still insists we treat him as if he were the real son of Zorlyn Gorst VIII."

Arano barely suppressed a gasp of surprise. The Bromidian emperor, the leader of the insurrection, a clone? How could it be? All at once, the subtle clues fell into place. The pirates had been raiding Biomek's stashes of equipment and technology, and had managed to obtain DNA information on the entire line of the Bromidian emperors, going back for at least four generations. The Coalition had been correct in the original assessment that no shuttles had left the star fortress of Rystoria before its destruction. Gorst VIII and his descendants were truly dead. Arano decided to risk the tiny glow and activate the video feed. One of the Chrysarthi guards approached the scientist.

"Emperor Hanse said the plan would work, and it will. By creating the Bromidian leader who would overthrow the existing government, we have started a conflict with the Coalition. Even now, the battle rages overhead. This entire section of the galaxy will be ours. So do not question the word of our emperor, or I will kill you where you stand."

"Yes," one of the Bromidians said, "it will work. And we who founded the reformed Tycon Mar will take our place in the new ruling order. But for now, we need to work together to find a solution to this problem. It wouldn't do to have our little plan collapse over the death of one man, even if he is a clone."

Arano shut down the video feed and removed the earpiece, allowing the system to continue recording the lab. He motioned his team away from the door, and briefly told them what he had heard.

"We need to get this information public," Laron said. "The Bromidian people follow Gorst out of fear, but also because they believe he is the true descendant of Zorlyn Gorst VIII. If we reveal this to the public, they will turn on the New Dawn Leadership."

"And plunge them into civil war," Lain said. "We need to avoid that, or we will play right into the hands of the Chrysarthi."

"What if we only revealed it to the military, at least at first?" Alyna suggested. "If they turn against New Dawn, we can overthrow the insurrectionist government with hardly a shot being fired. Once we have things under control, and Lentin is placed in command of the government, we can reveal the truth to the populace."

"It's devious," Videre said with a toothy grin. "I like it."

"You would," Lain said dryly, rolling his eyes.

"Okay, let's take these guys out," Arano said.

Once more, they approached the lab, projectile pistols in hand. They gathered in a tight knot just outside the door, each knowing which part of the room to cover. Arano held up three fingers, taking them away one at a time in a silent count, then kicked the door open. They burst in, pistols blazing with a silence that belied the violence in their weapons. One guard managed to draw his pistol, firing a single reflexive shot as a bullet struck him in the center of his chest. He tumbled to the ground, the last to fall, and Arano surveyed the carnage.

While his teammates searched for useful intelligence, Arano removed the memory rod from the recording device. His teammates uncovered copious evidence regarding the Chrysarthi conspiracy, including technical documents regarding the date and location where the Gorst clone had been created. There were even dispatches between the contingent of scientists and a liaison within the Chrysarthi government. They gathered what they could and returned to the hallway to find their way out.

When they reentered the kitchen, Arano sensed something was wrong. He held up a hand for caution and sank to one knee. "We're being watched," he warned.

"I'll check," said Enton, creeping forward on his stomach. He edged his way to the front of the bakery, rose up slightly, and peered out the bottom of a large window.

A blast from a laser rifle burst through the window, striking Enton in the forehead. His skull shattered, and he tumbled backward to land supine, mouth and eyes wide open. Videre restrained Xalen, who tried to rush to his father's aid.

"Stay down," Videre shouted. "We can't help him now. We need to find a safe way out. We'll deal with his killer soon enough!"

Several more shots rang out, with their besiegers firing blindly into the bakery in an effort to keep the Avengers pinned down. Arano rallied his soldiers, maneuvering them into covered positions where they could return fire when the enemy moved in to try and overrun them. He made Xalen stay at his side, where he could keep an eye on him. Ducking into the open and immediately back under cover, Arano tried to locate the points where the incoming fire was originating.

Xalen tensed, raising his head and pursing his lips as if whistling. Arano opened his mouth to offer an admonition to the young Latyrian, but stopped, realizing Xalen was communicating with another Latyrian.

"Stay down," Xalen yelled sharply. "This is about to get messy."

The bakery was rocked by a tremendous explosion, shattering the front windows and showering the Avengers with shards of broken glass. His ears ringing, Arano tried to brush off the larger fragments. The sound of intense weapon fire somehow permeated the fog in his ears, accompanied by piercing screams of pain. For several long minutes, the battle raged on, with the Avengers able to offer only token assistance. At last, the guns fell silent, and the familiar voice of Lentin came through the ruined bakery.

"Let's go, Viper! We're all here!"

Arano climbed out from under the counter to face his friend, totally dumbfounded. Lentin laughed out loud, coming forward to grasp Arano's shoulders firmly in celebration. "When word was passed to me regarding the importance of this mission, I decided the time had come to be the leader you want me to be. I rallied the entire RLF together, and we hid in ambush, waiting to help if you got into trouble."

Arano's eyebrows shot up in wonder. "How many troops do we have?"

"Those clerics did one hell of a good job. This group numbers five hundred, and there are a thousand more hitting other targets as we speak."

"Arano," Laron said, stepping across piles of debris, "we need to get this information out as soon as possible. I just turned on my subspace Comm, and the fleet is engaged in a losing battle over Rystoria 2 right now. The Chrysarthi ships are employing technology beyond anything we've ever seen before. It looks like the fleet's only chance is for us to get the Bromidian ships to turn on their allies."

Lentin snapped his fingers. "The prison! There is a subspace transceiver located on the roof, and it has access to the military frequencies."

"We'll need a way in," Videre warned. "If we try to force our way in with troops, we may end up damaging the transceiver."

"Wait," Arano said excitedly, holding up one finger. "Xalen, do you know what your people did with the prison hovercar I stole?"

Xalen nodded grimly, grief over his fallen father sending tears down his cheeks. "Yes, I do."

The rain-soaked streets of Notron were masked in a dense, roiling bank of fog, obscuring everything beyond twenty meters. The hovercar glided along the deserted thoroughfares, passing several army checkpoints unchallenged. Lentin stood at the helm, piloting the vehicle with one arm dangling casually out the side of the driver's compartment. He waved enthusiastically to the troops on the street, who seemed to be rushing about as if they were expecting a full-scale invasion. Arano watched from his concealed position in the cramped cargo bay, using his recording tube as a periscope. His Avenger companions were crammed in with him, all trying to get a view of his small display screen.

The lights of the prison were visible through the fog long before the walls came into sight, and Lentin slowed the hovercar, approaching the gates cautiously. There was an expanded retinue of soldiers at the gate, all well-armed, likely in response to the attacks in the city by the RLF. With such a contingent at the checkpoint, they could easily conduct a search of the entire vehicle and find the Avengers, ending the whole scheme before it ever got started. Arano hoped Xalen remembered his next part in the plan. The hovercar jolted to a stop, waiting for the approach of the guards.

"State your business."

Lentin leaned down from his perch. "Good evening," he said pleasantly. "I'm just returning from a prisoner transfer to the facility at Haxle. What's going on? I would have sworn I heard an explosion earlier, but in all this fog, I couldn't see anything."

Arano watched the guard relax, shoulders lowering as the tension left his body. "Some type of terrorist activity, we believe. We're all on heightened alert here. I apologize for the inconvenience, but we'll need to search your vehicle."

Lentin raised a hand to protest, but his challenge was interrupted by an explosion in a building directly across the street. A mushroom cloud of fire and smoke boiled into the night sky, lighting the fog with an eerie ruddy glow. The soldiers dove for cover, and Lentin ducked in his seat. Unseen, several people opened fire with laser rifles, some of the beams striking the rear of the hovercar, others exploding against the concrete barricades. Most of the soldiers poured out through the gates, taking up positions and returning fire, while the primary guard frantically motioned Lentin through the perimeter. In a feigned show of panic, Lentin accelerated away as fast as the damaged hovercar would travel, making a desperate rush for the motorpool directly to their front.

The enormous main doors of the facility shuddered once and slowly crawled together. Lentin maintained a breakneck speed, bearing down on the shrinking gap. They reached the doors, and one side of the hovercar skimmed the edge of the sliding portal, sending the car into a spin. They slammed into the far wall of the motorpool, knocking the occupants sprawling. Arano was actually laughing when he climbed from the cargo hold.

"Lentin, I never knew you could drive like that."

"Yeah," he replied with a shaky voice. "Neither did I."

"Which way to the transceiver?" Laron asked.

Lentin checked his hand-drawn map. "It isn't far."

They raced through the prison complex, meeting only minimal resistance. It seemed the series of bombings, combined with Xalen's assault outside the prison, had drawn most of the guards to the perimeter. They burst inside the room housing the subspace transceiver to find it was not even guarded. While Arano established security, Lentin hurried to the array of controls aligned along the far wall. With the assistance of two RLF soldiers, he activated the link.

"Attention, Bromidian soldiers. My name is Lentin, and I am the leader of the Rystoria Liberation Front . . ."

Kish kept a tight grip on the arm of the commander's chair, struggling to keep her seat under the barrage of fire the ship was taking.

"Vic, get those fighters off our six!"

"I'm trying! The targeting computer is damaged, so I'm having to target manually. The way they're moving, I'm having trouble tracking them."

"Hang on!" Kish sent the ship into a sudden vertical dive, then reversed the ship's course. The fighters scattered, breaking off their attack.

"Rear shields are critical," Pelos said. "I'm transferring power from the targeting computer and long-range scanners, to boost the rear shields. It would help if we could shut them down for a time."

"Can't do that right now," Kish said. "Give me what you can."

"More fighters are coming in, one-one-nine-mark-two-seven," Imatt announced.

Kish continued her evasive maneuvers, trying to keep the fighters from consolidating their attack. Her wing of assault ships had long since been disabled or destroyed, and the *Intrepid* was flying without the benefit of an escort. She swung the ship about once more, realizing too late they were cut off from the rest of the fleet.

"Two Bromidian frigates directly in front of us," Pelos shouted. "We've lost rear shields!"

Kish checked the tactical display, searching for a way out, then realized the enemy had stopped firing. She beckoned to an equally confused Pelos, who held his palms up with uncertainty.

"Hold on," Lon said. "There's a transmission coming through on the Bromidian Comm frequency, but it's not scrambled. Patching it through now."

The screen wavered and Lentin appeared, standing beside a contingent of Avengers and RLF troops. "*. . . proof of their duplicity. Based upon this, we can conclude beyond a doubt that the leaders of New Dawn are part of a conspiracy to throw our world into chaos, allowing the Chrysarthi to conquer us at their leisure. The Bromidian people fell into line behind Gorst because he was believed to be the legitimate son of our former emperor. We now know this to be untrue. Will you continue to allow yourself to be used to satisfy the power for hunger of an undeserving few, or will you cast off the puppet strings and fight for a free Rystoria?*"

Lentin bent to a computer in front of him, tapping several controls, and then he straightened. "*Bromidian soldiers: the choice is yours. I have transmitted copies of the proof I have shown you, along with much I haven't the time to display here. I must be going. I leave it to you to turn the tide against the deceivers.*"

The screen went blank. Kish sat in silent apprehension, staring through the haze of smoke permeating the bridge of the *Intrepid*, wondering what the Bromidians would do. To her side, she heard Pelos key in the instructions to the ship's computer, temporarily shutting down the shields to allow the system to recover. The only sounds were the heavy breathing of her worried shipmates, the crackle of electrical discharges from damaged equipment, and occasional warning chirps from the computer, telling of damage to the various systems. A hazy smoke drifted lazily through the air. Her tactical display flickered on and off, and she slammed a small fist on the panel. It flashed once more, then came on to stay. The Bromidian ships were regrouping, but they had not powered down their weapons. She could do nothing but wait.

A Bromidian frigate broke formation and made a run on the Chrysarthi ships. Kish never knew if the ship would have fired on the Chrysarthi or not, because the hapless frigate was rapidly destroyed by a hail of torpedoes from their former allies. There was a moment of hesitation, as if every ship's commander in both the Coalition and Bromidian fleets was stunned by the turn of events. The lull didn't last; the Bromidian ships turned as one and attacked the badly outnumbered Chrysarthi fleet. Despite their technological advantage, Kish didn't believe the ships would stand up to the heavy pounding being delivered by the Bromidians, especially if the Coalition fleet joined them.

The Comm beeped once more. "This is Admiral Aradle. All ships, attack the Chrysarthi fleet!"

Bromidian ships were exploding at an alarming rate. But first one Chrysarthi ship, and then another, was destroyed, a process hastened by the arrival of the Coalition ships. Kish had saved a fair portion of their allotment of torpedoes, and Imatt fired them blindly into the aft portion of a battle cruiser's starboard hull. The ship's shields held at first, but under a heavy barrage from the *Intrepid* and other Coalition ships, the battle cruiser's hull was finally exposed. Impact after impact struck true, and several massive explosions rocked it on all decks. One final detonation split the massive ship in half, and it disappeared in a ball of flame.

The other Chrysarthi ships turned and disappeared almost immediately into their wormholes. The remaining Coalition and Bromidian ships stirred about aimlessly before rendezvousing over Rystoria 2. For the day, at least, the battle was won.

His face distorted in rage, the clone who was Gorst IX staggered along a hallway beneath the imperial palace, accompanied by his usual retinue of bodyguards. His physician, an overweight Bromidian who did not seem to be used to physical exertion, wheezed heavily as he trotted along beside him. A glance at a sign on the wall told him they were close to their destination, a shuttle bay where he would make his escape.

Bitter resentment welled up in his throat.

Escape? Escape to where? Escape from what?

For he was a clone, and a defective one, at that. At best, he had another three months of life remaining. But better to die alone than at the hands of these insurrectionist rebels. He might not be the real descendant of the Gorst line, but he was close enough. Their blood coursed through his veins, and by right, rule of the Bromidian people should be his. And as the door to the shuttle bay hissed open, he vowed that he would reclaim his rightful position before he died.

One of his bodyguards keyed the entry code on the door to his private shuttle, but the ship's computer beeped a warning in response: the code was incorrect. The bodyguard tried again, with the same results. The hulking Bromidian turned to his companions, his insectoid face expressing confusion.

Several murky figures materialized from the shadows in the

shuttle bay. They glided into a tight formation around the Bro-midians, the ghostly figures pinning Gorst and his escort against his ship. Although he couldn't see their faces, hidden as they were in the cowls of their dark robes, Gorst knew their presence could mean only one thing.

ARANO SAT IN RAPT ATTENTION, LISTENING TO the diplomats before him hammering out a new treaty of cooperation between Rystoria's restored diplomatic government and the Coalition High Council. The mutual defense pact would have been a complete surprise several weeks prior, with both sides under the mistaken belief that there was no other power around to threaten their security. But with the discovery of the Chrysarthi, everything had changed.

Lentin had been installed as the provisional head of the new government, a position confirmed a month later in a general election. He had been selected by an overwhelming majority of the Bromidian population, and he was well on the way to stabilizing the planet. There was still a small level of unrest, with a few disjointed factions opposing the restored government, but he seemed to have the situation in hand. Of course, the Avengers teams were still busy. Many of the insurrection's leaders had escaped and were being hunted down. Top on Arano's list was Ustin Shiba, the shadowy Osiris, but his trail had gone cold. The good news on that front was the violent demise of the Gorst IX clone. While trying to escape the palace, his retinue was ambushed and slaughtered by Kian assassins.

Arano and Alyna had a tearful reunion with Aunt Nebra and their daughter, Nicole, and after a week of convalescence, had reluctantly returned to work. Arano regretfully confided in Alyna about the possibility of his retirement. He had served the Coalition faithfully for many years, and he thought it might be time for him to step away from it all. He intended to continue assisting the military as an advisor, but he wanted to spend more time with his family.

That evening, they attended a banquet for political leaders from both the Coalition and the Bromidian governments. Arano sat with Alyna at his side, Nicole on her lap, talking to Lentin and Laron. Lentin appeared quite unsettled, looking like the weight of the galaxy hung on his shoulders.

"I have no doubt the Chrysarthi will return, and my people will be their first target. Not only are we the closest to the sector they seem to hail from, but our fleet turned on them in the battle. They won't forget what they'll perceive as treachery."

"The Coalition will be at your side, Lentin," Laron promised him. "This mutual defense pact ensures it. We all recognize the threat the Chrysarthi pose."

"I just hope we can analyze the battle data and come up with a solution to the weapons and shield advantages they have," Arano said. "If they come at us with a large fleet, we'll be in trouble."

"Not necessarily," Lentin said. "We have one thing they don't."

"What's that?"

Lentin took Arano's arm firmly in his own. "Unity. Dedication to a cause. And most of all, we have the one driving force that nothing in this galaxy can conquer. Freedom."

Arano felt a steeling of his own resolve, and he took Lentin's forearm in a firm warrior's grasp. "My friend, I couldn't have said it better. There's nothing a free people can't accomplish."

He experienced a strange euphoria, thinking of all his team had accomplished in the previous two years; of the lives lost and sacrifices made—all in the name of freedom. Perhaps he wasn't quite as ready for retirement as he'd thought.

THE KILLING FROST

SCOTT GAMBOE

There is an uneasy peace between the United Systems Coalition and the Bromidian Empire. But it is constantly strained by the actions of a group of renegade Bromidians who call themselves Rising Sun, and an elite Coalition military group known as the Avengers has been fighting a covert war against them for years.

Captain Arano Lakeland leads one of the teams. His motivation, vengeance. Revenge against the Rising Sun's invasion of his homeworld and the subsequent slaughter of his family. His actions, however, in his relentless quest to see the Bromidian empire brought to its knees, have won him the enmity of Grand High Councilor Balor Tient, a corrupt man holding one of the most powerful positions in the Coalition.

To further complicate matters, Arano's efforts to prove a connection between Rising Sun and the Bromidian government are being hampered by both a traitor in the Coalition bureaucracy, and the Coalition's desire for peace at any price. And now it is a race against time as Arano and his companions try to survive long enough to solve a series of brutal murders, expose the traitor in their midst, and unite various factions with the Coalition. And if he fails?

Cataclysmic war that will engulf the entire galaxy.

ISBN# 9781932815986
Mass Market Paperback / Science Fiction
US $6.99 / CDN $9.99
Available Now
www.scottgamboe.net

The Piaras Legacy

Scott Gamboe

LONG AGO, SO THE LEGENDS SAY, THE NECROMANCER Volnor invaded the continent of Pelacia. His legions of undead soldiers ravaged the land unchecked, until the three nations united and pushed their evil foes back into the Desert of Malator.

But that was centuries ago, and few people still believe the tale. Other, more worldly matters occupy their time, such as recent attacks by renegade Kobolds. But Elac, an Elf who makes his way as a merchant, is too concerned with his business affairs to become involved in international politics. Until a marauding band of Kobolds attacks Elac's caravan and he finds himself running for his life.

Befriended by an Elven warrior named Rilen, he travels to Unity, the seat of power on the Pelacian continent. There he is joined by a diverse group of companions, and he sets out on an epic quest to solve the riddle of his heritage and save the land from the growing evil that threatens to engulf it.

ISBN# 9781933836256
Trade Paperback / Fantasy
US $15.95 / CDN $17.95
Available Now
www.scottgamboe.net

LEAPFROG

STEVE HENDRY

In a test to the human race, highly advanced aliens decide to offer free secrets that will enable universal space travel without time or distance constraints. Earth snaps at the challenge and collectively musters resources to develop the most advanced starship ever built on Earth, which is appropriately named, Leapfrog, for the technological jump over existing science. Unfortunately, corrupt secret services, greedy politicians, and overly wary generals condemn this mission from the start.

While in deep cryogenic sleep, the crew of Leapfrog encounters a disastrous meteor shower that destroys the main engines. Thousands of years pass while the stricken ship slowly meanders its way back to earth with two hundred and seventy five humans solidly frozen in deep suspended animation.

As the crew finally awakens, they find Earth is no longer the same. Seeking clues as to what has happened; the survivors attempt to re-colonize, only to discover that a new ultra-evolved creature now predominates and ruthlessly rules the top of the food chain. The explorers are forced to abandon their derelict starship and face a horrifying battle among cannibal Neanderthals and the ultra-evolved creatures, barely escaping with their lives.

ISBN# 9781933836508
Trade Paperback / Science Fiction
US $15.95 / CDN $17.95
Available Now
www.stevehendry.com

Be in the know on the latest
Medallion Press news by becoming a
Medallion Press Insider!

<u>As an Insider you'll receive:</u>

• Our FREE expanded monthly newsletter,
giving you more insight into Medallion Press

• Advanced press releases and breaking news

• Greater access to all of your favorite
Medallion authors

Joining is easy, just visit our Web site at
<u>www.medallionpress.com</u> and click on the
Medallion Press Insider tab.

m e d a l l i o n p r e s s . c o m